Kitty Hawk and the Hunt for Hemingway's Ghost

Book Two of the Kitty Hawk Flying Detective Agency Series

Iain Reading

This page is dedicated to everyone who loves
Taylor Swift's music as much as I do

Other books by this author:

Kitty Hawk and the Curse of the Yukon Gold
Kitty Hawk and the Hunt for Hemingway's Ghost
Kitty Hawk and the Icelandic Intrigue
Kitty Hawk and the Tragedy of the RMS Titanic
The Guild of the Wizards of Waterfire
The Hemingway Complex (non-fiction)

www.kittyhawkworld.com
www.wizardsofwaterfire.com
www.iainreading.com
www.secretworldonline.com

TABLE OF CONTENTS

Prologue

Holding On By My Fingertips

I was literally holding on by my fingertips in a cramped, dark little space surrounded by thick brick walls on all sides. It felt as though I was suspended in a vertical tomb. I heard the sound of footsteps approaching from somewhere above me—footsteps that I hoped would pass by without stopping or (worse yet) noticing I was there.

I couldn't see how anyone could possibly notice me, but I wasn't taking any chances, so I lowered myself into the narrow brick opening as far as I could go until I was completely out of sight. My fingers burned painfully under the weight of my body, so I braced my feet against the walls to take the pressure off. It helped a little, but I didn't want to push too hard and risk knocking another piece of masonry loose so that it could crash down on me and alert someone of my presence. That was, after all, the exact reason I found myself in my current predicament. The brick walls around me were a hundred and fifty years old, and even though they were as solid as rock in most places, they were still remarkably fragile in others— a fact that I'd learned the hard way just a few minutes earlier.

I shifted my weight carefully to take a little pressure off my fingers, and I winced in horror when a tiny pebble broke loose and plunged into the dark abyss beneath me. I braced myself for its impact and soon heard it plop almost silently into the pool of water below.

I breathed a deep sigh of relief that it hadn't made more noise than it did, but it also wasn't much comfort to know that the empty black space below me was actually full of water.

I thought the cisterns weren't in use anymore, I said to myself as I clung for dear life with even more earnestness now that I knew there was a deep pool of black water lurking below. If I fell down there, not only would it make a lot of noise, but I would surely drown before anyone could reach me.

The crackle of a handheld radio from close above startled me, nearly making me jump and lose my grip. The sound of footsteps suddenly stopped, and I heard voices echoing off the thick walls.

"Citadel, Citadel, this is Cuba Libré, over," a faint crackly voice on the radio said.

"This is Citadel, go ahead, over," replied another voice that sounded like it was coming from directly above me.

I panicked. The voice sounded so close. *Oh my god, oh my god, oh my god—please don't see me, please don't hear me—please, bricks, don't break off now.*

I remained completely frozen in place, terrified to move a single muscle. My fingers burned from the pressure, but I didn't dare move to alleviate the pain. If even a tiny pebble like the one that just fell was knocked loose now, there was no way the person talking on the radio just above me wouldn't hear it.

Oh god, please don't hear me, please don't hear me, I repeated to myself over and over in my head like a mantra as I listened to the radio conversation taking place above.

"Citadel, you need to advise us about what's going on," the voice at the other end of the radio said. "And tell us what to do out here, over."

"I lost them," the voice just above me snapped back in reply. "I have no idea where the hell they disappeared to, and I can't find any trace of them anywhere."

There was a long silence, and my heart jumped into my throat as my imagination ran wild.

What if he just noticed me and switched his radio off, I said to myself in a panic. *Maybe that's why it's suddenly so quiet.*

"Okay, Citadel," the voice at the other end of the radio finally answered. "In that case we're going to abort any further operations and get the hell out of here right now."

I breathed another sigh of relief and stayed frozen in place, waiting for the conversation to be over and for the person above me to continue on his way.

"Understood," the voice replied. "I'll sort things out at this end, and we'll see you at rendezvous in a few days."

"Roger that," the voice at the other end replied, peppered with static. "Over and out."

There was silence for another long, tense moment, and my imagination raced with crazy, stupid panic all over again, convinced that at any second I would see a pair of hands reach over the ledge and grab me.

There was another burst of radio static followed by another long silence before I heard the sound of footsteps again, this time echoing and making their way briskly into the distance. I wondered for a moment where they were heading but quickly decided that I really didn't care as long as it was somewhere far away from me. My fingertips were on fire, and as soon as the sound of the footsteps faded away, I counted slowly to two hundred and then very carefully pulled my body up and out into the open.

I knelt at the top of the ledge and massaged my fingers while listening intently to make sure that no one was hiding just around the next corner or doubling back to catch me. But there was nothing to hear except the sound of the wind wailing mournfully through the labyrinth of archways and openings that surrounded me. It was such a desperate and hollow sound. It sent chills down my spine, but unless there were ghosts somewhere in the vicinity, the emptiness of the howling wind meant that the coast was clear. I wasn't taking any chances, however, so I made myself count to two hundred very slowly before climbing all the way out and into the open air.

Once I was free, I took a second to stick my head back into the opening to see if I could spot the surface of the water below. I strained my eyes to see in the darkness, but it was impossible. In fact, the space was so small and narrow that I doubted I would have been able to see anything even in daylight, much less in the middle of the night.

Thank god, I didn't fall down there, I said to myself, shivering horribly as I stared down into the inky well of darkness. It was the idea of dying a horrible death by drowning in that enclosed black space that bothered me, not the idea of getting wet. I was already planning to go for a bit of a risky night swim of my own in another minute or two.

Chapter Zero

An Exciting Prospect But Also A Little Frightening

From: Kitty Hawk <kittyhawk@kittyhawkworld.com>
To: Charlie Lewis <chlewis@alaska.net>
Subject: Greetings from Quebec City!

Dear Charlie,

Hello from Quebec City! (Or maybe I should say, "Bonjour!"?)

You wouldn't believe how beautiful and amazing (and big) this country of mine is. Too bad you're not Canadian so that it could be your country too. Ha ha ha. But don't worry, tomorrow I'm off to visit your country as well, and I'm sure it's every bit as amazing as mine.

As you know, I'm meeting my dad tomorrow, and we're heading south for a little vacation. I'll be sure to think of you all the way up there in the cold Alaskan wilderness while I'm sitting on some beautiful island somewhere watching the sunset from the comfort of a white-sand beach with a cold drink in my hand.

I'll be sad to leave Canada behind, though. Just a few more days now and I'll be farther from home than I've ever been in my entire life. It's an exciting prospect but also a little frightening.

I will write whenever I can. Thank you so much for everything. I will never be able to thank you enough for what you've made possible. Without you, none of this would be happening, and I need you to know how much I appreciate it.

Take care of yourself, Charlie. Talk to you soon.

k.

Chapter One

There's No Turning Back Now

It was so impossible to believe this was really happening that I had trouble convincing myself sometimes, but I was actually doing it. I was actually flying around the world. And if I ever doubted it and wondered if it was perhaps all just a dream, the only thing I needed to do to convince myself that I was on the adventure of a lifetime was to look out of the windows of my trusty De Havilland Beaver to see the spectacularly beautiful landscape of North America passing beneath me.

Not that it had been easy, of course. Getting this far had required an unbelievable amount of work—much more than I expected when I first daydreamed the idea over a couple of cups of coffee in my parents' kitchen in Tofino.

Fortunately, my mom and dad helped me with a lot of the planning and preparations. Excruciatingly detailed flight plans had to be drafted. Telephone calls had to be made and letters sent to various governments and local authorities. Complicated arrangements had to be made to ensure that I always had fuel no matter where I was. Every single stop along the way had to be planned and settled in advance, including possible alternatives in case of emergency. And all of this required navigating a nightmare of bureaucratic red tape that I definitely could not have done by myself.

Then there was my plane. That had to be prepared as well, of course. And I never could have imagined all the work required to get it ready.

First there was the plane itself. My parents insisted (and rightly so) that the entire plane be checked thoroughly to make sure everything was in the best possible shape for the long flight ahead of me. Fortunately, there is a company in Seattle that specializes in aircraft maintenance for the De Havilland Beaver, so my parents and I flew down to spend a few days there while they checked my plane over and made various modifications. My father even arranged for the mechanics to spend a day with me going over various basic maintenance and repair operations while I furiously scribbled everything in one of my notebooks.

Next were the additional fuel tanks to extend my flying range. Without those, I wouldn't be going anywhere since several of the legs of my planned route around the world were longer than the normal operating range of the De Havilland Beaver. Without additional tanks and the extended range they made possible, I simply couldn't do it. Fortunately for me (again), a company just an hour's flight from Tofino specializes in custom fuel tanks, and they were able to install one for me.

After completing these modifications to my plane, I then had to get used to flying it all over again. The added weight of the extra fuel subtly altered the flight characteristics of the place, which took some getting used to. But of course, the previous summer I'd flown with a ton of gold on board, so the added weight and slight sluggishness of the plane was nothing I hadn't experienced before.

Finally, there were the emergency preparations. A friend of my father's who'd been flying De Havilland Beavers for more than thirty years took me through every possible emergency situation we could think of and taught me how to handle myself and the aircraft under various extreme circumstances. He also helped us install special transponder beacons and navigational gear in the plane in addition to all the other emergency gear—a life raft and life vests in the passenger compartment; spare parts for the plane; emergency food supplies; flare guns—everything I could possibly think of plus a bit more.

"It's not the things we've thought of that worry me," my father said. "It's the things we *haven't* thought of."

And he was right, of course.

All of these modifications and supplies were also not cheap, and the whole trip was made possible by a donation from Charlie and his brothers from the charity trust fund they'd set up using the gold that had been stolen from the Clara Nevada more than a hundred years before. I'd stayed in touch with them since our adventure through Alaska and the Yukon the previous summer, but I have to admit that Charlie was the best emailer of the bunch, and it was with him that I maintained an almost daily correspondence.

The planning and preparations for my solo flight around the world seemed to flash by in a complete blur. I'd chosen March 17th as my departure date because that was the same day that Amelia Earhart had begun her own flight around the world in 1937. That would give me enough time to get ready, but March had seemed a long way off in the fall when I'd first had the idea to make the flight. Soon it was Christmas, then Valentine's Day, and March was just around the corner.

At least I wasn't on a deadline, however. My flight around the world wasn't a race to set some a speed record or to prove anything. Part of my plan was to make several stops along the way to visit places that I'd always wanted to see. Overall, the whole flight would take longer than a year to complete, but I was still determined to set out on March 17 if I could do it. And thanks to my father and mother, Charlie and his brothers, my best friend Skeena and my father's friends, and everyone else who chipped in to help, by March I was ready and out on the water near the seaplane base in downtown Tofino, waiting for takeoff.

It seemed like half the town had come out to see me off. My parents were there, of course, plus Skeena and her family—and she has a big family, with more cousins, aunts, and uncles than I've ever been able to keep track of. I saw familiar faces from around town in the crowd that had gathered on the pier to cheer me on. There were a few unfamiliar faces, too, including a lot of tourists who were in town for the annual whale festival, which is an event celebrating the annual northern migration of something like twenty thousand gray whales that swim right past us every year on their way from Mexico to feeding grounds in Alaska. There was even a reporter from the *Vancouver Sun* who flew over to take my picture and do an interview for a story in his newspaper.

It was all very overwhelming for me. I felt like a celebrity with people taking pictures from all sides with their camera phones and slapping me on the back to wish me luck as I waded through the crowd. I don't even know how all of them knew about my flight, but clearly, my epic undertaking had caught people's attention.

Amid the cheers and well wishes of the crowd of more than a hundred people, I said a tearful farewell to my parents and Skeena and climbed into the cockpit of my trusty De Havilland Beaver. I waved good-bye, started the engine, and taxied out onto the water to make my final checks before takeoff.

I have to admit that I was a bit nervous. My father and I had been to the plane early that morning to check everything out and taxi it over to the downtown seaplane base to refuel it for the flight. I knew that everything on the plane was in perfect order and that it was ready to go, but I wondered if I was ready. As I put my hand on the throttle lever, I realized the magnitude of what I was about to do and that I wasn't going to see my beautiful home in Tofino for a very long time.

Up ahead on the pier people held up signs saying things like "GOOD LUCK KITTY!" or "WE'LL MISS YOU!" and the reality of what I was about to do suddenly hit me. While I was sketching out all of the plans on paper, it was easy to think of the flight as some distant theoretical dream in the faraway future, but now it was real, and the thought of being away from home for such a long time in distant, exotic lands made it seem as though I would be gone a lifetime.

Was I ready for it?

"You can do this," I said to myself as I pushed the throttle forward. The engine grumbled roughly for a second then quickly smoothed out into a nice, clean roar as I raced across the water and picked up speed. For a moment I had flashbacks of my adventures the previous year, and I half-expected to see the tip of Amanda Phillpott's kayak emerging in front of me, aborting my takeoff, but she was nowhere around, and soon I was airborne, climbing into the sky above the beautiful islands and inlets of Clayquot Sound. Down below, the crowd on the dock cheered and waved their arms to say good-bye. I waved through the cockpit window and wobbled the wings of the plane to say good-bye.

This is it, I thought. *There's no turning back now.*

Chapter Two

A Little Detour

To get onto my route from Tofino and fly all the way around the world, I first had to fly all the way across Canada. It was somehow fitting that before I set out to explore the rest of the world I was able to explore and discover a bit of my own country first. And along the way, I would also be able to try out all of the many new systems and modifications we'd made to my plane to prepare it for my epic world flight. I could do all of the testing and shakedowns of the new gear without even leaving my own country since Canada is a big country—a really big country.

I am always amazed by the fact that it is much farther to fly from Tofino at the western end of Canada to the eastern end in Newfoundland than it is to fly from Newfoundland to Europe. People living in eastern Canada are considerably closer to Europe than they are the opposite end of their own country. And it was across this vast landscape that I had to fly.

The distance is so far from one end of Canada to the other that even with my newly installed extended-range fuel tanks, I still had to leapfrog my way across from city to city, refueling as I went.

My first stop was the city of Calgary—a massive sprawling city of suburbs and residential subdivisions spread out across the foothills of the Rocky Mountains—home to cowboys and the infamous Calgary Stampede.

I was hoping to see some people in cowboy hats when I arrived, and I wasn't disappointed. The attendant who helped me refuel was decked out in complete wannabe-cowboy attire—Wrangler jeans with a giant shiny belt buckle, cowboy shirt, and a beautiful white cowboy hat on his head.

The white cowboy hat was the symbol of Calgary, he told me, and he wrote down the names of some stores in town where I could find one—a souvenir of the first stop on my around-the-world adventure.

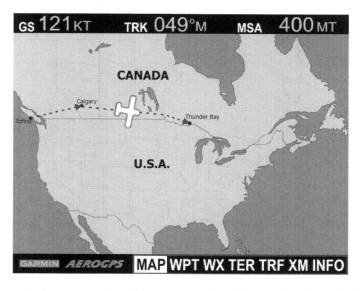

The next stop on my leapfrog across Canada was the city of Thunder Bay, Ontario, which is close to the border between the United States and Canada at the western edge of the Great Lakes. The flight from Calgary to Thunder Bay was an important test of my extended range because it was the first leg of my journey that really pushed the envelope of how far I could fly without stopping to refuel. My father and I had planned it this way. Even though we'd conducted extensive tests in Tofino, we figured that once I was on my way, it would be better to test things while flying over the safety of Canada. Thunder Bay was the ideal place to do that since the approach from the west was littered with thousands of isolated lakes and rivers that I could land on if I needed to.

Coming in for a landing on the westernmost lake of the Great Lakes—Lake Superior—I caught my first glimpse of Thunder Bay's famous "sleeping giant." Across from the city, the form of a giant man lying on his back rises up out of the water. It isn't a real man, of course, but a land formation that looks surprisingly like a giant sleeping human form.

I asked the attendant fueling my plane about the story of the giant. (These fueling attendants were turning out to be useful sources of information.)

"The local native Indian tribe..." he said, and then he paused and added with a smile, "...my tribe, the Ojibway, believed that the sleeping form was that of Nanabijou, the Spirit of Deep Waters. Long ago Nanabijou decided to reward the indigenous people of this region by giving them a rich silver mine. But he warned them that if they told the white man about its location, he would be turned to stone and the tribe would be forever cursed. For many years, the tribe kept the secret safe, but soon others noticed the beautiful silver ornaments and jewelry worn by the members of the tribe, and they wanted to know where the silver came from. But the Ojibway would not reveal their secret. So their enemies, the Sioux, had to resort to deception instead.

"One day a Sioux dressed as an Ojibway snuck into their village and was able to learn the secret location of the silver mine. He escaped undetected and made his way back to his own tribe, but he encountered two white traders along the way and decided to sell the secret to them instead. The secret was revealed, and after a thunderous storm, the sleeping form of Nanabijou arose from the lake and has remained there ever since."

"And what about the curse on your tribe?" I asked.

"Oh, I haven't noticed anything like that," he replied with a toothy grin, and he gestured to his expensive pickup parked on the shoreline.

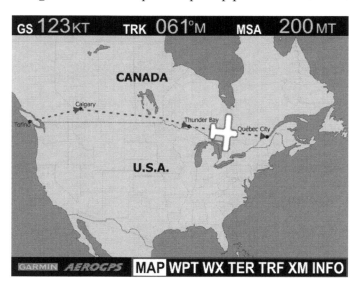

Taking off from Lake Superior the next morning I headed east toward the next stop on my journey across Canada—Quebec City. Once there my landing strip would be a river instead of a lake, but a river so massive that it was hard to believe that it really *was* a river—the St. Lawrence Seaway.

I suppose it shouldn't have surprised me that the river connecting the Great Lakes to the ocean would be so huge. I mean, the Great Lakes have a lot of water. And wherever all that water goes must be pretty big, right? Nonetheless, I was still stunned by the sheer size of this enormous mass of water flowing out toward the Atlantic Ocean.

After tying up to refuel, I asked the fueling attendant about the river and he told me that Quebec City marks the point where the river technically ends and becomes a massive, narrow tidal estuary that leads hundreds of miles out to the Atlantic Ocean.

"Ten or twelve million liters of water flow past here every second," he said. I looked out across the river to the distant shoreline on the opposite side and tried to comprehend such a colossal amount of water in constant motion, every second and every minute of every day.

That night, after I'd explored the city a bit and was making my way back to the plane to sleep in the makeshift bunk we'd installed in the passenger cabin, I decided to take a detour and wandered around the old walled city of Quebec. It felt as if I had been transported into another world. I had no idea that any place in North America could feel so European, for lack of a better word. I suppose in North America any place that has buildings more than a hundred years old feels European, but as I walked through the winding, narrow, cobbled streets in the late evening and heard French being spoken around me, it felt as if I was wandering through the streets of Paris. As a fog rolled in off the river and the dark alleyways and thoroughfares took on a slightly ominous atmosphere, I was suddenly Sherlock Holmes wandering the streets of London in search of Moriarty.

But those real cities of imagination—Paris and London and beyond— were still miles ahead of me on that particular night. Before I reached them, I had to make a little detour first.

Chapter Three

After A Vacation With My Father I Needed A Vacation

My father met me the next morning in Quebec City. It was part of our plan that he would fly out and meet me so that we could carefully evaluate the performance of the plane on the flight thus far, not to mention evaluate how *I* was performing and holding up over such vast distances and during such long flights. That way we could make any necessary corrections before I set out completely on my own and left Canada far behind me.

There was another reason for meeting up with my dad in Quebec: we'd planned a little detour that would take us out of the cold wind and rain of late March in Canada for a few weeks in a warmer climate farther south. We were going to the Caribbean!

Yes, I know. The Caribbean was not really along the way considering how my around-the-world flight was planned—taking a northerly route via Greenland, Iceland, and Ireland. But because I'd been so insistent on setting out in mid-March to honor Amelia Earhart, that meant that I would reach the northern waters of the Atlantic Ocean at exactly the moment when the winter storms were still gradually blowing themselves out. I might spend weeks in various locations waiting for an opening in the weather to hop safely from Newfoundland to Greenland to Iceland. The idea of spending weeks in Newfoundland waiting for that perfect moment to arrive was not quite as appealing as my parents' suggestion of island hopping through the Caribbean to pass the time.

My father caught a commercial flight out to Quebec City to meet me, and from there we would fly down to Miami together where my mother would be waiting for us. Mom decided to meet us in Florida and avoid all the "airplane talk" that would inevitably fill the entire flight south as Dad and I discussed how everything on my plane was working. This was probably a wise move since I don't think my dad and I stopped talking about it for longer than two minutes the whole way down. He even took the wheel and did some of the flying along the way. He insisted that he did so to give me a bit of rest before I had to fly hundreds of hours around the world, but I think he actually just wanted to fly his old plane for a while. My trusty De Havilland Beaver was a hand-me-down that used to belong to him, after all.

Chapter Four

Aruba, Jamaica, Oooh I Wanna Take Ya

Knowing how utterly exhausted I would be after a two-week "vacation" with my father, I'd already planned to take a little vacation by myself—a vacation where all the sightseeing would be done at my own pace, and there would still be plenty of time for lying on the beach, reading, swimming, and just plain old relaxing. I had found the perfect place to do all of that: Key West, Florida.

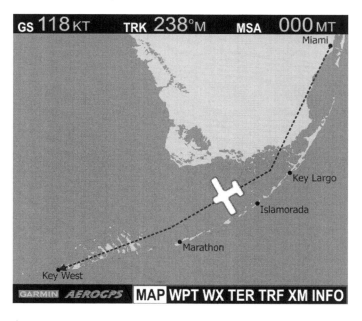

After kissing my parents good-bye in Miami, I found myself flying south with the vast expanse of swamp known as the Florida Everglades stretching out past the horizon on my right. Off to my left there were beautiful white sand beaches lining the coast and lots of human development—shopping malls, fast-food restaurants, and miles upon miles of houses and condominiums. Gradually all this development thinned out, and I could see the Gulf of Mexico slowly coming into view.

It felt like I was entering a completely different world—a world of water. Passing over the coastline of North America and out over the Florida Keys, I was stunned by the view that stretched out before me. Crystal-clear waters in a hundred different shades of gorgeous blue dotted with thousands of tiny green islands made such incredible view that I simply had to gasp at the beauty of it. And somewhere out at the end of all these islands was my destination—Key West.

Passing close to one of the larger islands along the way I noticed a familiar name on my GPS screen—Key Largo. The name was familiar, but I couldn't figure out why at first.

Did something famous happen there? I wondered.

Then it came to me. It was one of the places mentioned in that Beach Boys song my mom listened to sometimes.

What the heck is the name of that song? I asked myself. *The one that sounds like a Caribbean travel guide.*

"Key Largo, Montego, baby why don't we go," I sang quietly to myself. "Just off the Florida Keys...."

I struggled to remember the song's title, but it was no use. I couldn't remember it. In fact, I couldn't remember the rest of the words either.

After passing over some larger islands, I banked my plane into a turn toward the west. For the rest of the trip I would more or less follow the Overseas Highway, which is an unbelievably long road that connects the main islands of the Florida Keys using a series of long bridges, including one called Seven Mile Bridge, which I assumed was probably seven miles long. I'd read on the Internet the night before that long before the highways were built, there was the Overseas Railroad, which was a railroad that ran straight out over the islands and water and connected Miami to Key West. Passengers could board an overnight train in New York City, ride south, and then wake up one morning with sunshine and beautiful blue seas passing outside of their compartment windows.

That railroad had been partly destroyed by a hurricane in the 1930s and was never rebuilt, but down below me I could still see its stone arched bridges running parallel to the modern highway. Cars and trains no longer drove along these old relics, but they'd found new life as platforms for fishermen or as walking paths for locals and tourists to take an early morning stroll out over the water.

As I flew south, I marveled at the breathtaking beauty of the world that surrounded me. It was completely unreal—like something from a fantasy movie or a video game where the world is so fantastical that it almost defies imagination. What I was seeing outside of the windows of my seaplane was exactly like that—it defied imagination to think that such a place as this existed so close to the swamps and modern city developments that I'd been flying over just a half hour earlier.

Of course, there is development in the Keys too. For example, I clearly saw a Burger King down on the ground somewhere, but somehow the Keys seemed different from the crowded and bustling cities I'd left behind me. It seemed more laid back here, or at least it looked that way from a couple thousand feet in the air. I'd have to wait and see what it was like at ground level.

I wouldn't have long to wait because before I knew it, after passing over a few more long bridges and a couple hundred more tiny islands, I was descending into Key West for a nice landing and tying my plane up at a dock where I'd made arrangements to leave it for a few days.

It wasn't a long walk into town, but with the heat and humidity and my heavy duffel bag stuffed full of clothes, I wondered if I should take a taxi instead.

"Why not?" suggested the little voice in my head. "Mom and Dad are paying for it anyway."

It was true. My father felt bad for exhausting me with his intense travel planning, so he and my mom gave me a good-luck present for my around-the-world flight and booked me into a luxurious resort hotel for a few days where I could finally just sit by the pool and lie around on the beach. All expenses were paid by them, of course, including a couple of trips to the spa. (I made sure to clarify that last bit, groaning about how much I needed a massage after Dad's brutal sightseeing schedule.)

All expenses paid definitely includes a taxi, I told myself with a grin as I hopped into a cab that took me right to the front door of my resort. I didn't see much of the city along the way, but I would have plenty of time to do all of that later. At that moment, I couldn't wait to get changed and go for a swim, so after checking in, I threw my bag on the bed of my room and headed for the water.

Should I swim in the pool or in the ocean? This was the most challenging question that I planned to answer for the next few days.

"I will do both," I said to myself and headed down to the resort's private beach for a plunge into the clear waters of the Atlantic Ocean followed by another swim just steps away in the hotel swimming pool.

Refreshed by all that swimming, I then embarked on an intense schedule of relaxation. I found a comfortable reclining chair in the shade and spent the rest of the afternoon alternately reading and snoozing. This was followed by another quick swim in the pool then back to my room to watch a movie on television while I ate a cheeseburger from room service in my bed.

After that there was more time for reading and sleeping (mostly sleeping) until the next morning when I went for an early morning swim in the ocean followed by another swim in the pool, then a shower and breakfast before heading to the resort's spa for a massage and pedicure. After that, I continued with my intense schedule before heading back to the room for an afternoon nap followed by two more swims in the ocean and pool plus more reading and sleeping at poolside.

I finished the book I was reading just as the sun began to sink low in the sky, so for a while I just sat there and stared out at the ocean for a while.

Maybe Dad is right, I thought after gazing at water and sky for what seemed like forever. *Maybe there is a limit to how much laziness and relaxing a person can enjoy.*

Don't tell my Dad, but as much as I enjoyed not having to do anything, I was actually starting to get a little bored and antsy. I felt like I should be doing something instead of just lying around all the time.

Tomorrow I will actually do something, I told myself. *I will go see the city and find myself some new books to read.*

I headed back to my room for a shower and some more room service (a Caesar salad). As I sat there in the middle of the king-sized bed munching on my salad and watching reruns of *The Big Bang Theory,* I was tempted to abandon my plans of exploration and continue with my plans of laziness.

No! I told myself firmly. *I'll go crazy if I spend another day doing nothing. Tomorrow I will get out of here and start exploring Key West.*

Chapter Five

I Told You I Was Sick

I decided to get an early start on seeing the city to avoid as much of the midday heat as I could. Walking through the quiet early morning streets lined with palm trees and telephone poles brought me to the corner of South and Whitehead Streets where a crowd of people lingered around a large concrete pylon painted black, red, and yellow.

90 Miles to Cuba
SOUTHERNMOST
POINT
CONTINENTAL
U.S.A.
Key West, FL
Home of the Sunset

Even as early as it was many tourists had already gathered to line up and patiently wait their turn to be photographed standing next to the monument. I stood and watched for a while as the line of people inched forward and each group scurried over to have its picture taken.

As I stood there, I realized that there was something not quite right about the marker. It declared itself to be the southernmost point in the United States, but if I wasn't mistaken, the house to the left of the marker was actually farther south—and to be honest, I sincerely hoped I wasn't mistaken since, as a pilot, I pride myself on my excellent sense of direction.

I pulled out my map of Key West to check whether I was right or not. It was just a simple tourist map ("Not to be used for navigation" it read—as though you'd use a map covered with cartoon conch shell advertisements for navigating the high seas), but it clearly showed that I was correct—the house and yard next to the concrete marker were definitely farther south. In fact, all the land off to the side of the marker stretching out to the tip of a peninsula was much farther south as well.

I guess they meant the Southernmost Point Where There Was Some Free Space To Put Up A Marker For Tourists, I thought cynically as I reached for my iPhone to take a picture. I tried to get a shot without any people in the frame by timing it between groups of posing tourists, but the line moved too quickly, and I had to settle for one with a family of complete strangers in matching tracksuits standing in front of the marker. I couldn't stand around all day, after all. I had a city to see.

Leaving the *almost* Southernmost Point behind me, I navigated to my next stop through narrow streets lined with colorfully painted clapboard houses snuggled behind white picket fences and seas of lush, green, tropical vegetation. In some places, the exotic palm and Banyan trees grew so thick that they nearly choked out the sun and blue sky above me, but they also provided some welcome shade in the growing heat of the day.

Following some advice from my father, I was on my way to the Key West Cemetery. My father always says that one of the best ways to get to know the character of a city is to visit one of its cemeteries—the idea being that by seeing a city in death, you get some insight into what the city is like in life.

At the main gate, a bearded maintenance worker pointed me to a metal box with a hinged lid containing a free printed map of the cemetery. I took one and set off on a walking tour.

The cemetery was unlike anything I'd seen before. It was like a miniature city all to itself, complete with numbered avenues and streets with names like Violet, Laurel, and Pauline Street. Underneath the scant shade of several towering palm trees, many of the graves were stacked above ground like strange, macabre filing cabinets.

"Why are some of the graves above ground?" I asked the bearded maintenance guy who was repairing a cracked and broken tomb nearby.

"The ground's too hard," he replied with a cackle of laughter, clanking the tip of his shovel against the hard stone underneath our feet. "The whole island's built on fossilized coral, so here in Key Weird, you have to build up and stack the graves like condominium buildings."

"Key Weird?" I replied, grinning.

The maintenance man grinned through his scraggly facial hair. "I've lived here my whole life," he said, giving me a wink before he returned to his repair work. "And it's still weird to me."

I watched him for a moment before continuing my walking tour. The cemetery was certainly unusual—its white and gray tombs cracked and baking in the tropical sun—but I am not sure I would call it weird.

Maybe a little bit funny, I thought as I read an inscription on a large family crypt that stood like a little house in one corner of the cemetery.

GLORIA M. RUSSELL
MAY 22, 1926—DECEMBER 27, 2000
"I'M JUST RESTING MY EYES"

"Or maybe it *is* a little weird, after all," I said to myself as I stopped to read another unusual inscription.

I TOLD YOU I WAS SICK
B. P. ROBERTS
MAY 17, 1929—JUNE 18, 1979

As I stood there laughing to myself, I was a bit worried that I was being disrespectful, but I soon learned that it was stupid of me to worry. Clearly some of Key West's former citizens had a sense of humor.

But not all of Key West's former inhabitants were buried in its cemetery, and after slipping through a side gate of the cemetery, I headed out into the world of the living to track down the memory of another person who had once called the city home. I was headed west down to the corner of Olivia and Whitehead Streets where Key West's most famous resident had once lived—Ernest Hemingway.

Chapter Six

Six-Toed Cats and Hemingway's Last Penny

"Ernest Hemingway bought this house in 1931 for the unheard-of low price of only eight thousand dollars," the tour guide told us. "And by 'bought' I mean that Hemingway didn't actually pay for it himself but rather his wife's uncle bought it for them as a wedding present."

I found myself standing with a crowd of other sweaty tourists in the sticky heat of Hemingway's dining room listening to a handsome young man named James take us on a tour of the house and museum.

Hemingway's house is a beautiful, old two-story colonial mansion— white with green shutters on all the windows and an amazing verandah porch circling the entire structure on the upper floor. It stands at the middle of a lush garden surrounded on all sides by a low brick wall that separates it from the street and the adjacent properties.

"The brick wall was built in 1935," James continued, "to keep out the tourists after the author's home was listed in a local tourist guide as number eighteen out of forty-eight things to see in Key West. This distinction was very flattering, Hemingway said, but he was a modest and retiring chap who had no desire to compete with other tourist attractions, such as the Sponge Lofts (#13 on the list), the Ice Factory (#4) or the 627-pound Jewfish in the Key West Aquarium (#9). Besides, the added attention made it very difficult to keep up with his writing deadlines."

I chuckled at this story along with the rest of the group.

"You might notice," James continued. "That we have many mechanical fans here at the Hemingway Home."

I actually *had* noticed. In fact, I was trying to maneuver myself into the corner of the room in front of the stream of air being produced by one such fan at that very moment.

"We have oscillating fans," James said, "and box fans in windows, as well as desk fans. But there's one kind of fan that we *don't* have here. And it's the kind of fan you'd probably most expect to see."

We all stared at him dumbly for a moment until he pointed silently to the ceiling where a chandelier hung directly over his head.

"Ceiling fans," James said simply. "There are no ceiling fans here in the house because when the young couple first moved in, Hemingway's second wife Pauline replaced all the ceiling fans with her collection of chandeliers—much to the consternation of Papa Hemingway himself and a topic which surely caused some heated discussions between the two."

I groaned inwardly at this terrible pun, and the rest of the group groaned audibly.

Undeterred, James called out, "Now, on with the tour!" He took us through the rest of the ground floor of the house, explaining some of the many photographs and posters covering every inch of available space on the walls. From there he led us up the stairs and into the master bedroom. The room was full of natural light streaming in through large arched windows, and there was a door leading directly out onto the verandah. At the other end of the room, against the wall, stood a large bed neatly made up with a rumpled-looking white bed cover. The bed was adorned by an ornate headboard carved from dark wood, but it was roped off to discourage us from getting too close. Ignoring the barrier, however, was a large black and gray tomcat that was happily curled up on one of the pillows having a nap.

"This is Hemingway's bedroom," James explained. "And this is Hemingway's bed with its beautiful carved wooden headboard made from the gates of a monastery in Spain that happened to catch Papa's eye on one of his many trips there. This is where he slept every night—or should I say every night that he wasn't in Spain, Havana, Africa, Idaho, Bimini, or elsewhere, which was quite a lot of the time.

"But even while he was off traveling the world, Key West was home for him from 1931 until 1940 when the breakup with his wife Pauline began in earnest, and he crossed over to Cuba to live with the woman who would soon become his third wife—Martha Gellhorn. With Hemingway in Cuba and the divorce becoming final in November 1940, Pauline continued to live in the house in Key West with their two sons until her death in 1951. After her death, Hemingway never moved back to Key West but sometimes stayed here as he shuttled back and forth to Cuba. Following Hemingway's own death in 1961, the house was sold to a private owner. But even though Hemingway was no longer living here, the house remained high on the list of 'Things To See In Key West' and eventually the new owner became tired of answering her door to find curious tourists standing on the porch asking to see the house. She eventually moved out of the main house, and it was opened as the museum you see here today."

James took a few steps closer to the bed.

"But although Hemingway no longer sleeps here," he said, gesturing to the sleeping tomcat at the top of the bed, "the bed is still put to good use by one of our many famous cats here at the museum."

James reached down to stroke the cat's head lovingly. The cat was completely unfazed and continued snoozing on the pillow.

"The little fellow's name is Buster Keaton, after the famous silent film star," James said. "Hemingway would often name his cats after famous people, and we try to keep up the tradition because the cats you see around the house and garden are descendants of one of the so-called six-toed cats that Hemingway was so very fond of."

Six-toed cats? I asked myself, raising my eyebrows.

"If you look closely at Buster, here," James said, "you can see that he actually has *seven* toes instead of five or six."

I leaned over for a closer look. *One, two, three, four, five, six...seven,* I counted. *Seven toes.*

"Cats normally have five toes on their front feet, of course," James continued. "But many of the cats you will see here today are special polydactyl cats that have six, seven, or even eight toes."

That is so weird, I thought, unable to take my eyes off the strange sight of a cat with so many toes.

"But let's leave Buster alone so he can sleep," James said, ushering us outside through the nearby door.

We shuffled out onto the verandah, which overlooks the back part of Hemingway's garden and a large, blue swimming pool. Through the lush trees and yellow bamboo to my left, I could see a small, two-story building with a sloped, red-shingled roof and stairs leading to the upper floor.

"Through the trees here you can see the estate's old carriage house," James said, pointing to the unique building. "It was here that Hemingway worked on such masterpieces as *The Snows of Kilimanjaro, The Green Hills Of Africa*, and his definitive Key West book, *To Have And Have Not.*

"Back in Hemingway's time," James said, taking a few steps over and putting his hand on the iron railing. "He had a special bridge built connecting his bedroom directly to his writing studio. He would wake up early in the morning, before the day got too hot, and walk straight across the garden to his studio and get to work. But unfortunately for us the bridge is no longer there, so we'll have to walk around to the other side of the building and take the stairs."

James led our group like sheep slowly around the outside porch of the house to the other side where some stairs led to the ground level. From there he led us over to the foot of the metal staircase leading up to Hemingway's writing room on the top floor of the carriage house.

"There's only space for two or three people at a time to view Hemingway's writing room," James said, pointing up the staircase to a doorway at the top. "So just take your time and go up and have a look, and then let's all meet over by the swimming pool where we will end the tour."

One by one, each of us in the tour group trundled single-file up the narrow staircase to have a look. While I waited my turn, I stopped to pet one of the six-toed cats sleeping at the edge of the shingled roof.

When it was my turn, I stepped up into a small caged-off viewing area just inside the doorway and got my first look at the room where Hemingway once worked. It is a simple room, but it takes up the entire upper floor of the carriage house. There are open windows on all sides letting in plenty of natural light and air, and a pair of French doors at the opposite end. Various bookshelves filled with knickknacks surrounded the center of the room, and various animal heads (presumably from Hemingway's many hunting activities) hung from the walls. On my left was an old-fashioned steamer trunk with the simple initials *E.H.* stenciled on the top, and in the middle of the room stood a simple, round wooden table with a small, lonely typewriter sitting on top of it.

I have to admit that I felt a little bit in awe standing there on that quiet spring morning in the tropical heat of Key West (don't worry, there was a fan in Hemingway's writing room too, even though people weren't allowed inside the room itself). I didn't know whether any of the furniture or decorations were authentic, but if nothing else, this was certainly the room where Hemingway had once written some of the books and stories and magazine articles that millions of people have enjoyed and that made him a legend.

"But of course, let's not forget that you have never read any of those books or stories or magazine articles," the little voice in my head reminded me.

Thanks for ruining the moment, I told myself. *But don't worry. After the tour, I plan to visit the bookstore and buy some of his books, and see what the fuss is all about.*

I took a few pictures with my iPhone and then carefully descended the other side of the stairs and headed toward the swimming pool to catch up with James and the rest of the tour group. The pool was much larger than I'd thought when I'd seen it from a distance upstairs. In fact, as far as privately owned backyard swimming pools go, it was absolutely huge. I'd never seen such a large pool in someone's yard before in my life. It was also wonderfully inviting on such a hot and muggy day. To my eyes, it looked like the perfect place to be.

"Sadly, this is where our tour ends," James said after his entire group had joined us at the head of the swimming pool. "But before you go, let me just tell you one last story—one about the swimming pool you see here at the Hemingway home.

"Construction on the pool began in 1937 and was completed the following year. At the time, it was the only swimming pool anywhere within a hundred miles or more, which of course also made it the southernmost swimming pool in the United States at the time. The pool was built at enormous expense, which was partly due to the fact that the city of Key West is built on top of an island of fossilized coral, and it required a great deal of effort to dig the pool's foundations. All told, the cost of the pool was twenty thousand dollars, and by that I mean twenty thousand 1938 dollars, which is more like three hundred thousand dollars nowadays. And of course, when evaluating the cost, we shouldn't forget that the entire house and property had cost only eight thousand dollars when purchased a few years earlier.

"Hemingway always wanted to have a swimming pool here in Key West, but by the time construction started, he was off working as a war correspondent during the Spanish Civil War, and it was his wife Pauline who had to oversee the swimming pool project.

"As the story goes, when Hemingway finally returned home, he found a nearly completed pool sitting right where his personal boxing ring used to stand. That infuriated him, but when he heard how much it had cost, he supposedly turned red, pulled a penny from his pocket, and said to Pauline, 'You've spent everything but my last penny on this pool, so you might as well have that too!'. With that he flung the penny on the ground and stormed off, fuming and angry."

Everyone in the group laughed.

"Now, I don't know if that story is true or not," James said, leaning closer to us and lowering his voice as though he were imparting some mysterious secret. "But if it is, it's not really very fair to Pauline, since her uncle probably carried most of the cost of the pool anyway, just as he'd bought the house for them in the first place. But whether it's true or not, have a look down at the foot of this post here. As a memorial to his angry outburst, Pauline preserved Hemingway's last penny here in the pavement at the head of the swimming pool."

I turned to look where James was pointing along with everyone else in the group. Sure enough, embedded into the cement was a single, shiny copper penny— Hemingway's last penny.

Chapter Seven

A Midnight Stroll Through The Streets Of Key Weird

"You've never read Hemingway before?!?" James asked me incredulously. "Not ever?!? How is that even possible?"

After ending his tour at the edge of the swimming pool, I waited patiently while the crowd slowly dispersed and listened as James answered some questions from a few lingering people from his group.

"Does anyone ever use the pool?"

Answer: "No, unfortunately the pool is off-limits to the public and is just for show."

"How did Hemingway die?"

Answer: "He committed suicide in 1961 at his home in Ketchum, Idaho. He was 61 years old."

"How many cats are living here?"

Answer: "We have forty or fifty cats here. There is also a cat cemetery of previous inhabitants on the opposite side of the gardens."

Finally, I was able to ask a question of my own when everyone else drifted off to stroll around the grounds or return to the house for another look.

"What books would you recommend for someone who's never read Hemingway before?" I asked after introducing myself.

I could have asked this same question to the lady at the counter in the bookstore underneath Hemingway's writing room, but just between you and me, James was really quite good looking and had a bit of a Johnny Depp thing going on that I liked.

(What? Can't a girl flirt a little bit?)

"Didn't they make you read *The Old Man And The Sea* in school?" James asked, continuing in his disbelief that I'd never read Hemingway before.

"We read Shakespeare," I replied, trying to think of what books they'd made us read instead. "And *Lord Of The Flies*. And *Never Cry Wolf*."

"*Never Cry Wolf*?" James asked.

"I think it's a Canadian book," I said. "I'm from Canada."

James shook his head in mock disapproval. "What are they teaching you up there in Canada if you've never read Hemingway before?" he asked, grinning.

I shrugged my shoulders.

"Fortunately for you," James continued, gesturing comically like a car salesman toward the unassuming door leading into the gift shop and bookstore, "we have an excellent selection of Hemingway on sale right here."

I laughed.

"That was my plan," I replied. "And that's why I asked you what books you would suggest for a first-time reader."

James stroked his thin Johnny Depp goatee pensively and thought about this for a moment. "Well, *The Old Man And The Sea* for sure," he said. "And of course you must read *A Farewell To Arms, For Whom The Bell Tolls*, and maybe a collection of stories with *The Snows of Kilimanjaro*."

I jotted down the titles on my notepad while he was speaking and looked up when he finished.

"Anything else?" I asked.

James thought a bit longer before shaking his head. "That's probably enough to get you started," he said. "Hemingway isn't for everybody, so you'll have to see if he suits you or not. For some people his writing fits them like a glove while for others it's a little too much of men trying too hard to be macho."

I laughed again, intrigued by his description of Hemingway's writing style.

"Okay," I said, closing my notebook and wrapping my arms around it. "Thank you so much."

"Jackie in the bookstore can also suggest some other books as well," James suggested.

"Perfect," I replied with a nod, continuing to stand there, nervously kicking the ground with the toe of my sandal. I didn't know what else to say, but I also didn't want the conversation to end.

James smiled at me. "Listen, do you maybe want to have lunch with me tomorrow?" he asked casually. "I could regale you with stories of the great Ernest Hemingway."

I thought you'd never ask, I said to myself.

I blushed. "I'd like that."

"Good," James said. "How about we meet at Sloppy Joe's at noon?"

I pulled open my notebook again and scribbled the name of the restaurant.

"Sloppy Joe's," I repeated as I wrote. "What's the address?"

James laughed. "You've never read Hemingway *and* you're a tourist in Key West who's never been to Sloppy Joe's?" he asked, teasing. "What is this world coming to?"

I shrugged my shoulders and grinned.

"I have to do another tour," James said, "but meet me tomorrow at noon at the corner of Duval and Greene, okay?"

I nodded. "Twelve o'clock," I said. "See you there."

I watched as James headed to the front of the house, and then he turned and waved good-bye. When he disappeared around a corner, I turned on my heels and headed for the bookstore.

I enjoyed wandering through the store and was able to find all the titles that James had suggested plus a couple more that the lady behind the counter recommended as well. I stacked them up at the cash register, and after paying in cash, I grabbed the heavy bag and headed out onto the streets of Key West.

As I made my way across town to my hotel, I could think of nothing but lying by the edge of the pool overlooking the beach and getting a start on some of my newly acquired reading material. But when I stopped in my room to change clothes, the sight of my comfy bed quickly put an end to my poolside ambitions. Before I knew it, I was under the covers and three pages into the first chapter of *The Snows of Kilimanjaro*. Unfortunately, three pages were as far as I got before I drifted off into a deep and peaceful sleep.

I am a fanatical devotee of afternoon naps. The only problem with them is when I sleep for too long and wake up in the middle of the night, tossing and turning for hours because I've screwed up my normal sleeping schedule.

And that's exactly what happened. I woke up some time well after midnight and flopped around restlessly for the next two hours before finally deciding to go out for a walk to make myself tired again. This is how I found myself on the dark streets of Key West at 2:30 in the morning, walking aimlessly down Duval Street and starting to get a better idea of what the cemetery maintenance guy had meant when he referred to the city as Key Weird.

It all started when a woman dressed in tinfoil and high heels strolled past me singing something that sounded distinctly like a show tune.

"Chicks and ducks and geese better scurry," she sang as she floated past me on the sidewalk, "when I take you out in my surrey, when I take you out in my surrey with the fringe—on top!" She leaned in toward me to belt out the last two words, scaring me nearly out of my wits.

I watched her continue down the street and vanish around the next corner past the ice cream shop.

"Maybe this wasn't such a good idea," the little voice in my head commented. "What would your dad say if he knew you were wandering around the streets of a strange city in the middle of the night?"

"You're not kidding about it being a strange city," I muttered under my breath as I continued up the street.

Hardly two minutes passed before the next unusual Key West character cycled past me on a bike covered in blinking Christmas lights. He was wearing a Santa hat on his head, which fit in with his festive bike motif even though it was a little bit out of season. At least he was wearing normal clothes made out of fabric instead of tinfoil.

"Good evening, young lady," he called out cheerfully. "Merry Christmas!"

"Merry Christmas," I replied, watching as he pedaled past and down the street behind me. I didn't have the heart to tell him that Christmas was still more than half a year away. Surely, he knew that already, right?

As I approached the next intersection, I came across the third installment in my evening of Key Weird entertainment. This time is was a virtually naked man wearing nothing but a tiny Speedo swimsuit and a bright red cape, flapping his way down the middle of the road on a pair of roller skates.

This is getting a little too weird, I said to myself as I rounded the corner of Duval and Olivia Streets. *But the concierge at the hotel did tell me that Duval Street was the heart of Key West's strange nightlife, after all.*

I decided to walk back to the hotel on what I hoped was a quieter and less bizarre street. One block over was Whitehead Street with the Hemingway House on the corner. From there I could head straight to the southernmost point and back to my hotel.

Walking along the low brick wall that surrounded the Hemingway House, I passed the sign at the main entrance and stopped to pull myself up to my tiptoes and peer over the wall. I was hoping to see one of the six-toed cats prowling through the garden, but it was too dark. I couldn't see a thing.

Lowering myself down again, I continued down Whitehead Street when I heard a strange sound floating in the air, barely audible over the sound of the wind blowing through the branches of the palm trees and bamboo. It sounded exactly like a typewriter.

I stopped in my tracks to listen more carefully. At first I thought that maybe it was just the clacking of bamboo stalks hitting together as they swung back and forth in the breeze, but then I distinctly heard the sound of a bell and the shudder of a typewriter carriage being slammed back to the left so that the typist could begin a new line of text. I'd played with my grandmother's typewriter enough times as a kid to recognize that archaic sound anywhere.

"Maybe it *is* just the bamboo," the little voice in my head suggested. "And the bell you heard was just someone's wind chime or something."

I continued listening carefully, and after a few moments, I was rewarded with the telltale sound of the bell and carriage banging home once again. The clattering sound of the wind rustling the palm fronds almost drowned it out, but I was right—it was definitely the sound of a typewriter, and it was coming from somewhere in the direction of Hemingway's house.

Pulling myself up to my tiptoes again, I peered over the wall and into the yard for a second time. The wind continued to wrestle the trees back and forth, and I caught a hint of illumination peeking through the distant branches. It looked like a dim, flickering light coming from the windows of Hemingway's writing room.

Just then, a truck turned the corner and accelerated loudly down the street behind me. As the noise of the truck faded into the distance, I turned to look up at Hemingway's writing room again, but the mysterious flickering light in the windows had disappeared, and the only sound I could hear was the lonely sound of the wind in the trees.

I waited for a few seconds, expecting the sound of the typewriter to return, but as those seconds turned into several long minutes, I soon had to wonder whether I had ever actually heard or seen anything at all. The wind was slowly dying down, and there wasn't much sound of anything anymore except the cheers and yells of drunken revelers one street over on Duval.

"You probably just imagined it," the little voice in my head suggested. "It was probably just the sound of the wind and a reflection from a streetlight or something."

"I don't know," I whispered to myself, yawning as I reluctantly dragged myself away and continued down Whitehead Street toward my hotel. "I am pretty sure I heard a typewriter."

"Why would anyone need such a thing nowadays?" the little voice in my head asked. "It's so old fashioned. Who on earth would use a typewriter?"

"Hemingway did," I replied simply.

Chapter Eight

The Ghost Of Ernest Hemingway

I didn't have to be a psychic to know what James was thinking—the look on his face said it all. He thought I was a complete lunatic.

The two of us were sitting across from each other at a table near the back corner of Sloppy Joe's Bar in the heart of downtown Key West. Sloppy Joe's, a sign proclaimed, is a Key West tradition, and judging from how crowded and busy it was, that was certainly true. It is also a sort of touristic shrine to Ernest Hemingway, with photographs and knickknacks from his life hanging from every square inch of wall space while Hemingway's grim, white-bearded face stares down at you from the bar's logo painted on the back wall.

It was there in Sloppy Joe's that the great author once came to drink and get drunk while living in Key West.

"Although, in fairness," James told me, "Hemingway spent more time at the bar's original location just up the street. Once the bar moved to its current location in 1937, Hemingway was off covering the Spanish Civil War and didn't spend much time in Key West. But the bar was still owned by his good friend Joe Russell, and the name itself—Sloppy Joe's—was also an idea of Hemingway's."

Sloppy Joe's Bar is located very nearly at the northern end of the infamous Duval Street, and that morning I walked the entire length of it from my hotel. I didn't have any more bizarre experiences along the way, so I wondered if maybe the events of the previous night had been a strange dream.

"I swear to god, James," I told him. "I heard the sound of a typewriter, and there was a strange flickering light coming from the windows of Hemingway's writing room."

James looked at me again with that dubious smile and then glanced up as the waitress arrived with our food and set it on the table in front of us. First, there was a basket of conch fritters for the two of us to share followed by small bowls of conch chowder and the specialty of the house—sloppy joe sandwiches.

"What exactly *is* a conch?" I asked James, reaching over to grab a ball of fried dough from the basket between us to examine it closely.

"It's a type of sea snail," James said, grabbing a fritter and dipping it in

Key lime mustard sauce before taking a bite.

"A sea snail?" I replied, making a face and looking askance at the fritter. I wasn't sure I wanted to taste it now.

"You can find their shells all over the place," James explained, pointing to a large curved seashell on the bar—the kind that you always see people in movies blowing through like a horn. "We make lots of different things from them."

I smelled the fritter and took a single, tentative bite. It tasted like fried dough.

"It doesn't really taste like anything," I observed, taking another bite, this time with some Key lime mustard. "Just like dough. And I can't taste the lime in the Key lime mustard, either."

James shook his head in a dramatic show of mock disappointment that made me laugh. "Barbarian," he muttered under his breath.

"The conch chowder is good, though," I said after tasting a heaping spoonful of the chunky, hot, and salty tomato broth. "It's *really* good, actually."

As someone who grew up on the ocean, I was a big fan of all forms of clam chowder, and the conch chowder was very similar to that, just with sea snails instead of clams. I took another spoonful and savored the warm and salty flavors of the ocean as they passed over my tongue. It was actually *really* good—definitely much better than the conch fritters.

"I should probably tell you that we pronounce it *conk*," James said, stuffing another mustard-dipped fritter into his mouth. "Not *conch*."

"Conk," I repeated aloud, trying out the unfamiliar pronunciation.

"I wouldn't want people to think you're a tourist or something," James explained, pushing the basket of fritters away and picking up his sloppy joe sandwich to take a bite.

I looked down to examine my own sloppy joe, lifting up the top of the round bun to see what was inside. It was ground beef in a red chili-tomato sauce.

"This is just a sloppy joe," I observed, looking up at James.

He stopped midbite to look across at me.

"Uh, yeah," he replied hesitantly, then he kept chewing and staring at me as if to say, *And your point is...?*

I rolled my eyes at him. "I mean, this is just a sloppy joe like we'd make at home," I explained. "That's what we call a ground beef sandwich like this."

James watched me patiently as the realization finally set in. Sloppy Joe's Bar was where the name of the sandwich came from in the first place.

"Oh, I get it," I said. "This is where the name comes from!"

James and I both laughed at my dim-wittedness for a second before taking another bite of our sloppy joes.

There was something about James that I really liked—something comfortable and kind that put me completely at ease. Normally I would have blushed and felt horribly stupid for not realizing that Sloppy Joe's was where the generic name for the sandwich came from, but I didn't feel embarrassed at all. We just laughed about it together, and it was funny instead of embarrassing. Around him, I felt relaxed and comfortable. It felt more like a very good friendship rather than anything romantic, though, despite the serious Johnny Depp thing he had going on.

The two of us continued eating and chatting for a while, laughing our way through our conch fritters and sloppy joes until there was nothing but empty baskets on the table.

"Time for dessert," James said, pulling out a menu and holding it up for me.

I was so full of food that I couldn't imagine eating another bite, but the lure of something sweet was irresistible, so I leaned across the table to look at what was on offer.

DESSERT
Key Lime Pie
$4.95—with Raspberry sauce add .50—with Chocolate sauce add .50

"Not much choice, is there?" I commented wryly. "Key Lime Pie it is."

James ordered two slices of pie—one for me, one for him—and in no time the waitress brought over a pair of pale yellow-green slices of cream pie topped with whipped cream and a thin slice of lime. Forking a bit off the tip, I took my first taste and fell instantly in love. The sensation was amazing. The fusion of the smooth and creamy cool filling with a subtle sour bite of lime was a perfect combination. Too soon, I'd finished my own piece and was forking tiny slivers off the side of James's plate as well.

"This is so good," I said, my mouth half full of pie. I felt like such a pig, but I didn't care. I felt perfectly relaxed and comfortable around James, although in hindsight I am not sure why that meant I had to eat like a pig and talk with my mouth full.

"It's the official pie of the state of Florida," James quipped as he pushed his plate over toward me so I could finish off what was left.

I laughed. "I saw a sign for a shop selling it on Duval Street last night," I said. "Right before I heard the typewriter at the Hemingway House."

"Yes, right, the typewriter," James said, the dubious smile returning to his face. "I thought we were finished with that."

"You don't believe me!" I protested.

James shrugged his shoulders doubtfully and opened his mouth to say something but he was interrupted by the sound of a ragged and throaty old voice speaking from behind us.

"I believe her!" the ragged old voice croaked.

James and I both turned around to see a decrepit and weathered old man sitting alone at the table behind us. He looked like something that should be standing in the corner of a dusty shop where antique maritime artifacts are sold. He was thin and creaky looking with wisps of white hair sticking up at odd angles from his head and shoulders, sprouting in an unruly fashion from beneath his sleeveless undershirt.

"I believe her," the old man croaked again, poking a bony finger into the air for emphasis. "It's Hemingway's ghost."

"Hemingway's ghost?" James replied, nearly choking with laughter as he took a sip of his iced tea.

"That's what I said: Hemingway's ghost!" the old man snapped, his forehead and crazy bushy eyebrows furrowing in impatience. "I seen him just yesterday, clear as day out there on the *Pilar*, riding the Stream."

"The stream?" I asked, confused. "The Pilar?"

James leaned toward me. "He means the Gulf Stream," he explained. "And the *Pilar* was Hemingway's boat. He's claiming that he saw Hemingway and his boat last night out in the Gulf Stream."

"I'm not claiming anything!" the old man snapped again. "I saw it with my own two eyes! It was closing in on sunset, and across the water I seen the *Pilar* and him right up on there on the flying bridge."

James leaned over again. "A flying bridge is the upper deck control station on a boat," he explained. That one I knew already, but I didn't say anything.

"Hemingway's been dead for more than half a century, old-timer," someone shouted from the bar. "And the *Pilar* is down in Cuba at his house where he left it."

"Don't you think I know Papa's been dead now fifty years?" the old-timer shouted back. "But I know what I seen. It's Hemingway's ghost, I'm telling you. And he's come back!"

"Woooooo! A ghost! And he's got a score to settle with you!" the voice over at the bar replied, laughing with his friends before they returned to their beers.

The old man ignored them and leaned forward to look me straight in the eyes. Waggling his unsteady skeleton of a finger in the air, he pointed up to the wall behind me.

I turned to look up and saw a large oil painting of a tough-looking old-fashioned boat with beautiful dark wood sides and a black hull carving its way through an ocean of deep, rich blue.

"It was him," the old man said with authoritative finality, "*and* the *Pilar*."

Chapter Nine

On The Hunt For Hemingway's Ghost

The next morning I found myself once again at the controls of my trusty De Havilland Beaver, flying a few hundred feet off the beautiful clear blue waters and heading northeast out of Key West.

All the talk the previous day about the Gulf Stream had made me curious, so when I got back to my hotel later in the afternoon, I sat down to do some research. And what I discovered absolutely fascinated me.

When I'd flown down to Key West from Miami, I'd followed the line of the Florida Keys as they curved gracefully from the tip of Florida down to the southwest. What I discovered (thanks to Google) is that a few miles offshore and running parallel to this long arc of islands is a system of coral reefs that is the third largest barrier reef system in the world. This reef system protects the islands by keeping the water calm and flat, which is perfect for boaters and fisherman, and it also makes the whole area a fantastic snorkeling and scuba-diving paradise.

But what really fascinated me (here's where you can safely call me a nerd, I guess) was the discovery that running all the way from the mainland and past Key West is a moving channel of water that travels from northeast to southwest, flowing slowly between the island chain and the outer coral reefs. This channel, I was delighted to read, is named Hawk Channel.

A great name, if I do say so myself.

You're probably wondering what's so interesting about a big moving channel of water, right? Well, what I think is so fascinating is that just outside of this coral reef system and the Hawk Channel current is another river of seawater that runs in the opposite direction. This current is the Gulf Stream, which runs from the Gulf of Mexico, through the Florida Straits between Florida and Cuba, and up the east coast of the United States and Canada, carrying warm water north and shaping the climate and weather of half the western hemisphere.

I loved the idea that someone could hop in a boat all the way up near the top of Florida and ride the slow moving current in the Hawk Channel all the way down to Key West, sipping icy drinks and relaxing on the calm azure waters as they went. And then for the return trip they could just pop out past the reef line where the much stronger Gulf Stream current flows in the opposite direction, and they could ride that all the way back to where they started their boat trip.

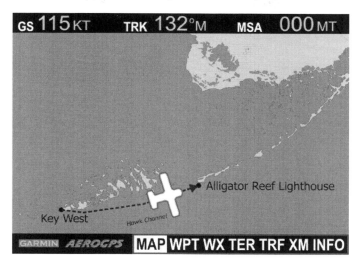

I am totally romanticizing the whole thing, of course, but the idea made me want to rush out and sign up for a university degree in oceanographic currents so that I could understand the entire fascinating process. I wanted to buy a boat and experience it for myself, but since I *do* have a seaplane, I decided to take it up and have a look for myself from the air.

As I headed for the outer reef, I passed over beds of sea grass and coral that formed weird patterns underneath the surface of the water. Up ahead a line of whitecapped surf stretched across the horizon, marking the divider line of coral reefs separating the Hawk Channel from the open water and the Gulf Stream. Passing over this barrier, I swung gradually into a turn and flew parallel to the reef on a heading of just slightly north of due east.

As the seafloor dropped out of sight, the color of the water changed dramatically from clear aqua to a deep purplish blue. Off to my left along the reef line the water was a beautiful and ever-changing concoction of a million shades of blue, each more breathtaking than the last, but out over the Stream, the color remained constant, solid, and dependable instead of flamboyant, and I thought it was all the more beautiful because of that.

I tried to imagine the power of the enormous river of water that was flowing beneath me. I imagined myself flowing along with it, drifting up the coast of Florida to Canada, Greenland, Iceland, and beyond.

"This Gulf Stream is really making you philosophical," the little voice in my head commented.

I smiled dreamily. I don't know what it was, but there was something wonderful and comforting about that flowing river of deep purple-blue far below me.

Up ahead of me to the left I saw a strange spindly iron structure rising up out of the water. It was a lighthouse built right out on the reef to warn off approaching ships.

I glanced over at my GPS. Alligator Reef Lighthouse it was called.

That sounds like as good a place as any to turn around and head back home, I thought as I put myself into a slow turn toward Key West, crossing over the outer reef and over the Hawk Channel.

Seven Mile Bridge lay stretched out before me. I'd seen it just a few days before on my flight down from Miami, and it was an amazing sight all over again, reaching almost to the vanishing point beyond the horizon in the distance.

As I drew closer to the bridge, I did a double take, blinking hard as I looked down at the world of islands, boats, and water beneath me. Just ahead, I saw a boat making for the bridge, heading for a gap between the support pylons so that it could cross underneath to the other side.

It was a strange boat, and that's why it caught my eye. For some reason almost every modern pleasure boat is bright and dazzling white in color. I have no idea why that is, but the boat down below me was much darker in color. It looked almost black, in fact.

Just before it passed under the surface of the bridge and out of my sight, I was able to get a closer look at the strange boat. I saw that it was old and wooden with deep brown sides and a lower hull painted completely black. It was just like the boat I'd seen the previous day at lunch in an oil painting hanging on the wall of Sloppy Joe's Bar. It was Ernest Hemingway's boat—the *Pilar*.

Chapter Ten

Talk About An Anticlimactic Moment

I couldn't believe what I had just seen—or at least what I *thought* I'd seen. Was I going crazy, or was it really Ernest Hemingway's boat that I'd just seen disappear under Seven Mile Bridge?

The seconds ticked heavily by as I peered out the window waiting for the boat to emerge out the opposite side.

"Where is it?" the little voice in my head asked impatiently.

I don't know, I said to myself, my heart in my throat. *But it has to come out again. It can't just disappear.*

"Isn't that what ghost ships do?" the little voice replied.

Then I saw it again, emerging on the opposite side of the bridge and making a slight turn to head up along the side of the island.

I examined it carefully, the shape and colors and design, and compared all of that against my memory of the boat that I'd seen the day before in the oil painting in Sloppy Joe's Bar. As far as I could tell, the two boats were identical.

As I passed overhead, I peered down at the occupants of the boat. There were two of them. Near the back of the vessel, a blonde woman was kneeling next to a pair of large fish that were spread out on the deck in front of her. There was nothing unusual about her at all, but the man who was on the flying bridge steering the boat made me wonder if I was completely losing my mind. Standing at the wheel on a platform built on top of the boat's main cabin was a shirtless man, barrel-chested with thin white hair and a close-cropped white beard. The man at the wheel of the boat was Ernest Hemingway.

No, I said to myself in disbelief. *That just isn't possible.*

But there he was all the same. At first, I couldn't believe it, but as my plane swept overhead, I looked down and saw with my own two eyes that Ernest Hemingway was at the wheel of his own boat, cruising fast up the western side of the Florida Keys.

"There has to be some logical explanation for this," I said aloud as I turned to take another look at him. Hemingway was still there, standing proudly at the wheel of his boat, his feet spread apart in something like a boxer's stance.

I pulled back on the controls of my plane and climbed to a higher altitude where I could think things through without drawing too much attention to myself.

Let's just be rational about this, I said to myself. *Obviously, it's not really the ghost of Ernest Hemingway and his boat down there.*

"Why not?" the little voice in my head asked.

Because ghosts don't go driving around in broad daylight or go fishing in the morning, I replied. *Nor do they wave at other boaters when they pass by them, like Hemingway is doing down there right now.*

Far below me, Hemingway had just raised his hand in greeting as he cruised past a couple of fisherman out in their small boat. The fisherman waved back, so it was obvious that I wasn't the only person who could see him.

"Maybe he's a friendly ghost?" the little voice in my head suggested.

I ignored the comment.

Obviously, it's someone who looks exactly like Hemingway, I reasoned. *And he has a boat exactly like Hemingway's.*

I nodded to myself. That was it. That was all it was.

"So what now?" the little voice in my head asked.

I watched as Hemingway slowed down and then turned into a sheltered bay where he motored the boat slowly to a set of docks next to a fish restaurant.

"If he ties up there at those docks, I'm going down for a closer look," I told myself resolutely.

Sure enough, Hemingway did exactly as I'd predicted and pulled up his boat into a vacant berth. His blonde companion jumped off the back and expertly tied it to the dock.

Without wasting another second, I got on the radio to the small local airport and arranged a place where I could land nearby and leave my plane for a few hours. Seaplanes are not exactly built for stealth—my brightly painted De Havilland Beaver rumbling up to the dock next to Hemingway's boat would be as subtle as an elephant in a china shop—so I immediately vetoed the idea of setting down in the same bay where Hemingway was docked. Fortunately, there were plenty of marinas in the area, and the helpful air traffic controller even sent a taxi out to wait for me after I touched down. Thanks to his assistance, I soon found myself at a waterside table at the fish restaurant with a menu in my hands. As I pretended to read the menu, I sneaked peeks over at the dock where Hemingway was unloading some equipment while his partner worked nearby at the fish table, cleaning and gutting their morning's catch.

"What'll it be, honey?" the waitress asked me.

I looked down at the menu again. I wasn't hungry enough for lunch, but I had to get something so I could continue my surveillance. I scanned down the menu to the dessert section.

"Key Lime Pie," I said, "and a lemonade. Thank you."

"Uh huh," the waitress replied, taking my menu and scribbling my order down on a notepad before heading for the kitchen.

Across the water next door Hemingway had finished unloading his gear and was now pushing a wheelbarrow full of tackle boxes and scuba tanks up the dock.

"Make way for the great Ernest Hemingway!" he bellowed, sending a pack of seagulls scrambling into the air. His blonde companion rolled her eyes and smacked him on the butt as he rolled past.

Funny guy, I thought. *But who is he? And what's his story?*

"Here you go, honey," the waitress said, returning quickly with my drink and a slice of pie.

"Thank you," I said.

"Uh huh," she replied and whisked off to help another customer.

Keeping my eye on Hemingway as he disappeared around a corner with his wheelbarrow, I took a forkful of pie and had a taste. I wouldn't have thought it possible, but the Key lime pie was even more delicious than the one I'd had the day before at Sloppy Joe's. I couldn't believe that I'd gone my whole life without ever having eaten Key lime pie.

Hemingway soon returned to where his boat was docked and strode over to talk with his blonde partner who was just finishing up with cleaning their fish. They talked together for a few moments in low voices that I was too far away to overhear, and then they finished packing their fish and headed up the dock out of sight.

I lingered over my pie and watched their boat bobbing gently at the dock in the swells as I waited for them to return. Five minutes passed, then ten and fifteen, but still no sign of them. After twenty minutes, I'd already finished my pie and was busy crunching the ice in my lemonade.

"Do you need a refill, honey?" the waitress asked as she cleared my plate from the table.

I shook my head. "No, thank you. Just the check, please."

It appears that the Hemingways aren't coming back for a while, I thought. *So I'm gonna get a closer look at that boat.*

I paid my bill and casually strolled over to the dock where the *Pilar* was tied up.

"Beautiful boat, isn't it?" I heard a voice say from behind me.

I turned around to see an attractive middle-aged woman standing on a twin-hulled catamaran sailing boat. She had on white shorts and a yellow windbreaker, and was busy washing down the decks of the boat with a hose.

"It's the *Pilar*," I replied in awe, trying to sound like I knew what I was talking about.

"Not quite," the woman said, smiling as she turned down her hose and let the stream of fresh water flow into the ocean. She gestured toward the back of the boat, and I took a few steps over so that I could see where she was pointing. Painted on the stern was the boat's name:

THE OLD MAN
Cape Fear, NC

"There's also a few little details here and there that aren't quite accurate," the woman said. "They've installed a couple of cutaway openings for dive ladders on the back sides, for example, and there are fittings for a Bimini top upstairs that Hemingway never had, but all in all it's a pretty good imitation of the *Pilar*."

I nodded and pretended I knew what she was talking about.

"I'm Cassie," the woman said, jumping down onto the dock next to me. She wiped her hands on her shorts and held one out for me.

"Nice to meet you," I replied, shaking her hand. "I'm Kitty."

"The boat's been in their family for years," the woman continued. "It's an original Wheeler Playmate cruiser, just like the *Pilar*, and it's been passed down from father to son with modern conveniences and modifications made by the family along the way."

"The family?" I asked. *Did she mean the Hemingway family?*

"The Tifts," she replied. "They're the owners of this boat—Kevin and Kristina Tift. They were just here a second ago; you could have met them, but now they won't be back until this evening. They always head off in late afternoon, stay out overnight, and come back to do some fishing the next morning."

"I saw them from over at the restaurant," I said. "I thought it was Hemingway's ghost."

Cassie laughed hard. "Not quite," she said. "But Kevin's in town for the annual Hemingway look-alike contest down in Key West, so I think he figured he'd show up a couple months early, relax, and do some fishing and diving and start creating some buzz so he can win the contest."

So that's it, I thought. *That solves the entire mystery. It isn't Hemingway's ghost, nor is it Hemingway's boat. It's just some guy with a boat like Hemingway's who's in town trying to win a look-alike contest.*

Talk about an anticlimactic moment.

"So what do we do now?" the little voice in my head asked.

I shrugged.

I guess we'll head back to Key West, I replied. *Maybe I can go to that pie shop and start a quest for the world's best Key Lime Pie?*

Chapter Eleven

Welcome To Fort Jefferson

The next morning I found myself flying out across the open waters west of Key West. It was a beautiful morning with blue skies and occasional wisps of clouds chasing the wind all around me.

"If there is one place that you absolutely must visit while you are here," James had told me, "it is the Dry Tortugas."

And so, thanks to some help from James and a permit from the National Park Service, that is exactly where I was headed on that gorgeous sunny morning.

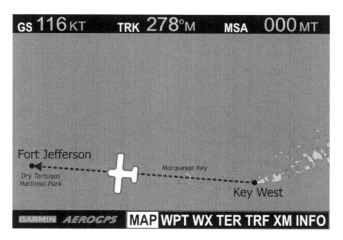

"Most people think that the Florida Keys end in Key West," James had told me, "because of that *Mile Zero* sign on Whitehead Street that marks the end of US Route 1. But the Keys actually keep going for another seventy miles west, all the way out to one of the most surreal and amazing places you will ever see — Fort Jefferson and the Dry Tortugas National Park."

As I headed west, I found myself flying over water so clear that it was like flying over the surface of some enormous sapphire speckled and flecked with the most perfect shades of color you've ever seen. At first, I could see tiny islands covered in mangrove trees dotting the horizon, but as I made my way farther west, the islands gradually thinned out and left me surrounded in a world of nothing but a million shades of blue.

I was flying barely five hundred feet off the water, staying low so that I could spot stingrays and sharks. The water was so shallow and clear that when I looked straight down past the pontoons of my plane, I was sometimes able to spot them swimming along with me.

"The last major islands you'll pass over on the way out are the Marquesas Keys," James said. "But after that there is nothing but water all the way to the Tortugas—shallow at first over an area called the Quicksands, but bottoming out into slightly deeper waters in Rebecca Channel."

The Quicksands were the area that I was flying over now, having left the large half-moon-shaped islands of the Marquesas behind me. Down below, an enormous desert of underwater sand dunes shifted and drifted with the tides until I finally reached the point where the bottom slid out from underneath and the water grew deeper.

Not long after I reached the deeper channel I began to see tiny patches of white up ahead on the horizon. I thought at first that it might be the whitecaps of waves breaking on the reef that I knew was up there somewhere, but somehow this white was more solid than that. And as I drew closer, I could see that the bright patches were actually tiny white sand islands, barren except for a few small tufts of grass growing on them. These islands, James had told me, marked the beginning of the Dry Tortugas. I knew that I was getting close.

Off to my left I finally saw my destination—Fort Jefferson. A long reef line of breaking waves stretched over from the left and ended near another low-lying chain of islands with white sands, grass, and mangrove trees. These islands were so small and low that they were barely sticking out of the ocean. But it wasn't the islands and their shabby vegetation that really caught my attention. It was what stood at the head of the islands that absolutely took my breath away. It was an enormous, manmade fortress of brick and mortar rising up out of the sea in the middle of nowhere, so completely covering the island it was built on that it looked like it was floating on the water.

But of course that was an illusion. Such a massive structure could never float. It was made of brick, after all, and it was absolutely gigantic. It was built in the shape of a hexagon with fortified towers at each corner, and each of its six sides was lined with dozens upon dozens of gunports.

I circled around the fortress to the south, unable to take my eyes off it as I crossed over the line of waves at the reef and banked down to come in for a perfect landing on the surface of the smooth water. Up ahead of me near the fortress a couple of larger seaplanes were sitting on the beach, leaving me in no doubt as to where I was supposed to tie up.

As I taxied across the water, I watched in amazement as the walls of the mammoth structure scrolled past. It was like a fantasy world come to life. I could hardly believe that such a place existed.

Closing in on the seaplane beach, I made one final sharp turn with my water rudders to spin the plane around before shutting down the engine. I climbed out of the cockpit and hopped down onto the pontoons then grabbed a paddle from its storage place. Unlike the two seaplanes that were parked farther down (De Havilland Otters, just like my father's, and big brother planes to my trusty De Havilland Beaver), I couldn't reverse pitch on my propeller to go backward, so I was left to paddle my way to the beach using nothing but my muscles.

At home in Canada on family picnics and other occasions my father would sometimes tease me from the shoreline as I struggled and paddled furiously after he'd neatly turned his own Otter seaplane around and backed it up to the beach under power. We always laughed at the pictures he took of his little girl feverishly paddling a big seaplane around as if it was a canoe.

But paddling a seaplane is not as difficult as it might seem, despite looking completely ridiculous, and in no time the back tips of my pontoons were running aground, and I was able to jump across to dry sand.

Once I was on the beach, I looked up to see a female park ranger walking toward me.

"Howdy," she called out, reaching down to pull a fixed nylon line out of the grass and handing it to me.

"Thank you!" I replied taking the rope from her and pulling my plane up into a solid position on the sand. Once I was confident that it was secure, I tied it off with the fixed lines and let the whole plane rotate slightly with the wind so that it would settle into the slack on the rope and pull it tight.

Perfect, I thought, dusting my hands off and walking up the beach to where the ranger was waiting for me.

"We've been expecting you," the ranger said, holding out her hand to shake mine. "Welcome to Fort Jefferson."

Chapter Twelve

A Completely Surreal Place In The Middle Of Nowhere

Seeing the fortress at ground level was just as amazing as seeing it from the air. When I stood close to its towering walls, it absolutely dominated every line of sight. I was eager to start exploring, but first I had to take care of making a home for myself for the coming few days. There are no hotels on the Dry Tortugas, and anyone who plans to stay the night has to rough it at the island's small campground.

"You came at a good time," Ranger Penny told me as she helped unload my tent and other camping supplies from the back of my plane and onto a wheeled cart. "Things are pretty quiet right now. After a few days around here, you'll forget about everything you left behind in the civilized world."

"Sounds perfect to me," I said, and then I grabbed the handles of the cart and followed her to the campground.

"Everything here at the Dry Tortugas is on the 'take only photographs, leave only footprints' principle," Penny explained as we passed the front side of the fortress. "Everything you bring in you have to take out again, which I doubt will be a problem for you, of course, since you have your own ride. Most of our visitors come out on the daily ferry service or in their own boats. I can't remember ever having anyone out here that had her own seaplane."

"What about the seaplanes parked over next to me?" I asked, nodding toward the pair of De Havilland Otters beached next to me.

Ranger Penny nodded. "Those are commercial sight-seeing flights," she said. "And in case you're interested, today is pizza day, so if you want them to bring you anything out on the last flight, just let me know."

I laughed. "I just got here!" I said. "I was looking forward to getting as far away from pizza as I could for a while."

Ducking under some trees Penny led me to an open clearing scattered with picnic tables and barbecue grills. It was a tiny campground, and with only a couple of other tents snuggled under the trees nearby, I had it almost completely to myself.

"No campfires allowed," Penny said, showing me where I could pitch my tent. "But feel free to use the barbecue grills. The compost toilets are up over that way, but they're closed during the day when the ferry's here, so just use the bathrooms on the boat during the daytime. That's about it for now, I guess. Just drop your camping fee envelope up at the post as soon as you can, and have a great stay."

"Thank you," I said, and I began unloading my supplies onto the ground.

Ranger Penny took a few steps away, and then turned around and said, "The ferry operators will be running a tour of the fort in about an hour and a half. If you're interested, I am sure they won't mind having you tag along."

"That would be awesome—thank you," I replied. A half hour meant that I would have plenty of time to get my camp set up and have a look around before joining the tour.

"Just meet them up at the Fort Jefferson sign at 11:45," Penny said, and then with a friendly, "See you around," she headed toward the docks.

I looked down at my pile of camping gear then longingly over at the fortress. I was really keen to have a look around and not be stuck there setting up my camp.

I'll just do the tent, I thought, compromising with myself. *Then I'll throw everything else inside it and go exploring.*

I pulled my tent from its bag and laid it out on the ground to figure out how to put it together. It was brand new, and I'd never actually set it up before, so I have to admit that it was a bit of a puzzle.

I could hear my father's voice in my head. *I told you so*, he was saying. *I told you we should have put it up at least one time before you left*. As usual, my father had tried to be thorough, but a tent, I insisted, was something I could surely figure out on my own.

Now I wasn't so sure, however.

"I was starting to wonder when we'd get new neighbors," I heard a friendly voice say from off to my right. I turned and saw a heavyset white-haired man in his fifties carrying a fishing rod and pushing past the trees next to me. He smiled brightly and ambled over to where I stood next to my rumpled tent with a look of obvious exasperation on my face. "Having some trouble?" he asked, grinning and pointing down to the lifeless jumble of nylon fabric and polycarbonate poles lying at my feet.

I blushed. "Maybe a little bit," I admitted. "I've put up plenty of tents in my life, but this one's brand new and a bit more high-tech than I'm used to."

"That usually makes them easier to put up," the man replied, leaning his fishing rod up against the bushes and wiping his palms on his trousers. He stuck a big, calloused hand out toward me. "Jack Hall," he said, introducing himself.

"Kitty Hawk," I replied, shaking his hand. He had a solid, confident handshake that my father would have appreciated.

"Somewhere around here is my wife, Jodi," Jack said, kneeling down to take a closer look at my unassembled tent. "And to be honest, she's the one who always sets up our tents, but I am sure that between the two of us we can figure it out."

I laughed and knelt down next to him.

"I'm sure," I replied.

He pointed to the diagram on the tent's instructions with his index finger. "You see?" he said, indicating the simplicity of the tent's assembly instructions. "The more high-tech they are, the easier they are to put up."

Together we flipped out the support poles, which snapped easily into locked position, and then we threaded them through the loops on the outside of the tent and bent them into perfect support arches before grounding them at the corners.

"Voila!" Jack said after we positioned the rain shell canopy over the top and pegged everything to the ground at the corners. "Home sweet home."

"Thank you so much," I said, admiring my new home away from home and tossing my sleeping bag and other gear inside it.

Jack scoffed. "No thanks necessary," he said. "You'd have figured it out yourself anyway."

"Still—I appreciate the company."

Jack walked over to the trees to grab his fishing rod. "I'd better get back and find my wife," he said, smiling. "But once you're settled, come over for a chat and some tea if you like. We're this bright yellow tent right over here."

"You can count on it," I said, smiling in return and waving as he walked off.

Looking at my watch, I saw that I had just enough time for some limited exploration before the tour started, so I pulled on a hat to protect me from the sun and set off toward the fort.

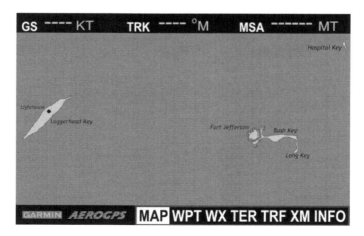

On two of its six straight sides, Fort Jefferson was surrounded by a small, low-lying island called Garden Key where the docks and campground were located. Farther to the east, Garden Key was connected to two more low islands called Bush Key and Long Key.

I had seen from the air that the fortress itself was surrounded by a wide moat that ran along the side of its walls on all six sides. This moat was formed by a low brick wall that circled the entire fort about fifty feet out from the main structure. I had seen people walking on the moat wall, and that seemed to be the perfect place to start my exploration. A walk around the entire circumference of the fort would bring me back around with plenty of time to make the tour.

I started from the end of the wall nearest to the camping area and headed in a clockwise direction. To my left was the island's south beach where some snorkelers from the ferry were already in the water with their heads down, investigating the lively underwater world next to the moat wall. As I walked along, I could see schools of small fish and coral in the clear waters beneath me.

Off to my right across the moat was the fortress itself, its brick face looming three stories above me and lined with the dozens of gunports I'd seen when I'd come in for a landing. I counted the ports along the wall facing me and did some quick calculations in my head, remembering to multiply by six for each face of the fortress walls. The fort must have been an absolute terror back in the day because there was room for hundreds upon hundreds of cannons facing out from all sides.

As I rounded the corner of the first tower, I looked out across the open water toward one side with another nearly identical face of the fort on the other. Off in the distance across the water I saw a lighthouse on a tiny island called Loggerhead Key, but that was the only other land I could see anywhere. Everything else was water all around me.

I continued along the moat wall to the far side of the fort, examining the fortress walls as I went. In some places, the brickwork of the fort was crumbling and dilapidated.

Is the damage the result of some long forgotten battle that took place here? I thought, the blinding sun making me a bit philosophical. *Or is it simply the result of the classic battle that we all fight against the passage of time?*

The sun was relentless and brutal out on the exposed moat wall where there was not even a hope of finding shade anywhere. I reminded myself to be careful not to get sunburned on my very first day.

As I continued around the fort, I was almost relieved when I turned the last corner and the north beach of the island came into view. It was lonely out there on the far side of the fortress with nothing but the sound of the gentle lapping of the waves to keep you company and the endless water stretched out in front of you.

Up ahead the tail of my plane came into view as I rounded the last tower and returned to where I'd started. Off in the distance past my plane I could see a handful of private boats riding at anchor in the harbor and the whitecaps of the waves breaking on the reef farther out.

"What a completely surreal place this is," I said to myself, reflecting on the utter strangeness of my current surroundings. "Why would they build this massive fortress all the way out here in the middle of nowhere?"

I hoped that question would be answered shortly as I reached the Fort Jefferson sign at the front side of the fort and joined a small group of people who had already gathered for the 11:45 tour.

Chapter Thirteen

Why In The World Would They Build This Place?

"The Dry Tortugas got their name from none other than the famous Spanish explorer Ponce de León," Sandy, the tour guide, told us. She was a young woman in her midtwenties with short brown hair and a nose ring wearing a loose-fitting tan shirt with shorts and serious-looking dark brown hiking boots.

"Ponce de León first visited this area in the year 1513 on his famous quest to find the Fountain of Youth. He didn't find it here, of course, but he and his crew did notice the abundance of sea turtles living in the area and named this chain of small islands *Las Tortugas*—Spanish for *The Turtles*. The word *Dry* was later added to the name on mariners' charts to indicate the complete lack of fresh water on the islands.

"Five hundred years later that lack of fresh water remains as true as it was when Ponce de León first visited. Everything you see here on the islands—food, water, fuel, and so on—has to be brought here from somewhere else. And that includes bricks, which, as you can see from the large structure in front of you, meant that they had to bring an awful lot of bricks here."

Sandy turned around and pointed to the intimidating walls of the fortress looming behind her.

"All of these bricks," she said, gesturing dramatically, "had to be brought here from the outside world. And that's a lot of bricks, let me tell you—more than sixteen million in total, which makes Fort Jefferson the largest masonry structure in all of the Americas—both north and south."

Sandy took a step closer to the fort and pointed up toward the top level of the walls. "Some of you might notice a difference in color between the bricks making up the first two levels of the fort and those used to build the top level," she said.

I looked up at the walls of the fortress and noticed that she was right. The lower two thirds of the walls were made up of pale reddish-yellow bricks whereas the bricks at the top level of the structure were of a much darker shade of red.

"The reason for this is because when they first started building the fort in 1846, they shipped all the bricks here from a brickworks factory in Pensacola, which is in the northwest corner of Florida near Alabama,"

Sandy explained. "Construction on the fort took many, many years, of course, and by the time the Civil War began in 1861, the fort was still not finished. This was a problem for the builders since Fort Jefferson itself was in the hands of the northern Union army, and their brick supplier in Pensacola was now part of enemy territory in the southern Confederacy. This meant that to finish the construction of the fort they had to ship bricks here from much farther away, across thousands of miles from all the way up in Maine.

"But, in fact, the construction of the fort was never actually completed," Sandy said. "Before I explain that, let's head across the moat and through the entrance to the fort to get a closer look at the inside."

We followed Sandy across a narrow bridge to the main (and only) entrance to Fort Jefferson, after which we passed through a heavily fortified series of archways and doors and out into the enormous inner yard of the fortress. A few gnarly and twisted weather-beaten trees were scattered here and there across the yard, but other than those and a handful of small buildings and ruins, the inner yard was nothing but wide-open space. The huge grassy lawn surrounded on all sides by the mesmerizing, recurring pattern of archways and gunports looked more like the inside of a sports stadium than a military fortress.

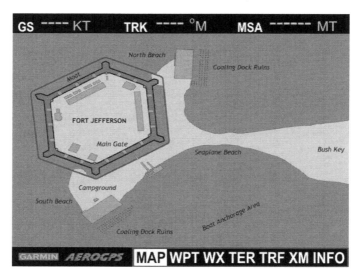

"Before we talk about why they never finished building the fortress," Sandy said, gathering us around her in the shade of one of the ancient-looking trees, "I want to talk a little bit about why they built this massive structure out here in the first place. And the reason was nothing more than simple geography."

"You might have noticed on the way out here that the Dry Tortugas are kind of in the middle of nowhere," Sandy said, and a few people in the tour group nodded and laughed. "But in fact the Dry Tortugas lie right at the heart of several very important shipping lanes. To the north and west lie the Gulf of Mexico and various important ports in Florida, Mississippi, Louisiana, and Texas. But even more important is the fact that to the south lies Cuba, and between here and there the Dry Tortugas mark the western entrance to the Straits of Florida, through which flows the Gulf Stream current that carries ships all the way up the eastern seaboard of the United States and beyond to Europe.

"Where we are standing right now is a perfect spot to control access to these vital shipping lanes and ports," Sandy said, pointing to the ground. "What makes it an even *more* perfect location is the fact that the Dry Tortugas form a natural harbor. The calm, shallow water surrounding the islands is protected by the reefs, yet the water is deep enough for heavier warships to anchor here for resupply before they range out into the open water and maintain control of the shipping lanes.

"In the early days of the United States—long before the invention of airplanes and before the establishment of any kind of substantial navy— this geographic location made the Dry Tortugas a vital place for the young nation to control and occupy. After the United States bought Florida from Spain in 1821, the US Navy sent some men here to scout things out and report on the possibility of building a fort. The report of their first scouting mission in 1825 basically stated that it was completely unfit to build anything here; it's miles from civilization; there's no fresh water, and there are hardly any islands here—just a few tiny patches of sand barely sticking out of the ocean, which probably can't bear the weight of a fortress anyway. And that was the end of it, but a few years later in 1829, a completely different scouting mission explored the Tortugas and came back with a completely different report. The scouts concluded that it was a perfect location because there's perfect anchorage here, and if we didn't control it, someone else would, which meant that US shipping enterprises in the Gulf of Mexico would be gravely threatened. So the decision was made to build a fortress here, and after a series of lengthy bureaucratic delays, the construction finally began in 1846.

"But don't forget," Sandy said. "That there was no water here—not then, not now. So how could they expect to build and maintain a garrison of hundreds of men and resupply warships out here if there was no fresh water?"

Sandy looked around at each of us with a smile on her face.

"The answer," she said, "is revealed at the next stop on our tour. Follow me!"

We followed Sandy across the inner yard and underneath the open archways on the far side of the fort. Off to both sides of us passageways of arches lined the side of the fortress, each successive opening designed to hold a single large cannon pointed out through a small gunport in the outside wall.

"As you can see, Fort Jefferson was designed to withstand incredibly massive assaults by enemy forces," Sandy said, smacking the thick walls with the palm of her hand. "These walls are fifty feet high and eight feet thick but they're designed to do more than just protect the fort from attack—they also serve as an ingenious water filtering and collection system.

"Two levels far above us, rainwater filters down through the sand and stones on the curved tiled roofs of the upper archways. The water then flows down into drainpipes and through the superstructure of the fort down to this level and through specially designed replaceable filters," Sandy said, stepping over and indicating an opening in one of the support pillars where the special water filters would once have been placed.

"After this final filtering process the water then would flow down into giant cisterns underneath the walls of the fort where it was collected and could later be used as drinking water. In total there are one hundred and nine of these cisterns all around the circumference of the fort with an overall capacity of one and a half million gallons of fresh water."

Sandy took a step back from the support pillar and looked at us. "Pretty clever, huh?" she said.

I nodded along with the others in the group. It *was* pretty clever and I was impressed.

"There was only one small problem," Sandy continued, her face looking sad. "The fort was too heavy."

Too heavy? I thought. *What does that mean?*

"The designers of the fort were clever, that's for sure," Sandy explained. "But what they didn't expect was that this enormous structure would weigh so incredibly much that it would actually cause the island beneath it to sink. As the immense weight of all the millions of bricks pressed down and the structure began to settle, the cisterns underneath began to crack open, letting in salty seawater and contaminating their fresh water supply—and so ended their ingenious solution for providing drinking water for the Dry Tortugas."

You've got to be kidding, I thought to myself, sticking my head into the filter opening and trying to see down into the darkness below as the group shuffled off to the next stop on the tour.

Sandy led us up a narrow spiral staircase that brought us to the top of the fortress where the view was absolutely spectacular. We had a commanding view in both directions: We could see the enormous inner yard of the fortress behind us, and the speckled blue waters and coral reefs in front of us stretched endlessly to the horizon.

"Great view, isn't it?" Sandy asked. "And pretty much everything you can see from up here is part of the protected areas of the Dry Tortugas National Park. The park covers more than a hundred square miles in total, but ninety-eight percent of that is under water."

Sandy walked along the fortress wall and over to the edge of one of the corner towers. We had a nice view along the side of the fort to the moat wall where a couple of snorkelers were swimming past.

"Fort Jefferson was built to accommodate a lot of firepower," Sandy said, pointing to the rows of gunports lining the fortress wall. "There were four hundred and twenty heavy artillery pieces, to be exact. But as it turned out, because they never finished building the fort, they also never fully outfitted the place with weapons.

"If you look down at these gunports here, you will see that many of the openings look as though they've suffered some battle damage. But Fort Jefferson has never been attacked, and this damage is not actually damage at all. These jagged holes are simply the result of the fortress having been left unfinished. You see, in 1875, the US government finally decided to pack up their operations and send everyone home, thus leaving the fort completely abandoned until the twentieth century when it was declared a national monument and later a full-fledged national park.

Sandy then gestured at the honeycomb of archways and passages of the colossal structure and said, "But you're probably wondering why in the world they would go to so much trouble to build this place only to abandon it in the end."

I looked around at the tour group, nodding along with the others. That was exactly what I was wondering.

"After thirty years of construction plagued with setbacks and problems," Sandy said, "and coping with cracking cisterns and harsh conditions and mosquitoes and yellow fever epidemics—after so many challenges, they still forged on, determined to complete the fortress, but then something happened that finally defeated Fort Jefferson. And that was the introduction of rifled artillery shells."

To my right a middle-aged man smiled and nodded in understanding.

I didn't get it.

What are rifled artillery shells? I wondered.

"Everyone knows cannonballs, right?" Sandy asked, holding her hands up to indicate the spherical shape of a cannonball. "For hundreds of years, cannonballs were fired from cannons, and they worked fine until the second half of the nineteenth century when the armies of the world began converting to a more modern type of artillery shell—the kind that is shaped like a bullet and spins through the air thanks to rifled grooves inside the cannon barrels. This spin stabilizes the projectile in flight, a discovery that allowed for much more accurate and powerful new artillery weapons to be developed—new weapons that were so powerful, in fact, that they would cut through the walls of this fortress like butter.

"As this innovation became more widespread in the various armies throughout the world, Fort Jefferson was slowly rendered obsolete," Sandy said. "The federal government finally came to its senses and realized that the old girl was more trouble than she was worth, and the whole thing was closed down."

Chapter Fourteen

And I Thought I Was Coming Here To Relax

After the tour ended, I spent some time wandering through the fortress on my own exploring its various nooks and crannies. Nearly all of it was open to the public, I discovered, except for a few areas where the handful of national park staff members lived.

I learned from one of the park rangers that the fort is staffed by eight to ten rangers who live at the fort full-time, staying there in shifts of varying lengths before heading back to the mainland on their days off. As I looked around at the beautiful surroundings, felt the warm sun on my skin, and contemplated a swim in the cool clear waters, I imagined this to be a highly coveted posting for a national park ranger.

"Not really, actually," a park ranger named Roger told me, stroking his bushy salt-and-pepper beard for a moment before answering. "Most people like their gadgets too much, I suppose. And out here things are pretty quiet and isolated."

Quiet and isolated sounded perfect to me, at least for a few days anyway. I had plenty of books with me, after all.

I got a much better idea of what Roger meant by "quiet" when the ferry headed back to Key West in the late afternoon and took most of the park's visitors with it. This was followed shortly afterward by the last seaplane of the day roaring across the waters of the harbor and taking to the skies to head home. After that, only the rangers and a handful of overnight campers were left on the island—plus, of course, the tens of thousands of Magnificent Frigatebirds that were noisily nesting over on the adjacent two islands that were closed to the public. (The word Magnificent, Roger had told me, was not an adjective used to describe them. It was actually part of their proper name.)

The fortress was closed at sunset, and as night began to fall over the Tortugas, those of us who were intrepid campers found comfortable spots on the beach or along the moat wall to watch the sky turn from bright blue to brilliant pink and shimmering gold, and finally to the deep indigo blue of twilight.

The sunset was amazing, but the stars that came out afterward were even more beautiful, and I must have spent half the night lying out on the sand watching them sparkle and shine through the inky black canopy of the night sky. I'd rarely seen so many stars in my life, not even in Canada where I'd had plenty of chances for excellent stargazing. Eventually I dragged myself back to bed, zipping up my tent for the night and reading a couple of pages in the darkness on my Kindle Paperwhite before falling asleep.

I wasn't asleep for long, though, because the dawn came early, and soon the cocktail lounge chattering of the Frigatebirds from over on Bush Key was in full swing. I was still tired, but my excitement to get started on another day in the Dry Tortugas got me out of bed, and soon I was sitting cross-legged in the grass just outside my tent eating a can of cold beans for breakfast.

"Why don't you come over and join us?" I heard a voice say from the bushes off to my right. I looked up to see an attractive woman in her early fifties walking toward me. "I'm Jodi," she said with a gentle smile, her friendly face perfectly framed by her shoulder-length dark brown hair. "Jack's wife. I believe the two of you met yesterday."

I smiled. "Good to meet you," I replied, shaking Jodi's hand, and then I followed her to their picnic table just on the other side of the bushes where Jack was waiting.

"Good morning!" Jack said in a stage whisper as the two of us sat down across from him. It was still quite early, and he was trying not to disturb the other campers. "Help yourself to anything you want," he said, waving his hand over their elaborate spread of camping breakfast.

I looked down at my can of beans.

"No, no," I replied. "I'm fine with my beans. I can't take any of your food." I knew that campers coming to the Dry Tortugas on the ferry were limited in how much food and supplies they could bring with them.

"Don't be crazy," Jack scoffed. "Help yourself. We've got plenty more on our boat."

"Your boat?" I asked.

Jack nodded. "The *Tradewind*, she's called," he said, gesturing past the trees and out to the water beyond where several boats were riding at anchor. "We've got plenty of space and a kitchen on board, but when we're down here in the Tortugas, we like to take the dinghy ashore and rough it along with all the other campers."

I looked down at my can of beans again then back at their selection of bread and various toppings.

"Just help yourself to whatever you," Jack insisted, holding up a jar of peanut butter to entice me.

I resisted for a few moments longer, but eventually caved in to temptation. I was suddenly in the mood for a peanut butter sandwich.

"I don't have much to offer in return," I said, taking the jar of peanut butter and a couple slices of Wonder Bread from Jack. "I only brought beans and corn and Spam out here with me."

"I love Spam!" Jack replied, smiling. "Bring it along tomorrow for breakfast and we'll call it even."

"It's a deal," I said, spreading a thick layer of peanut butter on my bread and looking for something to put on top. Jack and Jodi had an extensive selection of jams and jellies, but in the end, I opted for a classic PB & J with grape jelly.

"Do you come here often?" I asked after swallowing the first delicious bite of my sandwich.

Jodi nodded. "Ever since Jack retired from the police force and we bought the boat, we come down here for camping at least a couple times a year, from up near Fort Myers where we live."

"And what brings you here?" Jack asked as he started a peanut butter sandwich of his own. "We're dying to know your story ever since we saw you fly in yesterday on that fancy plane of yours."

"Jack!" Jodi scolded, turning to me to apologize. "I'm sorry for my husband's nosiness and terrible manners."

"What?" Jack protested. "I'm curious! I've never met anyone with her own plane before, much less someone so young."

"Don't worry, I really don't mind," I replied, smiling, and then I told them about my upcoming flight around the world, which would take eighteen months to complete.

Jack looked impressed. "That's quite an undertaking," he said. "I don't even know what I'm going to do later today, much less a year from now."

I laughed again. "I have no idea what I'm doing later today either," I said. "So don't feel too bad."

"Snorkeling," Jack and Jodi both answered at the same time.

"You definitely have to go snorkeling up along the moat wall," Jodi added. "It's beautiful. And if you hit the water before the ferry arrives, there will be fewer people around."

"And when you get bored of that, you can come fishing with me from the dock for a while," Jack suggested.

"It sounds like I have a busy day ahead of me!" I grinned. "And I thought I was coming here to relax."

Chapter Fifteen

The Popular Wisdom About Barracudas

I thanked Jodi and Jack for having me over for breakfast, and then I returned to my tent to change into a swimsuit. They were right; snorkeling sounded like a perfect way to spend the morning.

With my fins, mask, and laminated fish chart in hand, plus a generous layer of sunscreen, I waded into the ocean just off the south beach. The water was deliciously cool against the heat of the day, and I was soon snorkeling my way clockwise around the fortress.

Underwater was a completely different and magical world. Coral had grown along the side of the moat wall creating perfect hiding places for a hundred different types of colorful fish. The sea floor was littered with jumbles of fallen bricks, and here and there, large sections of collapsed wall were scattered, encrusted with coral and looking like the ruins of some long-vanished ancient civilization.

Up ahead of me a swirling school of small white fish twisted and turned to make a hole, and I swam directly through them. As I continued farther, they swirled around again behind me, seamlessly sealing the breach and leaving me surrounded on all sides by tens of thousands of fish all moving together in perfect harmony like one single living being. They were so close that I could almost grab them, but every time I reached out with my hands, the cloud of sparkling fish ducked away, just out of reach, only to return again when I pulled my hands back.

I swam clear of the sea of white fish and past a small group of black and yellow striped Sergeant Majors moving along the moat wall in search of food. Farther down some bright yellow and purple Spanish hogfish ducked in and out of the branches of coral and past some beautiful purple sea fans waving gracefully back and forth in the current.

I stopped for a while, mesmerized by the waving motion of the sea fans. My breath caught in my throat for a moment as a cow-nosed stingray flew past like some graceful underwater bird. It turned and circled back, diving down and smoothly skimming the bottom as it went. I was a bit nervous as it passed directly underneath me with its stinger clearly visible at the base of its long, thin tail, but I knew what friendly and gentle creatures rays are and told myself not to worry. Besides, the ray was at the sea bottom as I floated above it at the surface, well out of reach of its stinger.

The water wasn't very deep—maybe seven or eight feet at the most, with perfect visibility for snorkeling. Near the bottom, I could see some larger fish meandering their way through the bricks and coral. I took a deep breath and free-dived down to the bottom for a closer look, equalizing the pressure in my ears as I went. According to my fish chart, these larger fish were mostly various types of groupers and red and white hogfish who quickly sized me up before wiggling quickly off to a safer distance.

As I slowly paddled my way around the moat wall, I could hardly keep up with checking my fish chart to figure out the names of all the fish that were swirling around me, but I didn't need my chart to identify the next one I came across. Up ahead, slowly coming into view at the edge of my visibility, I saw the long dark form of a barracuda heading my way.

My heart jumped into my throat, and I completely froze. I couldn't believe how big it was—nearly a meter long and so dark that it looked almost black.

What do I do? What do I do? I screamed to myself.

The barracuda didn't move; it floated almost motionless just beneath the surface of the water, long and thin and powerful with razor-sharp teeth jutting out of its partly opened mouth.

Just don't panic, I told myself as I made a wide circle around him. He looked at me as I swam around him, watching carefully and curiously, but he didn't move, and I breathed easier again once I managed to put some distance between us.

I'll have to remember to do a Google search about barracuda when I'm back in civilization again, I thought after I completed my snorkel around the fort and was back on the beach toweling myself dry.

"You've only been here for a day and already you're missing the Internet," the little voice in my head observed.

True, I conceded as I looked at the postcard-perfect views that surrounded me on every side. *But I wouldn't trade all of this for anything.*

As it turned out, however, Jodi was as good a source of information about barracudas as Google might have been. She and I went snorkeling together later that afternoon, and I took her around to the place where I'd seen the barracuda earlier in the day. He was still there, floating motionlessly just beneath the surface of the water, and I was again amazed at how big and powerful he looked.

"There's really no need to worry," Jodi told me. "Barracuda have a fierce reputation, but it's not like they go around attacking humans for no reason. Millions of people swim around them every year without any problem."

"I guess that's true," I agreed.

"The popular wisdom about barracudas says that they are attracted to shiny objects in the water," Jodi added. "And just in case there is some truth to that I always make sure I don't wear any rings or shiny necklaces when I go swimming or snorkeling."

I didn't have any jewelry on either, so I guessed that I was safe too.

The two of us headed for the beach, but as we swam off, I happened to glance back and saw the barracuda following behind us. My heart leaped into my throat again, and I tugged on Jodi's sleeve. She looked back then nodded and gave me a sign that everything was okay. We continued to shore with me nervously keeping an eye out behind us until the barracuda finally swam off.

"Barracuda are sometimes lazy," Jodi explained, after we reached the sandy beach again. "Even though they are lightning fast predators who are fully capable of hunting on their own, they sometimes find it easier to follow along behind some of the ocean's larger predators so they can pick up the scraps left behind.

I looked at her with a dubious expression, unconvinced.

"That's all he was doing," she explained, smiling. "He probably thought we were a couple of sharks and was just following along in case there were any leftovers."

"How could he think *we* were sharks?" I asked in amazement.

Jodi shrugged. "Barracudas also don't have very good eyesight," she said. "That's why they often come so close and just stare at you. They can't see you very well otherwise."

You see? I told myself as the two of us walked to the campground. *Who needs Google?*

I said good-bye to Jodi and headed to my tent to change clothes and grab a book. I found a nice spot in the shade of the mangrove trees and read for a while. After reading a few chapters I wandered up to where Jack was fishing from the side of the dock, and I chatted with him for a bit. He eventually got tired of fishing, and after saying good-bye, I went off to wander through the fortress again for the rest of the afternoon until it closed.

All in all, it was a perfect, lazy day in the Dry Tortugas.

When the sun began to sink lower in the sky, I once again found a nice, comfortable spot on the sand at the end of the beach from which I could watch another spectacular sunset and the stars slowly coming out far above me. I lay back in the sand and was looking forward to another night of stargazing, but I didn't quite make it. My lack of sleep from the previous night finally caught up with me, and before I knew it, I was out like a light, fast asleep under a black sky filled with a billion stars.

Chapter Sixteen

The Word *Ghost* Suddenly Seemed Very Appropriate

The next thing I knew I was waking up to a cold, dark world all around me. At first, I was confused and had no idea where I was, but as I slowly emerged from the drunkenness of sleep, I remembered that I was sitting at the end of a beach on one of the islands of the Dry Tortugas.

I yawned and stretched my arms, working the kinks out of my back as I scooted up against the concrete wall nearby and pulled my knees up to my chin. I thought about going back to my tent right away but decided to sit there for a while to enjoy the stars and come fully awake. In my sleepy condition, I was liable to break my leg in the process of stumbling through the dark bushes on the way to my tent.

As I sat there, I looked out across the water toward the lighthouse on Loggerhead Key and watched its dazzlingly bright beam sweeping in circles through the darkness.

One one thousand... two one thousand... three... four....

I started counting as the light flashed directly at me. *Eighteen one thousand... nineteen one thousand... twenty one thousand.*

The beam flashed again for a split second, blinding me with its light before swinging on through its endless circles.

Twenty seconds, I thought and yawned again. The lighthouse beam rotated once every twenty seconds. Maybe between its light and the harbor light on the fortress I could find my way safely back to my tent without a flashlight.

I looked up at the trees behind me to see how dark it would be if I returned to my tent before daylight, and I was startled to see the thin, narrow beam of a powerful flashlight shoot out across the water from somewhere almost directly above me. As I craned my neck to look up, I heard the almost imperceptible sound of something scraping across gravel, like the sole of someone's shoe twisting on loose stones.

I froze.

Someone was on the platform above me, and he or she was shining a light across the water—three quick flashes followed by one longer burst.

I turned my head to track the sweep of the beam into the distance, and I saw something very strange—or at least I *thought* I saw something very strange. I couldn't be certain because it disappeared almost immediately.

It looked like a strange, eerie blue-green glow from beneath the surface of the water, like some weird radioactive monster from a science fiction movie. For an instant, it was there, far off in the distance, and in the next instant it was gone, leaving me squinting into the blackness and wondering if I'd actually seen anything at all.

From somewhere through the trees behind me I heard another noise, this time louder and more obvious, like the sound of someone who is trying to be quiet, but not trying *too* hard at it, if you know what I mean.

There was a sharp crack of a twig and the sound of fabric tearing followed by a whispered cry of frustration. "Oh, dammit," I heard a familiar whisper say from somewhere off through the trees. You can never be sure who is speaking when you hear whispering, but to my ears, it sounded a lot like Jack.

I cocked my head to the side and listened carefully as Jack (or whomever it was) continued shuffling through the trees, the wobbly beam of their flashlight glinting through the trees.

What in the world is he doing? I thought. *And what is going on out here in the middle of the night?*

I heard footsteps walking along a wooden surface followed by the sound of a door opening and closing, and then it finally dawned on me. He was going to the bathroom. Up through the trees behind me were the compost outhouses that the campers used.

I heard some other sounds during the next minute or two, but I'll spare you the intricate details and just say that after a few more interesting noises, the wooden door opened and closed again, and Jack (or whomever) made his way through the trees to the campsite. Over the faint sound of the wind and waves, I heard the very distant zipping of a tent door closing and (I think) a few more sounds of someone flopping around a bit, but then it was quiet once again.

So if that was Jack going to the bathroom, I asked myself, *who is on the wall above me?*

I pondered this question as I waited breathlessly, crouching motionless against the base of the concrete supporting wall of the disused dock and helipad above me.

The minutes passed slowly by without a sight or sound of anyone or anything, and I started to wonder if maybe I'd just imagined all of it, but then after exactly five minutes, I saw a single long burst of light pierce the darkness above me and shoot out across the water. I knew it was exactly five minutes because I had counted the cycles of the lighthouse beam on Loggerhead Key. There had been exactly fifteen of them since the last noises I'd heard of someone settling heavily into his or her sleeping bag at the campsite.

The precision in timing of the light beam above me made me wonder if it was some sort of automated navigational light.

But how would an automated light know to start counting once Jack stopped flopping around in his sleeping bag? I asked myself. *That can't be what it is. Whatever the light is for, it's a human flashing it.*

I turned my head and looked out across the water to where I'd seen the unearthly blue glow a few minutes earlier. At first, there was nothing but blackness, but then I saw it again—an incredibly peculiar, almost alien bluish-green glow floating on the surface of the water in the distance so far away and dim that I could barely see it at all.

The beam from the lighthouse flashed in my eyes as it circled around, and I shut them tightly out of reflex. When I opened them again, I tried to determine what was causing the glow in the water, but I had to wait for the purple spots in my vision to dissipate. I was blinded for a few moments, so I started counting in my head to time the light so that I could avoid being blinded again the next time it came around.

One one thousand… two one thousand… three one thousand….

"Maybe it's some kind of phosphorescent algae," the little voice in my head suggested.

I shook my head. *That isn't it. I've seen that plenty of times in Tofino, and this is way too bright for that. Eighteen one thousand… nineteen one thousand… twenty.*

I blinked hard to close my eyes and shut out the flash of light from the lighthouse at the instant it passed over me, then opened them again.

Besides, phosphorescent algae don't respond to a person standing on the shore sending signals with his flashlight, I continued. *And that's exactly what that was—a signal.*

Something very strange was going on, but I had absolutely no idea what it could possibly be. To my eyes, the eerie blue glow was so strange and completely unfamiliar that I could only equate it to being some radioactive movie monster or some other kind of paranormal activity, like a ghost maybe.

A ghost?

The thought sent a shiver down my spine, and as my eyes adjusted to the dark, I noticed something else on the water that I hadn't noticed before—there was a boat out there.

I blinked again, shutting out the light and preserving my night vision. I opened my eyes and peered into the blackness, averting my vision ever so slightly to the left of where I was looking so that I could see better in the darkness—a little trick I learned in astronomy club. The light sensors on the periphery of your vision are much more sensitive than the ones near the middle, so if you want to see something better in the dark, just look slightly to the left or right of it instead of directly at it.

It was definitely a boat—a boat with all its running lights switched off—and a hull that was almost blacker than the black water that surrounded it. I continued to squint and stare, and as I slowly made out its basic outline and shape, my use of the word *ghost* to describe the eerie glow in the water suddenly seemed very appropriate.

It was Hemingway's boat out there in the water.

It was the *Pilar*.

Chapter Seventeen

Secret Radioactive Government Super Squids

I couldn't believe what I was seeing, and my eyes instinctively flicked over to look directly at the boat again. It faded and almost disappeared from sight. I glanced a bit to the left again and watched it reappear. I struggled to make out its silhouette with my peripheral vision. I couldn't be one hundred percent sure, but with every passing moment I became more and more convinced that I was right—it was the *Pilar*.

But why is it out there? I asked myself. *And what is this weird bluish glow in the water?*

I kept watching, completely stumped and fascinated by the bizarre spectacle that was playing out before my eyes. I wished that I could climb onto the platform above me to get a better look, but whatever was going on with the boat had something to do with whoever was on the concrete platform above me sending signals with his flashlight, so I stayed motionless and silent, and continued watching.

Ten minutes passed, then twenty. The sweeping beam of the lighthouse on Loggerhead Key counted the minutes and seconds off like a precision watch.

A pale glow crept into the eastern sky from the horizon. It was almost sunrise. I'd been out here on the sand the entire night.

I panicked at the thought of daylight giving away my position. I silently pulled myself closer to the base of the concrete wall.

As it turned out, there was no reason to worry, because after a few more minutes, the strange glow in the water disappeared, and the water was completely dark again.

What do I do now? I thought with rising panic. I was growing increasingly nervous as the sky brightened gradually with every passing minute.

Finally, the stillness was broken, and I saw the flashlight beam shoot out once again from somewhere above my head. Three long bursts of light flashed across the water, and a few seconds later, I heard the faint and distant rumble of a boat engine starting up.

I watched in fascination as the *Pilar* slowly made its way across the water, and three more long bursts of light shot out over my head as the boat disappeared from view behind the fortress. The sound of the engine faded completely as it passed behind the wall, but I waited and listened until I eventually heard it again far off in the distance through the trees behind me. It was so faint that it was almost not there, but I was sure that I could hear it powering up a little and moving faster until it faded away into nothingness.

I was concentrating so closely on the sound of the boat in the distance that I was startled again by a sound much closer—the sound of soft footsteps on the loose gravel somewhere up above me. I continued to sit motionless, pulled tightly out of view at the base of the wall, until the sound of footsteps also faded away. I strained to hear what direction the person had headed, but it was impossible to tell, and once the footsteps reached the soft sand and grass at the opposite end of the platform, I couldn't hear anything anymore.

I wasn't sure what I should do. With every passing minute, the sky in the east grew brighter, and from the direction of Bush Key, I could hear a few of the nesting birds waking up and starting a brand new day of bird noise.

Okay, here's the plan, I told myself. *I'll sneak up to where the outhouses are, then I'll just walk normally to my tent as if nothing happened. If anyone sees me, he'll just think I'm going to the bathroom, which will be true since I've been sitting out here all night without a break.*

It was a good plan, and my nearly bursting bladder convinced me to put it into immediate effect. I pushed myself to my feet, steadying myself with one hand on the concrete wall as I climbed up the sand to the trees. Stepping carefully along the grass and around the bushes, I pushed myself up to the outhouse platform and used the railing to stand to my feet.

Once I was finished, I confidently pushed the door open and noisily plodded down the ramps toward my tent, whistling nonchalantly as I went.

"You don't have to make *extra* noise," the little voice in my head observed sarcastically. "And you certainly don't need to whistle."

I stopped my stupid whistling and reached down to unzip my tent and crawl inside. Kicking off my sandals at the door, I zipped the mesh closed behind me and slid into my sleeping bag.

I lay awake for a long while, turning restlessly from side to side as I pondered everything I'd just seen, trying in vain to figure it out. It wasn't that I didn't have any ideas about what might have been going on. The problem was that every idea I had was completely ridiculous.

I wondered whether I had accidentally stumbled onto some secret government experiments with radioactive super squids. I had already established that Hemingway's ghost was, in fact, some guy named Kevin who was in town to win a Hemingway look-alike contest, but what was he doing out here in the Dry Tortugas? Was *he* doing experiments on radioactive super squids? Was it even him in the boat? Maybe it *was* Hemingway's ghost after all. I didn't really get a very good look at the boat, nor did I get a good look at who was signaling from the shoreline. Was it one of my fellow campers, or one of the park rangers?

Or was it someone else entirely? I thought, my mind taking a sudden turn down an eerie path. *Maybe what was standing on the platform above me wasn't even human.*

Goosebumps crawled all over my skin at the thought of having been so close to something supernatural.

Maybe it was a ghost? I thought. Or *maybe an alien? Maybe there's a crashed UFO out there in the water?!?*

And so it went, my imagination running wild and jumping from one absurd explanation to the next until I finally fell asleep.

Chapter Eighteen

The Tuna Witch Wahoo Whacker

I emerged from my tent several hours later when the ferry arrived and the sound of people moving around the island woke me up. After a few stretches to get my blood flowing, I walked over to Jack and Jodi's campsite to see if they might still be having breakfast. I had promised them some of my Spam that morning, after all, but they had long since finished their breakfast and started on their day already.

No surprise there, I thought wryly. *It's almost eleven.*

Walking down to the beach, I looked across the water to where I'd seen Hemingway's boat earlier that morning before it had puttered off under the cover of darkness. By the light of day, everything seemed much less ominous, and I felt pretty stupid for letting my imagination run wild.

There's probably some completely harmless explanation for the whole thing, I told myself, even though I knew that it was almost certainly not true. Whatever the explanation might be, I doubted very much that it was something innocent. Innocent explanations never involve the use of secret flashlight signals in the middle of the night.

The thought of someone flashing signals from the concrete platform reminded me to go directly there to check things out. Maybe I could find something that would help me figure out the identity of the mysterious accomplice.

Climbing the concrete wall above the brick pylons where I'd been sitting the night before, I pulled myself onto a large open rectangle that jutted out over the water. The surface was collapsed in some places and overgrown with weeds here and there, but it was still solid enough to serve as an emergency helipad for the fortress as well as to support a couple of large generators that were housed at the far end.

On the eastern side of the platform was a grid of support piles for the dock that used to be located there. Sandy the tour guide had told us that in the 1800s, the docks had been used for loading US Navy ships with coal and other supplies. I had snorkeled around those support piles the day before as if I was swimming through an underwater slalom, and I had admired the beautiful coral that had grown over them during the past century.

I walked over to the corner of the platform just above the spot where

I'd been sitting the night before, and I snooped around for clues. The surface had collapsed slightly on the inside and formed a perfect hiding place with a commanding view of the water, the fortress, and the entire south beach. The depression was deep enough for anyone to duck down out of sight behind the brick wall and remain hidden.

It's also a perfect place for someone to signal a boat with a flashlight, I thought, climbing down into the corner. The angle from there to where I'd seen the boat the night before was such that no one on land would have seen the light—no one except me.

I bent over to inspect the collapsed surface of the concrete platform and noticed what looked like someone's buttprint in the sand. There were also a number of footprints in the sand underneath, but you know how sand is—it's not very good for retaining footprints that are of any use to amateur detectives. People's butts, on the other hand, are the perfect shape for imprinting on sandy surfaces, and unless I was mistaken, that was exactly what I was looking at.

But what does that prove? I asked myself. *That someone sat in the sand out here? People probably sit in the sand up here every day to watch the sunset; not to mention that a buttprint is hardly the kind of evidence that would hold up in a court of law.*

"What are you, an actor on a show you've just made up called *CSI Dry Tortugas*?" the little voice in my head asked. "Who said anything about a court of law?"

You know what I mean, I snapped, standing upright again and thinking through the clues that I'd found. It wasn't much use, however. All I had was some vague evidence that someone might have been up here the night before, but that really didn't get me anywhere since that much I knew already because I'd seen him flashing signals.

"Good morning!" I heard a voice call out from behind me. I spun around to see Jack walking along the platform toward me with a pair of fishing rods in one hand and a tackle box in the other. "We missed you at breakfast," he said.

"Sorry," I replied, laughing. "I slept in a bit, I guess."

"Not to worry," Jack said. "Maybe tomorrow. But I saw you up here and wondered if you wanted to come out and keep me company for a bit while I do some fishing."

"I'd love to," I replied, and the two us headed for the dock.

"Jodi's out with the birders by Bush Key," Jack said. "But she'll come over and join me when she's finished. She was hoping the two of you could go out snorkeling again."

"The birders?" I asked. "What do you mean?"

Jack stretched his fishing rods out and pointed to a crowd of people a few hundred yards away who were standing near my seaplane on the narrow stretch of sand that connected Garden Key and Fort Jefferson to Bush Key. A large sign lettered *ISLAND CLOSED* was posted in the middle of the narrow corridor of sand, and the entire group was standing behind it, cameras and telescopes mounted on tripods at the ready as though some amazing and incredible thing was about to happen.

"Those birders," Jack said, rolling his eyes a little bit.

"I don't understand what you mean," I replied.

Jack looked at me. "Birders—people who watch birds."

I stopped in my tracks and looked over at the eager group of people crowded on the beach. They looked like fans at a rock concert.

"Is that why they're standing there like that?" I asked in disbelief. "Just to see some birds?"

"Not just *some* birds," Jack replied. "Magnificent Frigatebirds, Brown Noddies, Sooty Terns, Belted Kingfishers, and let's not forget the magnificent Masked Booby."

I laughed loudly, startling a nearby family eating some sandwiches at one of the picnic tables.

"I thought the Frigatebird was magnificent," I said, still laughing and drawing attention to myself.

"Oh he is," Jack replied, also laughing. "Even more than the boobies are."

The nearby mother and father scowled at us, and Jack and I made a quick escape in the direction of the dock.

"Oh dear," Jack said as we slowly recovered from our laughing fit. "Jodi would kill me if she heard me making fun of one of her hobbies like that. She already gets enough teasing about her yoga."

"Hey!" I replied sternly. "There's nothing funny about yoga!"

I reminded myself to ask Jodi about yoga, because it occurred to me that early morning out on the Dry Tortugas, before any of the day's tourists showed up, would be a perfect time to do some yoga in this amazingly peaceful place.

Jack raised his hands in submission. "Sorry, sorry," he said. "I'd better not offend both the birders *and* the yoga people on the same day."

"Apology accepted," I replied, grinning.

"Now come over here and help me pick a lure," Jack said. "Because if you think bird names are funny, then you're going to laugh your head off at the names that some of these have."

"Oh yah?" I asked, intrigued. "Like what?"

"This one's a Fathead Junior," Jack said, pointing to an interesting specimen, and as he pulled various brightly colored fishing lures from his tackle box and displayed them with maximum showmanship, he named each one. "This is my Candy Scooter Chugger Head...and my collection of Crappie Lipless Rattles...and let's not forget my favorite lure, the Badonk-a-donk."

I laughed and laughed as he pulled out one lure after another, each with a more ridiculous name than the last.

"And what about this one?" I carefully picked up a pointy-headed one with black and red stringy things attached to it.

"That's the Tuna Witch Wahoo Whacker," he replied, making me laugh even harder.

"What the heck is going on over here?" a voice asked from behind us.

Jack and I turned to see Jodi walking over with a small telescope on a tripod tucked under her arm and a big smile on her face. "Is Jack boring you by showing off his collection of fishing lures?"

"I would hardly call it boring her," Jack protested. "Look how much she's laughing!"

"It's true," I admitted, slowly bringing my laughter under control as Jack and Jodi showed me how to fit a lure at the end of a fishing line and cast off the dock into the water below.

As I stood there with Jodi and Jack quietly casting off their fishing lines and reeling them in, I thought about telling them what I'd seen the night before. I'd almost opened my mouth to ask Jack whether he'd ever noticed anything strange happening out on the water in the middle of the night when it suddenly occurred to me that I really had no idea who it was that had gone to the bathroom in the middle of the night. At the time it had *sounded* like Jack whispering and complaining, but as I said, when it comes to whispers, it's nearly impossible to recognize someone's voice. It could have been just about anyone going to the bathroom, just as it could have been anyone sitting at the top of the concrete wall flashing signals out to the boat. For all I knew it was one of them.

I snapped my mouth shut and didn't say a word. I decided that for the moment I was going to keep the whole thing to myself until I managed to figure it out.

Chapter Nineteen

The Old Man And The Sea

After a bit of fishing and a lunch of Spam sandwiches with Jack and Jodi, I wandered off by myself through the fortress again. I needed some time to think, but I wanted to get away from the relentless sun because it was starting to bake me to a crisp. I climbed one of the spiral staircases to the second level and walked in the shade of the fortress from each gun casemate to the next with a nice brisk breeze to keep me cool.

Let's recap what I know about last night, I told myself as I restlessly paced the second floor of the fortress.

I knew that I'd seen a strange radioactive glow in the water that looked like nothing I'd ever seen before, except maybe in the movies. Just a short distance away from that strange, eerie glow was *The Old Man*, the boat I'd seen in the town on Marathon Key a few days earlier—the boat that was outfitted to look exactly like Hemingway's boat, the *Pilar*, and the man who was outfitted to look exactly like the great Ernext Hemingway himself.

I admitted to myself that it was possible that the boat I'd seen at night was a different boat from *The Old Man* that belonged to Kevin and Kristina Tift, but the outline I'd seen in the darkness was lowriding, old-fashioned, and shaped just like *The Old Man*. Of course, there had to be other similar types of boats in the world, and anyone up to no good trying to keep his boat invisible at night would probably also choose a low riding boat with a black hull. I also had to admit that it was remotely possible that maybe it wasn't the *Pilar* replica but the actual *Pilar* that I'd seen floating out on the water close to that unearthly and ghostly glow, complete with the actual honest-to-goodness ghost of Hemingway working the controls on the flying bridge. But as far as working hypotheses went, I basically discounted this one as unworthy of serious consideration.

As for the identity of the mysterious signaler on the shoreline, I knew far less. All I really knew was that he used a flashlight for signaling, and based on the prints I'd found in the sand, he had a normal sized butt. But unfortunately, nearly everyone has a normal sized butt, so that really didn't tell me anything of importance.

What *was* important, however, was the fact that he'd been signaling the boat in the first place. That single fact alone was what made the entire incident so suspicious. As I'd already told myself, innocent explanations never involve the use of secret signals. And it was the apparent reason for the signal that made it even more suspicious. The signal had come right before I'd heard someone stumbling through the trees on their way to the bathroom. Clearly the purpose of it was to tell whomever it was out there on the water to *stop* doing whatever they were doing because there was someone on shore stumbling around who might see them.

The timing of the second signal was also a convincing clue. It had come exactly five minutes after the danger of being spotted had passed. I knew that if I was in charge of a conspiracy involving secret nighttime experiments with radioactive squids, and my job was to sit up on the wall and signal when the coast was clear, I would probably make it a rule to wait five minutes after the last sign of trouble before giving the okay to continue.

It was all very suspicious; that much I knew, but that didn't help me get any closer to figuring out exactly *what* was going on. All I knew was that some people were up to no good, and whatever it was they were doing had something to do with a strange, science fiction kind of glow emanating from the water.

I stopped walking for a moment and stared out across the water through one of the unfinished gunports; I was thinking of all the science fiction movies I had seen. Something about that blue-green glow seemed very familiar.

And then it came to me. It *was* in a movie I once saw—a movie by the same guy who directed *Avatar*, only this movie was filmed completely underwater.

"Night scuba diving!" I said to myself in excited realization. "They're scuba diving out there!"

The answer was so obvious that I felt ridiculous for not thinking of it already. The weird blue-green glow was produced by underwater diving lights not radioactive alien squid or some other ridiculous explanation.

Shaking my head at my stupidity, I descended the stairs to the first level of the fort and wandered across the yard toward the entrance.

After walking across the moat, I spotted one of the park rangers working on a boat that was tied up at the dock. In his crisp tan uniform, he looked like someone who knew what went on around here, so I decided to walk over and ask him a few questions.

"Look at this," the ranger said when he saw me approaching. He pointed to one of the hoses from the boat that was spraying water into the ocean.

I took a few more steps and peered over the side of the dock. At the back of the boat, a huge fat mammal with a big, flat beaver-like tail had come to the surface and put its wrinkled, whiskery face into the stream of water from the hose. As I stood there watching in amazement, it rolled over onto its algae-covered back and floated in the water with its too-short flippers resting happily on its tummy.

"What the heck is it?!?" I asked.

"It's a manatee," the ranger said. He turned toward me and I read his name off his nametag. Patrick, it read. "They like to drink the fresh water from the hose," he said.

"I've lived by the ocean my entire life," I replied, kneeling down for a closer look at the strange animal. "But I have never seen such a bizarre creature before."

"You must be from up north, right?" Patrick asked.

"Tofino," I replied, getting to my feet again. When I saw the puzzled expression on his face, I added, "It's in Canada."

Patrick nodded. "That's why," he said. "You're too far north. The manatees don't like the cold. They only live in the warm waters close to the equator."

"Really?" I replied, looking at the huge blob of a creature below me. "They're so fat. I would have guessed they were built for the arctic."

Patrick shook his head. "Nope," he replied as the manatee finished drinking and swam off at a leisurely pace before disappearing from view under the boat. "They stick to the warm waters, although you virtually *never* see them this far out from the rest of the Keys, and they prefer the fresh water of Florida's natural springs. I hope this little guy isn't lost. He's far from fresh water; that's probably why he's so desperate for a drink."

The shapeless blob of a manatee was hardly what I would call little, but I agreed with Patrick—I did hope he wasn't lost.

"Anyway, what can I do for ya?" Patrick asked, returning to his chores on the boat. "You looked like you were coming over with a question before Mr. Manatee interrupted us."

I nodded and looked down again at the back of the boat just in case the manatee had returned. He wasn't there, but as I turned my head to take a look, something unusual caught my eye.

"Is this your boat?" I asked, looking up toward Patrick, wrinkling my forehead and trying to process what it was that I was seeing.

"You bet," Patrick replied proudly. "She's a real beauty, isn't she?"

"She sure is," I replied, trying to sound suitably reverent yet casual as my mind was racing.

The boat certainly *was* beautiful, there was no doubt about that at all. It was a single-masted, brilliant white sailing boat with clean, sleek lines and a low hull that looked like it was built for speed. But what really made me take notice was the boat's name that was emblazoned boldly on the back end:

AND THE SEA
Cape Fear, NC

Cape Fear, North Carolina, I thought to myself, trying to keep myself from grinning at the significance of it. *I've seen that name somewhere before.... haven't I?*

I spent a few more minutes chatting with Patrick about his boat, asking a few polite questions before thanking him for his time and retreating to a shady picnic table nearby. I didn't say a word about the strange goings-on that I'd witnessed the night before because after noticing the name of his boat, I realized that Patrick the park ranger must somehow be connected to Kevin Tift, the Ernest Hemingway look-alike who was cruising around the Florida Keys in a boat that was a replica of the *Pilar*.

Kevin's boat—the *Pilar* replica—was named *The Old Man*, and now I'd just discovered that the name of Patrick's sailing boat was *And The Sea*.

The Old Man And The Sea.

Just like the story by Ernest Hemingway.

And just in case I needed any further convincing, both boats had the same unusual port of registry clearly painted on them—Cape Fear, North Carolina.

I couldn't believe it. Kevin and Patrick were probably brothers, or maybe father and son because Kevin looked like he might be old enough to have a son in his thirties.

I'll bet a million dollars, I said to myself as I watched Patrick working down at the dock, *that if I marched down there and asked him his name, he'd introduce himself as Patrick Tift, a lifelong fan of the writings of the great Ernest Hemingway.*

It all made sense. While Kevin and his wife were performing their night dives from *The Old Man*, Patrick was on the shore keeping a lookout so that he could alert them at the first sign of trouble. Three quick flashes of the flashlight, and in an instant, the diving lights go dark and no one on shore sees a thing. Without lights, *The Old Man's* pitch-black hull and dark wood sides were impossible to see at night. After all, I'd had a hard enough time making it out in the darkness when I already knew it was there.

I nodded to myself and felt proud about my discovery and for putting it all together, but it didn't take long to realize that I still had no idea whatsoever what was going on. They were scuba diving at night and didn't want anyone to find out about it, but why?

What could it be? I wondered as I sat from a distance watching Patrick tend to his sailboat. Whatever it was, I was determined to find out.

Chapter Twenty

Going For A Swim

I spent most of the rest of the day in my tent, sleeping as much as possible before the sun went down so that I would be wide-awake and alert once nighttime fell. I ventured out shortly before nightfall and joined the rest of the campers on the beach to watch the daily spectacle of the sunset.

I found Jack and Jodi sitting on a pair of camping chairs, and I sat down on the sand next to them. The three of us talked, joked, and laughed until long after darkness set in and the stars filled the sky overhead. Eventually the two of them began to yawn, so we said good night and headed to our tents.

I climbed inside mine but left the zipper door hanging open behind me. I didn't want to make any noise whatsoever when I crawled outside again later.

Settling down on my air mattress, I pulled my sleeping bag half over me and read for a while to pass the time until the sounds of the other campers gradually dwindled to nothing, and the silence of the night set in. I continued reading for a while longer, keeping the brightness on my Kindle at its lowest setting so that I wouldn't attract any attention, but shortly after midnight, I shut that down too and just lay there, waiting and listening.

The time passed slowly, with each minute dragging out like an eternity as I closed my eyes and strained to hear any signs of activity or movement in the night.

One o'clock came and went, and I was starting to wonder if maybe there was a flaw in my plan. I had assumed that if I waited long enough, Kevin and his fake *Pilar* would return to do whatever it was he and Patrick were doing the night before, and that Patrick would take up his position at the end of the concrete pier as a lookout. But as the minutes dragged on, I realized that there was no reason to think that there would be a repeat of the previous night's intrigue. I had no idea what they had been doing, after all. It could've been something mundane and routine.

And then I heard it—the low and almost inaudible rumble of a boat engine idling on the water. I listened as it continued for a few minutes longer before shutting down and plunging the world into silence again.

I waited and listened. I had also expected to hear the footsteps of someone walking out on the cement platform to keep lookout, but I didn't hear anything.

Patrick's probably already out there, and I just didn't hear him, I told myself. *He must be. He would be there waiting before the boat arrived, wouldn't he?*

Slowly, slowly, slowly I pulled myself to my knees and carefully crawled out of my tent and into the cool night air. It took me several minutes to weave and twist my way out of the tent without making any noise, but soon I was free and padding silently across the grass.

I knew that Patrick most likely would be keeping a sharp lookout in the direction of the campground, so earlier in the day I had staked out an approach that would take me around the trees at the opposite end of the platform and far from his sight from the other end where he would be positioned again, hopefully.

It was too risky to walk across the concrete platform itself—that would make too much noise, and I would be too exposed—but a small beach at the end would allow me to sneak down the sand and keep position behind the cement wall with just my head poking up above it. That meant that if I needed to, I could duck down whenever I wanted and disappear completely from sight.

It was a perfect plan, but I hadn't counted on how impossible it would be to see the other end of the platform where I'd assumed Patrick would be sitting. My night vision had been adjusting for hours, and yet as hard as I tried, I simply could not see a single thing. It was simply too dark. I had a completely clear line of sight, but there was not enough light to see anything.

What made it worse was the fact that I'd also misjudged the viewing angle out to the boat on the water. If I stood on my tiptoes and made soft, short jumps into the air, I could catch a faint glimpse of the blue-green glow out across the water, but I couldn't really see what was going on, and of course it was too risky to keep jumping up and down, even on the quiet sand. The motion alone would attract attention, even if I did manage to stay completely silent, because something else I hadn't anticipated was the harbor light that was shining down from behind me on top of the walls of Fort Jefferson. It didn't give off very much light, but it would be enough for Patrick to see me if I was jumping up and down repeatedly.

I leaned up against the cold concrete wall and peered across the platform into the darkness, hoping to catch a glimpse of something—a bit of motion as Patrick adjusted himself on the sand, perhaps, or anything that would confirm my suspicions that he was there.

But it was hopeless. I couldn't see a thing.

"So what now?" the little voice in my head asked.

I need to figure out Plan B, I replied, ducking down to sneak back to the cover of the trees. *And I think I have a pretty good idea of what that will be.*

I made my way carefully back to my tent and pulled off the black lightweight hoodie and black cargo pants that I'd been wearing as camouflage in the darkness. After a bit of twisting and contorting to get myself into the tent, I changed clothes as quickly as I could and crawled outside again.

I crouched in the grass for a few moments with my eyes and ears on full alert as I scanned the world around me for any signs of danger. I waited thirty seconds then a minute more, but there was nothing. The coast was clear.

I reached down and silently grabbed my snorkel gear bag, which I had stowed beside the tent, and I unzipped it carefully, one zipper tooth at a time until I was able to pull out my mask and fins.

"Please tell me you're doing what I think you're doing," the little voice in my head said.

I'm not sure what you think I'm doing, I replied, crouching and sneaking along the edge of the trees to the beach at the far end of the concrete pier. *But, yes, I am.*

I was going for a swim.

Chapter Twenty-One

Plan B It Is, Then

Staying low and close to the tree line, I made my way around to the far end of the platform. With my snorkel gear under my arm, I sneaked across to the corner of the concrete wall and climbed down to the beach below where I'd been standing a few minutes earlier.

I peered over the top of the wall and tried one last time to see if I could make anything out at the other end of the pier, but nothing had changed. It was just as inky black and indistinguishable as it had been a few minutes before.

Plan B it is, then, I said to myself as I ducked down and made my way over to the edge of the water. The quiet sound of the small waves lapping against the pier was indistinguishable from the sound of my wading carefully into the water. I continued until it was deep enough for me to float, then I pushed off and pulled on my fins.

Well done, I congratulated myself as I silently swam farther out into the ocean, carefully paddling with outstretched arms until the water was deep enough to use my flippers.

I stuffed my mask and snorkel under the snug-fitting shirt I was wearing. I'd brought them with me in case I might need them, but for the moment, I was worried that breathing through the snorkel would make enough noise for Patrick to hear me from the dock.

Keeping my fins well submerged, I silently flippered to the corner of the concrete wall. Ahead of me, I could see the dock pilings lined up in orderly rows just a short distance out from the concrete platform, providing me with perfect cover to circle around and make my way to the end. From there, I hoped I would be able to see Patrick on the corner of the wall near the beach and have a clear view across the open water to *The Old Man* and the strange blue glow of their clandestine diving operation.

I pushed myself from one post to the next, being careful to keep my hands off and to use my flippers as much as possible so that I wouldn't disturb the coral. I might be on a secret mission, but that didn't mean that I should be going around ruining a hundred years of coral growth, right?

As I neared the end of the line of pilings, I could see the blue-green glow coming into view from across the water. Farther in the distance, the pulsing beam of the lighthouse on Loggerhead Key counted off the minutes and seconds in wide, sweeping arcs of light. As I rode the crests and troughs of the tiny waves, my line of sight across the water also rose and fell, giving me a perfect, clear view every second or two.

My view of the top of the platform, however, was not so good. From my position behind the corner piling of the long vanished coaling dock, I still couldn't see a thing on the concrete pier.

Dammit, I'm going to have to swim a bit farther out, I thought and pushed myself off the last support post then propelled myself into the open water.

I assumed that from his vantage point on the platform, Patrick's attention would be focused on the campground, and he would probably also be keeping an eye on the boats anchored in the harbor just in case anyone out there decided to get up in the middle of the night to go to the bathroom or something. Presumably, the last place he would be looking was out on the open water away from the pier where I was currently floating.

Even if he did happen to glance my way, I was still not worried. Back at my tent, I had chosen a black rash vest shirt with long sleeves to cover my upper body. Not only would it keep me warm, but it would also camouflage me as much as possible in the black water. I knew that I was almost invisible out here, even if someone was looking directly at me, and as a last resort, I could always dive under the surface to disappear completely if I had to.

As I swam farther out, my view of the corner of the concrete platform became clearer. I pulled myself up and held my position, treading water as I squinted through the darkness.

It was unbelievably difficult to see anything. It was so dark up there, and with every slight gust of wind I caught a glimpse of motion and was fooled for a second until I realized it was just the trees moving. But eventually, after a few minutes, I finally saw something useful.

Yes! I cried to myself triumphantly as I caught sight of some human movement on the platform. It couldn't possibly have been the wind in the trees this time. It looked like someone reaching up with his hand to wipe his face or push the hair out of his eyes.

Finally, I knew where to look.

I paddled in place some more and peered into the night. There was definitely someone up there leaning against the corner of the wall, looking in the direction of the campground.

I knew it, I said to myself, smiling from ear to ear. It was too dark to make anything out except for the person's silhouette, but that was all I needed. Now I knew that there was definitely someone standing directly above where I'd fallen asleep on the beach the night before.

I used my flippers to swivel in place and turned to look out across the water over toward the boat and the blue-green glow. Bobbing on the surface of the water was not the best option for gaining a clear view, but at least I could still make out the eerie glow and the blacker-than-night outline of *The Old Man.*

As I watched the action on the water, I glanced now and then at Patrick on the concrete pier just in case he turned to look in my direction, but he didn't. He just continued to lean nearly motionless against the corner of the wall.

If I swim even closer, I'll have a much better view, I thought to myself.

"Don't even think of it," the little voice in my head warned.

Too late, I responded, and I put my head forward to start paddling toward the blue-green glow.

Chapter Twenty-Two

The Safest Place For Me To Be

"This is completely insane," the little voice in my head complained as I swam through the pitch-black water farther and farther away from the safety of Fort Jefferson and Garden Key.

What's the problem? I asked myself as I pulled out my snorkel and mask and fitted them over my head, carefully clearing the snorkel of excess water as quietly as possible. *In the daytime, I swam pretty far out to the coral heads at the edge of the snorkeling area.*

"Yes, but this isn't daytime, is it?" the little voice replied then fell silent.

I wasn't worried. In calm, flat waters like this with no current, I could swim almost indefinitely, especially with a pair of flippers on. The snorkel and mask also made things easier, but I realized that swimming with my face down in the black water where I couldn't see a thing was somewhat disconcerting, so after a minute or two, I took the mask off again and stuffed it under my shirt.

I glanced back at the concrete pier just to make sure that Patrick couldn't see me. It only took one look for me to realize that it would be completely impossible for him to spot me because I was already too far out, and if I couldn't see him, there was no way he could see me.

Turning forward again, I swam a bit stronger toward the blue-green glow while off to my right the lighthouse on Loggerhead Key kept up its never-ending circles of light.

One one thousand... two one thousand... three one thousand... four....

I counted the seconds after the lighthouse flashed in my direction to establish a rhythm for swimming; I made long, powerful strokes with my arms on the odd numbers and kicked twice per second with my feet.

Kick kick, kick kick, stroke; kick kick, kick kick, stroke... *eighteen one thousand... nineteen one thousand... twenty...* flash... *one one thousand... two one thousand... three one thousand... four....*

Overhead, a billion beautiful stars filled the sky from horizon to horizon. I rolled over to swim on my back for a while and admired the dazzling sky filled with brilliant diamonds. Stretching across the canopy of night, the Milky Way looked brighter and closer than I'd ever seen it before. It seemed as if I could almost reach out and run my fingers across it. Out of the corner of my eye, I caught some movement and turned to watch a satellite cutting its way across the heavens like a lantern at the masthead of some distant sailing vessel navigating through the stars.

It was such a beautiful sight that I was reluctant to roll over to my front, but unfortunately, I couldn't see where I was going when I was swimming on my back, so out of necessity, I flipped over.

One one thousand... two one thousand... three one thousand... four....

I was swimming strongly across the open water making good progress. The only problem was that the boat and the glow didn't seem to be getting closer as quickly as the fortress was grower smaller and smaller behind me. They were apparently a bit farther out than I'd thought.

It doesn't matter, I thought to myself, and I concentrated on maintaining the rhythm of my swimming. *Nothing to worry about.*

At the horizon I could see flashes of lightning from a distant storm. I reminded myself to keep an eye on that in case it was headed this way, and then I turned my eyes forward again to make sure I was swimming straight toward the eerie glow ahead.

Then suddenly everything went black.

In the blink of an eye the strange blue-green glow in the water suddenly flicked into blackness, leaving me without a reference point to swim toward.

"What the hell?" I whispered under my breath as I stopped dead in the water and swam in place.

I turned to look back at the fortress to see what was going on. Was someone going to the bathroom? Is that what was happening?

I couldn't see a thing. I was too far away.

Do they see me? I thought, panicking. I knew it was impossible, but in my split second of fear, I wasn't so sure.

I turned in the direction of the boat and tried to see if it was visible. I thought I could make it out, black against the blackness of its surroundings, but I wasn't certain that I was seeing what I thought I was seeing.

If worse comes to worst, I thought. *I have the lighthouse and the harbor light on Fort Jefferson to guide me home. But why did they shut the lights down on the boat? Are they done for the night already?*

I assumed that it was too early for them to be finished, but in truth, I only had the previous night's experience to guide me. I had no idea what they were doing, so I obviously also had no idea when they would eventually call it quits and head for home.

All I could do was wait, glancing back and forth between the boat and the fortress, watching for the all-clear signal from Patrick and listening for the sound of the boat's engine being started before its driver headed back to civilization.

I counted the cycles of the lighthouse to keep track of how much time had passed. Eight or nine minutes after the glow had first disappeared into the darkness, I finally saw a flash of light coming from the direction of the fortress—a single, long burst of light that pierced the darkness and disappeared—the same all-clear signal that I'd seen the night before.

I turned quickly and scanned the water, holding my breath and waiting for the glow to reappear. After a few long moments, it did, and I was able to breathe a heavy sigh of relief.

Someone probably just went to the bathroom at the campground, I assumed. *Maybe it was Jack again?*

I started swimming forward, quickly falling into my rhythm in time with the lighthouse beam.

I was getting closer now. With every strong push of my arms, the glow in front of me grew brighter and the silhouette of the nearby boat loomed larger. I stopped for a moment and reached under my shirt to pull out my snorkel, fitting the mask over my eyes as I continued to kick forward with my legs.

I leaned forward and stuck my face in the water to see what I could see. Sure enough, a bright blue glow was filling the water, and it was exactly what I'd expected—a set of underwater diving lights with thick clouds of bubbles filling the water and floating to the surface.

I pulled my head out the water and looked toward the outline of the boat. It was very close now, and I could reach it in just a few minutes.

"How much farther are you planning to go?" the little voice in my head asked in alarm.

I thought about this for a moment.

If I wanted to see what was going on, I would have to get fairly close. That much was certain. But I didn't want to get too close and have anyone see me. Doing both was going to be a tricky balance.

Unless... I thought to myself, pondering my options.

"Unless what?" the little voice asked warily.

...unless the safest place isn't out here in the open water. Maybe I would be better off right up next to the boat?

Chapter Twenty-Three

One More Loaf Of Bread

It makes perfect sense, I told myself. *Instead of floating out here in the middle of the water where anyone on the boat can see me, I'll just swim so close to it that I'll be completely out of sight. No one will see me.*

"No one except anyone who's in the water with you," the little voice in my head reminded me. "Like the person who's scuba diving, perhaps?"

I still wasn't worried.

Their attention will be on whatever they're doing down there, I told myself. *They won't be looking straight up on the off chance that someone might have swum all the way out here in the middle of the night to see what they're doing.*

It made perfect sense. At least it did to me, anyway. And that's all that mattered.

I decided to make for the boat's anchor line first. It stretched away from the front of the boat into the darkness. It would give me something to hold on to while I floated in place for a while and checked out what was going on down below.

As I paddled slowly and carefully to the anchor line, I kept one eye on the boat to make sure no one was looking over the side. In the low lighting on the back deck, I could see someone moving around, but I couldn't see who it was or what he was doing.

When I reached the anchor line, I held on to it tightly with one hand while I adjusted my mask and peered underneath the surface. A short distance beyond the back of the boat, I could see someone moving around on the sea floor with a pair of powerful dive lights. Judging from the small clouds of air bubbles rising to the surface, there appeared to be only one diver, which made sense to me since I assumed it was just the two of them on the boat—Kevin and Kristina—and one of them was definitely on deck. But it occurred to me that I actually didn't know for sure whether anyone else was with them.

I'll never know as long as I stay here hanging off the bowline, I thought. It was obvious that I was going to need a better vantage point if I wanted to see what was going on.

I pulled myself forward with the anchor line and floated carefully over to the starboard side of the boat. This side was the farthest from the fortress *and* from the diver underwater, which I hoped meant that it was the best place for me to see without being seen.

Just above the waterline along the length of the wooden hull of the boat was a raised, beveled edge with brass trim. I was sure it was originally designed for decoration, but I was immediately thankful that it was there because it was perfect for me to hold on to and steady myself as I worked my way along the side of the hull. I returned to where I'd started until I was even with the pilothouse and just a few feet from the back end of the boat. Ahead of me was an opening in the side of the boat that gave me a fairly good view of what was taking place on deck. Actually, I could see across the deck to the opposite side of the boat where a blonde woman was leaning next to another opening and peering into the darkness toward Fort Jefferson. I assumed she was keeping a lookout for any signals from her accomplice on the shore, and I breathed a bit easier because that meant that her attention was focused in the exact opposite direction from where I was floating.

I lowered my head into the water to check things out down below. The scene that met my eyes was so completely surreal that I almost could not believe what I was seeing. Millions of air bubbles filled the water, each one illuminated and sparkling from the strange, eerie glow coming from the sea floor. The entire area was bathed in a deep blue light that looked so unearthly and strange that for a moment my breath caught in my throat at the beauty of it.

The source of the light was a pair of dive lights fixed on spindly mechanical arms that were attached to a pair of air tanks strapped onto the back of a solitary scuba diver. The water was not even ten feet at the most, and thanks to that, I had a nearly perfect view.

The diver, who I assumed was Kevin, was kneeling down in the sand right in the midst of a forest of coral that was growing on what appeared to be man-made ruins and debris lining the ocean floor. Spiky, thin structures laced with coral shot up from the bottom at strange angles, and scattered in the sand were what appeared to be bricks.

In his left hand, the diver was holding a kind of strange and clumsy weapon, a sort of gun that he was pointing underneath the ruins. Moving the device from side to side for a while, he used his other hand to poke around and occasionally reach up to adjust his dive lights to a better angle.

Suddenly he stopped and leaned in closer to the ruins, fanning the water with his hands for a few seconds before pointing his strange gun into a crevice and pulling the trigger. As he did this a cloud of sand and sediment blew out in a mini underwater explosion and filled the water for a few moments before it was gradually carried away by the slow tidal current. The gun was apparently some kind of underwater fan that he was using to clear away deposits of sediment and sand so that he could see more clearly.

I watched in fascination as he continued working, slowly moving along the edge of the ruins, alternately waving his strange gun around as he sifted through the debris then using it to blow off the sand and sediment so that he could take a closer look before moving on.

He was obviously looking for something. But for what?

I lifted my head out of the water and eased forward to peek through the opening and check on Kristina. She hadn't moved, and she was still keeping a lookout in the direction of the fortress.

Feeling reassured that I was undetected, I returned to watching the underwater operations taking place down on the sea floor. Kevin continued with his search, repeating the same actions until finally there was a break in his routine. I suddenly saw his body tense. He leaned forward to look closely at something, and then he dropped his underwater fan and reached down with both hands to pull something free from the ruins, which took a bit of struggling on his part. He looked like a human-octopus mutant with his various pieces of equipment floating free in the water around him but remaining tethered to his scuba tanks as he jerked and pulled on something underneath the coral-encrusted ruins.

He finally pulled it free, and after the dust settled, I saw that it was a large, black brick. It didn't look very special, so I expected him to set it aside and continue with his excavations, but instead of doing that, he hefted the brick up into his arms and reached for a net bag that was hanging down from the boat nearby.

As Kevin turned to do this, he almost looked in my direction, so with my heart almost jumping into my throat, I slowly pushed along the length of the hull until I was safely out of his line of sight. Once I was safe again, I continued watching as he wrapped the net bag around the brick. Kevin had to struggle a bit to get the brick into the bag because it was fairly big—at least a foot and a half long and almost a foot across. When he finally got it secured in the bag, he reached up to pull three times on the line. Kristina pulled the brick to the surface and Kevin along with it. As he rose up on the line, riding it like an elevator, I could see that he was wearing only diving socks and no flippers. With his heavy weight belts and gear, it was probably difficult for him to swim, so it made sense that he would hitch a ride on the line back to the boat.

When he reached the port side ladder, Kevin switched off his dive lights and climbed up to the boat. The world was plunged into darkness again, but the glow of the small light on deck was enough to see by as I eased forward and peeked through the opening at the two of them.

I watched as Kevin stripped off his mask and dive tanks, setting them aside and disengaging straps and hoses as he went.

"Another one," I heard him say as he worked quickly to switch out his dive tanks for a fresh pair. "And just in time too. I was almost out of air."

Kristina nodded and slid the brick across the deck; then she wrapped it in towels and moved it out of the way.

Why did they bring this brick onto the boat? I wondered. There were plenty of other bricks littering the sand down on the sea floor, after all. Granted, most of them were smaller than this particular one and yellowish-green in color, but there were other large, black bricks down on the bottom. What was so special about this one?

Kristina pulled a radio from her back pocket and held it up to her mouth.

"Citadel, Citadel, come in, this is the Cuba Libré, over," Kristina said into the radio then waited for a reply.

"This is Citadel," the reply squawked through the tiny radio speaker. "Go ahead, over."

"One more loaf of bread up," Kristina said simply. "But still no luck and we're prepping for the last dive of the night, over."

"Roger that," the reply came, and Kristina slipped the radio back into her pocket.

A loaf of bread? I asked myself in confusion. *What the heck are they talking about?*

Chapter Twenty-Four

Finding What They Were Looking For

Holding my position just off to the side of the opening, I watched as Kevin finished changing his scuba tanks and pulled the entire heavy set of gear onto his shoulders again. He reached for his mask and spat twice on the inside, wiping the saliva around the lenses to keep them from fogging. He turned to Kristina before he put the mask on, and she used two fingers to smear a layer of Vaseline all over his moustache so that the seal on his face mask wouldn't leak.

With all of that out of the way, Kevin nodded curtly and plunged off the side of the boat again, slowly descending to the bottom. He switched his dive lights on again and made his way toward the edge of the ruins where he resumed his methodical and repetitious search routine.

I watched for a while, but nothing new was happening, so I pulled myself along the hull of the boat to see what Kristina was up to. I had expected to see her at the side of the boat again, keeping a careful watch toward the fortress, but instead of that she was kneeling down on deck with a stack of towels and the large black brick in front of her. She had positioned herself so that she still had a view of the fortress, and that worked to my advantage because it meant that her back was turned completely toward me.

I pulled myself a bit closer and watched what she was doing. Using several towels, she carefully cleaned the brick by first wiping its flat top side and then removing layer after layer of the ugly, black muck that was covering it.

What exactly are they doing? I wondered. Kevin was obviously looking for something, although God knows what it was. The only thing I knew was that apparently some of the bricks from the collapsed ruin were more interesting than others; they were worth bringing to the surface so that Kristina could clean them and dry them.

Why doesn't she just let the brick air dry? I wondered, as I watched Kristina unroll some paper towels and work carefully to get every last bit of water out of every nook and cranny on the ragged surface of the brick.

Eventually she was satisfied with her work, and she put the brick on a new, clean, dry towel and tossed everything else into a hamper at a corner of the pilothouse. She then kneeled down again and placed a binder full of various papers on the deck next to her. From the binder she took out a clean sheet of paper and placed it on the surface of the brick.

She grabbed a small, black rectangle from a plastic case next to her knees and rubbed the surface of the paper thoroughly with it for a few minutes. Afterward, she put the rectangle back in the case and set the paper down on the bench next to her while she carefully wrapped the brick in a towel.

Suddenly, a gust of wind caught the edge of the paper and blew it across the floor, pinning it for a few seconds against the side of the boat.

I stared at the paper, and it finally dawned on me what Kristina had been doing. She had made a pencil rubbing of the surface of the brick, just like we used to do sometimes in art class in grade school, but she had used a small triangle of graphite instead of a pencil.

I turned my head to the side to get a better look at the rubbing. The light was dim but I could still make out a series of etched markings imprinted on the paper from the surface of the brick.

What the hell?!? I blinked my eyes and tried to make sense of the various bizarre markings. Some of them seemed to be made up of familiar characters and numbers, but the rest of the markings were unlike anything I'd ever seen before. *What does all of that mean?*

I didn't have much time to think about it because almost immediately Kristina reached over to grab the paper before it blew away. She carefully folded it and inserted it into a plastic sleeve in the binder full of papers.

Once she was done that, she climbed to her feet and disappeared from view carrying the binder, and then she returned and slid the towel-wrapped brick into a corner. With everything in order, she returned to her spot at the side of the boat and continued her lookout in the direction of the fortress.

I slowly pushed myself out of sight and looked into the water to see what Kevin was doing. Nothing much had changed. He was still busy working at the sea bottom, moving along the edge of the ruins for a second time over areas that he'd already covered.

After several minutes, my good sense told me that I shouldn't push my luck and that I should start my long swim back to Fort Jefferson, but my stubborn curiosity wouldn't allow me to leave—not yet anyway. Despite all that I'd seen that night, I still had no idea what was going on or what they were looking for, so against my better judgment, I decided to stick around a little longer.

About half an hour later, my stubbornness paid off. Kevin suddenly stopped sweeping the sea floor with the fan gun and brought it close to his face. After examining it for a moment, he smacked it on the side with the palm of his hand.

It didn't take a genius to decipher his body language.

He pointed it downward and pulled the trigger; sand blew everywhere as the fan spun quickly. Again, he pulled it up to his face and examined it closely, and then he pushed a couple of buttons on the top before smacking it again.

What's the problem? I wondered. *It looked like it was working fine.*

Apparently satisfied that he'd smacked it into proper working order, Kevin pointed the gun toward the hole he'd been sweeping, and his body suddenly froze. I could see every muscle in his body tense as he waved the fan gun back and forth over the hole. Apparently, the device was more than just a fan, and Kevin had found something that he'd missed before.

I watched as he stuffed the muzzle of the gun into the hole and blew sand off everything. A miniature sandstorm brewed across the sea bottom and Kevin nearly disappeared in the cloud of sediment swirling all around him.

When the water was clear again, Kevin adjusted his dive lights and pointed them straight into the hole under the ruins. He reached deep inside, his arms disappearing nearly to his shoulders as he strained and pulled out another of the unusual black bricks.

I backed off down the side of the hull of the boat, expecting Kevin to turn around and load this new brick into the net bag behind him, but this time he simply set the brick aside and reached down again, tugging and pulling until another brick emerged from the hole. He set that one aside as well, and then he leaned down and pulled yet another one out. This one he finally loaded into the net bag and pulled excitedly on the line to get a ride up to the surface, checking his air gauges as he went.

"Bingo," I heard Kevin say as he climbed onto the bottom rung of the dive ladder and handed the brick up to Kristina, who plunked it down onto the deck with a solid thud.

"Oh, my god, you're kidding," Kristina replied, her voice breathless and excited.

Whatever it was they were looking for, they had apparently just found it.

Chapter Twenty-Five

Not Just One, But Two Of Them

Kevin didn't waste much time at the surface, and before I could duck out of sight, he stepped off the swim ladder and dove to the bottom of the ocean. I cursed myself for getting so close and nearly being seen, but I didn't have to worry—Kevin's full attention was focused on getting back to work.

I watched as he loaded another black brick into the net bag and tugged three times on the line, checking his gauges again as Kristina pulled him up to the boat. I stayed hidden near the bow just in case Kevin made a quick descent again. I could hear the muffled thud of the brick being placed on the deck, and then almost immediately afterward Kevin headed down again.

One more to go, I thought to myself as I waited for Kevin to load the last brick and head up again. I could tell that he was worried about his air supply because he kept looking down nervously at his gauges.

Instead of loading the last brick and sending it up to the boat, however, Kevin dropped to his knees and angled his dive lights to get a better view into the hole while he poked around under the ruins.

From my vantage point, I couldn't see exactly *what* he was grabbing, but each item was small enough to fit in the palm of his hand as he quickly stuffed it into a nylon bag wrapped around his wrist.

He managed to recover five or ten of the objects before his body suddenly tensed again and he stood to his feet. The flow of bubbles from his scuba regulator suddenly ceased, and he looked down one last time at his gauges. He was out of air.

I expected him to shoot for the surface immediately, but instead he calmly and carefully placed the remaining brick into the opening of the hole and quickly shoveled piles of sand on top of it until it looked like any of the other bricks and debris lying on the bottom of the ocean. Only then, did he yank on the line above his head and let Kristina pull him to the surface.

As Kristina hauled Kevin up to the boat, I could see the small nylon bag clutched in his fist. Out of air and obviously pressed for time, he apparently didn't notice that one of the objects from the bag he was guarding so carefully happened to fall out just as he was yanked up to the surface. I watched as the small object twisted and tumbled down through the water, bucking tiny currents as it went. It looked like some kind of magical stone that glowed with its own inner light—a greenish-blue iridescent glow that seemed to originate from somewhere deep inside it. I couldn't take my eyes off it; I was hypnotized by its beautiful incandescence as it spun downward to the bottom, finally coming to rest in the sand, nestled against some small yellow-green bricks on the ocean floor that formed a kind of random pattern that more or less resembled the shape of a crooked letter H.

I had only a second or two to see where it fell before Kevin's dive lights switched off and the world plunged into darkness. I pulled my head up out of the water, and as my eyes adjusted, I could see that it was not quite as dark as it had been before. Off to the east a faint glow was growing at the horizon as sunrise rapidly approached.

I could hear Kevin grunting and pulling himself onboard again. I slid down along the hull of the boat so that I could see what was going on.

I heard the ripping of Velcro and a faint clinking clatter as Kevin poured the objects from the bag into the cupped palms of Kristina's hands.

"Oh, my god, they're unbelievable!" she squealed as she examined them more closely.

"We need to get out of here," Kevin said, his voice serious as he quickly stripped off his dive gear. "We'll have to continue tomorrow. I'm out of air, and the sun's coming up."

Kristina nodded and quickly poured the handful of objects into the nylon bag before handing it to Kevin. She pulled the radio from her back pocket and held it up to her mouth.

"Citadel, Citadel, this is Cuba Libré, over." Her voice was all business again.

"This is Citadel, go ahead, over."

"Two more loaves of bread up," Kristina said simply, pausing for a moment. "And we've found the gumdrops."

There was silence for a long moment before the reply finally came.

"That's incredible!" the voice at the other end replied. The voice was definitely Patrick. I could recognize it better now that there was some emotion in his voice. "That's incredible!" he repeated. "Are we finished? Do we have them all?"

"Negative," Kristina replied. "But we're out of air, and it's getting late, so we're going to bug on out of here and get the rest tomorrow, over."

"Roger that," Patrick said after another long pause. "Have a safe trip home, over and out."

When Patrick signed off, I suddenly realized that I needed to get out of there fast. In no time at all Kevin and Kristina would be pulling up anchor and starting their engines to head for home. Unfortunately, in my excitement, I hadn't thought that far ahead, and I wasn't sure exactly what my escape plan should be.

Just don't panic, I told myself as I swam away from the boat, past the anchor line, and out into open water. Somewhere up ahead was the reef rim, which marked the dividing line between the calm waters I was currently swimming in and the open water of the Hawk Channel. Because of the reef, Kevin and Kristina would have to head in the opposite direction that I needed to go, so it seemed like a safe direction to swim for the time being.

I watched from a distance as they started the boat's engines and puttered forward. In the dim lights from the boat's pilothouse, I saw Kristina climb onto the bow to guide the anchor line up until it was securely locked in place. She gave a thumbs-up to Kevin, and he powered up the engines a little more, making a slow turn before rumbling off in the opposite direction.

I watched as the boat gradually melted away into the predawn darkness, disappearing from view until nothing but the faint sound of its engine remained.

Out of the corner of my eye, I caught a flash of light, then three long bursts of light shot out across the water from the corner of the concrete pier at the fortress. I didn't know what that signal meant, but I assumed it wasn't a danger signal since I could hear the boat engine motoring toward the opposite side of the fort.

Maybe it means something like good-bye, good luck, see you tomorrow, I thought with a chuckle.

I was just about to start my long swim back to Fort Jefferson when I suddenly saw the same flashing signal for a second time—three long bursts and then nothing—but this signal wasn't coming from the concrete platform where I'd just seen it a few seconds before. It was coming from somewhere along the top of the fortification walls, most likely near the second corner of the six-sided fortress from what I could make out in the dim light. That meant that it was much too far away for the same person to have made both signals.

And that meant that there wasn't just *one* accomplice standing lookout at the fort. There were *two* of them.

Chapter Twenty-Six

Hey, Look Out Up There

Did I see that right?!? I peered toward the fortress and replayed in my mind the two signals that I'd just seen. In the predawn light, I could see the faint outlines of the fort, and I was positive that the first signal had come from over toward the right, low to the water at the spot on the concrete pier where I'd seen someone standing earlier. But the second signal had come from much farther off to the left, almost at the opposite end of the fortress and higher up, possibly at the top of one of the corner tower bastions.

I wasn't very surprised to discover that another person was involved— maybe even more. But one thing was certain: this was probably not the best time to worry about it. I was alone and floating out in the middle of a dark ocean with a long swim ahead of me.

I'd better get going or it'll be daylight by the time I'm back at the campsite, I told myself, and I put my head down to start swimming.

It didn't take me long to fall into a steady rhythm again. I passed the time by thinking about everything I'd seen that night, and a million questions were running through my head.

What's the significance of the brick ruin that Kevin was searching through so carefully? What are they looking for?

"They were looking for loaves of bread and gumdrops," I muttered when I turned my head to take a breath.

But what exactly are the "loaves of bread?" Why are some of the bricks special enough to bring up to the boat and the others are not?

My mind continued to spin with questions as I continued swimming. I thought about the crazy markings on the "loaf of bread" that I'd seen from the pencil rubbing. I thought about the strangely luminous "gumdrops" that Kevin had collected from underneath the ruin. I thought about the ruin itself. *Maybe it was part of the fortress, or the remains of some lost sunken city.*

My breath caught in my throat at this last thought.

A sunken city?

It was difficult to keep my imagination from running wild after the surreal night I'd just had. I knew better than to think the next thought that popped into my head, but I just couldn't stop it.

Atlantis! My heart pounded heavily in my chest. *Was I just swimming over the ruins of the lost city of Atlantis?!?*

I have to tell you, swimming out there in the open water, surrounded by the inky black ocean and the diamond-like stars in the velvet sky, I was in the perfect place to think all sorts of crazy things, and believe them too.

But then something even crazier happened.

"Hey, look out up there," I suddenly heard a voice say from somewhere very close by. It was almost as though someone was speaking directly into my ear.

I stopped abruptly, spinning around in a panic, left then right then left again in an effort to see who had spoken. There was nothing; no one in the water close by; no boats or swimmers. There was simply nothing.

"Who's there?!?" I said aloud, my voice cracking with fear as my heart pounded two hundred beats a second. "Who are you?!?"

I continued spinning, looking around on all sides as the panic rose inside of me.

Who is out here with me? And why can't I see them? Are they underwater? Are they reaching up to grab me from under the surface at this very second? Oh my god, if they are, I won't know it until their hands clasp my legs and drag me under!

I kicked and thrashed with my flippers, trying to push those imaginary hands away. I could almost feel them, cold and clammy, wrapping around my ankles. My mind spiraled into a complete panic, and the only thing I knew was that I had to get out of there. I looked all around me, desperately trying to find the harbor light from the fortress so that I could start swimming for it as fast as I could.

Finally, I saw it, and a cold, hard realization washed over me. All the while that I'd been swimming along and letting my mind wander, the tidal current had been getting stronger and had pulled me far out into the ocean away from the fort. I was going to have to swim very hard in order to make it back before exhaustion set in.

I put my head down and started swimming for the harbor light as though my life depended on it—and maybe it did, because I wasn't sure how strong the current was.

Fortunately, the current wasn't too bad. I was quickly able to swim out of it and into the more tranquil waters that surrounded the fortress. Of course, I was helped by the fear that someone was in the water with me somewhere, chasing me down and reaching for me with icy hands. I knew that this was ridiculous thinking and that the voice I'd heard was probably just some trick of the wind, but it had sounded so real and so close that I found it hard to shake the uneasy feeling that it had given me.

As I got closer to the fortress, my panic subsided, and I wondered about the two lookouts I'd seen earlier. Were they still there? Could they see me swimming in the early-morning light?

They must be long gone by now, I reassured myself. *With that boat gone, there's no reason for them to keep standing around, right?*

I knew this had to be true, but I still didn't take any chances. I swam as quietly as I could for the last few hundred feet, keeping my eyes peeled for any sign of movement as I approached the concrete wall at the end of the beach. As far as I could see, the coast was clear, so I pulled off my fins and waded the rest of the way up to the sand before trotting silently back across the grass to my tent.

What a night! I thought as I peeled off my wet clothes and quickly toweled myself dry. I climbed into my warm sleeping bag, shivering uncontrollably, although I didn't know if that was from cold, fear, or just sheer exhaustion. It took me a long time to settle down and relax. My mind was racing a hundred miles an hour. As much as I tried to make sense of everything I'd just experienced, I couldn't. It was simply too much. I had a tiny handful of pieces to an enormous puzzle, and no matter how hard I tried, I just couldn't figure out how they all fit together.

I needed more pieces to the puzzle, and I already had a few ideas about where I would find them.

Chapter Twenty-Seven

Spam And Eggs

After only a few hours of sleep, I forced myself out of bed. I wanted to make an early start on the day so I could catch Jack and Jodi for breakfast.

"Good morning," Jodi said as I appeared around the corner of the bushes between our tents. A short distance away Jack was trying to cook something on one of the campground's iron barbecue stands, swearing a lot and producing a lot of smoke as he did so.

"What's going on?" I asked, nodding over toward Jack.

Jodi rolled her eyes. "He's trying to make scrambled eggs on the barbecue," she replied.

"Oh!" I replied, raising my eyebrows. "I didn't know that was possible."

"It's not," Jodi assured me in a droll tone of voice.

"Oh, come on!" Jack complained to no one in particular as the first few drops of a passing rain shower began to fall.

"Help yourself to anything you want," Jodi said, ignoring Jack and inviting me to sit at the picnic table across from her. The two of them had brought their own canopy tent to cover their table, so she and I were safe from the rain. Jack and his eggs, however, were not.

"I don't mind if I do," I replied, grabbing the peanut butter, and Jodi and I laughed at Jack's antics.

"Are you serious?" Jack said again to no one in particular as the rain *really* started to come down. "Give me a break!"

Jodi and I watched Jack struggle with his eggs for a few more minutes, surrounded by a growing cloud of steam as the rain doused the coals in the grill. But it was hopeless, and eventually Jack gave up and ran over to the shelter of the canopy with a frying pan full of soggy egg soup in his hand.

"Good morning," he said glumly. "So much for my eggs."

"I brought Spam," I suggested helpfully, holding the can up to show him.

"Oh, excellent," Jack said, setting his frying pan down on the grass and taking the can of Spam from me. "You know what goes great with Spam?"

"What?" I asked.

"Eggs!" he replied, making me laugh.

Jack slid onto the picnic table bench, and the three of us sat for a while watching the rain grow steadily into a complete downpour before quickly slacking off again. It was a typical Dry Tortugas rain shower, and soon the sun was out again, shining brightly overhead.

Jack hadn't given up on his eggs.

"I'm going out to the boat to make some proper eggs," he announced, grabbing the can of Spam from the picnic table.

"Take Kitty with you," Jodi suggested. "She's not seen the boat."

"Sure, if you want to come," Jack asked, looking over at me.

"I'd actually love to," I replied. I was curious to see what kind of boat they had.

Jack and I headed down to the beach where their small two-person dinghy was tied up. He pulled off the tarp that was covering it and we jumped in and headed out across the water toward the cluster of boats anchored nearby.

"Which one's yours?" I asked, looking from one boat to the next and trying to guess.

"This is my baby, the *Tradewind*," Jack said, pointing to a sleek new cabin cruiser that looked like something a movie star would use to cruise around the Caribbean.

"Are you kidding me?" I replied in awe. "This isn't a boat—it's a yacht! It's the kind of thing millionaires own. Didn't you say you were a retired policeman?"

"It's not quite big enough to be a yacht," Jack replied, patting the *Tradewind* affectionately on the side of the hull as we pulled alongside. "But it's perfect for Jodi and me."

Jack shut down the dinghy's engine and tied us up at the back of the *Tradewind*. He climbed onto the fantail and turned around to help me climb aboard after him.

"This is incredible," I said as Jack opened the door for me and I stepped into the main cabin. "When you said you had a kitchen on your boat, I thought you were kidding." Their boat had an actual kitchen. It was a small one, of course, but a real kitchen all the same.

Jack opened drawers and cabinets and pulled out some eggs and a frying pan before starting up the electric stove. Reaching down into a small fridge he grabbed some milk and cottage cheese and smelled both of them to make sure they hadn't gone bad. When he was done with all of that, he started some coffee brewing before preparing the eggs.

"Do you want some too?" Jack asked.

I shook my head. "No, thanks," I answered.

"You don't know what you're missing," Jack replied.

I watched as he cut the Spam into tiny cubes and whipped together some eggs, milk, and a tablespoon of cottage cheese in a bowl. He poured this entire concoction into the sizzling frying pan and sprinkled the Spam on top.

"Why don't you sleep out here instead of in your tent?" I asked, pointing down into the master bedroom where they had a real bed and even a bathroom with a shower.

Jack shrugged. "Even millionaires go camping sometimes," he joked as he finished scrambling his eggs, topping them off with salt and pepper before putting them into a small Tupperware container.

I offered to help wash up, but Jack had it all under control, quickly cleaning up and pouring the freshly brewed coffee into a thermos to take back to the campsite. In less than ten minutes, he'd made eggs and coffee, and we were puttering across the harbor in the dinghy.

We found Jodi waiting for us at the picnic table. "Are you happy now that you've got your eggs?" she asked, teasing.

"The more important question is whether *you* are happy," Jack replied, pulling out the thermos of fresh coffee.

Jodi's eyes lit up at the sight of it. "Coffee! Thank you!" she said excitedly, standing up to give Jack a sloppy kiss.

"And now we can have a proper breakfast," Jack announced solemnly as he sat down and pulled out his container of freshly scrambled eggs. He divided them between himself and Jodi and left a small bit for me off to the side. "I call these spambled eggs," he said. "You have to try."

I laughed and picked up a fork to sample a little bit. "Oh, these *are* good," I replied. "I never had scrambled eggs with cottage cheese mixed in before."

"Secret family recipe," Jack said, giving me a wink.

It started to rain a bit again, but we were safe and dry under the canopy, so we ate breakfast in silence and watched the rain. I pulled my knees up to my chest and savored the warmth of the fresh coffee. I hadn't had a cup of coffee in days.

"Can I ask you a favor?" I asked Jack as I looked out at the rain.

"Sure thing," Jack replied. "Name it."

"Can I borrow your dinghy for a couple of hours this morning? I just want to check things out around the fort, and I promise not to be long because I'm planning to fly into Key West for some groceries later this morning."

"Of course," Jack said, "but on one condition."

"More Spam?" I asked, joking.

Jack laughed. "Fuel, actually," he replied. "Since you're flying to civilization, if you could refill my jerry can with some gas, I'd very much appreciate it. I'll pay you, of course."

"Sure, I'll be glad to," I said.

"Oh, and some Doritos," Jack added.

I laughed. "Okay. Doritos too."

"And some fresh bread," Jodi suggested.

"No problem," I replied.

"What about some KFC?" Jack asked. "Flying here doesn't take long, so it should still be warm by the time it gets here. We could have chicken night, the three of us."

I laughed again. "I'd like that, actually," I replied.

"We'll make a list," Jodi suggested helpfully, and she began to clear the breakfast table. I helped her clean things up a bit before Jack took me down to the dinghy and showed me how everything worked.

The dinghy was small, but the most important thing was that it had an outboard motor. After the previous night's activities, I'd had enough of swimming for the time being.

Chapter Twenty-Eight

Third Time's The Charm

"This might be trickier than I thought," I said to myself as I motored out across the water in Jack's little dinghy. My plan was simple: I would motor out to where *The Old Man* had been anchored the night before so that I could snorkel around a bit and check things out in the daylight. With bright sunlight to illuminate the sea bottom instead of just a pair of dive lights, I would be able to see everything a lot more clearly.

The only flaw in my plan was how I was going to figure out exactly *where* in the open water the boat had been anchored the night before. I knew the general direction and could guess at the approximate location, but without the glow of the dive lights to guide me, it would be tricky finding the exact spot.

After puttering back and forth aimlessly a few times, I tried to be a little more scientific and attempted to orient myself by the relative positions of the lighthouse on Loggerhead Key and Fort Jefferson. Looking back and forth between these two landmarks, I slowly moved myself into what I thought might be the right position.

I peered over the side of the dinghy and down through the shallow water below, looking for signs of scattered bricks and ruins, but I couldn't see a thing. The reflection of the sun on the surface of the water was blinding.

I put on my snorkel mask and leaned down again to stick my face right into the water. The world beneath was instantly revealed in perfect clarity. Directly underneath my little dinghy was a snorkeler's dream world with brightly colored fish and coral all around. Parrot fish, Sergeant Majors, and Yellow-tailed Jacks swam against a backdrop of coral and sea fans waving in the current. A group of fifty or sixty dark blue fish whirled and swam together in unison, moving from place to place to feed with the sunlight flashing off them like a cloud of neon color.

For a moment I nearly forgot why I'd come out there and just spent a few minutes watching this magical underwater world in action.

Okay, let's get down to business, I finally told myself sternly, and I scanned around for any sign of the brick ruin that I'd seen the night before. I peered through the water from every angle around the boat, but

I couldn't see anything like it anywhere; just coral and sea grass as far as the eye could see.

I looked across the water to judge my position relative to the lighthouse and fort.

Maybe it's a bit farther this way, I thought, and I puttered toward the lighthouse. I let go of the throttle and stuck my face into the water again. It was the same as before—a million beautiful colors of fish and coral, but no sign of any bricks or ruins.

How about a bit farther this way? Once again, I motored the dinghy farther out from the fortress.

I leaned down to check underwater again, but there was still only fish and coral.

I pulled my head up and tried to think of a better plan.

Maybe I can look down into the water as I drive the dinghy.

It was worth a try, so I slid back in the boat to get closer to the outboard motor where I could operate it while I leaned over the side of the dinghy with my face in the water. I gave the motor a bit of gas, and soon I was cruising around like an idiot, with one hand on the throttle, my butt sticking up in the air, and my face in the water, all while skimming over sea grass and coral.

Schools of fish ducked and turned, coiling gracefully out of my way as I plowed through the water. The underwater world below was an ever-changing wonderland of life and activity, but I still wasn't finding what I was looking for. And of course I couldn't steer the boat straight while I was doubled over leaning into the water, so I was zigzagging all over the place as I maneuvered around.

This isn't working, I finally admitted to myself after several minutes of haphazard searching. I leaned over the side of the dinghy and warmed myself in the sun while I tried to figure out what to do next.

I had to admit it—this was no way to conduct a proper search. That much was clear. My scientific nature told me that the best method would be to divide the ocean floor into an orderly search grid that I could methodically work my way through until I found what I was looking for. It was a good idea in theory, but how was I supposed to do that in reality?

I could get the GPS unit out of my plane, I thought. *But then what would I do? Draw a map and design a search grid?*

The whole thing was getting too complicated, and I was probably much happier just sitting in the warm sun drifting along lazily; maybe I would even do some snorkeling.

Maybe I will just get lucky, I thought, gunning the engine in frustration and motoring over to a random spot on the water. I leaned over the side and put my face into the water to check things out.

Nope, I said to myself. There was nothing there.

I gunned the engine again, turned the rudder, and headed out to another random spot. I leaned over the side and looked again. Still no luck.

Strike two, I thought. *And if anyone's watching me from the shore, they must think I am completely crazy.*

But they say the third time is a charm, and after motoring over to yet another random location, I stuck my head in the water and found myself staring at a scattered debris field of bricks and coral-encrusted ruins.

I couldn't believe my eyes.

I'd actually found it.

Chapter Twenty-Nine

Gumdrops And Barracudas

At first, I was sure that my eyes were fooling me, but after blinking hard a few times, I became convinced that what I was seeing was real. Directly beneath me the sandy bottom was littered with wreckage and debris, all of it scattered across the sea floor and overgrown with coral. These were definitely the same bricks and ruins that I'd seen the night before, but by the clear light of day, I could instantly saw that it actually wasn't a ruin at all—it was the wreckage of a sunken ship.

Not that what I was looking at resembled anything even remotely shaped like a ship. The debris was too scattered and coral-encrusted to resemble much of anything, but what gave it away was a large four-bladed propeller situated at what I assumed was the stern of what was once a ship. I hadn't noticed that propeller the night before, and thanks to all the bricks scattered among the wreckage, my brain had concluded that I was looking at the ruins of a submerged city.

My heart sank. It wasn't the lost city of Atlantis after all—not that I had actually believed that in the first place, but it had been a nice daydream.

A sunken ship is mysterious and exciting too, I reminded myself, and I pulled my head out of the water and sat upright. *But if I want to go snorkeling and get a better look, I first need to figure out what to do with this dinghy.*

I looked around in vain for some way to secure the little boat, but there was nothing around to tie it to. It didn't have an anchor, so I couldn't secure it that way either.

I'll just have to pull it around with me, I decided, pulling on my mask and fins and wrapping the dinghy's towline around my wrist before rolling off into the water.

The dinghy was small and light, so it was no problem to tow it around behind me as I swam slowly back and forth over the entire site. As I did so, I started to get a sense of the extent of the wreck. It was about a hundred feet from bow to stern with a junkyard of scrap metal and other completely unrecognizable debris scattered in between. The whole thing was in such bad shape and was so overgrown with coral that if it wasn't for the propeller, I might not have recognized it as a shipwreck at all.

In my imagination, a shipwreck was supposed to be like something out of *The Pirates of the Caribbean*—a majestic sailing ship with towering masts and billowing sails. But this boat was nothing like that at all. It had engines, not sails, and the wreck itself was just a big giant mess.

It's probably some kind of workboat from when they were building the fortress, I guessed. *That would explain why bricks are scattered everywhere.*

As I swam back and forth, I noticed that the wreck looked as though it had been stripped down some time after it sank. Other than the propeller, there was no sign of any other equipment that you'd normally expect to find on a sunken ship. I supposed that it was possible that anything of value was covered in coral, and I couldn't see it, but that wasn't what it looked like to me. To my eyes, it looked like the ship had been stripped clean of parts and anything useful after it sank.

I guess that's no surprise, I thought, hanging motionless in the water and staring below me as I thought things through. *Everyone must know that the wreck is out here because it's in such shallow water and so close to Fort Jefferson.*

But if the ship had already been stripped of everything of value long ago, what was Kevin looking for on his secret night dives? I knew they'd found some large bricks with strange writing on them that they'd called loaves of bread.

And don't forget the "gumdrops," I reminded myself.

That gave me an idea.

I swam back and forth again, but this time with a purpose. I was looking for the bricks that I'd seen the night before scattered in the shape of a crooked letter H. I'd seen one of the "gumdrops" fall into the sand there. If I could find that, then maybe I could see what a "gumdrop" actually was.

It took me a while to find the spot, but eventually the shifting sand and sea grass parted to reveal the H-shaped pile of debris. Assuming the "gumdrop" hadn't been washed away with the tide, I should find it buried in the sand right at the inside bottom corner of the H.

I took three or four very deep breaths and filled my lungs with as much oxygen as possible before kicking my feet up and heading for the bottom, clasping my fingers over my nose to equalize my ears as I descended.

Sticking my fingers into the sand I dug around for a while trying to find the "gumdrop," but I couldn't find anything. The tide had shifted the sands, half burying everything. I dug around a bit more until my air ran out, and then I kicked up and returned to the surface.

Maybe I'm doing this the wrong way, I thought, remembering the handheld underwater fan that Kevin had used to clear away the sand. I gave my lungs a moment to recover then took a few more deep breaths and free-dived down to the bottom again.

This time I didn't uselessly move the piles of sand from one place to another by digging. Instead, I waved my hand back and forth to blow the sand off of the bricks and debris. This method worked much better than digging, but I still couldn't find anything, and soon I had to return to the surface for air.

Panting and wheezing from the lack of oxygen, I clung to the side of the dinghy to take a rest. The search was hard work, but my fanning technique was working well, so as soon as I finished catching my breath, I would head down again.

Taking a big lungful of air, I ducked under the water and was about to kick my feet up into a dive when I saw something at the bottom that almost made my heart stop. It was a barracuda, a big one, and it was weaving in and out of the wreckage.

Damn it, I thought. *Why now?*

I watched from the surface as the huge barracuda swam casually through the wreck, slowly stalking some small white fish nearby. With lightning speed, he coiled his body to the side and seized one of the small fish in his mouth, striking and biting so fast that I almost couldn't see it.

"Oh my god!" I said to myself, amazed at the speed of the attack. It was incredible that something so big could move so fast.

The barracuda ignored the other fish and swam along the length of the wreck, passing over the H-shaped cluster of bricks below me and swimming a bit farther beyond to the ship's propeller where he stopped.

I waited, hoping he would swim off again and go somewhere else, but he stayed right where he was, floating motionless in the shade of the propeller, perfectly still except for the barely perceptible fluttering of his fins.

I waited some more, still hoping, but after a while, it was clear that he wasn't going anywhere.

"Well, I'm not giving up now," I muttered to myself. "Not because of some stupid barracuda."

But my talk was a lot tougher than I felt on the inside, and somehow I couldn't quite bring myself to ignore him and head for the bottom again.

I remembered what Jodi had told me the other day: that barracudas had a much worse reputation than they actually deserved. After all, millions of people swim around them every year without being attacked.

"That's all fine and dandy," I said to myself. "But those people aren't staring down at a gigantic barracuda like this one, are they?"

Actually, I didn't know if he really *was* considered gigantic or not, as barracudas go. Maybe this one was actually normal sized for a barracuda, or even considered small. I had only seen two in real life—this one and the one two days earlier—and they were both huge as far as I was concerned. In fact, for all I knew they were the same gigantic barracuda.

But I couldn't just sit there all day waiting for him to swim off. I had to get on with it, but I was still nervous. I'd seen how fast he could attack, and I certainly didn't want him coming after me.

Don't be stupid, I told myself. *He couldn't care less about you. To him you're not food. Besides, he just ate, so he won't be hungry again for a while, right?*

That logic made sense, and I was tired of being timid, so I finally convinced myself just to take a deep breath and dive.

Here we go, I thought as I kicked my feet up and plunged down to the sea floor, keeping an eye on Mr. Barracuda as I descended. Thankfully, he didn't move an inch.

Once I reached the bottom, I immediately started fanning the sand like crazy, and after thirty or forty seconds, I was rewarded for my hard work and courage. With tiny clouds of sand and silt filling the water around me, I cleared a spot alongside one of the bricks and caught a sudden flash of green hiding underneath. For a moment, I forgot all about the giant barracuda lurking nearby and stared at the most beautiful green that I'd ever seen—a color so heart stopping and radiant that it almost looked alive.

Chapter Thirty

You Are Really Losing It

Underwater, the color palette is skewed, and nearly everything looks kind of bluish-green no matter what color it actually is. Green objects don't really stand out all that much, but this flash of green was different. It was so intense and glowing with color that when it caught the light of the sun, it seemed to be burning with a kind of magical green fire from deep within.

I fanned even harder with the palm of my hand, and as the sand blew off some more in great swirling clouds, I saw a small vibrant green stone lying beneath me. I reached down carefully and picked it up for a closer look. It was roughly the size of my thumb and was heavy with uneven, irregular edges and smooth faces like a crystal.

The stone looked completely magical as though it had been forged deep within the earth and possessed supernatural powers. It left me completely hypnotized as I turned it over in the palm of my hand. I was so mesmerized that I forgot that I was underwater and needed to breathe. I'd stayed down too long, and I'd forgotten not only about the barracuda, but also about the fact that I was not a fish and that I needed air.

Clutching the stone tightly in my fist, I rocketed to the surface and exploded out of the water, gasping and choking. I reached for the side of the dinghy and hung from it with one arm while I struggled to catch my breath.

As I floated, I opened my palm and stared down at the stone again, completely amazed by its ancient and primeval beauty.

What in the world is it? I wondered. The stone glinted in the sunlight and gave off so much light and radiance that I wondered if it actually *was* glowing all by itself. I let go of the dinghy for a second and cupped my hands around it so I could peek between my fingers and see it in the dark. I was about to put my eye up to the gap between my palms when a frightening thought occurred to me.

What if it's radioactive? I nearly dropped the stone in horror at the thought. The idea that it might be radioactive wasn't so farfetched, I reasoned, because it looked like a piece of Kryptonite or something else entirely otherworldly.

Fortunately, my good sense returned, and I clutched the stone even tighter in my palm. I reminded myself that Kevin and Kristina had been handling these stones the night before with bare hands, so obviously this stone wasn't dangerous to touch. I cupped my palms together again and peered between the gaps in my fingers. The stone was completely black in the darkness of my cupped palms—no radioactive glow. Despite what it looked like in the sunlight, the stone was most definitely not glowing by itself. Somehow, this disappointed me. On the bright side, however, that meant that it couldn't be radioactive, but it also meant that it probably wasn't magical, either, but it sure was beautiful.

I tucked the stone securely into my pocket and reached down to pull off my fins. I climbed into the dinghy and started the engine. When I reached the fortress, I dragged the little boat onto the beach and tied it where I'd found it.

"I see you were out exploring the Brick Wreck," I heard a voice say behind me as I was covering the dinghy with its tarp. I spun around to see one of the park rangers standing at the edge of the grass above me. At first glance, my heart skipped a beat because I thought it was Patrick, but it wasn't. It was one of the older rangers, the tall one named Roger with the bushy salt-and-pepper beard. I'd spoken to earlier. He smiled brightly and walked down to the sand to help me secure the tarp over the boat.

"The Brick Wreck?" I asked.

"Out by Bird Key," he replied, stretching his long arm to point across the water to where I'd come from. "I saw you were having some trouble finding it at first."

"Oh, yes," I replied, still a bit confused. "The shipwreck with the bricks. I didn't know it had a name."

Roger shrugged. "The Brick Wreck is just what we call it," he explained. "No one actually knows its real name or even how it got there."

"Oh yah?" I replied, intrigued.

Roger nodded. "Thanks to the bricks in the wreckage, we know it's got something to do with the construction of Fort Jefferson," he said, pointing over to the fortress. "The bricks on the wreck are the same type that was used to build the fortress, at least until the start of the Civil War in 1861, that is, when they changed brick suppliers. So we know the ship must have sunk some time before that. And thanks to some other bricks they found from the wreck's steam engines that were produced in 1857, we also know that the ship must have sunk sometime after that."

"So, it wrecked sometime between 1857 and 1861," I replied, thinking this over.

"But that's about all we know," Roger continued. "We don't know the ship's real name or what happened to it. We only know approximately when it might have sunk and that it was apparently run aground on purpose."

"Run aground on purpose?" I asked in surprise. "Why would anyone do that?"

Roger shrugged again. "We have no idea," he replied. "We only know that's what happened because of the damage to the ship. In order to cause the kind of damage it sustained, the boat had to have been running under power at the time, and since anyone involved with the work here at the fortress would have known these waters like the back of his hand, the only logical conclusion we can come to is that someone must have grounded her intentionally."

I nodded thoughtfully and looked out across the water to where the mysterious Brick Wreck was lying just beneath the surface.

"And what about the contents of the wreck," I said cautiously. "Was anything valuable found on the ship?"

I tried to sound casual, not wanting to reveal that I knew anything. For all I knew Roger was best friends with Patrick, and he was the mysterious second signaler I'd seen on the fortress the night before.

Roger laughed heartily, throwing his head back and holding his belly like some sort of skinny hippie Santa Claus.

"Valuable?" he replied. "Not unless you're a collector of rare bricks. And if you are, I've got sixteen million of them right here I can sell you."

Roger wished me a good day and headed off to return to his duties. "Valuable," I heard him mutter, and he was still laughing quietly to himself as he wandered off. "That's a laugh."

Roger's reaction said it all. He was definitely not part of the conspiracy. But of course I still had no idea who *was*, so I strolled over to the north beach to sit by myself for a while to think things through.

I sat down in the sand and took a quick look around to make sure no one was watching me before I pulled the beautiful green stone out of my pocket to have another look at it.

As I held it in my hand, I felt hypnotized somehow, almost as though I couldn't take my eyes off it. I rolled it around in my palm and watched, mesmerized, as its radiance transformed from one second to the next like a shapeshifter.

Was I going crazy, or did it almost look alive? When I closed my palms around it, I could feel its warmth, and I could almost hear it speaking to me in some ancient, unearthly language.

You are really losing it, I told myself, and I stuffed the stone quickly into my pocket. *It's not alive! It's just a rock or a crystal or something! But whatever it is, it's not alive, and it's definitely not speaking to you!*

I knew that logically, but it still felt as if there was more to the stone than its physical properties. There was something special about these stones, and even before I'd gotten out of bed that morning I had formulated a plan to find out what that was. And now that I actually had one in my possession, I was even more determined to put that plan into action.

Chapter Thirty-One

As Long As No One Sees Me I'll Be Fine

Forty-five minutes later, I was in the air and flying in the direction of Key West. On the seat next to me were an empty jerry can from Jack and a handwritten note from Jodi with their satellite phone number and a short shopping list. Safely tucked away in my pocket was the mysterious green stone. I could feel its weight pressing reassuringly against my thigh. I forced myself to resist the urge to pull it out to look at it while I was flying. The last thing I needed was to crash my plane because I was staring stupidly at some green rock.

But it was more than just some stupid green rock, and I knew it. There was something special about it and all the others like it—something that made them worth all the effort that Kevin and his accomplices were putting into secretly scuba diving for them in the middle of the night.

I looked down at the GPS and adjusted my course a bit toward the northeast, letting Key West pass slowly by on my right-hand side. The place where I was headed was a bit farther up the Keys to the town that I'd visited a few days before where Kevin and Kristina had moored their boat. According to my GPS, the town was called Marathon, and I was betting that I'd find their boat tied up there again this morning.

I continued following the endless island chain of the Florida Keys until I reached Seven Mile Bridge. Just beyond that was the marina and fish restaurant where I'd watched Kevin and Kristina unload their boat.

As I approached the marina, I made a slow turn so that I could look out my window at the sheltered bay below; I peered down anxiously to see if their boat was there.

"Bingo!" I muttered to myself. *The Old Man* was right where I'd expected it to be.

I banked my plane around and got on the radio to the local airport. I talked to the same air-traffic controller I'd spoken to before, and he directed me to the same dock on the other side of the island where I'd parked my plane the first time. Just as he'd done for me the first time I was in town, he called his friend, the taxi driver, and as soon as I was on the ground, a taxi was waiting for me. It was a total déjà vu moment.

"You must really love this restaurant," the taxi driver said after I piled into the back seat of his cab. "You keep coming back."

"Best Key lime pie in the Florida Keys," I replied with a smile.

"Ayah," the driver responded keenly. "You got that right."

The taxi raced through the small town, and soon I was back at the same table in the same restaurant overlooking the same docks drinking a nice cold iced tea and enjoying a slice of Key lime pie.

I lingered over my food so that I could stake out the action at the marina next door. Kevin and Kristina were nowhere in sight, but their boat was there, rocking softly in the water at the dock.

That woman I met before—she told me something about Kevin and Kristina the last time I was here. What was it? I struggled to recall my conversation with Cassie, the owner of the sailing catamaran who I'd talked to on my previous visit, and then I remembered. She had said something about how Kevin and Kristina always stayed out overnight and returned every morning, but were never around during the daytime.

I couldn't remember exactly what she'd said, but it was something like that, and I was counting on it being true because my plan depended on it.

I sipped my iced tea and kept watch over the docks. It was a quiet day, and except for the occasional party of fisherman coming and going, there didn't seem to be much of anyone around.

"More iced tea, honey?" the waitress asked as she passed by my table.

"Yes, please," I replied, nodding.

"Uh huh," she replied, grabbing my glass to get a refill.

It wasn't just the marina that was quiet. The restaurant was strangely quiet as well. Only a few other tables were occupied in the entire place, and my waitress seemed to be the only one waiting tables.

The quieter the better, I thought. I was counting on things being quiet, because after I checked things out for a while longer, I planned to go over to Kevin and Kristina's boat and finally get some answers. Somewhere on that boat (or so I hoped) was a binder full of papers and pencil rubbings like the one I'd seen Kristina make the night before. That binder held all the answers. And I was going to find it.

"What if it's not there?" the little voice in my head asked. "What if they took it with them when they left the boat?"

Then I'll turn around and leave, I replied, *and I'll figure out something else instead.*

"And what if the boat is locked?" the little voice asked.

Then I'll turn around and leave, I repeated.

"What if they *didn't* leave the boat after all and are on board sleeping?" the little voice asked persistently.

Then at least the binder will still be there, and I'll read it before I leave, I replied, exasperated.

But the little voice was right. A million things could go wrong with my plan. I was going to have to be very careful.

"But you do realize that you'll be breaking the law," the little voice reminded me. "Trespassing on someone's boat is illegal."

I know, I replied, nodding to myself. *But as long as no one sees me sneak on board, I'll be fine.*

Chapter Thirty-Two

Too Late To Wimp Out Now

After paying my restaurant bill, I walked slowly to the docks in an effort to look casual, as though my being there was the most natural thing in the world.

I'm only going to get one shot at this, I told myself. *I can't make it seem like I'm sneaking around by looking over my shoulder to make sure no one's watching. I have to just walk straight out on the dock and hop straight up onto their boat as if that's exactly what I'm supposed to be doing. Anything else will look suspicious.*

I had to time it perfectly. If anyone was around when I hopped on the boat, they might see me and know that I didn't belong there despite how nonchalantly I might act.

I stepped onto the dock and knelt down to pretend to fix my shoes while I checked everything out. There was no one in sight anywhere—so far, so good.

As I made my way down the dock, I tried not to walk too fast, just in case I looked like I was hurrying. Of course, I didn't want to walk too slowly, either, and look like I was deliberately trying to take my time. I had to walk at the perfect pace and with all the confidence I could possibly project as the boat was mine.

Just twenty more feet to go, I said to myself as the distance closed between the boat and me. *Ten feet...and five....*

When I reached the back of the boat, I took one last casual look around then put my hands on the wooden sides and vaulted myself onto the deck. I landed solidly with both feet, which made a much louder thump than I'd planned to. If anyone were on board, he or she would have heard that and would be coming out to investigate soon.

But I didn't have time to worry about that. I was still betting there was no one on board, and my main concern at that moment was getting out of sight as quickly as possible.

I ducked into the pilothouse and moved about casually and confidently. Just past the captain's chair was a set of wood-paneled doors that led down into the interior of the boat. I walked over and twisted the door handle, and was incredibly relieved when the doors swung open to reveal a short flight of stairs that led down into the main cabin.

Thank god, I said to myself as I clambered down the stairs and pulled the doors closed behind me.

Small windows lined the top of the walls of the cabin, and a skylight in the roof provided most of the illumination, but the light was dim, and it took a moment for my eyes to adjust.

The main cabin of the boat was comprised of a simple food preparation area and a dining table for four with benches running along either side. On the opposite side of the cabin to my right was a small sofa built into the boat's hull that looked as if it could be pulled out into a bed. At the end of the room there appeared to be a small bathroom next an open doorway that led straight through into the sleeping quarters at the nose of the boat. The interior of the boat was quite small, and from where I was standing, it was immediately obvious that there was no one else on the boat.

I breathed a sigh of relief and walked quickly over to the side windows to peek outside and see if anyone had seen me jump onboard. As far as I could see, everything looked normal outside. There was no sign of anyone running over to arrest me or to ask me what I was doing. In fact, there was no sign of anyone at all except for a few customers having lunch at the restaurant, and they weren't paying the slightest bit of attention to what was going on over at the docks.

I was safe—at least for the moment.

I didn't waste a second to start my search for the binder full of papers. In the main cabin, there were several cabinets and storage spaces big enough to hold a binder, so I opened each one in turn and looked inside, but all I found was some grocery items, plates, drinking glasses, and a first-aid kit.

Makes sense, I thought. *This is the galley of the boat, after all.*

I moved into the sleeping cabin next. This room was even smaller since the walls angled forward and narrowed toward the front of the boat with the contour of the hull. An open skylight in the ceiling provided some natural light, but the corners of the room were dark.

On either side of me was a cozy little bunk built at waist height with drawers and compartments underneath. I pulled open each one of these, carefully lifting up piles of folded clothing to check underneath before putting everything back exactly as I'd found it.

The only place left was a wardrobe at the foot of one of the beds. I twisted the fastener of the door and pulled it open. Inside were various articles of clothing hanging from a bar across the top but nothing else. I pushed aside the clothing and found several pairs of shoes at the bottom on the floor, but that was all there was. The binder wasn't there.

I stood back and leaned against the railing at the side of the bed while I thought things over for a moment.

The bathroom, I thought. *I forgot to check in the bathroom.*

I returned to the main cabin and opened the door to the bathroom. Not surprisingly, there was nothing there; just a toilet and a sink.

I thought about where a good hiding place would be, and then I went through all the compartments and shelves in both cabins a second time, just to be absolutely sure that I hadn't missed anything. I checked more carefully the second time, but there were no binders hidden anywhere I looked—just clothing and food, plates and utensils, a first-aid kit and a flashlight. I hadn't noticed the flashlight the first time around, and I grabbed it and switched it on to search all the dark corners of the cabin.

I found an entire bookshelf in the main cabin that I hadn't noticed before, but it was full of worn-out, old paperback novels and a few comic books. No binder there either.

Don't they have navigational charts or logbooks or anything the least bit nautical? I asked myself. *They must have. It's a boat! But where?*

Before I even finished asking myself that question, I realized what the answer must be, and I cursed myself for being so stupid. The maps and charts (and the binder) must be up in some compartment in the pilothouse, not down here in the boat's living quarters.

I hurried over to the stairs that led up to the deck and poked my head out to look around the pilothouse. On the far side underneath the boat's steering console was a storage compartment that looked like a perfect place to store maps and charts and navigational logs.

Not to mention a perfect place to store a binder full of papers, I thought.

I now faced two problems to resolve as quickly as possible. The first was that the storage compartment was locked with a padlock—a fact that, under normal circumstances, would have been a serious problem, but fortunately, a set of keys was hanging from the padlock. The second problem was a little more serious. In order to look into that compartment, I would have to crawl out into the open where just about anyone would be able to see me.

It's too late to wimp out now, I thought, and I peeked out again to make sure the coast was clear. I scanned quickly around and saw that there was no one in sight anywhere on the docks, and over at the restaurant, the diners still seemed more interested in their lunch than what was going on elsewhere.

"It's now or never," I muttered, and I pushed open the cabin door. I scrambled across the pilothouse on my hands and knees, burning my palms and shins on the wood as I went. I turned the key and the padlock fell open, and I pulled it off to let the door swing free. The shelves inside the cabinet were piled high with various odds and ends: rolled-up charts and notebooks, Motorola radios, a couple of portable GPS systems, and the most important thing of all—a large black binder.

I grabbed the binder off the shelf and quickly tucked it under my arm before closing the compartment door and padlocking it again. Once that was done, I scurried across the deck and down the stairs into the main cabin where I closed the door behind me and rushed over to the side windows to see if anyone had spotted me. Outside it was business as usual, and I was still safe.

I breathed another sigh of relief and moved to the middle of the cabin to stand under the skylight where the light was best, and I opened the binder. It was filled with pencil rubbings and other papers that were somehow connected to Kevin and Kristina's secret nocturnal underwater explorations.

I was impressed. The binder was very organized, with plastic dividers separating the different sections and documents. At the very front of the binder was a plastic sleeve with a folded sheet of paper stuffed inside. I pulled the paper out and spread it out on the dining table. As I suspected, it was a pencil rubbing of one of the bricks. I'd only had a quick glance at the one Kristina had made the night before, and that had been from a distance, so I wasn't sure whether this was the same one, but it looked very similar.

What does it mean? I wondered as I examined the various markings. *What do all these Roman numerals and symbols represent?*

It didn't make any sense to me, but instead of trying to figure it out, I snapped a photo of it with my iPhone, and then I put the pencil rubbing in its plastic sleeve.

When I turned the page, I did a double take in surprise. If I thought the markings on the bricks were unusual and mysterious, then there were hardly any words to describe what I found next.

Covering the entire next page in the binder was the most bizarre handwriting I'd ever seen. It covered the entire page from top to bottom, running on and on with no punctuation marks, and as far as I could tell it wasn't even split into separate words. The lines of text contained very few breaks and consisted of a seemingly endless string of letters—and I wasn't even sure that I would call them letters because they weren't like any letters that I was familiar with. It was more like the kind of writing in some Hollywood fantasy movie—like elvish writing or something like that.

What the hell is this? I asked myself as I snapped another photo with my phone. *This doesn't help me at all.*

I flipped quickly through the rest of the binder to see what else was there, but it was all just more of the same: pencil rubbings of the strange brick markings and endless pages of bizarre handwriting. The only page in the entire binder that was different was a single page stuck at the very back that contained a poorly photocopied reproduction of a handwritten note:

The prize of Consolation
Carried by Rosario
Is with the Scottish Chief

Unlike the other handwriting in the binder, this one was at least written in English, but that didn't help it make any more sense to me. I could read the words, but their meaning completely escaped me.

What the is all this? I asked myself again and snapped yet another photo.

Unfortunately, I didn't have time to come up with an answer, because at that exact moment I felt the boat rock slightly and heard a heavy thump from somewhere up on deck behind me. My heart completely stopped and plunged into the pit of my stomach.

Someone had just climbed over the side of the boat and jumped down onto the back deck.

Chapter Thirty-Three

Completely Screwed

I froze like a deer caught in the headlights of an oncoming car, so hypnotized and stunned by the oncoming lights that it doesn't have the sense to move out of the way to safety.

I am completely screwed, I thought to myself as I whirled around in a panic, desperately looking for a place to hide. But there was no place big enough. It was a small boat, after all. If whoever was up there decided to come down into the cabin, he or she would find me for sure.

I leaned over to look through the open skylight in the sleeping cabin. I wondered if I might be able to climb up through there if I could be fast and quiet enough, but then I realized that I would be caught either way. Whoever was outside would either see me climbing out on deck or see my legs disappearing through the hole in the ceiling if they came into the cabin.

That plan wasn't going to work, and with the seconds ticking by and the sound of footsteps moving across the deck, I had to come up with something quick.

I can hide in the bathroom, I decided, and I reached for the door handle but immediately pulled my hand back when I realized that the person out there might come down to use the bathroom.

Maybe I can fit in the wardrobe, I thought, and I spun around to see if it was big enough, but I realized that even if I could fit inside, I would make too much noise getting in, what with all the shoes and coat hangers in the way.

But where? WHERE?!? My mind screamed when I heard the sound of footsteps approaching the cabin door and the outer handle being turned. I was out of time.

My eyes darted around in desperation, and I spotted the dining table in the main cabin with its benches running down either side.

Of course! I ducked underneath and quietly slid against the hull as far as I could go. I pulled my knees up to my chin and made myself as small as possible, hoping that the two benches and the table above me were enough to make me invisible.

I heard the door open and saw sunlight flooding into the cabin, but then it was blocked momentarily as someone plodded heavily down the stairs.

"Where the hell did I leave them?" I heard a male voice say to himself. It was Kevin.

Where did he leave what? I asked myself.

Then it suddenly came to me.

The keys, I thought, my heart sinking. *He came back for the keys.*

I cursed my stupidity. When I'd seen the keys hanging from the padlock I should have known that someone would probably be coming back for them.

I could hear Kevin pacing around the cabin and then pulling open drawers and cabinets in the kitchen. I couldn't understand why he wasn't looking in the most obvious place first—on the padlocked compartment in the pilothouse. For a moment I panicked, thinking that I'd somehow slipped the keys into my pocket when I'd unlocked the padlock, but then I remembered that I'd definitely locked the cabinet again and left the keys hanging in the lock.

Kevin pulled open a couple more cabinets then pounded up the steps to the pilothouse. "Oh, for god's sake, there they are!" he cried out, and I heard the rattle of keys.

I breathed a sigh of relief, but it was short-lived. I heard Kevin opening the compartment door and rummaging around inside the cabinet.

Oh my god, I thought, clutching the binder to my chest. *What if he's looking for the binder?!?*

Kevin stopped rummaging, and for a few moments, there was silence. My heart was pounding like a jackhammer while I strained to hear what he was doing.

"It's not here," Kevin said to no one in particular. At first, I thought he was just talking to himself, but then the conversation continued, and it was obvious that he was talking to someone else. "Yes, I looked in the wheelhouse cabinet," he said. "Where did you leave it?"

He was on the phone—probably talking to Kristina.

"Hang on, I'll check," Kevin said, and I heard him lumber down the stairs again and cross the main cabin. His legs flashed past me at the end of the table and disappeared into the sleeping quarters.

He was looking for the binder.

I had to do something. He might tear this place apart looking for the binder, and if he did, he'd definitely find me. It was risky, but I had to put the binder somewhere that he'd find it. Reaching out over the padded bench, I very carefully lifted the binder to the surface of the table and slowly pushed it down toward the end before yanking my hand back.

I could hear Kevin pulling open drawers in the sleeping cabin then slamming them shut again. "It's not in there either," he said in frustration. "I'll check the wheelhouse again. Maybe I'm blind."

Again, his legs passed by the end of the table as he pounded heavily across the wood floor. This time, however, he stopped in midstride and turned toward the table.

I held my breath, terrified.

"Found it," Kevin said, finally with a smile in his voice. "It was out on the kitchen table. I must have left it there when we were going through the manifests this morning."

Manifests? I thought, my ears perking up.

I could hear Kevin flipping through pages in the binder, stopping occasionally and pausing for a moment.

"You were right; it was the wrong number," Kevin said, and I heard him snap the binder closed. "I'll grab the duds now and head back. And tonight we'll go out on the town and celebrate."

Kevin ended his telephone call, and I saw him step back from the table, sliding a cell phone into the pocket of his shorts as he did so. He disappeared into the sleeping cabin again, and I could hear him going through the wardrobe. He pulled a couple of hangers off the rail and closed the door again before dashing past the end of the table one last time and pounding up the stairs to the deck.

"Hey, Hemingway!" I heard a familiar woman's voice yell sarcastically from somewhere outside. "Do you wanna keep your speed down when you come racing in here? You nearly pulled me off my moorings this morning!"

Why is that voice so familiar? I asked myself. *It must be that woman I met out here the other day. What was her name again?*

"Bite me, Cassie!" I heard Kevin shout, his voice full of anger. "Mind your own business!"

Cassie, right! I said to myself. *That's what her name was!*

I heard the sound of Kevin opening the padlocked compartment again and sliding something onto one of the shelves—the binder presumably. He then locked the cabinet again and walked over to close the cabin doors. The glare of sunlight streaming into the cabin was abruptly extinguished, and the room was dark again.

Oh my god, that was close, I said to myself as I breathed yet another heavy sigh of relief. *As soon as the coast is clear, I'm getting out of here.*

Or at least I *hoped* I would be, because just then, I heard the click of a deadbolt as Kevin locked the cabin door behind him before rushing off the boat and heading up the dock.

Chapter Thirty-Four

Let's See Them Trace Me Now

I hope that door unlocks from the inside, I thought as I sat underneath the dining table, silently waiting to hear if there was anything going on outside on the dock.

After about ten minutes of waiting, I finally decided that it was safe to venture out again. I carefully stretched my legs and crawled out from under the table. My right leg had fallen completely asleep, and I shook it around for a bit trying to get the blood flow going again.

When the pins and needles in my leg subsided, I pulled myself to my feet and walked over to the side windows. As far as I could see, the coast was clear. I wanted to get out of there as quickly as possible.

I went over to the cabin door to see if there was an interior release for the lock. There wasn't, and when I twisted the handle and pushed on the door, it didn't budge. I was definitely locked in.

"Well that really sucks," I said aloud, looking around the cabin for another way out. I remembered the open skylight in the sleeping cabin and walked over to check it out.

It should be possible, I thought, staring up at the sliver of blue sky that I could see above me. *It looks like the window pushes the whole way open, and if I stand on the edge of the bed, I should be able to pull myself through it.*

I climbed onto the bed and lifted myself up to peer out through the open skylight. The only problem I could see was Cassie. Her boat was docked directly in front of Kevin's, and she was out on her deck doing various boat chores.

I'll just have to be patient and wait until she leaves, I thought.

I kept a close eye on Cassie while I examined the release mechanisms on the skylight and figured out how they worked. I wanted to be ready to go for a quick getaway as soon as the opportunity presented itself.

I waited and waited—and waited. Cassie finished mopping and scrubbing the deck of her catamaran, and then she pulled off the mainsail and set it aside before unfurling a new one to replace it.

This is going to take forever, I thought, rolling my eyes. *What if Kevin comes back?*

But I had to wait. There was nothing else I could do.

Finally, I got my chance when Cassie disappeared down some stairs into the hull of her boat. Without wasting a second, I pulled the releases on the skylight and flipped it wide open. I pulled myself up through the hole with both hands, and just as I was about to pull my legs up after me, I looked over in horror as Cassie reappeared on the deck of her boat.

She stopped short and stared at me blankly for a second. Then she smiled a strange little smile and went back to her chores.

I hesitated for a moment, unsure what the expression on Cassie's face had meant. What I wanted to believe was that my secret was safe with her and she wasn't going to tell anyone, much less Kevin, that she'd seen me sneaking around his boat.

At least that's what I wanted to believe, but I really didn't care. I closed the skylight again and pulled myself to my feet, and then I shot a quick glance at Cassie. Her back was to me, and she was bending over working busily on the ropes of her new mainsail.

That was good enough for me. I jumped over the side of the boat and onto the dock. Without another look in her direction, I strode confidently to the end of the dock and headed for the restaurant next door. I asked the waitress if she would call me a cab, and while I waited impatiently, I looked across the water to the docks where Cassie was still busy with her sail.

Please don't tell anyone—at least not until I'm gone, I implored silently.

Once I was gone, she could tell anyone she wanted, because no one around here knew who I was anyway.

I heard the sound of tires on gravel and looked up to see a taxi pulling into the parking lot. It was time to make my getaway. I hopped in the cab and was about to tell the driver to take me across the island to my plane, but then I changed my mind. If Cassie did end up telling anyone that she had seen me, that person could trace the cab to where it had taken me. And that happened, it wouldn't be too difficult for someone to ask around and find out that a teen girl with bright red hair and an even brighter red seaplane had landed there.

Besides, I had some shopping to do.

I told the driver to drop me at the nearest large supermarket, and I went inside to get the various items on Jodi's list: bread, Danish pastries, peanut butter, and of course some Doritos for Jack. I then took another taxi to the local Kentucky Fried Chicken and ordered a big bucket of chicken with some macaroni salad and coleslaw before taking yet another taxi back to the marina and my plane.

Let's see them trace me now, I thought as I loaded the supplies onto the floor of the copilot's side of the cockpit. I grabbed Jack's jerry can from the seat and walked over to the corner gas station to fill it. Once filled, it was heavy and difficult to lug back to the plane, but it wasn't too far to walk. I slid it in behind the copilot's seat and closed the cargo door.

I was finally ready to get out of there. I climbed into the cockpit and looked toward the dock and the street beyond it one last time, half expecting to see the flashing blue and red lights of police cars speeding out to arrest me, but all was quiet. I was free to go, and within minutes, I was cruising across the harbor, my engine rumbling throatily as I let it warm up a bit before taking off.

As I taxied out, I saw off to my left some pelicans coming in for an awkward landing on the water. One of them had a fish in its mouth and tipped its head back to extend the billowy underbelly of its beak so that it could swallow. Florida was full of pelicans, and even though I'd never see such strange and clumsy-looking birds until I came here, I somehow felt a connection to them. The way they glided in for a landing on the surface of the water reminded me of a seaplane. They extended their feet like skis and skimmed across the water, gradually slowing down as they folded in their huge wings and giant beaks. It occurred to me that some people probably thought seaplanes like mine were awkward and clumsy too, but to me they were as graceful and beautiful as a ballet dancer, and so were the pelicans—the De Havilland seaplanes of the bird world.

I took one last look around before I turned into the wind and pushed the throttle up. The engine sprang into life, and I was soon skipping across the wave tops—blasting and slamming through until I got up enough speed for my pontoons to break the surface tension of the water.

After a few more bumps and jolts, I was finally airborne.

Chapter Thirty-Five

It Couldn't Possibly Be A Coincidence

My flight to Fort Jefferson took the better part of an hour, but it was uneventful and gave me a chance to relax and put on some music. I had to laugh at myself a little bit, flying along just a few hundred feet off the beautiful blue ocean, singing Taylor Swift songs at the top of my lungs. I could only wonder what the sharks and sea turtles I could see down below thought of that.

Once I landed at the fortress, I taxied up to the seaplane beach and neatly turned myself around, shutting down my engine and stepping out onto the pontoons to paddle into shore. A few tourists lined the beach to watch me, laughing good-naturedly as they snapped some photos. I shrugged and smiled at them and struck silly poses with my paddle.

"I've never seen anyone paddle a plane before," said a balding middle-aged man in a Hawaiian shirt with a big grin on his face as I jumped onto the beach and pulled my plane up to the sand.

"If you think that was cool, just watch what this guy does," I replied, tying my plane off securely. I pointed over to the large green and white De Havilland Turbo Otter seaplane that was coming in for a landing across the harbor.

The Otter came in for a textbook landing and taxied over toward us. He pulled in close and spun around at the last second so his nose was facing out from the beach. The pilot-side door opened, and a barefoot and bearded young pilot leaned out to look behind as he backed up.

With a healthy roar of the engine, he reversed the pitch on the propellers and neatly backed the plane onto the sand, then he shut down the engine and climbing onto a pontoon to tie off his plane.

"Now, how'd he do that?" the man in the Hawaiian shirt asked, looking over at me.

"Reverse thrust by twisting the propeller pitch," I explained, twisting my palms to demonstrate the principle before heading up the beach with my bag of groceries and bucket full of fried chicken.

I stopped at Jack and Jodi's campsite and left the bag on their picnic table. I couldn't see them around anywhere, and I was back earlier than the time I had told them I would return, so I headed to my tent for a bit of a rest until it was time for dinner.

I was relieved to finally lie down and take a break. For the first time since I'd been sneaking around Kevin and Kristina's boat, I could relax.

My body wanted a nap but I had too much to think about to fall asleep. I pulled out my iPhone and flipped through to the photos I'd taken a couple of hours earlier.

I first looked at the photo of the pencil rubbing of the brick markings.

At the far left and right of the image there were strange stick-figure symbols with meanings that I couldn't possibly fathom. They reminded me of designs that I'd seen on the Discovery Channel of the so-called Nazca Lines in Peru. Centuries ago, enormous geometrical patterns had been carved into the desert floor, and they were only visible from the air. These symbols were similar to that, and I wondered if the two were somehow connected.

Scattered in a couple of places around the image were several small, round markings that looked similar to the shield designs of coats of arms. I zoomed in and tried to make sense of them, but they were too faint and incomplete to decipher.

In the center of the image, there was a splotch mark that looked kind of like an infinity symbol (or maybe a peanut?), and just above that to the left was the notation *P1622*. I had no idea what that meant, but what caught my eye was that the numbers were from the Latin alphabet instead of Roman numerals like the rest of the numbers on the rubbing.

After examining all of the smaller markings on the image, I turned my attention to the two largest ones. They were comprised of two numbers, one at the top, the other at the bottom, written in two different styles and both using Roman numerals.

Or should I say that at first sight they *appeared* to be Roman numerals. Once I took a closer look at them and thought about it a little, I realized that they actually weren't Roman numerals at all.

The top one read:

See what I mean? They're Roman numerals, right?

Wrong.

At least two things are wrong, actually.

Firstly, there was no number U in the Roman numeral system as far as I could remember. (This was when I wished the Dry Tortugas had a Wi-Fi network. A simple Google search would have cleared up my uncertainty on this point in no time.)

The second problem was the letters IIII. I didn't need Google to tell me that the Roman numeral system never uses four Is to represent the number four. Four is written IV, not IIII.

The bottom number was equally confusing:

Once again, the letter U was in there, which wasn't actually a proper Roman numeral. But if these weren't Roman numerals, then what the heck were they?

I stared at the picture for a while longer, zooming in and zooming out, moving my finger around the screen to move the image around, but I just couldn't figure it out.

My mind was reeling, so I decided to move on to the next picture, the one with the strange handwriting.

Seeing the bizarre writing for a second time and having a closer look at it did not help my understanding whatsoever. It was so strange, in fact, that I wondered if it was handwriting at all.

It has to be handwriting, though, I thought. *It's too structured to be random squiggles.*

I closed my eyes and tried to think of any writing system past or present that looked anything like it. The closest I could come up with was Arabic, but I'd seen enough Arabic to know that that wasn't what this was.

Not to mention that Arabic reads from right to left, I mused. This writing didn't seem to have any structure at all. Instead, it was an unbroken string of characters running from one line to the next in an endless stream. Even in Arabic, the writing was separated into sentences and words, and this text did not seem to do that.

But if it wasn't Arabic or any other known language, then what in the world was it?

I suddenly had an idea—a silly idea, I will admit, but one that my mind seemed to keep coming back to again and again that day.

It's from Atlantis, I thought, unable to stop myself before the idea formed in my head. *This writing is from the lost civilization of Atlantis. That's why it looks so alien and strange, and yet it's still kind of familiar. The Atlanteans must have passed on their system of writing words and numbers to the other ancient civilizations, and those systems evolved into the forms of writing we use today. That's why it looks familiar.*

I knew it was crazy, but in some strange, twisted parallel universe, this probably sounded like a reasonable explanation. Then again, a parallel universe might be exactly what we were dealing with if we were talking about Atlantis.

My hand instinctively reached down to the side pocket of my shorts where the strange luminous green stone was still resting comfortingly against the side of my leg. I couldn't forget that whatever explanation there was, it had something to do with these beautiful green stones.

Knowing how mesmerizing the stone could be, I resisted the urge to pull it out and flipped to the last picture on my phone instead.

The prize of Consolation
Carried by Rosario
Is with the Scottish Chief

I closed my eyes and tried to figure the meaning of this cryptic message. What did it have to do with the other things I'd found—green stones, strange markings and numbers, and Atlantean handwriting?

Who is Rosario? I wondered. *And who is the Scottish chief?*

I had absolutely no idea.

I opened my eyes and stared at the note until the lines became blurry and crossed over one another the more I looked at them.

This is no use, I thought, and I checked the time. Soon I would have to meet up with Jack and Jodi for our feast of Kentucky Fried Chicken.

I flipped through the photos one last time and was about to lock my phone when I noticed something that I'd somehow missed before. At the top right-hand corner of the page of strange handwriting, the number *4717* was stamped in block-style letters. It was different and looked out of place from the rest.

"Four seven one seven," I muttered to myself, and I flipped back to the picture of the pencil rubbing.

I stared at the letters for a moment as I calculated in my head.

What if U is meant to be one thousand, I wondered.

I shook my head. That couldn't be right.

In Roman numerals, M equals one thousand, I said to myself. *Everyone knows that.*

But I couldn't stop thinking about it, because if U was meant to represent one thousand, and if IIII was the incorrectly written form of the number four, then that would make the number written at the top of the pencil rubbing also 4717.

My heart began to beat faster in excitement at having made this discovery. It had to be right. It couldn't possibly be a coincidence.

I flipped back to the page of strange writing again and stared at it some more. My heart took another leap when I noticed something else I'd missed before. Drawn in the left-hand margin was a stick-figure symbol that looked familiar; it was shaped like an S with a kind of tail hanging from it. I realized that the same symbol was at the far left of the previous image of the pencil rubbing.

Another coincidence? I asked myself. *There's no way. But what does all this tell me?*

Unfortunately, none of it actually told me much of any use except that whoever had made these markings used a strange system of Roman numerals and that the pencil rubbing and the page of strange handwriting had something to do with each other. But, of course, I'd already guessed that much from the fact that the two papers were filed right next to each other in the binder.

I sighed heavily and stared at the other Roman numeral at the bottom of the pencil rubbing.

If my theory about the character U was correct, then this number was supposed to be 2380.

"Two thousand three hundred eighty," I said, hoping that by saying the number aloud its meaning would become clear to me.

It didn't work. Speaking it didn't magically reveal its secrets. I still didn't have the slightest clue what these numbers meant.

Just then, my phone chirped and a reminder flashed on the screen in front of me. The only thing I knew for sure was that it was time to meet Jack and Jodi for dinner.

Chapter Thirty-Six

Maybe You'd Better Start At The Beginning

I crawled out of my tent and headed around the bushes to Jack and Jodi's campsite. I could already smell a barbecue burning and the smell of fried chicken. As I came around the corner I saw Jack over at the barbecue with a pair of tongs and the grill piled high with pieces of KFC chicken.

"Hey there!" Jack called out, waving to me with his barbecue tongs. "I'm just warming up the chicken a bit."

"Good idea," I replied. I had expected to be eating lukewarm chicken for dinner, but Jack's idea was much better.

"Thank you for the supplies," Jodi said as she walked over and began to set the table with plastic plates and utensils.

"No problem," I replied. "The jerry can of gas is still in my plane though. I didn't have enough hands to carry everything."

Jack waved me off with his tongs. "No rush," he said. "I'll get it from you tomorrow." He turned back to the grill and began to unload it, putting one piece of chicken at a time into the cardboard bucket. When he was finished, he poured some water over the coals to put them out before walking over to join Jodi and me at the picnic table.

The three of us helped ourselves to the freshly warmed chicken. I couldn't remember KFC ever tasting so good. It was greasy and made a huge mess all over my face and fingers, but it was so good. It was a perfect picnic dinner in perfect surroundings with my two new friends. It reminded me of when I was a kid, and my parents and I would drive out somewhere and have a KFC picnic. Unfortunately, those picnics were almost always rudely interrupted by the arrival of wasps. This would usually send my father screaming and running into the forest while my mother and I laughed our heads off and bravely waved the wasps away with our hands. But out in the Dry Tortugas there were no uninvited wasp guests to disturb us; just the sound of the waves and the birds calling to one another on Bush Key.

The three of us talked and laughed our way through half a bucket of chicken before calling it quits and pulling three lawn chairs onto the grass to sit and watch the last tourists of the day slowly making their way onto the ferry.

"What did you get up to today?" Jack asked as he arrived with some glasses and a fresh pitcher of sun-brewed iced tea that he'd made that afternoon.

I shrugged my shoulders. "Nothing much," I replied. "Just snooping around a little—trying to figure some stuff out."

"What kind of stuff?" Jodi asked, pouring a glass of tea and handing it to me.

I hesitated for a moment before answering. I still didn't know who was involved in this scheme with Kevin, Kristina, and Patrick. I knew that at least one other person was involved, but I had no idea who that was. Maybe it was Jack or Jodi? Or both?

That's completely ridiculous, I scolded myself and decided to show them the photos I'd taken earlier. Jodi had proven to be knowledgeable about barracudas, after all. Maybe she would have some insight into this as well.

"This kind of stuff," I replied, holding up my iPhone so that Jodi could see the photo of the pencil rubbing with its strange symbols and numbers.

Jodi leaned forward to look at the screen and then laughed. "You've been to the shipwreck museum," she said, leaning back in her chair again. "That's Jack's specialty, not mine."

I wasn't sure what she meant, but I turned the screen toward Jack, and he leaned forward to see the photo. He took the phone and put on his reading glasses to examine it more closely, smiling and nodding to himself as he did.

"Do you know what it is?!?" I asked, surprised.

"Yes, of course," he replied, handing my phone back to me. "It's some markings from an old-fashioned Spanish silver treasure ingot from one of the 1622 shipwrecks."

My head was spinning. In the span of only two short sentences, Jack had completely overloaded my brain with information.

Silver ingots?!? I thought. *1622 shipwrecks?!? Spanish treasure?!?*

I shook my head in confusion. To me an ingot meant something small, maybe the size of a chocolate bar, not something like a huge brick. "It's not an ingot," I protested. "This is from something much larger."

Jack continued nodding. "An ingot," he said again, holding out his hands about eighteen inches apart. "A silver bar about this big."

My thoughts were in a spin. I couldn't accept what I was hearing, and I shook my head again.

"But not silver," I replied, still protesting. "This was black, like burned toast, not silver."

Jack kept right on nodding, and even Jodi was nodding too. "That's right," they both said. "Silver."

"Silver reacts with seawater," Jack explained. "And after a long while underwater, it starts to turn black."

I stared down at the picture on my phone, trying to make sense of what they were telling me.

A bar of silver? I thought. *Is that what those huge bricks were? Is that even possible? They were enormous!*

As my mind struggled to accept what Jack was telling me, I thought of another thing he'd said that didn't make sense.

"What did you mean when you said it was a silver ingot from one of the 1622 shipwrecks?" I asked.

Jack pulled his chair up next to mine and leaned over to point at the photo, sliding his fingers to zoom in on the text that read *P1622*.

"P1622," Jack read, tapping his finger on the screen. "It's a foundary mark. It means the ingot was forged in the foundries at the Spanish silver mine in Potosí in the year 1622."

My mind was swirling with a million thoughts and questions occurring to me all at once. *What are the strange symbols? What's the deal with the Roman numerals? What do they mean?*

Jack seemed to read my mind and pointed down at my phone again to explain the various symbols.

"These weird marks over at the left and right are the insignias of the shippers and receivers," he explained. "Kind of like a personal logo or something like that. And this V over here is the mark of the silver master, who happened to be a Dutchman named De Vreder. This number up here at the top is the serial number of the bar—4717. This blob in the middle is called the assayer's bite, and it's where the assayer took a sample of this ingot to determine its purity, which was then recorded at the bottom along with the assayer's mark. You can see that this bar is of purity 2380 out of 2400—very pure, the same as nearly all of the Spanish silver from the New World. They had excellent purification processes."

I stared at Jack in disbelief.

"And finally," he said. "All these stamps everywhere, these are so-called *Quinto* stamps, which prove that the owner of this silver brick had paid the required twenty-percent tax to the Spanish crown. They stamped the ingots several times just in case the owner ever cut up the bar and sold it in bits and pieces."

I was speechless. I wanted to ask him how in the world he knew all of this, but there was an even more burning question on my mind: did he know anything about the strange handwriting?

I reached over and tapped the screen on the phone to the next picture.

"And this?" I asked, pointing at the bizarre Atlantean-Arabic scrawl of characters flowing across the page like waves on the ocean. "Do you also know what this strange handwriting is?"

Jack took the phone from me and peered down through his bifocals. As he looked at the image, he nodded in recognition, and to my profound surprise, he actually began to read the text right off the screen of my iPhone.

"*In Cartegena, on the twenty-fifth day of July of said year, the accountant Benido Marques Villido, in the name of Jacove de Vreder, silver master of the fleet and said galleon, confessed to having received from Señor Juan Francisco de Salvadore and accountant Don Alonso de Toledo, official judges of the royal treasury and of the royal chest in their charge, is deposited the proceeds from slave licenses, the silver bars following. Item: Bar number four thousand seven hundred and seventeen—purity two thousand three hundred and eighty—weight one hundred thirty six marks six ounces—value three hundred and twenty five thousand four hundred and sixty seven maravedis, from which will be deducted seven thousand three hundred and forty maravedis....*"

Jack looked up, rubbed his eyes, and pulled off his reading glasses, letting them hang around his neck on a string. "And so on, yada yada

yada," he said. "The text ends there, but you get the idea. This is the manifest entry that goes with the bar of silver you just showed me."

I took the phone from him and examined the handwriting again, trying to figure out how he could have possibly read all of that from the flowing stream of indecipherable text.

"This says all of that?" I asked, looking at Jack.

He nodded. "It's difficult to read," he said, still rubbing his eyes. "And what makes it even more difficult is that they didn't use punctuation, and they wrote out all their numbers in longhand. The point of using this procesal script was to prevent counterfeiting, but you can read it once you know how to. It's just Spanish, after all."

Spanish?!? I never would've believed it. I took a moment to process all that Jack had told me: procesal script, manifest entries, silver masters, assayers—it was all too much for me, and I just sat there speechless.

"I'm sorry," I said slowly, "but I am really not understanding any of this."

Jodi looked over at me and smiled sympathetically.

"You and me both, dear," she said. "These 1622 wrecks are Jack's obsession, and even after twenty years, I still don't know what he's talking about most of the time."

"The 1622 wrecks?" I asked. "I don't even know what *that* means."

Jodi looked over at Jack. "Maybe you'd better start at the beginning," she said, leaning over to pat him on the arm.

Chapter Thirty-Seven

The 1622 Spanish Treasure Fleet

"Strewn all across the coastal waters of Florida are hundreds upon hundreds of shipwrecks," Jack explained. "From down here in the Dry Tortugas stretching all along the Florida Keys and up the eastern seaboard of the United States, there are modern merchant ships, old warships, German U-Boats, pirate ships, sailing ships, you name it. And the reason for all these shipwrecks lies in the fact that just a few miles from where we are sitting right now the waters of the powerful Gulf Stream current begin their journey from the Gulf of Mexico all the way north and across to Europe."

So far so good, I thought. *At least I'm familiar with the Gulf Stream.*

"In those days, the same as now," Jack continued, "ships returning home to Europe would ride the current of the Gulf Stream and use it to shorten the time it took to cross the Atlantic Ocean. It was sometimes a dangerous business, but the added speed made it worth the risk. And what made it risky, particularly down here in Florida, is the fact that nearly the entire coastline is lined with an enormous system of shallow water reefs."

My ears perked up again. I knew about this as well.

"The third largest barrier reef system in the world," I said excitedly. "I read about this on the Internet!"

Jack nodded. "Exactly," he said. "And what makes it so dangerous is the combination of this system of underwater reefs with the yearly hurricane season. Back in the old days before satellites and radar systems, predicting the weather was almost completely based on guesswork and superstition. Ships got caught in hurricanes and storms all the time, and if you were on a sailing vessel without engines, that meant there was nothing you could do but ride it out, praying and hoping for the best. If you were lucky, you survived. If not, a ship might end up smashed on the reef and sent to the bottom along with all its passengers and cargo.

"And for the Spanish, that lost cargo often meant lost treasure," Jack continued, "because for hundreds of years after Columbus's discovery of the Americas, the Spanish were the true masters of the New World—the Caribbean Sea wasn't known as the Spanish Main for nothing, after all.

In those days, this was their turf, and from 1492 until the early 1800s, they shipped billions upon billions of dollars' worth of silver, gold, and other treasures back home to Spain. This made their ships a major target on the high seas, so the Spanish went to great lengths to protect them because if the treasure didn't make it through, they wouldn't be able to afford their various wars and other expensive luxuries at home.

"One of the ways Spain safeguarded the arrival of its goods and treasure was to organize ships into convoys that sailed under the protection of big, well-armed galleons. These treasure fleet convoys crossed the Atlantic from Spain to the New World and back again once a year on average.

"After the end of the winter storm season, the convoys left Spain and sailed across the Atlantic Ocean until they had safely reached the first islands of the Caribbean. From there one group of ships headed south to the ports of Cartagena and Portobello to pick up silver and gold from the mines of Peru. Another group sailed to Trujillo to pick up indigo from the Spanish plantations in Honduras and Guatemala. Yet another group sailed for Veracruz where china, silk, and spices from the Far East arrived after being shipped across the Pacific Ocean and transported overland from Acapulco. All these various groups of ships then regrouped in Havana in late summer and sailed together in a single heavily armed convoy, riding the Gulf Stream all the way back to Europe.

"It was a good system that worked very well for the Spanish for centuries because it protected them from pirates and ambushes by enemy ships from rival European nations. But what it couldn't protect them from was the unpredictable whims of the weather. Sometimes storms swept in out of nowhere scattering ships and sending countless billions to the bottom of the ocean.

"The dates and years that these ill-fated treasure fleets met their demise are well known to any shipwreck buff like me. Some of the more famous ones include the 1733 treasure fleet that was struck by a hurricane just off the Florida Keys near Islamorada and resulted in the sinking of more than a dozen ships. Then there's the 1715 treasure fleet that ran into a hurricane just off the Florida coast up near Vero Beach. The entire fleet sank just a hundred feet offshore, and coins from those wrecks still wash ashore to this day. But the most famous one of all is the fleet that sailed north from Havana on September 4th, 1622.

"The 1622 treasure fleet was plagued with bad luck and delays the entire year, and the ships arrived in Havana many weeks behind schedule. Discussions were held between the various captains and pilots to consider delaying the sailing until the following year. To sail so late in the year was considered foolhardy because it was already well into hurricane season, and the chances of being caught in a storm were much higher. But unfortunately, the treasure was desperately needed in Spain because the new young King, Philip IV, had inherited the debts and wars of his predecessor.

"The pilots and navigators looked to the skies to plot the upcoming celestial alignments and decided that the best weather would come in the early days of September at a time when the sun, moon, and planets would converge in the heavens. Preparations were made to sail, and as the sun rose on the morning of their departure, the captains and pilots anxiously looked to the skies. The weather was fair and clear, and the call went out that the fleet would set sail as planned.

"Less than twenty-four hours later," Jack said, leaning forward and taking a sip of his sun tea, "a hurricane would sweep down from out of nowhere and send its most valuable treasure ships straight to the bottom of the sea."

Chapter Thirty-Eight

I Was Just About To Get To That

Jack took another sip of his tea and Jodi handed him the pitcher so he could refill both of our glasses.

"In terms of lost numbers of ships, the 1622 fleet wasn't a total disaster," Jack continued. "Some of the ships had already sailed for Spain ahead of the main convoy, and these successfully escaped pirates and the storm. Even most of the ships caught in the terrifying winds of the hurricane were blown safely past the reefs west of the Tortugas where they managed to ride the storm out in the deep waters of the Gulf of Mexico. Unfortunately, for the king of Spain, however, most of that year's treasure was loaded on the heavy galleons, and those were caught right in the heart of the storm. As the hurricane winds increased, the galleons were blown helplessly toward the coral reefs.

"But there was nothing the sailors could do. Without engines or the ability to steer, these ships were powerless in the screaming winds, and they could only watch helplessly as the storm blew them closer and closer to the reef. As the enormous galleons were lifted with each passing wave, they could see the reef getting closer, and they knew that soon they would come crashing down on top of it. Passengers and crew alike knelt on the decks in the driving rain to pray that they would be spared, but it was hopeless. When their fragile wooden hulls smashed into the coral, the ships sank, and the passengers' fates were sealed. Hundreds died, and millions of dollars' worth of treasure sank to the bottom of the shallow waters.

"But just because the galleons sank didn't mean that the treasure was lost forever. It wasn't the first time the Spaniards had lost ships in a storm, and it certainly wouldn't be the last. They were experts at salvaging their own wrecked galleons, and as soon as the winds of the hurricane died down, the salvage operations began.

"The salvage ships soon found the sunken hull of one of the largest treasure galleons about forty miles east of the Dry Tortugas. They knew exactly where to look because the water was shallow enough that the ship's mizzenmast was sticking up above the surface, and five survivors of the storm were found clinging to it.

"But even though the tip of the tall mast was above water, the rest of the ship was not, and it was too deep to reach at the time, so the salvage operation turned its attention to finding another of the galleons that they believed had sunk nearby.

"Eyewitness accounts from survivors of the storm told of another ship sinking nearby, but no matter how much they searched for this other galleon, they couldn't find a trace of it. Frustrated, they turned west to search for traces of other wrecks from the storm. They sailed here to the Dry Tortugas, and over there near Loggerhead Key, they found the broken hull of another treasure ship sticking halfway out of the water where it had run aground. Some of the survivors of this wreck had waded ashore through the surf and had been living on the island without food and only rainwater to drink for three weeks.

"This wreck was easily salvageable since it wasn't even completely submerged, so the Spanish salvage team quickly set fire to the wreck and burned the hull to the waterline so they could more easily access the cargo decks. Once that was done, they sent divers down to grab anything of value and bring it to the surface.

"The Spanish were expert divers—or should I say that they were experts at finding other people to do their diving for them. Years earlier on an island off the coast of Venezuela, they had discovered an amazing tribe of indigenous people who were capable of diving down to immense depths with just a single breath, and they would come back up again with handfuls of pearls. The Spanish were so impressed by this feat that they rounded up the entire tribe and immediately enslaved them, putting them to work collecting pearls for the Spanish crown. Unfortunately, this tribe eventually died out from European diseases and the harsh conditions of their slavery, but the Spanish were not too bothered about that because by then they'd already found some other local tribes who could do their diving for them.

"Diving in those days was a tricky business. It wasn't like nowadays where just about anyone can strap on a scuba tank and jump into the water. The Spanish had no scuba tanks, but more important than that, they had no diving masks to help them see underwater. As far as diving goes, it's one thing to be able to breathe underwater, but being able to *see* is by far more important, especially when you are trying to find treasure.

"But hundreds of years before Jacques Cousteau and the dawn of modern scuba diving, the Spanish divers did have a few tricks up their sleeves. Lenses made from the polished shells of turtles were used by the slave divers and pushed into their eye sockets, thus allowing them a somewhat blurry window on the underwater world. But these lenses were hard on the eyes since the water pressure pushed them right up against the eyeballs and caused constant bruising all around the eye sockets.

"Another method used by the Spanish slaves to see underwater was to soak a sponge in oil and carry it down to the bottom. By squeezing the sponge and releasing droplets of oil into the water, a skilled diver could then catch a droplet on his eyeball, and as a result, he'd be able to see for a few seconds.

"And so, using these primitive methods, in just a few short weeks the Spaniards were able to salvage almost the entire contents of the wreck over there at Loggerhead Key. The only hiccup in the project came when a second hurricane swept through the area just a month after the first and sent the salvage crews scrambling for cover on the tiny island. But once the weather cleared again they resumed the salvage operations and were able to bring up nearly everything of value—silver bars, gold bars, pieces of eight, even the cannons."

"Pieces of eight?" I asked. "Are those like coins?"

"Exactly," Jack replied. "Until the 1800s, the basic unit of currency in Spain was called the *real*, and the most common coin in circulation was worth eight *reales*. That's where the name comes from."

Jack reached around to the back of his neck to undo the clasp of a silver chain he was wearing. He took it off and handed it over to me. Hanging from the end of the silver chain was a rough coin of brilliant, shining silver.

I held it in my hand and tested its weight. It was heavy for its size and had uneven edges, and there were impressions on each of its faces that I had to strain my eyes in order to make out.

"This is a four-real coin," Jack said, leaning over to explain the markings. "On this side is the Spanish royal crest, and on the other side is the shield of the Hapsburg Empire."

I flipped the coin over.

"On this side there's also the date the coin was minted and where," Jack said, pointing to various markings on the coin's face. "The Spaniards minted millions of coins just like this one at various mints in the New World. The coins were then packed into special treasure chests that were built with a dozen separate spring locks all around the lid that were turned simultaneously using a very large single key. That key was so difficult to turn that a team of horses was required to do it. In this way the Spanish ensured that no one would be able to open the treasure chests at sea, and they would be safe until they reached their final destinations."

"Pretty clever," I said, nodding as I examined Jack's coin in the palm of my hand. "So, where did this coin come from, then?"

Jack smiled. "I was just about to get to that part of the story," he said.

Chapter Thirty-Nine

The Archive Of The Indies

Jack looked at the silver coin on his chain and held it up so that it sparkled in the late afternoon sun.

"Even though the Spaniards were able to fully salvage the galleon they found here in the Tortugas," he said, continuing his story, "there were still two valuable wrecks that had sunk somewhere a few dozen miles east of here. So after they finished their operations on Loggerhead Key, they sailed to where they'd found the first wreck with its mizzenmast sticking out of the water.

"But thanks to the second hurricane that had struck while they were salvaging on Loggerhead Key, the first ship had apparently broken apart and the mizzenmast was long gone. There was no sign of it anywhere.

"The Spanish set up base on a nearby uninhabited island, and day after day they rowed back and forth towing grappling hooks behind their boats, trying to find the wreck again. Whenever the hooks snagged onto something, the divers jumped overboard and investigated, but the ships were never found. The loss of all that treasure was such a disaster for the Spanish Crown that the commander of the 1622 treasure fleet, the Marquis of Cadereita, sailed out to oversee the salvage efforts, but it was hopeless. The enormous treasure galleons had disappeared under the waves, and eventually the Spanish were forced to give up and head back home.

"But the two ships and their fortunes in treasure were not forgotten. A way simply *had* to be found to locate and salvage them, so four years later another salvage team was dispatched to the area. But this time they had a secret weapon—an underwater diving bell had been specially constructed that allowed a man to be pulled along underneath the sea, and he could look out the window for signs of wrecks as he went.

"This new invention worked very well, and it wasn't long before they found treasure. They even found the third galleon, the one that had eluded the earlier salvage operations, but no sign was ever found again of that first ship whose five survivors had clung so desperately to its mizzenmast after it sank.

"For the next twenty years, salvage operations continued on and off in the area and they recovered hundreds of silver ingots, dozens of bars of gold, and tens of thousands of pieces of eight. They were even able to raise some of the bronze cannons from their watery graves and restore them to working condition. But as time went on they found less and less treasure, and eventually the whole salvage operation was called off, despite the fact that the majority of treasure from the two ships had not been found.

"The ships were gone, but the missing treasure was not forgotten. Decades later the Spanish still listed the two ships' names—the *Santa Margarita* and the *Nuestra Señora de Atocha*—at the top of the list of unsalvaged wrecks in the New World. But as the years passed and the shifting sands at the bottom of the shallow waters covered their secrets, the memory of the two ships faded."

Jack paused and took another sip of his tea before leaning toward me and continuing with the story.

"Now, fast forward three hundred fifty years to the twentieth century and the early 1960s," he said. "For the first time in centuries there was the possibility that these long-lost treasure galleons could be found and their valuable cargos recovered. The age of modern scuba diving had just begun, and for the first time ordinary people like you and me could dive beneath the waves and explore the mysteries of the underwater world. The imaginations of a new breed of treasure hunter were fired, and they dreamed of finding a shipwreck and striking it rich. And at the top of the list of the hundreds of shipwrecks lining the shores of North America, the two that were considered the most desirable—and profitable—were the *Atocha* and the *Margarita*.

"The only problem was that after so many years no one had any idea where the ships were supposed to have sunk. The Spaniards who'd worked on the original salvage operations were obviously long since dead, and all that was left were documents containing tantalizing clues as to the whereabouts of the two galleons.

"One such clue was a record from the year 1622, dated shortly after the first disastrous hurricane. This document stated that the still visible mizzenmast of the *Atocha* was located 'near the last key of the Matecumbe.' To these eager new modern treasure hunters, that description seemed clear enough—it must have been referring to the two islands of the Florida Keys known as Upper and Lower Matecumbe.

"Unfortunately, it wasn't the right place—in fact it was more than a hundred miles away from the correct location. In the intervening centuries, it had somehow been forgotten that the Spanish had referred to the entire chain of the Florida Keys as the '*Matecumbe*', not just one or two of the individual islands. The two galleons had sunk near the last key of the entire Florida Keys and not halfway up the island chain toward the mainland where both Upper and Lower Matecumbe Keys are located.

"And so, while dozens of adventurous divers with bronze tans and hair bleached blonde by the sun scoured the sea floor near Upper and Lower Matecumbe Keys, a man named Eugene Lyon sat in a library on the opposite side of the world and flipped through dusty documents and books. All of them were looking for the same thing—the resting place of the *Atocha* and the *Margarita*—but only one of them would actually find it.

"For hundreds of years the Spanish had sailed the high seas and ruled their colonies in the New World with a gradually declining dominance. During all that time, records had been kept, contracts written up, and letters sent. In 1785, the Emperor of the Holy Roman Empire decided that all of these documents should be brought together in a single place for safekeeping. And this is how the *Archivo General de Indias*—the General Archive of the Indies—was born.

"In a large sixteenth-century building in Seville there are more than fifteen million pages of documents, ledgers, maps, and other records available to any researcher willing to take the time to sift through them and discover their secrets. No one ever could have guessed that it was in this building that the *Atocha* and the *Margarita* would be found, not in the waters off the Florida coast.

"As Eugene Lyon sat there in the archive in Seville reading document after document, he began to wonder if the treasure hunters in Florida were looking in the right place for these two lost galleons. As he read various archival documents and looked at modern maps as well as older ones hand drawn by the Spaniards, this man began to wonder about an island lying to the west of Key West called Marquesas Key.

"From the mainland all the way west to Marquesas Key, the Florida Keys consist of a group of islands that are more or less densely packed together into a single flowing archipelago. To the west of Marquesas Key, however, is a vast expanse of forty miles of open water until you reach the very few tiny islands of the Dry Tortugas that mark the true end of the Florida Keys. While not technically the *last* island in the Florida Keys, in realistic terms Marquesas Key more or less *did* mark the end of the island chain as far as the Spanish were concerned.

"Eugene wondered whether it was this island that was referred to by the Spanish when they wrote 'the last key of the Matecumbe.' He also wondered about the island's name—Marquesas Key. Where did the name come from? All islands have names that come from somewhere, after all. What was the story behind this particular name? Eugene wondered if the name might have originated at the time of the original salvage attempts. After all, in the months following the sinking of the ships, the commander of the treasure fleet, the Marquis of Cadereita, had overseen the salvage operations from a base camp set up on a nearby island. Could that island have been Marquesas Key, so named in honor of the Marquis of Cadereita?

"After examining thousands of pages of documents, Eugene was able to establish that this particular island had never been referred to as Marquesas Key *before* the year 1622. It was only *after* that point in time that the name began to be used.

"Eugene didn't know it yet," Jack said with a grin, "but he had just found the two long-lost Spanish treasure galleons."

Chapter Forty

The World's Greatest Treasure Hunter

"Eugene Lyon lived in Florida and was in Seville doing research for a thesis that had nothing to do with shipwrecks or treasure or anything like that," Jack continued. "But being a student with a family and in need of extra money, he made an agreement with a man named Mel Fisher to keep an eye out for any documents mentioning the *Atocha* or the *Margarita*. Fisher was a treasure hunter based in Florida, and he was absolutely desperate to find the two galleons and become famous as the world's greatest treasure hunter.

"Lyon wrote a paper explaining his conclusions about the location of the ships, and then he forwarded it to Fisher. After reading it, Fisher immediately moved his operation from the Matecumbe Keys to Key West and began searching the area off Marquesas Key instead.

"Finding treasure on the ocean floor is a tricky business," Jack explained, "particularly in the area around Marquesas Key. This particular area is called the quicksands because the underwater sands there move and shift with every tide, burying everything on the seafloor. But Fisher had a solution to this problem. He'd installed great big metal deflectors called mailboxes on the backs of his boats that could be lowered and fitted over the propellers. Then, when the boat engines were started, a flood of clear surface water was blasted down to the sea bottom where it dug holes straight through the sand and all the way down to bedrock. The sand is blown away in the process leaving only the heavier artifacts behind.

"And so they searched, day after day, just as the Spaniards had done more than three hundred years earlier. They searched using metal detectors towed behind the boats to find promising places to dig, and then they cleared away the sand with a blast from their propellers before sending divers down to take a look.

"When Fisher abandoned his searches in the Matecumbe Keys, the other treasure hunters there thought he was crazy, but as time went by, he began to find various artifacts and clues near Marquesas Key that suggested that he was on the right track. The first was an enormous iron anchor that could only have come from a ship as large as the *Atocha* or *Margarita*. This was followed by the discovery of thousands of Spanish coins minted in the years leading up to 1622 but none later than that date. They also found an astrolabe, which is a kind of mariner's instrument similar to a sextant that was used by the navigators on the 1622 fleet. Fisher was positive that he was on the trail of the *Atocha*, but his crews and the other treasure hunters were less convinced.

"For years the search and uncertainty continued until they finally found some silver bars, just like the one that you have a picture of on your phone," Jack said, pointing down at my iPhone. "By comparing the serial numbers and weights from the Spanish manifest documents with the numbers and weights of the actual bars, they'd found they were able to confirm that the bars of silver had come from the *Atocha*. Fisher's crews were now sure that they'd found her, but even then some of his fellow treasure hunters were still not convinced.

"The search continued, year after year, with various small finds being made here and there. They found a huge pile of silver coins at a place they later called the Bank of Spain. So many coins were found there, and thousands of them were fused together in block-shaped slabs from being stored so long in the treasure chests that originally held them, which rotted away over the years.

"And they also found small ingots of gold," Jack said, "and personal items such as religious icons or money chains."

"What are money chains?" I asked.

Jack looked over at me and smiled. "They are long gold chains—sometimes more than six feet long—that were worn by wealthy people, not only as decoration but also to avoid paying taxes. The law stated that gold jewelry could not be taxed, so the Spanish wore enormously long gold chains with standardized links whose weight corresponded to a unit of currency. If they needed to pay for something, they would just bend off one of the links and use that as money.

I laughed. "That's ridiculous!" I said. "Do you know how heavy a six-foot gold chain would be? Why didn't they just pay the taxes?"

Jack looked over his glasses at me.

"What if I told you that you could either give me twenty percent of everything you own or wear a big gold chain around your shoulders to avoid paying the tax? What would you do?"

I nodded. "Point taken," I conceded, and Jack continued with the story.

"Even after finding all of these things, the uncertainty remained, and many of Fisher's fellow treasure hunters were still not convinced that he'd actually found the *Atocha*. It was only when his crew discovered a series of bronze cannons at the bottom of the ocean with serial numbers matching those of the cannons on the *Atocha* that there was no longer any doubt. The remnants they'd found *had* to have come from the *Atocha*, but they had yet to find the actual ship itself.

"But then tragedy struck. Mel Fisher's son Dirk, who was captain of one of the search vessels, was killed along with his wife and another diver when their vessel capsized on July 20, 1975. Their deaths were a major blow to the operation, but somehow Fisher and his crew managed to keep the search going.

"For the next decade they found tantalizing clues and traces of the *Atocha* all over the seafloor near Marquesas Key, but they still didn't find the main hull or its valuable cargo of treasure. As the search continued, Fisher was forced to battle in the courts over ownership of the wrecks. The search ruined him financially and took a terrible personal toll.

"And yet they continued searching, making occasional small finds, and even discovering many priceless artifacts from the other lost galleon, the *Margarita*, but over and over again the money ran out, and Fisher was forced to scrape cash together from wherever he could get it in order to keep the search going for just a little bit longer.

"By the summer of 1985, Fisher's money had again run completely out, but as he always did, he somehow pulled together enough to keep the search going for another couple of weeks, but as it turned out, that was enough time to find the mother lode. On July 20, 1985, the lower hull of the *Atocha* and its cargo of treasure was finally found lying among the shifting sands on the seafloor—hundreds of silver bars stacked neatly on the bottom where they'd been sitting for more than three hundred fifty years. The search was finally over for Mel Fisher, and it was only later that anyone realized the significance of the date. Fisher's breakthrough discovery came exactly ten years to the day after the tragic accident that claimed the lives of his son, his son's wife, and one of his divers.

"All those silver bars and other treasure took months to be brought up and divided among Fisher's various investors. And even though the so-called mother lode had already been found, the search for treasure still continues to this day. The tides and storms of the past four centuries have scattered things over a very large area, and there is still plenty out there waiting to be found."

Jack leaned forward and held up his coin necklace again.

"That's where I got this," he said proudly, "diving on the *Atocha* and *Margarita* wreck sites last year."

My eyes opened wide as I looked at the coin with a new appreciation for what it represented.

"What is a coin like that worth?" I asked, reaching to touch the coin again.

Jack leaned back in his chair, shrugging. "It depends who's buying, I suppose—a few hundred dollars maybe; a couple thousand at most. But for me it's not how much it's worth that matters. It's the history of the thing that fascinates me and the fact that I plucked it from the bottom of the ocean with my own two hands where it had been hiding for almost four hundred years."

I took the coin in my hands again and nodded. "I know exactly what you mean," I said reverently.

Jack stood up from his chair to stretch his back. "I'm sorry for going on so long," he said. "But as Jodi can tell you, treasure hunting is one of my favorite subjects."

Jodi grinned and nodded in confirmation.

"Oh no, don't worry!" I replied. "It's an amazing story; thank you so much for telling me all that."

"You must have known half of it already," Jack said, "from when you went to the museum."

"The museum?" I asked, confused.

"The Mel Fisher museum in Key West," Jack said, gesturing to my iPhone, "where you took those photos."

"Oh, yeah, that," I replied with a nervous laugh. I looked down at my phone and wondered whether I should tell them where I'd *really* taken the photos. I had about a million different questions that I wanted to ask, but before I could make a decision about what to say, the moment was lost. We were interrupted by the sudden ringing of a telephone coming from inside Jack and Jodi's tent.

Chapter Forty-One

Life Without The Internet

"Isn't technology wonderful?" Jodi said, rolling her eyes as Jack jumped up from his chair and rushed over to their tent to answer the phone. He grabbed the handset from inside the tent flap and picked it up to answer.

Jodi and I watched as he listened to the voice on the other end and nodded his head. "We're actually not in the city anymore," Jack said. "We're out in the Tortugas, but we could easily make it in time. Just let me ask Jodi."

"What is it?" Jodi asked, looking slightly worried.

Jack waved his hand. "It's nothing bad; don't worry," he said. "It's Alex and Ginger. They just had a cancellation for a private showing out at David Wolkowsky's old house on Ballast Key, and they want to know if the two of us can make it tonight."

Jodi's eyes got wide and she smiled a wide smile.

"Definitely," she said. "But can we make it in time?"

Jack looked at the sky, gauging how much daylight they had before nightfall.

"We'd have to stay out on the boat overnight," he said. "But we can easily make it if we leave right away."

"We can get ready on the boat," Jodi said. "I'll drive while you shower, then you drive while I shower."

Jack nodded and put the phone up to his ear again.

"We're in," he said. "Where do we meet you?"

Jack listened a bit more while Jodi and I got up from our chairs and started clearing the table. He nodded a couple more times then said good-bye and hung up the phone.

"I'm sorry to eat and run like this, Kitty," Jodi said.

"Don't be crazy," I replied. "In fact, why don't you guys just get going and I'll clean this up."

Jodi hesitated.

"Seriously," I said as Jack came back from the tent carrying a small overnight bag. "Don't worry; I'm fine."

"We owe you one," Jack said. Jodi gave me a quick hug good-bye, and then the two of them hurried off toward the beach.

I watched them go and slowly began clearing all of our plates and garbage. I took my time and enjoyed the quiet of the evening. The ferry and its passengers were long gone, and the last seaplane of the day had just taxied out for takeoff, so things were about as quiet as they could possibly be at Fort Jefferson.

After I finished cleaning up, I wandered down to the beach to sit in the sand and watch the sun crawling lower in the sky. I thought about everything that Jack had told me and felt completely overwhelmed with information. I didn't even know where to begin sorting it in my head.

I was thinking about what Jack had told me about the markings from the silver bar. He'd said the bar was from the year 1622, but that actually didn't make any sense. What would a silver bar from 1622 be doing on a ship that sank in the 1860s?

It didn't sink, I reminded myself. *It was run aground on purpose.*

Not that it mattered how it ended up on the bottom of the ocean. What mattered was that it was off by about two hundred fifty years.

I wondered if maybe the silver bar had actually come from the wreck that Jack said had run aground on Loggerhead Key. The only problem was that Loggerhead Key was miles away, not to mention that Jack said the Spanish had completely salvaged that wreck shortly after the ship sank.

Maybe the phrase "completely salvaged" didn't mean the same in 1622 as it does nowadays, I thought. *And maybe it didn't sink as close to Loggerhead Key as everyone thinks.*

But Jack had said the survivors waded ashore from the wreck. That meant it had to have sunk pretty close to shore, and that definitely ruled out the site where the brick wreck had sunk.

It didn't sink, I reminded myself again. *It was run aground on purpose.*

I stopped suddenly and thought this last point through very carefully.

Someone ran it aground on purpose, I repeated slowly. *But why? And what were silver bars from a 1622 shipwreck doing on a boat from the 1860s?*

And then the answer came to me. I pictured Kevin carefully digging and excavating the area underneath the bottom of the wreck. The silver bars weren't *on* a wreck from the 1860s—they were *under* a wreck from the 1860s. Someone had run the boat aground over top of something that was already there, and they'd done it on purpose.

They must have known something was down there, I thought. *Something valuable enough to sacrifice an entire boat to keep it secret.*

I did some math in my head.

How much is a bar of silver that size worth? I wondered. *It can't be very much, can it? It's silver, after all, not gold. Silver isn't exactly a rare commodity.*

The previous summer I'd carried out a similar calculation involving the value of gold, but this time around, I was lacking too many important pieces of information to make a proper estimate. I had no idea how much a big brick of silver might weigh, nor did I know how much it was worth.

Just for the sake of argument, I said to myself. *Let's say that silver is twenty-five dollars an ounce, and one of those big silver bars weighs fifty pounds. How much would that be worth?*

The math seemed straightforward, but being from Canada, I was unfamiliar with pounds and ounces. I couldn't even estimate how much a brick might be worth because I had no idea how many ounces were in a pound.

ARGGGGHHHHHHHH!!! I cursed to myself.

Lack of Internet access can really be frustrating sometimes. I had no choice but to guess.

Let's say there's fifteen ounces to a pound, a bar of silver weighs fifty pounds, and silver is worth twenty-five dollars per ounce. How much is that? I struggled to make the calculation in my head and was surprised by the answer. *That's almost twenty thousand dollars! And if that's even close to being right, then one of those big silver bars is actually worth a lot of money.*

In fact, they would be worth so much money that they would justify organizing a secret nighttime scuba-diving operation to recover them.

And Kevin and Kristina have to do it in secret, I told myself. *Because the wreck is in the middle of a national park.*

I hadn't forgotten what the park ranger told me on my very first day in the Dry Tortugas. "Everything here is on the 'take only photographs, leave only footprints' principle," she'd said. And if taking a seashell or one of the sixteen million bricks from the fortress as a souvenir was frowned upon, then just think what they'd say about taking home a silver bar worth twenty thousand dollars or more, particularly when it also had immense historical significance.

I stood up from the beach and dusted myself off. Across the water to the west, the sun was getting low in the sky and casting long shadows across the sand.

I wandered over toward the entrance of Fort Jefferson. I knew that soon the rangers would clear out all the visitors and close the fortress for the night.

And when they did that, I needed to already be on the inside.

There was still more to this puzzle than I'd managed to figure out so far, and I felt like I was making progress. But I still had too many questions and not enough answers, and one of those questions was significant: Who was the other person signaling to Kevin's boat from up on the fortress?

The answer to that question was why I was heading into Fort Jefferson just before closing. That night I planned to find out.

Chapter Forty-Two

Maybe I Will Dream The Answer

I walked across the bridge over the moat and through the fortified archway leading into Fort Jefferson. I tried to look as casual as possible as I strolled around the fortress and searched for a good place to hide until the fort was closed.

Finding a hiding spot wasn't much of a problem. The fortress was a goldmine of hiding places—any group of kids from anywhere in the world would have a field day playing hide-and-seek there. The problem was deciding which one of the hundreds of perfect hiding spots to choose.

I finally settled on a perfect spot in the fort's unfinished powder magazine. The magazine was a separate building set off to one side of the inner yard and had several arched vaults where gunpowder had once been stored. I climbed over a small divider wall and slipped into one of the vaults at the end opposite the entrance. My assumption was that if one of the park rangers did happen to do a quick walk-through of the fort after closing, he or she probably wouldn't bother to climb down all the way to the very end to check if anyone was there. Tucked away in my hiding place, I could be reasonably confident that no one would find me, so I sat down on the grassy floor and leaned against the building's foundation to watch the sky growing dark through the open end of the building.

I had a very long wait ahead of me, so to pass the time I pulled the strange green stone out of my pocket again. I turned it over in my fingers and held it up to the light to watch it sparkle. In the dim light, the stone seemed to have lost nearly all of its amazing luminosity. It was as though it had run out of magic and energy.

Or maybe it never had any magic to begin with, I thought drolly. *After all, the strange markings from the silver bars were nothing more than serial numbers and shipping symbols, and the weird, wavy Atlantean handwriting turned out to be just Spanish.*

The dreamer in me had wanted to see all of these things as magical artifacts from a long-vanished civilization, but they were just ordinary things—some bars of silver and the bureaucratic paperwork that went with them.

I laughed cynically. It was almost as though I was disappointed by the fact that these things had simple, everyday explanations. But how could I possibly be disappointed? They were priceless objects of great historical significance, and that was exciting enough, wasn't it?

I'd let my imagination run away on me, that's all. But of course, if there was a simple explanation for the silver bars and squiggly handwriting, then the same was probably true for the beautiful green stone as well. I just couldn't figure out what that explanation was.

Judging from Kevin and Kristina's actions, they considered these strange green stones—these gumdrops, as they had called them—to be the primary goal of their nightly excavations, while the big silver bars seemed of secondary importance to them. And yet the silver bars were worth thousands of dollars. Did that mean these green stones were even *more* valuable than that?

How is that possible? I thought. *I've seen plenty of green crystal stones at rock and gem fairs, and they weren't very expensive. The only really truly valuable green stone that I know of is an emerald. But this rock is way too big for that.*

I looked down at the stone and wrinkled my forehead, thinking deeply.

Is it really too big to be an emerald? I asked myself. *Can that possibly be what it is? It's almost as big as my thumb. An emerald that big would be worth....*

My head began to swirl at this realization, and I didn't finish my thought. I looked closer at the stone and tried to compare it in my head to any emeralds that I'd seen before. The problem was that the only emeralds I'd ever seen were a mere fraction of the size of this stone, and they were cut and set into jewelry. Those emeralds were tiny compared to this, and yet as tiny as they were, they were still incredibly valuable. That meant that if the stone I was holding in my hand was an emerald, it must be worth an absolute fortune.

Forget the silver bars—they were only worth tens of thousands of dollars. Kevin had a handful of these huge green stones, and tonight he was going down to get more of them. If they were emeralds, then they would be worth *millions*—tens of millions, probably.

My head was spinning, and I felt so stupid for not figuring it out earlier. But how could I? Compared to the emeralds used in jewelry, these stones were absolutely enormous. I had no idea that emeralds could be so big. Then again, I was still not sure that these actually were emeralds. But what other possible explanation was there? They obviously weren't magic energy crystals from Atlantis.

They say that the simplest explanation is usually the right one. If the mysterious bricks from the wreck turned out to be silver bars from a long-lost sunken treasure fleet, then the green stones were probably treasure too, right? And what more typical green treasure gemstone is there than an emerald?

They must be emeralds, I conceded. *But that still doesn't explain what all of them are doing on the bottom of the ocean in the first place— buried underneath a steam-powered pre-Civil War shipwreck.*

I put the emerald in my pocket and leaned against the stone foundation. Clearly, I needed more answers before I could finally figure out this puzzle. In a few hours, I hoped to find some of those answers, but until then, the best thing I could do was to get some sleep.

I rested my head against the wall and closed my eyes. Visions of brilliant green jewels and dazzling silver bars danced in my head like sugarplum fairies.

Maybe I will dream the answer to all of this, I thought to myself, smiling as I drifted off to sleep.

Chapter Forty-Three

Into The Complete Velvet Blackness

I awoke hours later, cold and with a painfully stiff neck from leaning against the wall for so long. At first, I couldn't figure out where I was. The world around me was so completely black that I couldn't even see my hands in front of my face. It was only after I had woken up a bit that I was able to make sense of the blackness around me.

I pulled myself upright and sat forward so that I could rub the stiffness out of my shoulders. I took out my iPhone and switched it on to see what time it was. The display flashed with a light that seemed brighter than the sun compared to the black world around me. I squinted my eyes against the glare and covered the screen with my palm so that no one would see the light. In fact, I hoped that no one had seen it already.

Don't worry, I told myself. *It's not as bright as you think it is. It's just a cell phone.*

Spreading my fingers a tiny bit I was able to read the time on the screen. It was 12:14 a.m. Perfect timing. Kevin and Kristina were probably pulling up in their boat at that very moment, and their lookouts were already in place on the fortress. All I had to do to figure out the identity of the second signaler was to climb up to the top level of the fort and sneak around to the corner tower where I'd seen the second set of signals coming from.

I stretched my arms and legs and yawned quietly. As I moved my feet, a noise from somewhere close by made me jump in surprise.

What the hell was that?!? I asked myself as I spun my iPhone around and carefully spread my fingers to allow a bit of light to escape. A thin beam of light shot out and dimly illuminated the brick vault around me. Down at the base of the wall near my feet was a rat, sniffing around and chewing on something.

I kicked at the dirt until the rat scurried away. I'd known there were rats at the fortress (the rangers made sure to remind everyone to keep their food securely stored away and safe from the rats), but I hadn't actually seen one until now.

I shuddered at the thought that there might be more rats around. I switched off my phone to save the battery and slid it into my pocket before cautiously making my way out of the vault and up toward the entrance to the powder magazine.

I now understand why they close the fort at night, I thought as I carefully made my way through the darkness. *It would be incredibly easy to fall down in here and break my leg—or worse.*

I finally reached the entrance of the magazine and looked out into the inner yard of the fortress. At the top of the walls in front of me, the harbor light gave off some dim illumination that made it easier for me to see. I walked up along the side of the structure, stepping carefully and avoiding some cactus until I was able to peer around the corner and look over toward the park rangers' living quarters. As expected, there was no sign of light or life over there, but I knew that somewhere at the top of the wall, someone was sitting and waiting. Whoever it was, he or she would be keeping a sharp lookout for any activity in the fortress, so my best approach was to circle around through the fortified walls then up the stairs of the corner tower and onto the roof just behind them where there were plenty of low walls and ledges to cover my approach.

Sticking close to the powder magazine, I made my way over to the closest point next to the fortress wall and dashed across. From there I would be able to maneuver from the cover of one set of support pillars to the next, all the way around to the other side of the fort.

I picked my way through the darkness, careful not to make any noise on the rock-strewn paving stones beneath my feet. The lighthouse on Loggerhead Key continued its nightly vigil, and every twenty seconds a flash of pale light flickered through the gunports and gave me a momentary view of the path ahead. It was slow going, but I wasn't in a hurry. The most important thing was to be quiet and careful and not have anyone notice I was there.

After quite some time, I finally reached the bottom of the corner bastion tower where I'd seen the second signal coming from the night before. As I entered the spiral staircase, I realized that I was going to have a real problem climbing the stairs since there was absolutely no light whatsoever, and the only way I would be able to do it was by feeling my way with my hands.

I closed my eyes and tried to remember what the staircase had looked like when I'd seen it in daylight. I remembered a series of steps made of simple blocks of stone curving up to the right in a clockwise direction. Our tour guide, Sandy, had explained that it was built this way because most fighters were right-handed and the counterclockwise spiral down would provide an advantage to defenders on top with more space to swing their weapons.

This isn't too bad, I thought as I felt my way slowly up the staircase. The stairs were in good condition and swept clean, so I didn't have to worry too much about slipping or making any noise as I carefully padded along.

As I passed the exit that led to the second level of the fortress, a tiny bit of light leaked in from the darkness outside, but as I ascended toward the roof, I was plunged into complete velvet blackness again. My eyes were playing tricks on me, creating shimmers of color that flashed like sparks on my retinas.

On and on I went, reaching ahead to feel the next step and then carefully lifting my feet up to it. As I got closer to the top, I could finally see some light. It wasn't much illumination, of course, but it certainly seemed like a lot compared to the absolute blackness I'd been wading through.

As I reached the top steps, I was finally able to see again, and I cautiously poked my head over the edge to inspect my surroundings. It was a beautiful night with more stars than I could count shining brightly all over the sky. I turned toward the outside edge of the fort, expecting to see the outline of a human figure standing there silhouetted against the sky, but I squinted into the blackness and couldn't make anything out.

I climbed another step and tried again to see, straining my eyes against the darkness of the night, but I couldn't see anyone or anything.

I looked around a bit. The top of the fort was full of places to hide—the giant cannon directly in front of me, for example, or the low walls and ledges all around—but the signaler wouldn't be hiding. There was no one to hide *from* as far as he was concerned. He would have to be over by the outer rim of the fortress wall because that was the only place he would be able to see Kevin and Kristina's boat from this distance.

I pulled myself up even higher, really sticking my head out this time and painfully straining my eyes. But it was no use. No one was there. Between all the various sources of light—the stars, the harbor light, and the distant lighthouse on Loggerhead Key—I had a good enough view of the world around me to see that no one was on the roof of the fortress except me.

It doesn't make sense, I thought to myself. *This is where I saw the second set of signals coming from.*

I lowered myself onto the top step to sit and think things over for a minute. It was possible that Kevin and his gang had called things off for the night and weren't even out there. From where I was sitting, I actually couldn't see out across the water, so I didn't know if Kevin and Kristina were there or not.

I pulled myself back to my feet and hurried across the roof of the fortress to have a look. Keeping a sharp eye out, I climbed the closest ledge and snuck across the grass to the inside corner of the bastion tower. From there I had a clear view across the water toward the shipwreck site. To my surprise, I saw that there was no strange blue-green glow out there, nor did I see the dark outline of a boat. There was simply nothing there but water.

Maybe they called it off, I mused as I padded down to the top of the stairwell. *But why?*

Unfortunately, I didn't have much time to think about this question because I suddenly glimpsed a flash of light coming from somewhere below me. At first, I thought that my eyes were just playing tricks on me again, but when I realized that I wasn't just seeing things, I nearly had a heart attack. From down the dark stairwell below me I heard the sound of footsteps and saw the jittery light of a flashlight getting brighter and brighter.

Someone was climbing the stairs toward me.

Chapter Forty-Four

But If He's Up Here...?

I panicked. I only had a few precious seconds before whoever was climbing the stairs would emerge from the spiral staircase and see me standing there.

I had to hide, and fast. That part of the decision-making process was obvious, but I had to consider several other complicating factors in the few seconds I had before being discovered. Firstly, wherever I decided to hide, I had to get there quietly, or the person coming up the steps would be sure to hear me. That meant that I had to move quickly and quietly, which was not really a good combination considering how dark it was, but the longer I waited and the closer that person came, the more likely it was that he or she would hear me.

The second factor that my brain insisted on including in the decision-making process was the fact that wherever I chose to hide, I would want to have a clear view across the water so that I could see what was going on. I assumed that whoever was climbing the stairs toward me was the mysterious fourth accomplice who had been signaling from up here the night before. I further assumed that this person was coming up here for that same reason again. Clearly, I had come up here too early.

"Stop over-thinking it and just find a hiding spot!" the little voice in my head snapped impatiently.

I will, I will!!! I replied, still desperately trying to figure out where to hide. I had to find a good spot, because once I took cover, I certainly didn't want to be moving around again to find somewhere better.

As the footsteps drew dangerously close, I finally decided on a hiding place. I jumped onto the low brick ledge next to me and up to the soft grass above.

To my left was a low brick structure built on top of the wall, whose function I could only guess at, but for my immediate purposes, I decided that it would be a perfect hiding spot. The only thing *not* perfect about it was how far away it was. I had to be quick if I was going to get there before the person below me reached the top of the stairs.

I raced down the length of the fortress walls, lifting my feet carefully and quietly as I went. As I ran, I kept glancing over my shoulder, terrified that I would see the light of the flashlight and a person emerging from the top of the stairs.

Reaching the edge of the low structure, I quickly climbed on top and ducked behind the edge of its roof. I laid myself out flat in the sand and left only my head poking out at the end so that I could see along the wall to where I'd just come from.

And then I waited...and waited.

It seemed to take forever, but eventually I saw the beam of a dimmed flashlight at the top of the staircase, and the person holding it emerged into the open. He kept his light low and made his way across the top of the fort to the edge of the walls before sitting down in the grass.

I breathed a sigh of relief. He hadn't seen me or heard me. For the moment, I was safe.

So what do I do now? I asked myself as I silently watched the figure. It was too dark to see whom it was or what he was doing, but I suspected that both of us were just sitting and waiting for the same thing—for Kevin and Kristina to arrive in their boat.

The minutes ticked slowly by one after another until I started to wonder whether Kevin and Kristina were even coming. But then I heard the soft rumble of an engine in the distance approaching from the north. Slowly the sound circled around the fort, and the boat finally came into view.

The figure sitting in the sand suddenly stood to his feet, and I saw a beam of light shoot out toward the approaching boat. He flashed three times—three long bursts of light—and then all was darkness again. I imagined Patrick down at the pier flashing the same signal.

The boat slowly made its way over to the wreck site, its engines idling so quietly that I could hardly hear them at all. The boat's black hull made it difficult to see in the darkness, but thanks to the periodic flashes of the lighthouse on Loggerhead Key, I was able to follow its progress.

The boat finally stopped, and after a few more maneuvers to set the anchor, it shut its engine down, and there was silence again. The figure to my right was still standing at the edge of the fort as though waiting for something to happen. After a few seconds, I realized what it was.

"Citadel, Citadel, this is Cuba Libré, over," I heard a low crackly voice say. It was Kristina, radioing from the boat.

I propped up on my elbows so that I could hear better. Kristina's voice on the radio was so quiet that I could barely hear it.

"This is Citadel, go ahead, over," the figure to my right said into the radio. My mouth dropped open in surprise. I recognized that voice. It was Patrick standing lookout up here on top of the fortress, not some other mysterious fourth accomplice. I had assumed he was the one stationed at the concrete pier next to the beach and the campground.

But if Patrick's up here, I asked myself. *Then who's down there?*

Chapter Forty-Five

They Aren't Just Going To Call It A Night

"We're in position," Kristina's voice crackled over the radio. "Are we all clear?"

"All clear," Patrick replied. "Over and out."

As Patrick signed off, I turned to look toward the boat; I was waiting for the blue-green glow to appear as Kevin switched on his dive lights and headed for the bottom. After a few long moments, the eerie glow appeared, and I imagined Kevin floating down through a sea of bubbles to start his excavations.

I was surprised at how much better my view was from the top of the fortress walls. Thanks to the higher elevation, I was looking down on the water instead of flat across it, which meant I was able to clearly see the lights under the water and the air bubbles billowing on the surface. If I'd had such a good view the first time I'd seen it, I wouldn't have had any doubts about what was going on out there.

I turned to my right to see what Patrick was up to. Not much, as it turned out. He was sitting cross-legged on the grass again, keeping a close eye on things.

It suddenly occurred to me why he'd chosen this particular place to stand lookout. Down below at the opposite end of this side of the fort were the living quarters of the park rangers who lived here full time. I'd noticed it a couple of days before when I walked all the way around the moat wall. There were several living units with rudimentary balconies built into the gunports at that end, and those balconies looked straight out toward the sunset and the lighthouse on Loggerhead Key. This meant that they also happened to look straight out in the direction of where Kevin was conducting his underwater excavations.

Obviously, that was problematic, but from where Patrick was sitting, he could easily see if any of the rangers decided to get up in the middle of the night to sit on their balconies or otherwise move about the fortress. And if they did, he could signal Kristina to shut down the lights at the diving operation in an instant, just as I'd seen her do on that first night. Between him and his partner down on the pier watching the campground, they had all the bases covered.

So who is on the pier, then? I wondered again. *Who is the fourth accomplice in this little scheme of theirs?*

I'd stayed in the fortress that night to find out the answer to that question, but since Patrick was the one up here, I realized that I might as well have just stayed down at the beach and gone sneaking around there instead.

You're much safer up here, I told myself. *Lying comfortably and well hidden.*

That was true, but the only downside was that it was going to be a long night lying there watching the diving operation in the distance. I couldn't really see what they were doing from so far away, so it wasn't exactly exciting. It was so boring, in fact, that I could almost fall asleep.

Do NOT fall asleep! I commanded myself. *You'll snore or roll off or something, and Patrick will hear you.*

I forced myself to stay alert and awake, but it was difficult. I was lying on a patch of soft grass and sand with a nice cool breeze of wonderfully fresh air blowing over me. The air was cool, but I wasn't cold because the heat of the sun had warmed the rooftop sand all throughout the day, and even now, hours after sunset, I could feel the warmth.

I was relieved that I'd picked such a good hiding spot since I was going to be stuck there all night. Even after Kevin and Kristina motored off again and Patrick left, I was still going to be stuck there, because the only gate leading in and out of the fortress was locked until morning. Only when the fort reopened could I sneak out of it and return to my own bed to get some sleep.

I stared out across the water for a while and let my mind wander a little until I suddenly saw the eerie glow go dark. My body tensed, and I turned to look over at Patrick.

What happened? I wondered. *Did someone wake up to go to the bathroom?*

But Patrick didn't seem to be reacting. He was simply sitting there, exactly as before. I guessed that Kevin had probably just finished his first dive of the night.

After a few minutes, I heard the crackle of Patrick's radio.

"Citadel, this is Cuba Libré, over," I heard Kristina say.

"This is Citadel, go ahead, over," Patrick replied.

"It looks like we got most of what's down there," Kristina said. "I still have to count what we got just now, but it looks like most of them, over."

There was a moment of silence before Patrick responded.

"Are you going down for another try?" Patrick finally asked. "Or is that it? Do we have enough now? Are we going to call it off? Over."

Do they have enough of what? I asked myself. *Are they talking about the emeralds?*

"We've got all the loaves of bread we expected, but not all the gumdrops," Kristina replied. "We're going to give it one more try before we get the hell out of here, but I don't think we'll find much, over."

"Roger that," Patrick replied simply. "Over and out."

My mind raced to understand what was going on.

Have they really found all of the emeralds? I asked myself. *How do they know how many are supposed to be there? Are they really going to call it a night after just one more dive?*

"They aren't going to just call it a night," the little voice in my head observed. "After this next dive, they're going to call off the search forever."

I was shocked by this realization. They'd been sneaking around at night for a reason, and it was because what they were doing was illegal, and now that they'd found whatever it was they'd been looking for, they definitely weren't going to stick around or come back another night. This was it. After this, they were going to do exactly what Kristina said and get the hell out of there.

I can't let them do that! I said to myself angrily. They *can't just get away with this!*

Unfortunately, I really didn't have much choice. There was nothing I could do. I was stuck up on the roof of a fortress out in the middle of nowhere with no cell phone reception and no way out until morning, not to mention that Patrick was standing watch nearby. Until he left and morning came, I would just have to lie still and keep my mouth shut.

Chapter Forty-Six

We Can't Get Greedy

Maybe there's another way? I asked myself, poking my head up to look across the top of the fortress wall toward the entrance to the stairwell. A low brick ledge about four feet high at the base of the structure where I was hiding ran almost all the way to the top of the stairs. If I could somehow climb down off the roof and get behind that ledge, then I'd be invisible. Patrick was all the way out at the end of the corner almost fifty feet away, and his attention was focused on the boat. If I was careful, I could do it, and Patrick would never see me.

If I could just get to the stairs, then all I would have to do was climb down and circle around the walls to the entrance of the fortress. The door would be locked, of course, but it suddenly occurred to me that it was probably just locked from the inside with a big deadbolt or something. This wasn't Fort Knox, after all—it was a national park out in the middle of nowhere. There probably wasn't some advanced security system on the front door. I could probably just open it from the inside and slip out undetected.

I nodded to myself as I carefully thought this through, becoming more and more convinced that it was worth the risk.

I looked over toward Patrick. He was still sitting cross-legged in the grass and staring out across the water to where Kevin's dive lights were once again filling the water with the familiar blue-green glow. They'd started what was probably their last dive, and after that, they were out of here. If I didn't figure out a way to stop them, nobody would, because nobody else knew what they were doing. I had to do it. I had to get out of the fort now.

With my mind made up, I propped myself on my elbows and planned my route to the stairs.

First I'll climb carefully down off the roof of this structure, I told myself as I carefully pulled myself onto my knees, keeping one eye on Patrick at all times. My legs were stiff and my knees popped as I pivoted my weight onto my heels.

I crouched on the grass and used the brick wall on my right to keep balance as I carefully lifted my butt one small step at a time down the slope of the roof.

So far so good, I thought, smiling as I reached level ground again. *Just a short climb down from this little wall and I'm on top of the ledge.*

Still keeping a close eye on Patrick, I lowered myself into the dark shadows where the brick ledge met the slope of the roof. It was so dark in that corner that I doubted Patrick could see me even if he were standing directly in front of me, but I wasted no time climbing down behind the ledge and completely out of his sight.

I sat down at the base in the shadows for a few minutes to catch my breath. Moving so slowly and silently was more exhausting than I would have expected.

Once I was ready to go again, I stood to my feet and peeked over the ledge toward Patrick. He hadn't moved an inch.

Moving along behind the ledge was much easier going. Behind the safe cover of a solid brick wall to my left, I was able to move quickly almost all the way to the staircase. All I had to do was be careful not to make any noise and stop occasionally to peek over the wall to make sure Patrick was still where he was supposed to be.

It took just a minute or two of careful sneaking to reach the place where the wall ended, and soon I was crouched there, staring off toward the top of the staircase and wondering how I was going to cover the last five feet of open ground. There was nothing to hide behind. If Patrick happened to look over while I was dashing across, he would definitely see me. I would just have to make a run for it and hope for the best.

I had only one thing to my advantage: if Patrick *did* happen to look over, he would be staring directly into the harbor light on the opposite side of the fortress. As long as I stayed low enough, I might not be visible to him from this angle. Of course, the exact opposite was also true: if I didn't stay low enough, I would be silhouetted directly against the light, which would almost definitely get Patrick's attention.

I'll just have to stay really low, I told myself as I prepared to head across. *And take it nice and slow and easy.*

With one last deep breath, I left the shelter of the brick wall and headed out across the open ground toward the top of the stairs, waddling like a duck and using my hands for balance as I went. I must have looked ridiculous, but at that moment, I didn't care, and after a few of the longest seconds of my life, I finally reached the top of the steps and crouched down low, balancing myself with one hand on the brick wall next to me.

"Citadel, this is Cuba Libré, over," I heard Kristina's voice crackle distantly over Patrick's radio.

"This is Citadel, go ahead, over."

I paused and lowered myself into a sitting position at the top of the stairs to listen in on the conversation.

"We've found a few more," Kristina said. "I did a count, and we've got a hundred and twenty seven in total. We'll make one final quick check, but it looks like that might be it, over."

There was a long pause before Patrick responded.

"A hundred and twenty seven?" he asked, sounding disappointed.

"Afraid so," Kristina responded, followed by another long silence.

"There should be nearly a hundred more of them," Patrick finally said, sounding slightly confused. "What happened to the rest of them?"

Another long pause.

"Tides, currents—I don't know," Kevin's gruff voice replied. Apparently, he had taken the radio from Kristina. "But we can't get greedy. We've got enough."

"You're right," Patrick replied. "Of course you're right."

"I'm gonna take one last look to see if there's another pile of them somewhere," Kevin said. "And if I find anything, I've still got four more tanks of air to dig around for a couple more hours, but if I don't find anything on this next dive, we're gonna call it off, over."

Silhouetted against a backdrop of stars, I could see Patrick nodding his head as he raised the radio to his mouth again. With their conversation almost over, that was my cue to get out of there and start heading down the stairs while he was still talking on the radio.

I reached up to grab the brick wall next to me so that I could pull myself quietly to my feet, but as I transferred my weight to the wall, I suddenly felt a small piece of the cement mortar break off and fall. I gasped, and every muscle in my body tensed as I listened to it crash and crumble into pieces as it tumbled down the stairs.

Chapter Forty-Seven

Another Completely Obvious Trick

My heart fell straight down into the pit of my stomach as I listened to that piece of cement clattering and echoing down the stairs. I spun my head to look back at Patrick. He was still over at the end of the tower roof, and even though I couldn't tell in the darkness what direction he was looking, the odds were that he was staring straight over toward me.

Dammit, dammit, dammit! I screamed to myself. *How could I be so stupid?*

I stayed completely frozen in place, watching and waiting to see what Patrick would do. Maybe he thought that a piece of rubble had just randomly fallen off. It was an old fort, after all.

"Citadel?" I heard Kevin's voice say over the radio. "Are you still there, Citadel?"

"Stand by," Patrick responded curtly and keyed his radio off.

I didn't move a muscle as I breathlessly watched Patrick with my heart pounding in my throat.

Patrick took a couple of steps in my direction, switching on a flashlight as he did so. I quickly ducked my head down but kept watching. He swung the flashlight beam back and forth across the roof of the fortress, apparently searching for whatever had made the sound.

Didn't you hear all the echoes as that giant piece of cement flipped end over end down the stairs? I said to myself sarcastically. But apparently the sound hadn't been as loud for him as it was for me since he was scanning with his flashlight all along the brick ledge and giant artillery cannon directly behind him instead of over toward the stairs where I was sitting.

"What's going on up there, Citadel?" Kevin's voice hissed over the radio. "We see lights from your position and we've shut everything down out here. Is something wrong? Are you trying to signal us?"

"Stand by," Patrick responded again more forcefully. "I think someone's up here with me."

The radio went dead quiet, and Patrick continued to weave his light back and forth across the top of the fortress walls, drawing ever closer to where I was crouched at the top of the stairs.

And that's my cue to make a run for it, I thought. But still, I hesitated, and for a good reason. If I made a run for it into the blackness of the staircase beneath me, I was liable to fall and break my head.

But I had no choice. Any second now, Patrick was going to shine his flashlight directly over at me and see me. Darkness or not, I had do it.

Using my hands to steady myself on the steps, I backed down the staircase, keeping a very close eye on the flicker of Patrick's flashlight beam as I descended out of his direct line of sight.

One foot after the other, I continued down the stairs carefully, but I could see from the increasingly bright glare of the flashlight beam on the walls above me that Patrick was getting closer. At any moment, he would reach the top of the steps.

I made steady progress and soon had spiraled out of sight around the never-ending corners of the staircase. If Patrick looked down now, he would no longer be able to see me, but that didn't mean he wouldn't come after me.

Suddenly the entire stairwell was flooded with light, and I was able to see the stairs. I took advantage of the light and moved quickly and quietly downward.

"Hello?" Patrick called out. "Is anyone there?"

I stopped and held my breath while I waited to see what he would do.

"This is one of the national park rangers," Patrick said coolly, still shining his bright light down into the staircase. "If anyone is there, please identify yourself before someone gets hurt."

Patrick and I stayed frozen for a few moments in a tense standoff until I finally saw the flashlight beam wobble a bit and I heard Patrick take his first step down the stairs toward me. I could no longer afford to go slow. I really had to get moving now.

I scrambled quickly and quietly down the next few steps, but I was not as quiet as I had hoped, because I soon heard Patrick pounding down the stairs after me.

I forgot all about trying to be quiet and dashed down the stairs as fast as I could go. I could hear Patrick's heavy footfalls echoing off the brick walls, and as I approached the exit doorway leading to the second level of the fortress, I knew that I had to make a split-second decision. Should I exit at the second level or continue down the stairs to the ground level? Common sense dictated that I should continue all the way to the bottom where I could exit into the open yard instead of limiting myself to finding somewhere to hide on the second level. But I thought I would trick Patrick by not doing the obvious, so I dashed through the open doorway and out along the row of empty gun emplacements that lined the second level.

I made a sharp turn and raced past the seemingly endless line of archways leading to the fort's next corner tower. I could hear Patrick closing in behind me, thumping down the final steps to the exit at the second level.

I ducked behind one of the fort's foundation pillars and flattened myself against the bricks while I silently waited and listened carefully to see which way Patrick would go, hoping desperately that he would think I'd headed all the way to the bottom and then continue down after me.

No such luck, I thought, rolling my eyes as I saw the beam of his flashlight sweep across the second level, throwing complex shadows all over the walls as it shone through the various openings and archways.

It didn't matter. I hadn't *really* expected him to fall for such a completely obvious trick. But I had another completely obvious trick that I was hoping he would fall for hook, line, and sinker.

Chapter Forty-Eight

Hook, Line And Sinker

In order to execute my next clever plan, I somehow had to make it all the way down the side of the fortress to the next bastion tower where there was another staircase. I was already almost halfway there, but in order for my plan to work, I had to get to the next one with a decent head start on Patrick.

I have to make a run for it, I told myself. *And I have to do it pretty quickly because he's coming up behind me fast.*

Judging from the flashes of light on the walls, Patrick was making his way toward me from one empty gun emplacement to the next, shining his light around the corners to check things out before moving on to the next.

The design of the second level of the fort meant that there were only two ways to get from one bastion tower to the next. You either walked up the inside edge of the fort through a line of small arched doorways or you went up along the outside edge through each empty gun emplacement. Patrick was working his way along the inside edge, so my best bet was to make a run for it on the opposite side. That way, when he heard me break into a run, it would take him a few precious seconds before he could figure out where I was. I knew that I could easily outrun him, but every extra second would help.

I knelt down to gather a few good-sized rocks and then stood up again. I pulled my black hoodie over my hair to camouflage myself as much as possible in the darkness before I crouched over and prepared to run.

I watched the beam of Patrick's flashlight sweep around the corner and shine down into one of the empty casemates. The moment he did this, I took off running as fast as my feet would carry me along the line of empty gun emplacements.

It didn't take Patrick long to catch on, and within minutes, I saw a beam of light flashing from behind me and I heard the sound of heavy footfalls approaching fast.

"Hey!" I heard Patrick shout. "Hey, you! Stop!"

The light from Patrick's flashlight illuminated the path in front of me, and I narrowly missed tripping over a calcium stalagmite that had grown up from the floor after decades of dripping rainwater. My toes caught on the edge of the lump, and I stumbled for a few steps before regaining my stride and running at full tilt again.

I saw that I was quickly approaching the end of the line of archways. I passed the last pillar and turned in abruptly through the doorway to the stairs. The weaving beam from Patrick's flashlight behind me told me that he was following suit and planned to do the same thing.

After reaching the stairs, I immediately turned left and bolted up, feeling my way in the darkness from one step to the next as I went. At first, I didn't care how much noise I made, but after rounding the first corner of the spiral, I slowed down and continued upward, moving as quietly as I possibly could.

I kept a close eye on the flashing of Patrick's flashlight as he reached the entrance to the staircase. He paused there and tried to figure out which way I'd gone.

Please go down, please go down, I pleaded to myself, but he simply stood there flashing the light up and down the stairs. That was no problem for me. The longer he stood there, the better.

I continued up, silently pulling myself from one step to the next until I reached the open air at the top of the staircase.

Time for my obvious trick, I said to myself as I took one of the stones and threw it as hard as I could up and over the top of the staircase.

The rock sailed through the air and out over the inner yard of the fortress. I stayed completely still, not moving a muscle or even breathing as I waited to hear it land.

Crack.

I finally heard the sound of the rock hitting home somewhere outside the fortress at ground level. It must have hit the branch of a tree because it sounded exactly like a small twig breaking.

Patrick heard it too, and I immediately heard him pounding down the staircase, heading for the ground floor.

An oldie but goodie, I smiled to myself, proud of my clever little trick.

As Patrick continued down the stairs to the inner courtyard, I didn't waste a second. I ran the length of the sandy grass roof of the fortress. The soft soil allowed me to move fast and quiet in the direction I'd just come from, back to where Patrick had been standing lookout at the corner of the next bastion tower.

After slowing down for a few steps, I stopped and padded over to see what Patrick was doing. I could see the beam of his flashlight as he made his way along the casemates at ground level, heading for the fort's main gate in the opposite direction of where I was.

Perfect, I thought. He'd fallen for it hook, line, and sinker.

I moved to the outside edge of the fort where I was out of sight until I reached the staircase where all of this trouble had started. I looked out across the inner yard, trying to see where Patrick was, but his flashlight beam was nowhere to be seen.

It didn't matter. He obviously expected me to head for the main gate to make my escape, which made perfect sense because it was the only way in and out of the fortress.

Or was it the only way?

The plan that I'd concocted depended on me leaving the fort by a completely different route.

Chapter Forty-Nine

This Is It

Fort Jefferson was meant to be a virtually impregnable fortress, and its main gate was designed with exactly this concept in mind. The massive granite gate was originally accessible from the outside by a heavy drawbridge that could be raised up in the event of an attack. However, if attackers did manage to cross the moat, they would find themselves confronted with yet another heavy door on the inside and cannon fire coming at them from all sides. This entire heavily defended gate is probably one of the reasons that Fort Jefferson never came under enemy attack during its entire life as a military garrison.

The drawbridge may be gone, but just like in the old days, the modern-day main gate remains the only way for visitors to the park to get in and out of the fortress. Perhaps it would be better to say that it's the only way in and out of the fortress if you want to stay dry. After all, the fort is surrounded by water on all sides, and it is an easy jump from one of the ground-level gunports into the waters of the moat below. From there a person can swim around the entire fort or across the moat to the beach.

That was exactly what I planned to do. While Patrick was off on his wild goose chase at the main gate, I was going to head down the stairs to the main level, climb out of the nearest gunport, and jump into the moat below. From there I would swim around to the campground, and once I was absolutely sure that the coast was clear, I would sneak back to my tent and wait there until morning.

I would have felt a bit better if Jack were with me since Jack was an ex-cop, but with my black hoodie pulled over my head, I was pretty sure that Patrick couldn't possibly recognize me in the darkness. Even if he did and he tried to come pull me out of my tent, I would kick and scream so loud that it would wake up every other camper in two seconds flat.

I headed down into the inky black stairwell, feeling my way from step to step. It was an eerie feeling of déjà vu, but in no time I was back on solid ground again on the bottom level of the fort. I poked my head out and took a quick look before ducking out of the stairs to hide behind one of the support pillars in the first casemate.

Just ten feet away, an open gunport led to the outside world and freedom. In less than a minute, I would be floating free, safe, and invisible down in the black waters of the fort's moat.

I was just about to scramble across and out of the gunport when I heard the sound of footsteps coming quickly up from the line of casemates behind me. There was no light from a flashlight or any other indication that Patrick had doubled back toward me, but I could definitely hear someone coming up fast.

I panicked and frantically looked around in the darkness to find a place to hide. It was too late for me to duck into the stairwell. Whoever was coming up behind me would definitely see me dashing across the grass to the stairs.

I was stuck.

Suddenly I thought of the tour I'd taken on my first day in the Dry Tortugas. I remembered how the guide had explained to us about the clever water collection and filtration system they'd built into the walls. In every pillar around the whole fortress, an opening led to the water cisterns below. The idea of using freshwater cisterns might have failed miserably a hundred years ago, but that didn't change the fact that those openings were perfect hiding places—assuming, of course, that you didn't slip and fall all the way down into the cistern below.

I couldn't think of a better hiding place, so I quickly climbed into the nearest opening and braced my feet against the sides as I climbed backward. I lowered myself down far enough to keep the top of my head out of sight, and then I just held on by my fingertips, listening with every nerve on alert as the footsteps grew louder and closer.

I suddenly heard the soft crackle of a radio and Kevin's voice speaking at the other end. "Citadel, Citadel, this is Cuba Libré, over," he said.

The footsteps stopped and I heard Patrick replying nearby. "This is Citadel, go ahead, over," he said quietly.

"Citadel, you need to tell us what's going on," Kevin said. "We don't know what we're supposed to do out here, over."

"I lost them," Patrick snapped testily. "I have no idea where the hell they disappeared to, and I can't find any trace of anyone anywhere."

There was a long pause, and my fingers were burning from supporting my weight for so long.

"Okay, Citadel," Kevin replied calmly. "In that case, we're going to abort any further operations and get the hell out of here right now."

"Understood," Patrick replied. "I'll take care of things at this end, and we'll see you at rendezvous in a few days."

"Roger that," Kevin replied. "Over and out."

Patrick's radio gave a final burst of static and then fell silent as he resumed his brisk walk along the side of the fort. I listened as his footsteps approached, and then they passed frighteningly close before receding into the distance.

I waited until Patrick's footfalls had completely faded away, and then I waited a few minutes more for good measure before pulling myself up into the empty casemate. My fingertips felt like they were on fire, so I shook my hands out for a bit while I stood and listened to make sure that

Patrick hadn't doubled back yet again.

I couldn't hear a thing. The coast was clear, I hoped.

I sneaked across the open space to the nearest gunport, climbed up to the ledge, and squeezed my way out. As my head poked through to the other side, I realized immediately that I had a problem. The tiny ledge on the outside was too small for me to turn myself around. I couldn't climb out headfirst. I was going to have to go butt first instead.

How am I supposed to do that?!? I asked myself as I tried out various contorted positions and angles for backing myself out of the tiny opening.

Finally, I found a way to do it. By kneeling on all fours and twisting on my side, I was able to slowly push myself out of the opening a few inches at a time until my feet were hanging out in midair and the rest of my body was about to follow.

I continued to slither and slide my way out until I was hanging from the ledge by my fingertips and reaching down desperately with the tips of my toes to feel the surface of the water. No matter how far I stretched, I couldn't feel the water. It was obviously a bit farther down than I had thought.

Clawing at the face of the brick wall with my feet, I managed to reach into my pocket to take out my iPhone. I held it high above my head so that it would stay dry when I finally dropped down. But no matter what happened to my phone, anything was better than being stuck inside the fortress with Patrick

Okay, this is it, I said, and I let go and pushed myself into the darkness.

Chapter Fifty

So Much For That Idea

As it turned out, the drop wasn't that far after all. As soon as I let go, my feet almost immediately hit the surface of the water, and I plunged into the shallow moat. I scraped my knees a bit on the way down and tore a hole in my pants, but on the bright side, I barely got my hair wet, and my iPhone was still dry as a bone.

My hair was pulled into a ponytail, so I pulled the elastic band tight and slid my phone into the knot at the back of my head so that both of my hands were free.

I hoped that no one had heard my splashy entrance into the water. It hadn't been that loud, but I wasn't going to take any chances, so I treaded water next to the side of the fort for a few minutes and watched for any signs of life above me.

After a few minutes of watching and waiting, I decided that the coast was clear, and I swam along the side of the fortress, circling around the closest bastion tower and continuing around in the direction of the campground.

As I swam, I heard the faint sound of a boat engine powering up and roaring off into the distance. It was so soft and far away that at first I wasn't sure if it was real. It had been such a crazy night, and with the sound of the wind and waves in my ears, I wasn't sure whether I was just hearing things.

I stopped for a moment and listened. I nodded my head. It was definitely the sound of a boat—Kevin and Kristina's boat, to be exact.

"They're getting away!" the little voice in my head protested. "You have to stop them!"

There's nothing I can do right now, I told myself. *For the moment, all I can do is sneak back to my tent and wait for morning. The sun will be up in a few hours and so will the other campers. Once some other people are up and about, I'll walk over to my plane and get on the radio to the Coast Guard or the police and tell them what I know.*

I had considered sneaking over to my plane right away, but decided not to risk it. Even if I was able to walk along the seaplane beach without being spotted, I would still have to switch on my instruments to see what I was doing, and that would be clearly visible to anyone who might happen to look over.

I couldn't just jump into my plane and go chasing after Kevin and Kristina either. The sound of me starting my plane's engine out here in the quiet night would be about as subtle as setting off a string of firecrackers—not to mention that it was too dangerous to take off in the darkness anyway.

My plan is a good one, I reassured myself as I continued swimming. *And it's the best I can do under the circumstances.*

As I approached the last corner tower of the fortress—the one near the campground—I stayed as low in the water as possible and swam very slowly. I peeked around the corner and floated there for a while as I surveyed the scene.

Stretching into the immediate distance, the moat wall continued along the side of the fortress and past the beach and campground. Right at the spot where the beach met the wall, the wind and waves had built up a small pile of sand on the inner side of the moat. That was where I planned to climb out of the water because it would be easier and quieter than climbing up and over the moat wall, and because it was the closest point to the patches of trees and brush that made up the campground. Once I was out of the water, I would only be exposed for a few short steps before reaching the cover of the trees that would take me all the way back to my tent. If the coast was clear and I moved quickly enough, no one would ever see me.

But was the coast clear? That was the big question. I would be completely in the open when I dashed across the tiny stretch of sand, so before I made a move, I would have to be very sure that no one was around.

I swam up a bit closer, still moving slowly and keeping my head down in the water. I was starting to get a bit nervous. As I looked around in the darkness, it was simply impossible to tell if anyone was out there.

Out of the corner of my eye, I caught a flash of movement near one of the palm trees at the edge of the campground. I turned my head and held my breath as I strained to make out what was there. Was it just the wind blowing through the bushes, or something else?

I studied the darkness at the base of the tree for several minutes, but it was useless. Everything was black on black, and it was impossible to be sure of what I was seeing. I thought I could see the shape of a human being standing there, watching and waiting, but it might also just be the shapes of the trees and bushes playing tricks on my eyes.

But why would anyone be standing lookout like that at the campground? I asked myself. I was still convinced that Patrick hadn't seen me well enough to recognize who I was, so how would he know to wait for me at the campground?

I thought about this for a second then rolled my eyes at my own stupidity when I realized the obvious answer to my question. The only people spending the night out at Fort Jefferson were the park rangers and overnight campers, so Patrick knew that whomever he was chasing had to be one of the campers. He wasn't necessarily waiting for *me*—he was just waiting and hoping that whoever it was would eventually return to his or her tent.

So much for that idea, I said to myself after watching the shadows at the base of the palm tree for a bit longer. I still couldn't tell whether there was actually someone there or not, but I couldn't risk it. I would have to come up with another plan.

Chapter Fifty-One

A No-Brainer

Plan B was a no-brainer. After all, I was on an isolated island out in the middle of nowhere with only a handful of people on it and no idea which of them I could trust. I couldn't go back to my tent to wait for morning, nor could I go into the fortress to hide since it was locked. And to top it all off, somewhere out on the ocean, Kevin and Kristina were successfully making their escape under the cover of night.

I had no other choice but to reconsider the idea of heading for my plane right away and getting out of there as soon as possible. As I swam slowly along the side of the fortress in the direction I'd come from, I made myself rethink all the reasons I'd had for vetoing that plan in the first place.

The first problem was that starting the plane's engine would make so much noise that it would probably wake up everyone on the entire island. But if I pushed it off the beach before I cranked it up, I would already be out in the water by the time they could get to me, and they'd have to swim pretty fast to catch me.

Another problem was that once I was airborne I would eventually have to land somewhere, and attempting a water landing at night would be complete suicide. But I had enough fuel to stay up in the air and circle around until sunrise when it would be light enough to land. In the meantime, I could use the time to find Kevin and Kristina's boat to see which direction they were heading.

The only thing that I was really nervous about was the fact that I would have to take off in complete darkness. I knew there were a series of navigational pylons out in the harbor somewhere that marked the deepwater channel leading up to the fort. These markers weren't a problem in daylight, but at night, they would be completely invisible, and if I hit one of them, I was dead.

In theory it shouldn't be a problem, I told myself. *All the navigational markers will be on my GPS. I won't be able to see them, but I'll know where they are, and I'll be able to maneuver around them.*

In theory that was true, but the thought of roaring across the water on a completely blind takeoff run still made me pretty nervous.

All in all, it wasn't the best plan in the universe, but at the moment it was all I had. I just had to figure out a way to get to my plane without being spotted.

That might be a bit tricky, I admitted to myself.

There were two options: The first was to swim all the way around the entire fort to the north beach and then sneak across to my plane from there. It was a long way around, but I'd be in the moat and under cover of the fortress walls almost the entire way. The major obstacle in that plan would be right at the end when I'd be completely in the open and sneaking across a big wide area of low bushes and grass to get to the seaplane beach.

My second option was to swim from where I was out into the open water and make a wide circle around the south beach and concrete pier, past the handful of boats in the harbor, then finally across to the seaplane beach. Going that way had the advantage of keeping me hidden in the water the entire way and simply swimming up to my plane, untying it, and pushing off the beach before I climbed into the cockpit.

It was a good plan, but what frightened me about it was that I'd have to swim out in the open water where I ran the risk of the current carrying me out to sea. I'm not ashamed to admit that the thought of this scared me, but I was even more scared of trying to cross the open area on the other side of the fort.

I thought about this for a moment. I knew that as long as I swam fairly close to the shore (although not *too* close, of course) I should be okay.

With a confident nod to reassure myself, it was decided. I was going to swim to my plane by way of the open water.

The first step was to get across the moat wall. It was going to be difficult. The top of the wall was high above the water, and I would somehow have to pull myself up with my clothes soaking wet and heavy.

I swam over and took a quick look around to make sure no one was watching before I reached up and hung from the top edge of the moat wall, waiting for the flash of the lighthouse on Loggerhead Key. I knew that as soon as I saw it, I would have twenty seconds of darkness to get over the wall.

Go! I said to myself as the beam of light flashed over me. I strained to pull myself up, dripping water noisily as I went. I quickly rolled across the top of the wall, leaving a wet trail behind me as I went, and then lowered myself into the water on the other side.

Did anyone see me? I asked myself, looking around anxiously. *Did anyone hear me?*

I hovered near the wall and waited for a few minutes to see what would happen, half expecting to see Patrick come running down, but there was nothing but darkness and quiet. I was safe.

I wasted no time swimming parallel to the moat wall for a while until it turned inward at the next bastion tower. From there I continued straight out, swimming into open water with the south beach and concrete pier to my left.

I continued swimming quietly, making long powerful strokes with my arms and legs. It was exhausting to do with all my clothes on—much more than I'd expected—but at least there were no currents pulling me away from the fort. That was what had worried me the most.

I swam a bit closer to shore as I passed the end of the concrete pier where I'd first seen someone standing lookout two nights before.

Too bad for them that they aren't standing there now, I thought, smiling at the irony. *They might actually be able to see me.*

I continued past the dock pilings and out across the open channel toward the dim light on the masthead of the nearest boat. I could see four boats riding at anchor in the harbor, and my plan was to swim from one to the next on my way to the seaplane beach. The boats would provide me with cover, and I could hang off their anchor lines if I needed to rest.

Onward I swam to the nearest boat, then to the next one, and the next one. As I passed the third one, I could hear the sound of loud snoring coming from inside. I laughed quietly to myself. I'd forgotten that people were out here sleeping.

Finally, I reached the last boat and grabbed the anchor line to stop and catch my breath. I checked out the situation ahead of me on shore before I made the final swim to my plane. It looked like the coast was clear, but in the darkness, there was really no way of knowing for sure. I would just have to risk it and swim over to get my plane ready to fly as quietly as I could.

I took a deep breath and readied myself to go for it, but just as I was about to let go of the anchor line, I looked up at the bow and saw the name of the sailboat emblazoned there:

AND THE SEA
Cape Fear, NC

Chapter Fifty-Two

In Your Dreams, Paddy Boy

I was so startled at the sight of the name of the boat that I let go of the anchor line, jerking my hand away as if the line was a live wire that had just jolted me full of electricity. I couldn't believe it! It was Patrick's boat! I'd been hanging around having a rest while holding on to the anchor line of Patrick's boat.

Not that it made any difference—obviously, Patrick wasn't on the boat at that moment, nor was anyone else. But it still surprised me, although of course Patrick would have to keep his boat somewhere other than tied up to the dock.

I should sabotage his engine, I thought as I paddled around to the outboard motor mounted on the back of the boat. Once Patrick knew that he was busted, he might make a run for it, and I had a golden opportunity to strand him on the Dry Tortugas until the police came.

It was a good idea, but unfortunately, I had no clue exactly how I was supposed to do it. In the movies, they would have pulled out a knife and cut the fuel lines, but I didn't have a knife, and I would make so much noise trying to rip the fuel lines out by hand that everyone on the island would hear me. It was a good idea but ultimately too risky, so I decided just to swim to my plane as planned.

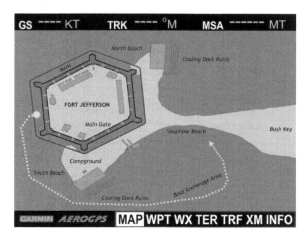

By kicking off from Patrick's boat, I was able to cover the remaining distance to the seaplane beach in a few strokes. As I approached, I swam slowly and silently while I kept a sharp lookout for anyone who might be lurking nearby. Fortunately, the terrain was only sand and grass, so there was nothing for anyone to hide behind. Even in the darkness, I could see that there was definitely no one around.

When I reached shallow water, I felt sand under my feet again and sighed with relief. I reached out to grab one of the pontoons of my plane to steady myself. Its cold metal surface had never felt as good as it did in that moment. I could have given it a big hug if there hadn't been more pressing things to deal with.

I waded around to the downwind side of the plane where the mooring lines were slack, and I quietly pulled the knots loose and let the rope float freely in the water. As I worked, I constantly scanned the shoreline for any sign of trouble, but thankfully, there was nothing.

So far, so good, I told myself as I waded around to the side of my plane that was farthest from the fortress. The mooring line on that side was pulled taut, so I grabbed it, braced my feet in the underwater sand, and pulled as hard as I could. Slowly but surely, the plane swung toward me, and the line went slack enough that I could untie it.

Now for the tricky part, I thought. I had to actually get out of the water and up into the cockpit to start the plane.

First, I took off my hoodie and gently squeezed a bit of water out of it. Without it on, I wasn't as heavy and dripping with water when I climbed onto the pontoon. Kneeling on the hoodie for a few moments, I listened nervously and scanned the shoreline as the excess water ran off me, making quiet trickling sounds on the hollow metal pontoon.

When most of the water had dripped off me, I pulled myself up the ladder and opened the cockpit door. I was worried that the hinges might squeak, so I swung it open only a couple of inches at a time until there was enough room for me to squeeze through.

But I didn't climb all the way into the plane just yet. Standing on the top step of the ladder and leaning across the pilot's seat, I very quietly went through the basic start-up procedures of priming the fuel lines and setting the controls. I wouldn't be able to do a proper preflight check of everything and would just have to have a bit of faith in my trusty seaplane, but if I wanted the engine to start, a few procedures had to be followed.

Once I finished everything that I could do quietly, I climbed down to the pontoon and swung my legs into the water. From that point on, everything I was about to do was going to make a lot of noise, and that meant it had to be done quickly and smoothly so I could get away from the beach as fast as possible.

Okay, it's now or never, I told myself, and I jumped into the water. I grabbed the struts of the plane's pontoon and dug my heels into the sandy bottom, pushing as hard as I could. The aluminum floats groaned and squealed as they slid off the sandy beach. The sound was a lot quieter than I'd expected it to be, but it was still plenty loud enough to get people's attention at the fort.

Sure enough, within a few seconds I saw the beam of a flashlight switch on near the fortress. As I continued pushing and heaving the boat off the beach, I watched the beam wobbling and swinging along toward me.

"Hey!" the person with the flashlight shouted as they ran toward me. "Hey, you! Stop!"

I gave the pontoons one last powerful shove to get the plane floating free and drifting out in the open water. I wanted to get far enough out that whoever was on shore would be unable to catch up, so when I pushed, I ended up pushing so hard that it felt like I pulled every muscle in my entire body.

The flashlight beam continued wobbling toward me, closing the distance between us fast, because whoever was holding it was sprinting along the edge of the water.

I'm gonna feel that tomorrow, I thought with a groan as I climbed into the cockpit. I slid into the pilot's seat and reached down to crank the starter.

One, two, three, four, five, I counted the rotations of the propeller before hitting the mag switch. The engine choked a few times then finally caught and sputtered powerfully into life.

The low power of the idling engine slowly pulled the plane away from the beach, but as I watched the beam of the flashlight getting closer, I wondered if it was enough.

"Please, please, please don't blow a gasket," I begged as I gently eased the throttle forward. If I gave it too much gas before the engine warmed up, it was likely that the engine would blow a gasket, and I would be left with a dead engine and no power at all.

The engine protested against the increased fuel flow, gargling throatily for a moment before settling down again into a strong idle. It was enough. The increased spin of the propeller was pulling me away from the beach much faster.

I pushed open the cockpit door with my foot and poked my head out to look behind me. The beach was now at least fifty feet away, then sixty, and seventy. The person with the flashlight ran up to the edge of the water and splashed a few steps out, pointing the beam directly toward me and temporarily blinding me.

"Hey, you! Return...beach immediately!" I thought that's what I heard him yell, but over the sound of the engine, I wasn't sure. He called out more threats, but all I heard was "...violation...federal law...arrested...!"

Yah right, I scoffed, and then I reached down to lower the water rudders, and gave the plane a little more gas.

I was cruising along at a pretty good clip now, taxiing into the harbor past the four anchored boats. Lights were beginning to appear on a couple of them as their owners were startled awake by the sudden commotion outside. On shore, I could see a few flashlight beams shining through the trees at the campground. People were waking up, and I wondered how Patrick was going to explain all of this once I got airborne and out of there.

I really could not care less what he tells people, I told myself as I looked down at my GPS to make sure I was giving any navigational hazards in the water a wide berth.

The lights being switched on around me were actually helpful, I realized. Between them, the lighthouse, and the harbor lights, I didn't feel like I was driving as blindly as I'd thought I would be. It was still pitch black outside, of course, but with some visual reference points around me, and my GPS telling me where the obstacles were, I felt a lot more confident about taking off.

I continued out into the open as far as I could go before turning into the wind for takeoff. As I swung around, I saw a flash of light out of the corner of my eye and was surprised to see a small Zodiac boat racing out toward me. Mounted on the front of it was a spotlight that was pointed directly at me, and as the boat rode up and down on my wake, the light flashed in and out of my eyes. In between the flashes, I could see Patrick at the controls, his maniacal face illuminated by the zodiac's instrument panel. I couldn't believe it. He was chasing after me and trying to maneuver around in front to block my takeoff run.

I laughed at him—the kind of laugh that can only come from having survived a very tense situation and knowing that you are in control of it. If Patrick honestly thought that he was going to stop me in that little tiny boat of his, then he was in for a big surprise.

"In your dreams, Paddy boy," I muttered under my breath, and I pushed the throttle forward.

Chapter Fifty-Three

A Strange And Alien Waterscape

The engine of my trusty De Havilland Beaver roared instantly into life, and I raced across the water, picking up speed with every passing second. It was probably just my imagination, but the engine sounded angry somehow, as though my faithful seaplane felt just as frustrated and annoyed (and relieved) as I did at that moment.

I looked down at my GPS one last time to make absolutely sure that I wasn't heading straight for some buoy or fixed navigational marker. It was perfectly clear, except, of course, for Patrick and his little Zodiac boat coming at me from the side.

I glanced over and checked my speed, making a quick calculation in my head to see whether he would make it in front of me before I was airborne. It was going to be close, so just to be absolutely sure, I adjusted my path a bit more to the right so that I definitely would not hit him. Besides, I didn't want his little boat to damage my plane.

"Come on, come on," I said nervously as I continued to rattle and bounce from one small wave to the next while picking up speed. I could feel that my plane was itching to get into the air, but it was still too early. I needed just a little bit more speed.

Finally, I pulled back on the controls, and my trusty De Havilland Beaver jumped into the air off the crest of the next wave. The rattling and bouncing disappeared, and suddenly I was skimming smoothly over the surface of the water, climbing into the dark skies over the Dry Tortugas. Down below I watched Patrick as he quickly reversed his engines and spun around to head back to the fortress.

"Nice try," I muttered to myself, chuckling at my own cleverness. "Next time don't bring a boat to an air race."

As I gained altitude, I looked back toward Fort Jefferson. I could see the beams of various flashlights moving around the campground and along the edge of the dock. My unexpected nighttime departure had apparently caused quite a ruckus at the fort, and I could just imagine the sleepy campers gossiping among themselves, trying to figure out what was going on.

"Sorry, guys," I said as I leveled off at a comfortable altitude of about five hundred feet.

I untangled my iPhone from inside of my ponytail and tossed it onto the seat next to me. I looked around the cabin for my hoodie then realized that in my rush to get airborne, I'd left it out on the pontoon. I glanced out of my window to see if it was still there, but of course, it was long gone.

Dammit, that was my favorite hoodie! I thought, frowning, but I had bigger things to worry about than lost hoodies. I had to figure out a way to find Kevin and Kristina's boat out on the open ocean.

I assumed that they would be heading east in the direction of Key West. It was a reasonable assumption since they wouldn't be heading south toward Cuba, after all, and there was nothing but the Gulf of Mexico for thousands miles to the west and north.

Definitely east, I thought to myself as I put my plane into a turn and leveled off on an easterly heading. I scanned all around me and up ahead to the horizon, but I couldn't make anything out.

I wondered whether they knew that I might be coming after them. Surely, Patrick or one of his accomplices at Fort Jefferson had already warned them.

Maybe he can't warn them? I thought to myself. After all, there was no cell phone service on the Tortugas, and unless he had a satellite phone or access to a radio set, he might not be able to reach them.

I was pretty sure that the National Park Service had a proper-sized radio at the fortress, but that didn't necessarily mean that Patrick would be able to access it. Obviously, their little scheme didn't involve the entire staff who lived out there. It could well be that he simply couldn't use the radio without appearing suspicious.

"Although Patrick probably has a radio on his boat anyway, and he is probably already talking on it to Kevin at this very moment," said the little voice in my head.

You're overthinking this, I thought, scolding myself. *First things first. Just concentrate on finding the boat.*

I continued scanning the horizon as I flew east, but I couldn't see anything at all. I tried to calculate in my head how far they could have gone since they'd left the fort, and wondered whether I should circle back and make another pass.

But then I finally saw what I was looking for. Up ahead at the horizon and off to my left I saw a set of lights that looked like a boat. I adjusted my course toward them and nodded to myself in satisfaction as I flew closer. It was definitely the running lights of a boat. I could see the green starboard light as well as the lights on the mast and stern quite clearly.

But then, suddenly, the lights were gone.

In the blink of an eye, they disappeared, and I was left with nothing but blackness all around me.

They must have seen me coming and switched their lights off. I cursed to myself after I figured out what they'd done. *How am I going to see them now?*

As I continued closer to the location where I'd last seen them, I strained my eyes to spot them. I'd had a lot of practice seeing in the dark over the last couple of days, but this time it was no use. There was no moon, and it was so dark that I couldn't even make out the surface of the water, much less a black-hulled boat motoring along in it.

Then I had an idea.

In a severe violation of aviation rules, I reached down to switch off my instrument panel and the plane's navigation lights. As soon as I flipped the switches, I was flying completely blind in utter blackness. I gave my eyes a few moments to adjust to the dark then looked out of my window again.

After a minute or two of scanning the blackness around me, I finally spotted what I'd been hoping to see. Off to the left a very faint smudge of blue light was streaked across the surface of the water. I made a slow turn to get closer, and the sheer beauty of it made me hold my breath for a moment. The strange light was a breathtaking blue so pale that it was barely visible at a distance, but as I got closer, it seemed as though I was looking down on the alien waterscape of some distant planet on the other side of the galaxy.

But as beautiful as it was, there was actually nothing unusual or alien about it at all. In fact, it is a common phenomenon that most sailors around the world are quite familiar with. The strange blue light was a trail of bioluminescent plankton and algae that had been churned up by the propellers of a boat—Kevin and Kristina's boat, to be exact, and it was leading me straight to where I wanted to go.

Chapter Fifty-Four

They Aren't People...

The luminous blue glow on the water was so breathtakingly beautiful that I was reluctant to switch on my instrument lights again, but flying in complete darkness was starting to make me nervous, not to mention that I didn't want the Coast Guard or the US military to think I was a drug-smuggling plane or something suspicious like that.

I switched on my lights again, blinking and giving my eyes some time to adjust before reaching over to grab my iPhone. I held it up and checked if I had a signal. I was getting close to Key West now, and I was relieved to see that I had one signal bar flickering faintly in and out but getter stronger as I flew farther east.

It will have to do, I said to myself, and I put the iPhone on my newly installed hands-free mount. I dug around through some papers on the copilot's seat until I found the shopping list that Jodi had written out for me the day before. Written at the bottom of it was the number for their satellite phone.

Punching the number into my phone, I hit the call button and listened through my airplane headset as it tried to connect. The first few times I dialed, the call failed, but on the fifth attempt, I finally got something.

"Come on, Jack," I muttered to myself as I listened to it ringing on the other end.

"Hello?" I heard a sleepy voice say at the other end of the line.

"Jack!" I cried out, more loudly than I intended. "It's me! Kitty!"

"Kitty?" Jack replied, sounding dazed and confused. "What time is it? Is it the middle of the night? It's dark outside."

"It *is* the middle of the night," I replied. "And I'm sorry to wake you, but I really need your help."

I could hear the sound of rustling and grunting on the other end of the line as Jack rolled out of bed.

"My help?" Jack asked, sounding instantly more awake and alert. "Is something wrong? Are you okay?"

"I'm fine, I'm fine," I replied. "But there's a situation that I need to talk to you about. I need to get some advice before I call the police or the Coast Guard."

Jack listened attentively while I quickly told him the whole story. I told him how I'd first noticed the mysterious glow in the water and how I swam out to see what it was; about the lookouts and flashlight signals from the shore; about the silver ingots and the emeralds, and about everything else that followed. I finished my story by telling Jack about being chased through the fortress by Patrick, and then I told him that Kevin and Kristina were escaping in their boat at that very moment. After I finished, Jack was quiet for a few moments, silently absorbing everything that I'd just told him.

"It's unbelievable, isn't it? " I asked as I waited for him to respond.

"Are you sure about all this?" Jack finally asked, speaking slowly. "It doesn't make any sense to find Spanish treasure on a Civil War-era steamboat. Are you sure that what they had was actually silver bars and emeralds?"

I reached down and patted the pocket of my cargo pants with the palm of my hand to feel the emerald that was still hidden in there.

"At first I wasn't sure about the emeralds," I replied, taking a deep breath before I told him the rest, "because the one I have is so big, and it doesn't look anything like the cut and polished emeralds you see in jewelry stores. But what else could it possibly be?"

"You actually have one of them?" Jack asked, surprised.

"Yeah," I replied. "I dove down and grabbed one yesterday."

Jack whistled in disbelief. "That's absolutely incredible," he said. "Do you have any idea what something like that is worth?"

"I have absolutely no idea," I answered honestly. "It's not like I was planning to keep it."

"And what about the silver bars?" Jack asked. "Are you sure they're Spanish treasure bars? Maybe they were just normal bricks, like you initially thought."

"You saw them yourself," I replied. "I showed you the photos of them on my phone, and you said the markings were from Spanish silver treasure bars."

"I thought those pictures were from the museum in Key West," Jack said, confused. "How did you get such good pictures of their paperwork?"

I cringed. Jack was an ex-cop, and I didn't really want to admit to him that I'd been trespassing illegally on Kevin and Kristina's boat. Oh well; it was too late now.

"I broke into their boat," I said sheepishly, "and I took the pictures there."

"What?!?" Jack asked. "You mean like breaking and entering?"

"Yes," I admitted. "But I didn't break anything. The door was unlocked."

"That doesn't make it any less illegal," Jack said with a disappointed sigh. "But I certainly hope you didn't do anything else even more illegal while you were on their boat."

I shook my head. "No sir," I replied. "I just took pictures—the two you saw plus a different one of a handwritten note."

"Another Spanish manifest document?" Jack asked.

"No, not like that," I replied, happy that the conversation was veering away from my short-lived criminal career. "This one was in English, like a poem almost, but it didn't really make any sense."

"What did it say?" Jack asked.

"Something like 'the consolation prize belonging to Rosario was given to the Scottish king'," I replied, trying to remember the exact words. "Hang on; I have to check the photo."

I reached down to my iPhone and flipped through my photos.

"The consolation prize?" Jack asked, a hint of excitement creeping into his voice. "The Scottish king? Rosario? Are you sure that's exactly what it said? Were those the exact words?"

I kept flipping until I reached the photo I wanted, and then I leaned down to read the text off the screen.

"You're right, sorry," I apologized. "I was close, but I didn't get the wording exactly right. It says 'The prize of consolation carried by Rosario is with the Scottish chief'."

Jack went completely silent, and I waited a long time for him to answer.

"Are you still there, Jack?" I asked, wondering if the connection had been dropped.

"I'm still here," Jack answered, breathless.

"Do you know what that means?" I asked. "Do you know who these people are—this Rosario and the Scottish chief?"

"They aren't people," Jack replied simply. "They're ships."

Chapter Fifty-Five

The Prize Of Consolacion

"Ships?" I replied in surprise. "How can they be ships?"

I leaned over again to reread the note off my iPhone screen. If the *Rosario* and the *Scottish Chief* were both ships instead of people, the note still read correctly, but that didn't mean it made any more sense.

"The *Rosario* was the *Nuestra Señora del Rosario*—a ship from the 1622 Spanish treasure fleet—the one that ran aground and sank out at Loggerhead Key," Jack explained.

"The ship that the Spanish found survivors from?" I asked. "The one that they salvaged all the treasure off of?"

"Exactly," Jack said. "That's the one."

"What about the *Scottish Chief*?" I asked. "That doesn't sound like a Spanish treasure ship."

"It's not," Jack agreed. "The *Scottish Chief* was a ship that delivered bricks to Fort Jefferson when they were still building the fortress."

"Bricks?!?" I asked excitedly, thinking about the wreck that Kevin (and I) had been diving on, where the seafloor was littered with bricks.

"Exactly!" Jack replied. "And it's commonly accepted that the *Scottish Chief* is the name of the so-called Brick Wreck just off Fort Jefferson where you say they were digging up silver bars and emeralds."

"And the Prize of Consolation?" I asked. "Is that also a ship?"

"Not exactly, no," Jack replied. "But the *Nuestra Señora de la Consolacion* was one of the ships lost in the hurricane that hit the 1622 fleet. It was just a small merchant vessel sailing home under the protection of the big guns on the treasure galleons, and according to witness accounts, it capsized during the early hours of the storm, sinking so fast out in the deep waters of the Gulf Stream that all the souls on board were quickly lost."

"But I don't understand," I said, interrupting. "Then what is the prize of Consolation?"

"I was about to get to that," Jack said, laughing. "Because even though the *Consolacion* was just a small merchant vessel and not a treasure ship, that didn't mean there wasn't any treasure on board. Thanks to letters and documents found by modern treasure hunters in the Archive of the Indies in Seville, we know that the brother of the *Consolacion*'s navigator was a merchant living in the New World, and that he had shipped a small number of silver bars to Spain aboard his brother's ship.

"But it might not have been just bars of silver that this merchant shipped home on the *Consolacion* because according to hints found in letters he later sent to his family after the loss of the treasure fleet, it appeared that he also shipped a large number of raw emeralds from the fabled Muzo mine in Columbia as well. The references to the emeralds in the letters are vague and inconclusive, however, but that's not surprising since no emeralds were ever listed on the *Consolacion*'s official manifest, and no taxes had been paid. Smuggling untaxed contraband carried the threat of incredibly harsh punishment, so it isn't surprising that he would not have written openly about it.

"Where the story gets complicated, however," Jack continued, "is right before the fleet sailed from Havana. At the last moment, the merchant's brother was transferred from his regular posting as navigator of the *Consolacion* and was sent to the *Rosario* instead. The reason for the switch was that the *Rosario* was a privately owned galleon and not one of the regular fleet ships. It had been commandeered earlier that year to bring the guard fleet up to full strength following a threat of increased enemy activity on the high seas.

"So the *Consolacion*'s navigator packed up his things and moved onto the larger and better armed *Rosario*," Jack said. "And along with him went a large wooden chest containing various personal items and navigational instruments. We know this because after the hurricane drove the *Rosario* aground at Loggerhead Key, the navigator was one of those who survived and participated in the salvage operation that followed.

"A few months later, he wrote to his brother to tell him the sad news that his fortune of silver bars had been lost. He also mentioned his belief that the chest containing his personal effects had been somehow recovered during the salvage operations and that some of the other crewmembers had stolen it. He lodged a complaint with the Marquis, and an investigation was launched, but the whole affair was forgotten after the suspects disappeared at sea without a trace when the second hurricane hit the area."

"Oh my god," I breathed in amazement. "And in that chest was the treasure?"

"That's right," Jack said. "Or at least that's how the story goes. The wooden chest contained more than just navigational charts, clothing, and astrolabes. According to the legend, it also contained his brother's silver bars and the contraband emeralds, carefully hidden underneath all of his personal items. In the crazy world of treasure hunter mythology, the contents of that chest are known as the prize of the *Consolacion*."

I was speechless. The implications of this were completely astounding, and although I still didn't have a clue how all these various revelations fit together, I felt like I was finally getting very close to the answer.

"I can't believe it," I said in amazement as I made a long, slow turn with my plane. While Jack and I had been talking I had been constantly making wide circles in the air over the area where I'd spotted Kevin and Kristina's boat. I couldn't see them down below at that exact moment, but I knew that they couldn't have gone far.

"The only question I have," Jack said, "is how...."

"Whoa!" I cried out, cutting Jack off in midsentence when I spotted a ball of fire and sparks exploding out of the water about half a mile in the distance. "What was that?!??"

"What is it?" Jack asked, sounding worried. "What happened?"

I banked over and headed to the inferno to get a closer look. As the blaze died down, I could make out the outline of a flaming boat sitting at an odd angle in the water.

It was Kevin and Kristina's boat. It was on fire and sinking quickly.

Chapter Fifty-Six
Am I Really Going To Do This?

"Oh my god, Jack! It's Kevin and Kristina!" I cried out. "I don't know what happened, but their boat just exploded."

"What?" Jack exclaimed. In the background, I could hear Jodi asking him what was going on, and he quickly explained.

I grabbed the controls of my plane and descended to an altitude of a few hundred feet off the water to make a low pass over the burning boat below me. I could see Kristina struggling to put a life jacket on Kevin who was still trying to stand at the controls in the open pilothouse.

"Kitty!" Jack said at the other end of the phone line. "Go to Channel 16. Kevin's making a distress call!"

I reached down to end the call and switch over to my radio. Almost immediately, I heard the desperate sound of Kevin's voice.

"Mayday, mayday, mayday, this is motor vessel *The Old Man*; I repeat, this is *The Old Man*," Kevin barked into his radio. "We've just hit the reef somewhere in the vicinity of Boca Grande Key. I don't know the exact position. We're going down by the head fast, and my radio and GPS are all underwater. There are two of us on board, and we need immediate assistance. Our emergency raft has been compromised. Both of us have our PFDs on, but there are sharks in the water. Repeat, there are sharks in the water, and we have no emergency raft."

I heard the sound of screams and shouts over the radio before the transmission fizzled and went dead. I looked out of my window and watched in horror as the burning boat down below rolled quickly onto its side, spilling Kevin and Kristina into the water.

"Oh my god!" I cried out as I watched the two of them clinging desperately to each other by the light of the dying flames.

I reached down to hit the radio transmit button on my flight control wheel.

"US Coast Guard, US Coast Guard, this is private aircraft Charlie Foxtrot Kilo Tango Yankee, come in please," I said.

"This is the United States Coast Guard Sector Key West, go ahead," a cool voice at the other end intoned after a few moments.

"Be advised that I am in the air over the location of the boating accident involving motor vessel *The Old Man*," I said calmly, giving them my exact position and describing the nature of the situation below.

"Understood aircraft Kilo Tango Yankee," the cool voice replied after I finished relaying all the details to them. "Please advise whether you are able to stay on site until assistance arrives, over."

"Affirmative," I said. "I can remain on site, over."

"Thank you Kilo Tango Yankee," the voice replied. "Continue to monitor Channel 16. United States Coast Guard Sector Key West, over and out."

"US Coast Guard, US Coast Guard, this is the motor vessel *Tradewind*," I heard Jack's voice over the radio as soon as I signed off. "I repeat this is motor vessel *Tradewind*, over."

"This is the United States Coast Guard Sector Key West. Go ahead, *Tradewind*," the same cool voice responded.

"Be advised that we are in the vicinity of Ballast Key and are already underway to the location of the accident to render possible assistance," Jack said. "Estimate arrival in approximately one five minutes; repeat, one five minutes, over."

"Understood, *Tradewind*," the voice replied. "We have a vessel and a helicopter en route right now, but you'll be on site well before we can get there. Proceed with caution and assist only if reasonable to do so, over."

"Affirmative," Jack answered. "*Tradewind*, out."

As soon as Jack signed off, I switched my headset to my phone and hit redial.

"We're on our way to you, Kitty," Jack said as soon as he picked up the phone. "Can you keep an eye on things until we get there?"

"Of course," I replied, turning my control wheel to circle around. "But you'd better hurry. They're freaking out in the water down there."

I finished my turn and cruised overhead again to see Kevin and Kristina flailing about in the water, waving their emergency lights all around them in a panic. I dipped down as low as I could for a closer look and was utterly stunned to see the sleek and deadly fin of a shark make a run straight at them. Kevin kicked and punched violently as the shark got close, and thankfully, he appeared to scare it off for the moment.

"Jack!" I cried, circling around for another pass. "You really have to hurry. There are sharks down there, and the two of them look like they're really in trouble!"

"Negative, Kitty," Jack responded sadly. "At best we're still more than twelve minutes out and there are reefs all around the area. I don't want to end up in the water the same as them."

"I know, Jack, but I don't think they're going to last that long!" I said, watching in terror as another shark made a pass at Kevin. Its fin cut through the water as it dashed in close and veered off at the last second into the darkness.

"You'll have to do something yourself," Jack replied. "We can't go any faster than we already are."

"Me?!?" I replied, not sure what I could do except helplessly watch the horrible scene unfolding beneath me. "What can I do?"

"You're a seaplane, right?" Jack asked. "And you must have an emergency life raft on board. Can't you land on the water and throw them your raft?"

I shook my head emphatically, looking out at the pitch-black world around me. Off to the east I could make out the city lights of Key West and the running lights of Jack's boat in the distance making straight for us, but down below there was nothing but blackness. The only thing I could see was the tiny circle of light given off by Kevin and Kristina's emergency lights as they thrashed around in the water below.

"I can't do it, Jack," I replied. "I can't see a thing out here. It would be complete suicide to try to land when I can't see the water."

"Understood, Kitty," Jack said with a resigned sigh. "We'll get there as soon as we can and pray for the best."

I was still shaking my head as I watched the scene of potential carnage unfolding below me. I couldn't just stand by, but under the circumstances, I didn't know what I could possibly do to help.

I looked around the cabin and made a quick assessment of my emergency gear stowed at the back in the cargo area. I had an inflatable life raft, and for a brief second I considered climbing back there and somehow throwing it out the window to Kevin and Kristina, but the idea was completely stupid. There was no way I could do all of that in midflight.

I should have landed before the boat sank, I told myself. *While the fire was still burning, I could see the water's surface.*

This thought gave me an idea—a completely insane idea that my father would kill me if he knew I was even thinking, much less considering. It was the kind of idea that only an incredibly desperate person would even think about trying.

"Oh, god," I sighed heavily as I looked over at the space behind the copilot's seat where Jack's jerry can full of gasoline was stowed. "Am I really going to do this? Am I completely out of my mind?"

Apparently I was.

Chapter Fifty-Seven

Please Proceed At Reasonable Speed And With Caution

Reaching behind the copilot's seat, I grunted and pulled the jerry can of gasoline up into the cockpit beside me.

"Oh my god, I must be crazy," I muttered as I made another turn and flew back toward Kevin and Kristina. Using them as my only visual reference point and watching my altimeter carefully, I descended as low as I possibly dared before leveling off.

I pulled the jerry can onto my lap and pushed the door open on my side far enough to jam the jerry can halfway out. I unscrewed the cap and winced as the cockpit was instantly filled with gasoline fumes blown around like a cyclone by the wind howling in through the half-open door.

From the copilot's side I grabbed an old, ripped-up T-shirt that I used as a rag for cleaning the plane. Using a plastic bag to keep my hand dry I twisted one end of the shirt and carefully dipped it into the jerry can to soak the tip in gasoline. I then flipped the fabric around and stuffed the dry part inside, leaving the gas-soaked end hanging free.

"There's a word for this kind of homemade bomb," I said to myself absently as I flipped the plastic bag off my hand and reached under my seat to grab my Zippo lighter. "We learned it in social studies class."

Flipping the cap of the lighter open, I flicked it and prepared to do the craziest thing I had ever done in my entire life. I had to flick the lighter a few times since it wouldn't ignite with all the wind blowing through the cabin, but on the fifth or sixth try, it finally caught for half a second, which was long enough to ignite the gas-soaked T-shirt.

"A Molotov cocktail—that's it," I thought, my voice unusually calm considering the incredibly dangerous stunt that I was about to pull.

Heaving the door open as wide as I could, I watched the jerry can fall free out into the open air. It bounced off the ladder and the pontoon on the way down, splashing gasoline and spitting fire like a dragon as it went. For an instant, I panicked that I'd just accidentally killed myself by setting my own plane on fire, but thankfully, the jerry can bounced away from the plane and tumbled end over end toward the water below. I gently pulled back on the controls and climbed a bit higher, slowly making a turn as I watched the flaming jerry can falling rapidly behind me.

The jerry can tumbled a few more times through the air then finally hit the surface of the water. I'm not sure exactly what I was expecting, but I suppose all the action movies I'd seen made me imagine a hellish inferno exploding into the sky. I was a little disappointed when all that happened was a giant tongue of flame that came shooting out of the top and setting a small section of the water's surface on fire.

It wasn't much, but it provided enough light for me to land by. But I had to be quick because the flames of my disappointingly small explosion were already starting to die out.

After circling around one final time, I headed in for a landing. Up ahead of me I watched the small lake of fire snaking across the water, bobbing and curling on the swells. For this to work, I not only had to time things just perfectly, but I also had to touch down almost directly on top of the flames. That was the only place that I could see where the sky ended and the water began.

"Careful, careful," I whispered to myself as I slowly descended toward the dying flames. I watched them get closer and closer until my pontoons finally touched down, carving their way through the fiery water and extinguishing the flames almost instantly with the wash from my propellers.

It was a bit of a rough landing, but as long as my plane hadn't caught fire, it would be a safe one. I hadn't even slowed down completely when I popped open my door and looked back along the length of the plane to see if anything was burning. It was all clear on my side, so I quickly pulled off my seatbelt and slid across to check the other side of the plane as well. It was all clear there too, and I was safe.

"That wasn't so bad," I muttered, chuckling as I scooted back into the pilot's seat. I didn't have a second to lose and immediately pushed my throttle forward to taxi over toward Kevin and Kristina. I'd thrown my little firebomb out in the water quite some distance away from them so they wouldn't get hurt, and now I had to get over to where they were frantically treading water.

My plane bounced and roared over the waves, and in no time, I reached the bright blue-white beams of their emergency lights. I shut my engine down and coasted the rest of the way in while I climbed into the cargo section of my plane to pull out my emergency raft.

"Thank god, thank god!" I could hear Kristina screaming as I opened the cargo door and pushed the raft out in front of me.

As the two of them splashed their way toward me, I stepped onto the outside ladder and pulled the raft's inflate handle. In a hissing shriek of compressed air, the raft morphed and ballooned into full size and floated out on the waves. The sea was a little bit rough so I kept one hand firmly on the ladder while I pushed the raft out with the other and held it next to my plane.

The two swimmers finally reached me, and Kevin was the first to scramble into the boat. I thought this was a bit unchivalrous of him, but he immediately turned around and yanked Kristina all the way up beside him in one quick, fluid motion.

Okay, I was wrong, I thought to myself with a smirk. *That was a lot more efficient than if he'd tried to push her up into the boat first.*

While the two of them settled into the raft, I tied it off and climbed into the pilot's seat. I kept an eye on them as I put on my radio headset.

"US Coast Guard, US Coast Guard, and motor vessel *Tradewind*, this is private aircraft Charlie Foxtrot Kilo Tango Yankee, come in, please," I said.

"This is the United States Coast Guard Sector Key West, go ahead," that same cool voice at the other end replied after a few seconds.

"Be advised that my seaplane is on the water at the site of the motor boat accident," I said. "I have deployed a life raft, and the two survivors are safely onboard. The situation here is secure for the moment, so please proceed at reasonable speed and with caution."

Chapter Fifty-Eight

Jack And His "Cop Face"

"Thank you Kilo Tango Yankee," the cool voice replied. "We'll see you soon. United States Coast Guard Sector Key West, over and out."

I climbed back to the cargo door and stepped onto the top rung of the outside ladder, grabbing the sides of the doorway to steady myself as the plane dipped and wobbled on the waves.

"Are you hurt?" I called over to the two soaking wet survivors in the life raft below me. In the glare of their lights, I couldn't see any blood or other signs of injury—just the two of them lying exhausted against the side of the raft.

Kevin shook his head. "We're okay—thank god you saved us," he said, breathing hard and pulling Kristina close to his body to keep her warm. "I have a bump on my head and a little nip on my ankle, but that's all."

"A nip on your ankle?" Kristina cried, sitting upright and leaning over to take a look. When she pulled up the leg of Kevin's trousers, I cringed at the sight of a series of teeth marks along the back of his lower calf and ankle. The bites were shallow, more like bruises than actual puncture wounds, but there was no doubt about it, a shark had definitely tried to take a bite out of Kevin.

I threw a first aid kit down to Kristina who quickly pulled out what she needed and got to work like a pro. "You're a lucky man," she said as she poured some disinfectant on Kevin's leg and wrapped a couple of layers of bandages around it. "You're hardly bleeding."

"If I was bleeding, we'd both be shark food already," Kevin said, leaning forward to help her finish tying off the bandage. "The blood in the water would have driven them into a real frenzy."

Once Kristina finished with the first aid, I threw a couple of blankets down to them. They wrapped themselves in them and rested against the side of the boat again, huddled together for warmth.

"The Coast Guard will be here soon," I said, taking a seat at the edge of the cargo door with my legs dangling outside of the plane.

Kevin nodded and grunted wearily in reply. "Thank you," he said.

The three of us sat uncomfortably in silence for a few long moments.

"I don't see any sharks around anymore," I observed, trying to make conversation.

"Maybe you scared them off with your crazy fireball landing," Kevin said, "or maybe the noise of the plane did it."

I nodded. "Maybe," I replied, and we fell into uncomfortable silence again while we waited for help to arrive. There wasn't much else to say, I supposed. I couldn't really make small talk with them. I could just imagine how that would go: *Hello, how are you? Nice weather we're having. Sorry you got bit by a shark, and by the way, the Coast Guard is coming to arrest you.*

At least I *assumed* that's what the Coast Guard would do once they got here and Jack and I explained things.

The police will have to head out to Fort Jefferson to arrest Patrick and the other person, whoever that is.

I still had no idea who was involved in this whole treasure scheme. I knew there were at least four of them—Kevin, Kristina, Patrick, and one other—but because I hadn't seen any sign of anyone other than Patrick out at the fort, I still had no idea who the mysterious fourth person was. In fact, since I hadn't seen any sign of him, maybe he wasn't even at the fortress that night at all. Maybe he was off somewhere else instead.

My heart stopped cold.

Maybe the mysterious fourth person isn't just one person, but TWO people, I thought suddenly, thinking of Jack and Jodi. *Is it possible that they are somehow involved in all of this?*

"No," I whispered under my breath. "It can't be!"

And yet, in some weird way, it actually made sense. How else would Jack know so much about these Spanish fleets and sunken treasures? And why would they sleep in a tent at the campground of Fort Jefferson instead of on their boat? Their boat was pretty nice, after all, and it was definitely not the kind of boat you'd expect a retired policeman to be able to afford.

My thoughts were interrupted by the distant sound of a motor coming from the east. I turned my head and saw the running lights of a cabin cruiser plowing its way through the water toward us. It was Jack and Jodi, and they were now only a couple of minutes away.

Beyond their boat I could also see the lights of a helicopter approaching fast from the direction of Key West. The staccato rhythm of its rotors grew louder by the second, and it was soon thundering directly overhead, blinding us with its bright searchlights and creating a hurricane of wind and sea spray.

Standing at the open doors of the helicopter a pair of rescue divers were ready to jump, so I put my arm over my head to give them the okay signal before quickly climbing into my plane to get on the radio. I explained to them that the situation was stable and that there was no need to risk putting their people in the water.

In fact, I thought to myself. *It's not that I'm not glad to see you, but until you showed up, the weather conditions out here were nice and calm. Now we have gale force winds from your rotors blasting us all over the place.*

The pilot thanked me and said that a Coast Guard cutter was on its way to pick up the survivors. He then signed off, and the helicopter climbed to a higher altitude, taking its cyclone of wind with it. It didn't head back to Key West, however, and continued to circle nearby, illuminating us with its bright searchlights as Jack and Jodi's boat pulled up.

Jodi appeared at the back of the boat and threw me a mooring line so that I could tie up to their boat and we wouldn't all float away on the current before the Coast Guard arrived. Jack also soon appeared after finishing setting the boat's anchor, and he gave me a friendly wave.

I waved back but watched the two of them cautiously. Jack leaned over the back of his boat to check the situation with Kevin and Kristina in the life raft below, and he had an expression on his face that I had never seen before. It was the deadly serious expression of someone who was sizing up a potentially dangerous situation the way you would look at a wild animal to figure out what you were up against to determine whether it was a threat.

That facial expression told me everything I needed to know. The way Jack's eyes narrowed and his jaw clenched as he looked down at Kevin and Kristina told me without a doubt that he and Jodi had nothing to do with the plan to steal the treasure.

Jack's facial expression was what I might best describe as his "cop face," and as I watched him staring down grimly at Kevin and Kristina, I almost felt sorry for them.

Chapter Fifty-Nine

More To The Situation Than Meets The Eye

Fortunately, we didn't have to wait too long for the Coast Guard cutter to show up. Within minutes, a sleek red and white ship pulled up close to us, and the helicopter finally thundered its way back toward Key West, leaving the air still and quiet once again.

I watched as the Coast Guard officials went about their work with amazing efficiency, quickly sending a Zodiac boat over with a towline so they could pull the life raft toward the cutter. Once the raft was secured at the side of their ship, a medic climbed down and helped Kevin into a sling so that he could be hauled onboard. By now, the bite-shaped area on his leg where the shark had bitten him was turning a disgusting shade of purple. It looked like it hurt, but he probably could have walked on his leg and climbed onboard by himself, but the Coast Guard wasn't taking any chances.

Kristina was next to go, and I watched her scramble up the rope ladder that was hanging down the side of the ship. I noticed that the zipper pockets of her cargo pants were bulging and stuffed full almost to the breaking point. I looked across at Jack and caught his eye, nodding subtly toward her. He looked at her and then nodded at me almost imperceptibly before disappearing into the cabin of his boat for a few minutes. When he came back out, he gave me a hand signal—first pointing at me, then himself, then over to the cutter. The two of us were apparently going over to talk to the Coast Guard.

After unloading Kevin and Kristina, the Coast Guard Zodiac motored over to my plane to pick me up, and then we went over to get Jack while Jodi stayed behind on their boat to keep an eye on things.

"Are you all right, Kitty?" Jack asked as we made our way over to the Coast Guard ship. "Is your plane all right?"

"Everything is perfect," I replied. "But why are we talking to the Coast Guard? What did you tell them?"

"I gave them a brief recap of the situation," Jack said as we pulled up next to the ship. "But I told them that you would have to fill them in on the details."

I nodded and climbed up the ladder with several of the crew helping me pull myself up on deck. Jack was right behind me, and once he was onboard, an officer led us through some corridors to a small briefing room behind the ship's bridge.

A handsome man in a smartly pressed uniform was leaning over a chart table when we arrived, and he straightened up to walk over and introduce himself.

"Welcome aboard," he said, shaking both of our hands. "I'm Lieutenant Commander Walsh."

"Good to meet you," Jack replied as Commander Walsh ushered us over to a small table in the corner of the room.

"I'm sorry we couldn't meet under better circumstances," Commander Walsh said, looking across at me and gesturing toward Jack. "But Mr. Hall, here, tells me that there is a bit more to this situation than meets the eye, and that you're the one who can explain it for us."

I nodded.

"Okay," Commander Walsh said. "Let me tell you what I know so far. Before we received this distress call and had to come out here to respond to it, the Coast Guard was contacted by radio by one of the park rangers over on Fort Jefferson. She told us that there had been some kind of break-in, and...."

"Wait a minute," I interrupted. "Did you say that she told you? Did you say that the park ranger was a woman?"

Commander Walsh looked confused, but he nodded. "Yes, that's right," he replied, pulling out a writing pad from his breast pocket to check his notes. "National Park Ranger Penelope Tift."

"Penny Tift," I said, laughing. "Ranger Penny. I met her when I first arrived at the fortress, but I didn't know her last name."

"Is that important?" Jack asked, leaning toward me.

"Her last name is Tift!" I replied. "Don't you see? Kevin, Kristina, Patrick, Penny—they're all related!"

Jack sat back to think this over.

"I'm afraid you've lost me now," Commander Walsh said. "All I know is that this ranger Penelope Tift called us to say that one of the campers out there had been spotted inside the fortress after hours, probably stealing some artifacts or something like that. But when the rangers attempted to apprehend this person, he or she made a run for it and escaped by seaplane, taking off at night and endangering the lives of several people in the process."

"That's ridiculous," Jack said.

Commander Walsh leaned across the table toward me. "I assume that the person who escaped by seaplane was you," he said. "But apparently there's more to the story than that."

I nodded and began to tell the entire story again for the second time that night. I told the story from the moment I'd first spotted Kevin and Kristina's boat near Key West all the way to the moment just fifteen minutes earlier when the Coast Guard cutter arrived on the scene to rescue the two of them from my life raft. But in telling the story this time, I left out none of the embarrassing details.

Commander Walsh listened carefully and took a few notes, keeping a straight face as I spoke (although he did raise his eyebrows a bit when I explained how I'd thrown a burning jerry can of gasoline out of the door of my plane). When I came to the end of the story, I reached into my pocket and pulled out the large emerald that was still tucked in there.

"And this is what they were after," I said, placing the raw gem on the table between us. "And I suspect that if you take a look in the pockets of the two survivors down below in your infirmary, you'll find dozens more just like this."

Jack leaned forward to take a closer look at the emerald. "That's unbelievable," he said, his eyes wide with excitement. "It's enormous!"

Commander Walsh picked up the emerald and held it up to the light. Sparkles of green danced across its surface, and it seemed to glow from deep within as he turned it around in his fingers.

"I think we'd better have a talk with Mr. and Mrs. Tift," he said.

Chapter Sixty

And That Is How We Knew

Lieutenant Commander Walsh led Jack and me down through the innards of the ship to the sick bay where Kevin and Kristina had been bandaged up, and now were resting on a pair of stark clean beds. Kevin's leg was resting in a harness suspended from the ceiling, and he struggled to pull himself upright as we entered the room.

"I'm Lieutenant Commander Walsh, commanding officer of this boat," Commander Walsh said. "And this is Jack Hall and Kitty Hawk who were kind enough to come to your rescue tonight."

Kevin nodded. "I'm Kevin Tift," he replied. "And this is my wife Kristina."

Commander Walsh pulled up a chair next to Kevin's bed and motioned for Jack and me to take a seat in some empty chairs at a table nearby. "Tift is a well-known name around Key West," Commander Walsh said. "But you folks aren't from around here, is that right?"

Kevin nodded again. "That's right," he said. "We're from North Carolina."

"Listen, I'm not gonna beat around the bushes here," Commander Walsh said, getting right to the point. "We were called out here on a rescue operation and the law requires us to investigate what happened to cause the accident that led to your boat foundering and putting the two of you in the water. But I've received differing information about what exactly was going on tonight, so I'm gonna be straight with you, and I'd appreciate it if you all would be just as straight with me."

"I appreciate that," Kevin replied with a heavy sigh. "And if we're being straight, I might as well say that the way things stand right now, they've gone way too far for us to lie our way out of it. But as for the cause of the boat accident, well, I doubt you'd believe me even if I told you."

"Just start at the beginning," Commander Walsh suggested. "For example, tell me why you were out here racing around through shark-infested waters in the middle of the night."

"Fair enough," Kevin replied, nodding over in my direction. "I'm sure that whatever this young lady here told you is all pretty accurate. My wife and I, with the help of our son and daughter-in-law out at Fort Jefferson, have been illegally salvaging a wreck in National Park waters for almost a week now. Every night when the weather was clear we'd head out there to dive on the wreck, and eventually we found what we were looking for."

Kevin glanced over at Kristina who nodded at him and stood up to empty her pants pockets onto a side table. Large handfuls of huge raw emeralds spilled out and clattered across the hard surface. In the harsh fluorescent light, they seemed to glow a beautiful and ethereal green.

Commander Walsh picked up one of the stones and examined it closely. "And these emeralds—are they from one of the 1622 Spanish wrecks?"

"Correct," Kevin replied, nodding.

"But I'm told that the area where you were diving contained a much later wreck than that," Commander Walsh said. "A wreck from the Civil War era."

"Also correct," Kevin replied.

Commander Walsh put the brilliant green stone on the table and leaned in toward Kevin.

"Then what I don't understand," he said, "is how you knew they were there."

Out of the corner of my eye, I saw Jack nodding along with Commander Walsh's question. He had apparently been wondering the same thing.

"You were right when you said that the name Tift is a well-known one in Key West," Kevin explained. "My family has roots in the Keys from way back. In fact, my great-great-great-grandfather and his brother actually took part in building Fort Jefferson."

"Is that right?" Commander Walsh asked, leaning back in his chair with a skeptical expression.

"Absolutely," Kevin replied. "Just before the Civil War, his brother and him owned a boat that was used to supply the fort with building materials. That boat was named the *Scottish Chief*, and it's sitting out there on the bottom of the ocean just past Fort Jefferson.

"My great-grandfather used to tell me that they'd sunk the boat out there on purpose when the war started so the Yankees wouldn't get their hands on it. My family were proud Southerners, and when they knew that war was coming, they figured that Fort Jefferson would likely stay in Union hands because the Southern armies wouldn't bother to capture such a well-fortified position. So, instead of letting their boat get captured by the Union and used against the Confederates, they sank it. That was a good story, but it wasn't entirely true."

"Mm-hmm," Walsh muttered, apparently thinking the same thing. "Go on," he said.

"The real truth was that my great-great-great-grandfather had found something. During his work out at the fort, he'd discovered the wreck of a large skiff sitting right there down on the seafloor, complete with a rotting wooden chest that he was convinced was loaded to the brim with treasure. He could see it down there through the crystal-clear waters, but there wasn't a thing he could do about it. The water wasn't very deep, but he had no way to see properly underwater without bringing in a diving bell. If he had done that, it would have aroused the suspicions of the Union troops over on Fort Jefferson. So he had to wait and make a plan.

"But there was also another problem too—the war. Before he was able to find a way to recover anything from this wreck, the war began. He knew the war might last for years, and he obviously didn't want the Northern army to get their hands on his treasure, so in desperation he did the only thing he could think of and ran his supply boat aground right on top of the earlier wreck to conceal it. His plan was to come back with proper salvage gear once the war was over.

"Sadly, my great-great-great-grandfather never lived long enough to see the end of the war, and the story of the sunken treasure chest was passed down to his son, and then to his son after that, and so on. But you know how things like that are; it's like playing the telephone game—the words and facts get mixed around, and at the end of it all, the meaning is completely changed. By the time the story was passed down a couple of times no one really could figure out the truth of it anymore so nothing was ever done and the wreck just sat out there rotting away.

"By the time my grandfather came along, my family was settled up in North Carolina, and he decided that he was going to figure this whole thing out. He spent years going through the papers that my great-great-great-grandfather left behind after he died. He traveled to Spain to do research, and he sifted through thousands of pages at the archives in Seville. What he finally figured out was that a chest full of silver bars and emeralds belonging to the brother of a navigator from the 1622 Spanish treasure fleet had been transferred to a ship called the *Rosario*. That ship sunk out in the Tortugas during the hurricane, and the chest was later recovered. But the handful of men who'd found the chest kept it secret from the other salvors. They knew that no one would ever notice or be able to prove that it was missing since it wasn't listed on the *Rosario*'s official manifest. So they decided to steal it, and they set off one night in a small sailing skiff. They were going to bury the chest like pirates on one of the nearby islands and come back for it later after the salvage operations were over. Unfortunately for them, however, a storm came up, their skiff sank, and the men involved in the plot all drowned. Because no one knew to even look for it, the treasure chest was lost.

"My grandfather managed to piece together all of this completely on his own, and the secret was finally uncovered after all those years. But that's when things started to go wrong, and everything turned into a tragic comedy of errors. Another war broke out, this time the Spanish Civil War, and even though my grandfather was simply a bystander, he had the bad luck to be in the wrong place at the wrong time during some of the initial fighting, and he was accidentally wounded. He ended up in a Spanish hospital where his wounds quickly turned bad, and he died. But before he died, he wrote a short letter to his wife back home in the United States—a letter that was written partly in a sort of code that only she would understand.

"But my grandmother never got the letter. You won't believe it, but she was killed in a one-car accident on a deserted country road on her way into town to pick up her mail from the post office. So the letter was given to her children, including my father, but no one had the slightest idea what the letter meant."

Kevin took a drink of water and shifted himself into a more comfortable position before continuing.

"The prize of *Consolation,* carried by *Rosario,* is with the *Scottish Chief,*" Kevin recited. "That's what the note said. And it became a sort of tragic family joke, like a poem that everyone knew but no one understood—that is, until the day my son Patrick decided to reconnect with his family's roots, and he took a job with the National Park Service at the Dry Tortugas. You can imagine the excited and frantic phone call I got from Patrick when he came across the information about the *Scottish Chief*, the *Rosario,* and the *Consolacion* as part of his new duties as a park ranger. All those mysterious names in my grandfather's letter had meaning. Finally, the stories and fates of the men and ships from centuries past came together and led us to a fortune in treasure that was sitting out there in shallow water just waiting for someone to unravel the secret and come get it.

"And that, in a nutshell," Kevin said, taking another sip of water as he came to the end of his incredible tale, "is how we knew that the treasure was there."

Chapter Sixty-One

People Back On Land Don't Understand These Things

For a few minutes, no one said a word as each of us silently absorbed Kevin's remarkable story. Lieutenant Commander Walsh jotted down a few more notes then leaned back and took a deep breath.

"Thank you for being so forthright, Mr. Tift," he said, finally. "Of course, you'll have to go over all of this again with the police and make an official statement once we take you back to Key West. We are just the Coast Guard, after all, but I appreciate your honesty, because it makes my job of deciding what I need to do much easier."

Kevin nodded in acknowledgement. "I know you're just doing your job here," Kevin agreed. "And I know what a tough job it is, so we certainly don't want to make it any more difficult for you."

"The only thing left that I need to know," Commander Walsh said, "is about the events leading up to the accident tonight that caused your boat to founder. You said I wouldn't believe it if you told me, but unfortunately, you do have to tell me."

Kevin glanced at Kristina, who gave him the slightest shrug of resignation, and then he met Walsh's eyes again. "Once we left Fort Jefferson," he began, "we headed east like we do every night, toward Key West and up to Marathon where we're staying.

"About an hour after we left the fort, we got a call from our daughter-in-law Penny telling us that one of their campers, a young woman with a seaplane, had just taken off in the middle of the night and was headed in our direction. Her and my son Patrick suspected that this girl had discovered what we were doing and was coming after us. I didn't really know what to make of all that, but pretty soon afterward, we saw the lights of a small plane coming up behind us, so we switched off all our lights to hide ourselves, and we continued in the darkness using only our satellite navigation system.

"We could see that this plane was tagging along with us the whole way, circling around and holding position above us. That's when we started to worry, but there was nothing we could do about it, so we just kept our lights off and turned north to make our way up the inside of the Keys to our mooring in Marathon. We hoped that the plane might lose us after we made the turn."

Kevin paused and looked over at Kristina again for a moment.

"That's when something very strange happened," Kevin said slowly. "Our navigation system suddenly started to act up, cutting in and out and changing our position. Kristina tried to check for loose wires or something else we could fix, but everything seemed okay. And that was when I heard...."

Kevin looked around at all of us, his mouth hanging open as he stopped in midsentence. Commander Walsh leaned forward and raised his eyebrows in anticipation.

"What did you hear?" Commander Walsh asked.

"I heard a voice," Kevin said. "As clear as day, I heard a voice say, 'Hey, look out up there,' and I spun around in confusion, trying to see where it was coming from, but there was no one there. Then I looked off the stern of the boat, and for a second, I thought I saw a human figure sitting on the back railing—a man was just casually sitting there silhouetted against the darkness beyond. In the time it took me to blink and take another look, the figure seemed to disappear into thin air.

A chill went down my spine.

"And that's when we hit the reef," Kevin said, finishing his story. "The fuel tanks ruptured and the boat exploded, taking our life raft out in the process. We barely had time to put our life jackets on and make a call for help before our boat went out from under us and sent us in the water swimming with the sharkies."

Kevin took a drink of water and looked over at me, smiling weakly.

"So as it turned out," he said, "we were pretty lucky that this young lady here was following us in her plane after all, because before we knew it, she swooped down out of the sky and saved us."

Kevin inhaled deeply and leaned back exhausted against a stack of pillows. After a few moments of silence, Kristina leaned forward and spoke for the first time that night.

"I heard the voice too," she said simply.

"I did too," I said after a moment's hesitation, surprising myself by admitting it to everyone. "I heard it when I was at Fort Jefferson last night. I was swimming back to the fort, and I had let my mind wander until I was dangerously off course in the darkness, and I heard a voice say the exact same thing—'Hey, look out up there.' But there was nothing or no one anywhere near me at the time."

Everyone stared at me.

"I think I know the voice too," Jack said, and I turned to look at him in surprise. "I mean, I've never heard it for myself, but in the 1970s when Mel Fisher and his crew were out here searching for the 1622 treasure ships, there was an accident, and one of their boats capsized and took the lives of Fisher's son and daughter-in-law, as well as another man. On that night, just before the boat flipped over, one of the survivors later said that he'd been woken up by the sound of a voice, and that's what saved him from being drowned. The voice said those exact same words."

Commander Walsh looked at each of us slowly in turn, a serious expression written on his face. I was pretty sure that he was thinking that we were all crazy.

"Men and women have been going to sea for thousands of years," he finally said. "And nearly every sailor has a tale of some strange thing that happened at sea. I could even tell you a few of my own, in fact, if I didn't think you'd lock me up in an asylum afterward. But folks back on land don't always understand these types of things, so if it's okay with all of you, I'm gonna leave this part out of my official report."

Chapter Sixty-Two

We'll Never Be Able To Prove It

After finishing our talk, Lieutenant Commander Walsh thanked us for our assistance and called for a Zodiac to take us back to Jack's boat. The Coast Guard would return to Key West with Kevin and Kristina onboard, and once the sun came up, the police would be heading out to Fort Jefferson to deal with Patrick and Penny. Jack and I would have to meet with the police later in the day to give our statements, but for the moment, the excitement was over, and we could return to Jack's boat where Jodi was waiting for us.

After saying good-bye to Commander Walsh, a Coast Guard sailor motored us across to where Jack's boat was anchored and my plane was tied up nearby. Jodi helped us climb onboard, and as the sky to the east began to get light, we watched as the Coast Guard cutter headed toward Key West, leaving us out there all by ourselves.

It was still too dark for me to take off again, so Jack and Jodi and I decided to make the best of the time and have breakfast out on the open water. As the sun rose over the crystal-clear turquoise ocean, we sat on the deck and ate peanut butter and jelly toast and scrambled eggs.

After breakfast, we sat and drank some fresh, strong coffee while we discussed what to do next. Jack and Jodi planned to head back to Fort Jefferson to dismantle their campsite. They had originally planned to stay for a few days longer, but in light of everything that had happened, they decided to head home, but not before inviting me to visit them on Sanibel Island on the west coast of Florida near where they lived. There were plenty of seashells, and it was quiet there, Jodi promised me, and after everything that I'd been through, that sounded absolutely perfect to my ears.

In the meantime, I planned to fly to Key West, check into a hotel, and arrange to give my statement to the police. My belongings were still at Fort Jefferson, but I was a little uncomfortable about returning there all by myself, so Jack and Jodi offered to tear down my tent for me and bring everything with them when they came to Key West later in the day.

The flight into Key West was a quick one, and soon I was in a taxi on my way to a hotel near the southernmost point that Jack had recommended. It wasn't fancy like the first one I'd stayed in, nor did it have a spa with massages and pedicures, but it did have air conditioning and a pool—sweet relief after the incessant heat I'd endured at Fort Jefferson—and that was good enough for me. I went for a swim and had a long nap before heading out on foot to the police station.

The walk to the police station was a lot longer and hotter than I'd expected, so by the time I arrived, I was exhausted and sweating. The detectives I met were laid back and friendly, and they took me to a blissfully cool air-conditioned room where they listened to my entire story, which was practically memorized by now because I was telling it for the third time that day. They asked a number of follow-up questions, which I answered as best I could before they thanked me for my time and promised to keep me informed of any future developments in the case.

"Don't expect much to come of it," one of the detectives said to me as he escorted me to the front of the police station. "As far as crimes go, this isn't really all that serious, and we talked to them this morning with their lawyers, and it seems that they will all plead guilty. In the end, they'll probably just pay a fine, and that will be it."

I nodded. He was right. In the grand scheme of things, stealing some treasure from a national park wasn't exactly a serious criminal offense.

"Just out of curiosity," the detective said as I gathered my things together. "I don't suppose you have any idea how many emeralds they took with them when they abandoned ship last night, do you?"

I shook my head. "I have no idea," I replied. "It was complete darkness, and I was flying a few hundred feet in the air. I didn't even suspect that they'd taken *anything* with them until I saw Kristina's bulging pockets when she climbed up on the Coast Guard ship."

"Too bad," the detective said, shaking his head.

"Why do you ask?" I replied.

"Because we'll never know whether or not we got them all," the detective replied with a sigh. "When Mr. and Mrs. Tift were here this morning, they cooperated with us and voluntarily turned over all of the stolen treasure that they had in their possession. Lieutenant Commander Walsh also gave us a pile of emeralds that he'd seized from them last night, but the rest of it went down with their boat, of course."

"Can't you just go down and get it?" I asked.

The detective shook his head doubtfully. "We already have some divers out there looking, but they aren't very optimistic," he replied. "The tides and current are pretty strong in that area, so whatever emeralds were on the boat when it sank are probably already scattered all over the place by now. I doubt we'll ever find them."

I laughed cynically.

"On the radio last night they talked about having found a hundred and twenty seven emeralds," I said. "How many did they end up turning over to you?"

"Sixty-two," the detective replied, "which still leaves more than half of the emeralds unaccounted for."

"So many missing?" I asked, laughing even more cynically than before.

The detective nodded his head. "And even if they *do* still have some emeralds hidden away somewhere," he said, "we'll never be able to prove it."

Chapter Sixty-Three

The Secret Is Still Perfectly Safe

And so my adventures in the Florida Keys came to an end. After leaving the police station, I walked back to my hotel, sweating the entire way as I made my way through the steamy and lush green back streets of Key West. When I got to my hotel, I went for another long, cool swim while I waited for Jack and Jodi to arrive with my stuff. After they did, the three of us strolled a few blocks down to the waterfront and had a lovely dinner on an open-deck restaurant overlooking the ocean.

Over flaming Ouzo shrimp and Mongolian barbecued lamb ribs, we laughed and talked while watching our last spectacular Key West sunset together. Early the next morning, Jack and Jodi would head northwest toward Sanibel Island, and I would meet up with them there later in the afternoon to spend a few more relaxing days on the beach before continuing with my around-the-world flight.

As the colorful sky slowly faded to black and the stars began to twinkle overhead, the three of us lingered for a long time over coffee and Key lime pie. It seemed like none of us wanted the evening to end. Even though I would spend the next few days with them, it somehow felt like a chapter of our lives would close forever once we finally stood up and headed home to bed. But like all perfect evenings, even this one eventually had to come to an end. Jack paid the check and waved away the handful of dollar bills that I was trying to force on him to pay my own share.

We wandered slowly back to my hotel where we said good-bye, and then Jack and Jodi headed toward the marina where their boat was tied up for the night. I stood on the front steps and watched them until they disappeared around the next corner, where they turned to give me one last wave.

Once again, I was alone, and I returned to my room to have a shower, call my parents, and flop into bed with the stack of new Hemingway books I'd bought a few days earlier. I flipped through them, reading the titles and trying to pick a suitable one to read first. After everything I'd been through that week, I decided that *The Old Man And The Sea* was the perfect choice.

He was an old man who fished alone in a skiff in the Gulf Stream, the book's opening lines began. *And he had gone eighty-four days now without taking a fish.*

That was about as far as I got before my mind began to wander. I couldn't help thinking back and reflecting on all the craziness of the past few days. The next thing I knew I was asleep, and I woke up hours later with the book propped against my face.

I laughed at my own stupidity and closed the book to put it away. Switching off the light, I rolled over and curled up in the blankets to try to fall back to sleep. Unfortunately, as usually happens when you fall asleep too early and wake up in the middle of the night, I tossed and turned but simply couldn't fall asleep again. I'd spent too many of the previous days awake all night and sleeping through part of the day.

After lying awake for what seemed like hours, I finally decided to go out on another nocturnal walkabout through the streets of Key Weird. A late night walk would make me tired, and it would give me the chance to say good-bye to the town on my own terms, without the hustle and bustle of tourist crowds getting in my way.

I headed out into the streets, but unlike my previous late-night stroll, I found Duval Street to be quiet and deserted. The only odd character I came across was the strange cycling Santa Claus I'd seen the last time I was here. From half a mile away, I saw his blinking Christmas lights approaching, and I smiled as he pedaled closer.

"Good to see you again, young lady!" he called out as he cycled past, giving me a tip of his Santa hat as he went. "And Merry Christmas!"

"Merry Christmas to you too!" I called out, feeling pretty festive as well. Christmas might have been six months away, but who's to say that it's not Christmas every day of the year?

I stopped and watched his blinking lights fade into the distance, and then I continued on my way feeling lighthearted and happy.

At the corner of Duval and Olivia, I turned onto Whitehead Street and walked around the low brick wall surrounding the Hemingway House. I stopped at the private access gate on the Olivia Street side of the house and tilted my head up to gaze at the window of Hemingway's writing studio, which I could see through the trees. I listened carefully for the sound of a ghostly typewriter, but the only thing I could hear was the rattle of the wind in the bamboo.

I chuckled to myself and continued around the corner past the front entrance to the grounds where a sign on the inside reminded visitors to *PLEASE DO NOT PICK UP CATS*. I kept on down the street and was almost at the end of the wall when I stopped dead in my tracks and spun around.

That was definitely the sound of a typewriter bell, I said to myself, putting my fingertips gingerly on top of the brick wall so I could pull myself up on tiptoe to hear better.

As I watched the maze of trees swayed back and forth in a hypnotic, tropical dance, I could see the same strange flickering light I'd seen before coming from the window of Ernest Hemingway's upstairs writing studio. And floating to me on the wind, almost completely disguised under the rustling of leaves and the clatter of bamboo stalks, was the poetic staccato of a manual typewriter. It wasn't just my imagination—I was absolutely certain of what I was hearing.

I looked up to examine the wire fence just inside the brick wall. It looked like it was designed with the purpose of keeping cats *in* rather than human beings out, so I quickly scrambled up the wall and over the fence, and grabbed a tree on the other side to lower myself onto a bench inside the garden.

As I dashed across the open stretch of grass, it occurred to me that for the second time in a week I was breaking and entering, but I didn't care. The action-filled days that I'd just experienced had bolstered my courage, not to mention that my sense of natural curiosity and nosiness were still fully intact. If there was a ghost up there, I was going to see it.

Keeping low along the border of the hedge running along the side of the house, I ducked through an opening and past the tacky cat drinking fountain made from a urinal salvaged from Sloppy Joe's Bar. Just a few steps farther and I was at the foot of the iron staircase leading up to the writing studio.

The sound of the typewriter was much louder now, and I could hear it pounding enthusiastically as I slinked up the creaky stairs to the door at the top.

This is it; it's now or never, I told myself, and I pushed the door open.

As the door peeled slowly open, I could see the studio beyond lit by the pale light of candles and moonlight. It looked pretty much the same as I remembered it from my previous visit on the house tour.

As the door opened wider, I saw the circular table at the center of the room. At the right side of the table, there was a stack of pages and an old black typewriter with a ghostly pair of hands thrashing away at it with maniacal fervor.

I gasped in surprise as the door fell the rest of the way open and revealed the rest of a ghostly human figure sitting at the heavy wooden chair in front of the table. The figure was silhouetted against the moonlight coming in from the French doors behind. I'd expected to see a heavyset and gray-haired old man with a beard sitting at the typewriter, so I was surprised to see that he looked more like Johnny Depp. But of course it wasn't either of them, nor was it a ghost. It was James.

"Kitty?!?" James cried out, startled half to death and clutching his chest as he saw me standing there in the doorway. By the light of the candles that he had set on the table and shelves around him, he'd looked like some kind of ghostly apparition, so I could only imagine how I must have looked to him when I appeared suddenly in the doorway like that.

"James!" I replied. "What are you doing in here?!?"

James quickly composed himself and walked quickly over toward me.

"Kitty," he said again in a loud whisper. "You can't be in here."

I laughed and rolled my eyes.

"Who's going to stop me?" I asked. "Is there a night watchman guarding the place or something?"

James looked at me. "Yes, there is, actually," he said, still whispering and looking out the door before closing it behind us. "His name is Paul, and he'll kill me if he finds you up here with me. I pay him to let me sneak up here at night, and he'd charge me double if he knew that someone was up here with me."

"But what are you doing up here?" I asked, keeping my voice low so Paul wouldn't hear us. "Are you writing something?"

James nodded and gave me an embarrassed little smile. "I'm writing a novel," he said. "And I know it's stupid to think that writing up here will somehow help make my work better, but it inspires me. The words flow so much more freely here than when I'm writing at home."

I smiled at James and surprised myself by leaning forward to give him a hug. "I understand that more than you can ever know," I replied. "And if you want to write a great American novel, then I think this is absolutely the most perfect place in the world to do that."

James looked relieved and grinned sheepishly.

"You won't tell anyone that I was up here, will you?" he asked.

I shook my head solemnly.

"Of course I won't," I assured him. "I will never tell a soul."

And I never did, at least not until this very moment when I decided to share this little secret with you, my dear friend and reader of this book. Because after how far you and I have traveled together, I know that James's secret is still perfectly safe, just between you and me.

Epilogue

A Land of Volcanoes and Vikings and Ice

From: Kitty Hawk <kittyhawk@kittyhawkworld.com>
To: Charlie Lewis <chlewis@alaska.net>
Subject: Tomorrow it all begins!

Dear Charlie,

I can't believe it! This is really it!!! My last night in Florida!!! Tomorrow I set off to see the rest of this big old world of ours.

The next time I write to you I will really be on my way, leaving friends and family behind me as I head out around the world. My first stop—a land of volcanoes and Vikings and ice!

k.

Some Further Reading (if you're interested)

<u>Tofino Whale Festival</u>: The Pacific Rim Whale Festival is an annual festival held every March in the coastal towns of western Vancouver Island (Tofino and Ucluelet mostly). The festival celebrates the annual migration of grey whales from their warm winter home in Baja to the summer feeding grounds up in Alaska. Over the course of a few weeks every year more than 20,000 grey whales make their way up the western coast of North America and up past Kitty Hawk's home in Tofino. They have all sorts of fun events and always have beautiful and iconic artwork for each year's festival poster. For more information check out their website at: www.pacificrimwhalefestival.com

<u>Amelia Earhart and March 17th</u>: On 17 March 1937 Amelia Earhart set out on her first attempt to fly around the world. Flying east-to-west she left Oakland, California and landed in Honolulu, Hawaii where her plane experienced some mechanical problems and needed to be grounded for repairs. After the plane was ready to fly again Amelia attempted to take off from the U.S. Naval base at Ford Island at Pearl Harbor but suffered an accident on take-off which damaged the plane and required that it to be shipped back to California by boat. That was the end of Amelia's first attempt but a couple months later she made a second try, that time flying west-to-east from Oakland to Miami and beyond until her eventual disappearance over the waters of the South Pacific.

<u>Calgary White Cowboy Hats</u>: Anyone who's grown up near Calgary, Alberta knows that the White Cowboy Hat is the city's iconic symbol. What you might not know, however, is that there's actually a story behind it. The "official" Calgary White Hat is made by Smithbilt Hats (www.smithbilthats.com) and the story below comes from their website:

"The first cowboy hat was made by John B. Stetson in 1863 to protect himself from the weather of the American West. Working cowboys quickly adopted Stetson's hardy hat, and the North West Mounted Police switched to a version of it when their pillbox hats proved inadequate for conditions in the Canadian West. In 1946, Calgary hatmaker Morris Shumiatcher of Smithbilt Hats introduced the first pure white cowboy hat, using felt imported from Russia.

"In 1948, the Calgary Stampeders won a chance to compete for the highest honour in Canadian football, the Grey Cup. A special train carried 250 excited Calgary fans and entertainers, a chuckwagon, and 12 horses to Toronto for the game against Ottawa. Many fans wore Shumiatcher's white hats, and the Mayor of Toronto was presented with one.

"A Calgary alderman, Don MacKay, was on that legendary trip East. A born promoter, MacKay began presenting white hats to visiting dignitaries after he became Mayor of Calgary in 1950, and a tradition was born. It was continued by the Calgary Motel Association during the late 1950s, and today Tourism Calgary oversees the presentation of thousands of white hats to visitors each year."

<u>The Sleeping Giant of Thunder Bay, Ontario</u>: If you ever drive (or fly by De Havilland Beaver) across Canada I highly recommend a stop to spend some time in Thunder Bay, Ontario. And if you do then you won't be able to miss the strange landform out across the waters of Lake Superior that looks remarkably like a giant sleeping human lying on his back. Try Googling "Sleeping Giant Thunder Bay" to see some pictures.

Québec City: And while you're driving (or flying) across Canada I would also highly recommend a stop in Québec City. Nowhere else in North America is quite like it and even though walled cities are a dime-a-dozen in Europe they are no less quaint and lovely. Québec City is no exception.

The Overseas Railroad: The overseas railroad was a railway line built by millionaire Henry Flagler that connected Miami and mainland Florida to the city of Key West. Built between 1905 and 1912 the railway crossed the Florida Keys from island to island for an incredible 156 miles, at some points spanning long open stretches where passengers might look out the window to see nothing but water and feel as if they were riding on a boat. With the completion of the railroad passengers in New York could board a sleeper train dubbed the *Havana Special* and ride all the way south to Key West to catch a ferry over to Havana, Cuba. The railroad operated from 1912 until 1935 when a hurricane destroyed parts of the line and service ended.

The Overseas Highway: Built on the remnants of Henry Flagler's Overseas Railroad the Overseas Highway is a 127 mile long stretch of bridges and road that connects mainland Florida to Key West. Driving the road is an unexpected and surreal experience as you leave the swamps of the Everglades behind you and set out across the islands and waters of the Florida Keys. For most of the time all you see are dense bushes on either side of you but occasionally the view opens up and allows you wonderful views out across the waters which have some of the best snorkeling and scuba diving in the world. The drive feels like you're slowly entering a different world and touristy Key West at the end of the line almost feels like a disappointment once you get there. Anyone who has ever done it will join me in highly recommending this particular road trip as one that is well worth doing in your lifetime.

Southernmost Point: As described in this book Key West is home to the so-called "Southernmost Point in the Continental United States". However, as is also hinted at in this book, the marker is not actually located at the southernmost point. That doesn't make it any less popular with tourists, however. Try Googling "Southernmost Point Key West" for some pictures of what the frequently photographer marker looks like as well as some information on the various controversies surrounding it.

Key West Cemetery: For anyone who might like to escape the craziness of "downtown" Key West I would definitely recommend a stroll through Key West's cemetery. It's a great place to spend a couple hours just walking around in the quiet neighbourhood and exploring some of the interesting and funny graves found there. Free maps are available at the entrance that will lead you to various historically significant or interesting graves.

Hemingway House Museum: No visit to Key West would be complete without a stop at Ernest Hemingway's former home, the Ernest Hemingway Home and Museum (in fact, that is probably the reason a lot of people go to Key West in the first place). The home and grounds are lovely to walk through on a hot Florida Keys afternoon and you can even rent the garden for weddings and other events. There are many tours running throughout the day that take you around the house and grounds, telling you stories very much like those contained in this book. There is also a great bookstore for anyone who is a fan of Uncle Ernie and of course there are also the cats (see below). Check out the museum's website at: www.hemingwayhome.com

Six-Toed Cats: Probably a bigger tourist attraction that Hemingway's former home are the six-toed cats who are now the only residents there. The are fifty or so cats roaming the grounds as well as a cat cemetery for those who are no longer with us. The cats come in all shapes and colours and are descendents of a six-toed cat that was once given to Ernest Hemingway as a gift. Many of them share the strange genetic mutation that causes them to have more toes than normal. Signs remind visitors not to pick up the cats, however they are very friendly and are usually open to sharing a bench with humans and getting some attention. There is some controversy surrounding the cats, however, including whether the keeping of them by the museum qualifies them as zoo animals. But the most controversial of the controversies is whether or not Ernest Hemingway himself ever actually kept any cats in Key West. His son, Patrick, once revealed in an interview that he couldn't recall any cats at the house in Key West, only at his father's house in Cuba. Whatever the truth is, the cats don't seem to care much and since they live in one of the most beautiful and largest properties in the city I certainly can't blame them.

Sloppy Joe's Bar: Perhaps just as big a tourist attraction as Hemingway's house and cats is his old watering hole, Sloppy Joe's Bar. Just like with the cats, however, there is also some controversy surrounding Sloppy Joe's as well. There are those that will remind you that the bar's current location at the corner of Duval and Greene is not where the great Ernest Hemingway would have spent much time. He would have spent far more time drinking down at the bar's former location just up Greene street at what is now Captain Tony's Saloon. But regardless of where Hemingway may have spent more time, the Sloppy Joe's as we know it today is nothing like the place where Hemingway would have spent his time drinking. The atmosphere of the bar is hot and loud, crowded with tourists and the kind of place that you absolutely cannot miss out on if you ever happen to visit Key West. The Conch Chowder is good and if you're a fan of Sloppy Joe sandwiches, then this is the place to go. Don't be turned off or blame me later. You can eat at a normal place any day of the year, after all. Sometimes we all need a good dose of what is tacky and touristic. Check out the Sloppy Joe menu and calendar of events (including details of the annual Hemingway Look-Alike Contest) at the bar's website: www.sloppyjoes.com

The Conch: As detailed in this book (and as anyone in Key West will tell you) the word is pronounced "conk" not "conch". That may seem a bit strange, but then again, so are these large sea snails whose beautiful spiral shells can be found throughout the world. In the Florida Keys and the Caribbean conch is an important food source of food. Asking a local about what kinds of dishes are made from conch is a bit like that scene in Forrest Gump where Bubba takes several days to list all of the ways that shrimp can be prepared. Conch can be used to make almost anything: soups, salads, sandwiches, burgers, stir frys, even eaten raw like sushi. For my part, however, it is the conch chowders that I find the most appealing.

Key Lime Pie: Proper Key Lime Pie is seriously good. Like, seriously. It gets its name from a variety of lime originally from Asia that was introduced to the Florida Keys by the Spanish. Traditional/official Key Lime Pies are made from this type of lime and there was once efforts to make it against the law to call a pie a "Key Lime Pie" unless it was made from actual Key Limes. If you live in North America there is a couple of well known makers of Key Lime Pie from Key West who will ship the pies directly to your door: www.keywestkeylimepieco.com and www.theoriginalkeylimepie.com

Hemingway's Boat - The Pilar: Ernest Hemingway's boat - the Pilar - is a real boat just as described in this book. Hemingway bought the boat in 1934 from Wheeler Shipbuilding near Coney Island in Brooklyn, New York. The boat was one of the company's standard models but Hemingway made a number of modifications to it both before it was delivered to him and afterwards. The most notable modifications were painting the hull black and the later addition of a so-called "flying bridge" on the roof of the boat's wheelhouse. In addition to fishing on the Pilar Hemingway also famously used the Pilar to conduct "U-boat patrols" during the Second World War and wrote about these activities in his book "Islands In The Stream" (although whether or not these patrols were anything more than just typical blustery Hemingway macho bravado is a matter of debate). The Pilar is currently mounted in a drydock at the Hemingway museum just outside of Havana. For an absolutely outstanding book about Hemingway's Pilar I suggest "Hemingway's Boat: Everything He Loved in Life, and Lost" by Paul Hendrickson.

The "Other" Pilar: For those unable to travel to Cuba to see the real Pilar there is another Pilar that can be found in the Bass Pro Shops sporting goods store located part way down the Florida Keys in the town of Islamorada. This particular Pilar is not entirely authentic, however. For example it is not made by the same company as Hemingway's boat was nor is it identically configured, but it does have one great advantage over the real thing which is that you can actually climb on board and explore inside (the real Pilar in Cuba is closed off and only visible to visitors from a distance). Despite it being "fake" I would still recommend stopping in to see it if you're ever driving down the Florida Keys (you can also stop in for lunch at the excellent fish restaurant next door - the Islamorada Fish Company). Just don't be fooled by the photos of Hemingway above the desk and typewriter in the corner of the boat's inside cabin - it is not Hemingway's boat and he certainly never wrote any stories there. More complete details regarding the differences between these two boats are part of the end-notes of the previously recommended book "Hemingway's Boat: Everything He Loved in Life, and Lost" by Paul Hendrickson.

The Gulf Stream: For hundreds of years after Columbus's "discovery" of the Americas the Spanish were well aware that a powerful ocean current flowed from the Gulf of Mexico and Florida north to Newfoundland and out across the Atlantic Ocean beyond. This current was routinely used by Spanish navigators to shorten the sailing time required to return to Europe from the New World. Hundreds of years later Benjamin Franklin also later played a major role in charting the current as part of his duties as postmaster of the North American colonies in the period before the American Revolution. The British, however, were slow to believe in its existence and continued to run against the current, thus adding weeks to the time required to cross the Atlantic. Check out http://rads.tudelft.nl/gulfstream/ for up-to-date information regarding the velocity of the Gulf Stream current.

<u>The Hawk Channel</u>: As described in this book, in addition to the powerful Gulf Stream current running west to east along the coast of the Florida Keys there is another, less powerful current running in the opposite direction closer to shore contained between the islands of the Keys and the outer reefs. This current is (appropriately) named the Hawk Channel and provides excellent sheltered waters for all sorts of water sports, fishing, diving and snorkelling. For a bit more information check out www.hawkchannel.com.

<u>Mile Zero - Key West Florida</u>: One of the most photographed street signs in Key West is the so-called Mile Zero sign which marks the start of U.S. Route 1 highway that runs for almost four thousand kilometres from Key West, Florida all the way to the Canadian border up in Maine. Try Googling "Mile Zero Key West" for some pictures.

<u>The Dry Tortugas and Fort Jefferson</u>: Entire books could be written (and surely have been) about the stunningly amazing place called Fort Jefferson and the Dry Tortugas. There simply are not enough words to describe how absolutely beautiful and surreal this place is (although I have tried to convey a tiny sense of it in this book). You only need to Google pictures of "Dry Tortugas Fort Jefferson" to see what I mean, but the pictures do not do justice to how utterly incredible this place is. It is, by far, one of the most unique and amazing places in the world and so easy to get to that everyone should visit it at least once in their lifetime.

<u>Fort Jefferson Water Cistern System</u>: As described in this book the fortress at Fort Jefferson has an ingenious system of water filtering and storage cisterns to provide fresh water to the Dry Tortugas. The fact that this system ultimately was a failure should not take away from the ingenuity of its design. An absolutely outstanding computer diagram of this system can be found at http://donfoley.com/?p=344.

<u>Barracuda</u>: The barracuda is one of the most feared fish in the world. I have even heard people say that they are more frightened of barracuda than of sharks. I am not sure about that - I am personally more worried about sharks than of barracuda - but the fact does remain that when you come face to face (and teeth to teeth) with a barracuda in the wild that it can be a somewhat unnerving experience. They are lightning fast in snapping up their prey and although in my experience they spend far more time floating motionless I know that they can be incredibly fast when they want to be. That said, however, I am not entirely convinced that they are really all that dangerous, even if you foolishly flaunt the conventional wisdom and wear flashy jewellery in the water around them. There are plenty of myths and stories about barracuda attacks but the fact remains that people swim around them all the time. You see them in the waters off the Florida Keys all the time and if they were generally that dangerous to be around the snorkelling and scuba diving industry of Florida would be ruined. Try Googling "barracuda" for more information on this fearsome looking fish, most of it inconclusive and contradictory.

<u>Bird Names and Fishing Lure Names</u>: As detailed in this book there are plenty of funny names for birds and fishing lures out there. If you don't believe me, try Googling them some time.

Brick Wreck / Scottish Chief: The so-called "Brick Wreck" (possibly the wreck of the "Scottish Chief") that is mentioned in this book is a real wreck in the shallow waters off of Fort Jefferson. Check out a bit more information about this fascinating wreck at the National Park Service website for the Dry Tortugas: www.nps.gov/drto/planyourvisit/upload/Bird%20Key%20Wreck.pdf

Spanish Silver Bar Markings: The silver bar markings in this book are fictional but they are based on a real system of markings used by the Spanish for their treasure fleets. The strange symbols, serial numbers and purity grades are accurate representations to those the Spanish used and are familiar to any treasure buff. Try Googling "Spanish Silver Treasure Bar Markings" for more.

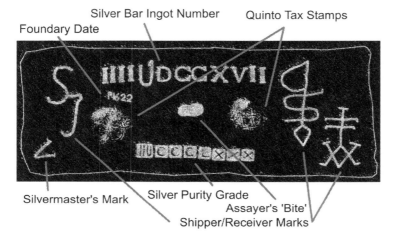

Procesal Writing: As described in this book this strange and virtually indecipherable form of writing was used by the Spanish bureaucrats in drawing up manifests for the Spanish treasure fleets to combat falsification of documents.

The 1622 and 1715 Spanish Treasure Fleets: As described in this book the lost 1622 and 1715 Spanish Treasure Fleets are two of the most infamous fleets for amateur and professional treasure hunters. Salvage on these wrecks has been conducted for decades (in fact, for centuries if you count the salvage conducted by the Spanish and others in the distant past) but year after year small amounts of treasure is still found in the shallow waters and beaches of Florida. For a couple of thousand dollars you can take a treasure hunting holiday and join a team in the waters near Marquesas Key for the wrecks of the Atocha and Santa Margarita. Or if you're more of a loner you can always grab a metal detector and join dozens of others scouring the beaches of eastern Florida after storms.

Modern Scuba Diving Equipment: Nowadays when you buy a cheap snorkel and mask set at a gas station anywhere on the roads of the Florida Keys it's easy to forget that such equipment did not always exist. We have Jacques Cousteau to thank for most of the innovations that are now standard-issue in modern snorkelling and scuba diving but I think it's also fascinating to imagine the primitive diving methods described in this book that were used by the Spanish salvors long before diving masks and scuba gear were invented.

<u>The Archive of the Indies</u>: The "Archivo General de Indias" is a real place just as described in this book. Tens of millions of pages of documents are housed in the archive and detail the history of the Spanish empire over the past five hundred years. Just as detailed in this book it was in this archive that Eugene Lyon painstakingly worked to uncover the secrets of the lost galleons of the 1622 treasure fleet. All of these records are available to the public and are even increasingly available online (thus eliminating the need to make a pilgrimage to Spain - although some would argue that this is all part of the experience). Check out the website in Spanish at http://en.www.mcu.es/archivos/MC/AGI/index.html

<u>Mel Fisher Museum / Mel Fisher Treasures</u>: No visit to Key West would be complete without a visit to the Mel Fisher Museum and the next door treasure shop Mel Fisher Treasures. This museum documents the long search for the 1622 treasure galleons conducted by Mel Fisher - the self-appointed "World's Greatest Treasure Hunter". The museum is interesting to visit and see the many amazing finds from the treasure fleets that were not ultimately distributed to investors as dividends. What remains for display is breathtaking and provides an incredible insight into the world of the Spanish New World. While you're there you can also visit the Mel Fisher Treasure store next door and maybe take home your own little piece of treasure. Check out the website for both at www.melfisher.com.

<u>How Much A Silver Bar Is Worth</u>: In the story our heroine is confused about the imperial system of measurements in her attempt to guesstimate the value of a silver bar. I am myself a child of the metric system so I can relate to her confusion, but just for the record I should probably set things straight. There are sixteen ounces in a pound and as of the publishing of this book silver is about $23 US an ounce. The silver bars from the 1622 treasure fleet varied in size but as detailed in this book the weight of each bar was carefully recorded in the ship manifests. A typical bar could weigh as much as 70 pounds which means in terms of the value of silver alone it would be worth more than $25,000. In terms of historical value it might be almost priceless.

<u>Bioluminescent Algae And Plankton</u>: Many people who have lived near or sailed on the seas and oceans of the world are familiar with the phenomena of bioluminescent life. Try Googling "Bioluminescent Algae Plankton" to see some images of this amazing natural occurrence. Of course in real life the effect is not as intense as in some of the photos, but it is amazing all the same.

<u>The Rosario, Spanish Chief and Consolacion</u>: The three ships that play such a major role in this story are all real vessels. Of course I have taken a little bit of artistic license in my attempt to craft a story around them but for the most part their histories are very much as detailed in this book. If you're interested in learning more about these ships, as well as the treasure galleons Atocha and Santa Margarita, there are several excellent books I would recommend on the topic of the search for the 1622 treasure fleets: "The Search for the Atocha" by Eugene Lyon; "Atocha Treasure Adventures: Sweat of the Sun, Tears of the Moon" by Syd Jones; "Treasure of Atocha: A Four Hundred Million Dollar Archaeological Adventure" by R. Duncan Mathewson; "Treasure - The Search for the Atocha" by Robert Daley.

Just in case you enjoyed this book, please allow me to try and entice you into reading another one by providing a couple of samples of new books that I am working on. The first sample is from a new book series that I am thinking of writing called...

The Guild of the Wizards of Waterfire

Prologue

The guilds had existed for two and a half thousand years, and it certainly wasn't the first time that tragedy had struck and claimed the life of an Elemental before their time. It had happened before, and it was sure to happen again, but for Virginia Soul, it was the first time that tragedy had struck so close to home in her own small world.

Since ancient times, the lighthouses had been the secret symbol of the elusive Guilds of the Waterfire Wizards. Standing strong as beacons of safety and stability where water meets fire, each one held the destructive power of the other at bay.

In the beginning, the lighthouses themselves had served the wizards as secret meeting places; each guild had constructed its own place of gathering and refuge. But as the guilds spread throughout the world and into places far from the sea, the image became more symbolic. The iconic form of the lighthouse began to appear everywhere—on walls and signs, over doorways, or cleverly hidden in corporate logos—just look around and you'll see what I'm talking about. But for those in the know, each lighthouse marks the location of a guild's secret meeting place.

Virginia's guild was no exception. Every Thursday at seven o'clock, she would ride out to the Shurgard Mini Storage building close to her home, type the access code into the keypad next to the entrance door, and climb the stairs to the secret room under the building's pretend lighthouse that the uninitiated simply dismissed as one of the company's marketing gimmicks.

But on this particular Thursday, Virginia wasn't there. She was somewhere else instead—the last place in the world that she wanted to be at that particular moment. She was standing in the rain in a cemetery wishing that she and the other mourners were in their secret room, safe and warm as they watched the rain streak down the windows outside. They would drink some hot tea and talk and laugh while playing games—Catan or Monopoly, maybe, or perhaps the ancient guild game of Pharos.

Every guild must consist of five members, or the guild must disband.

That was the rule, and it had been the rule since long before Virginia was ever born. It was a rule that stretched back as far as the very existence of the guilds themselves, for nearly two and a half thousand years.

Earth, air, fire, water, and ether.

Love and strife.

Everything had to exist in balance.

But at the moment, the only thing Virginia could feel was strife plunging its painful needles of memory deep into her broken heart. She looked across at Memphis Grey, her best friend, standing next to her at the side of the grave. Memphis was a mess, alternately wiping tears and raindrops from her face as she stared down at the lonely casket being lowered slowly into the ground. Strands of her intense blonde hair fell over her shoulders from underneath the fabric of the black hoodie that was pulled up to cover her face. She didn't want the others to see her cry. Virginia didn't care about that and just let the tears flow like rivers of sorrow. She cried just like the dark clouds that were hanging overhead.

Flickers of lightning licked at the corners of the sky, splitting the air and bathing the mourners in a stark, harsh light for an instant before another wave of thunder rumbled through the ground and sky.

Virginia leaned forward and looked past Memphis to the smaller figure at her side with tousled brown hair hanging wetly down into his eyes. Ithaca was Memphis's little brother, and seeing the two of them standing there in tears made Virginia's heart rip in two all over again. Ithaca was only two years younger than Memphis, and he was old enough to understand what death was, but just like the rest of them, it was the first time that something so tragic had struck so close and taken someone they loved so dearly out of their lives forever.

Virginia turned away from the sight of them and buried her face in her hands, sobbing loudly and coming close to completely losing it. Her eyes darted around the cemetery in a panic, looking for a way to escape. If only she could just push her way through the crowd of black-dressed mourners and make for the cover of the nearby trees. Then she could be alone with her thoughts and just listen to the rain, and remember.

As she grew anxious and was about to bolt, a warm hand patted her gently on the shoulder, instantly calming her and helping her to get her breathing under control. Virginia looked up to see Memphis and Ithaca's great-uncle, Winston. Winston Eric Waters was her mentor, and the leader of their guild. With droplets of waters dripping from his gray, speckled goatee, he smiled down at her, his brown eyes full of kindness but just as flecked with pain as hers were. He patted her on the shoulder again then left his hand there, its warmth and weight solid and reassuring against the rest of the world that seemed to be descending into chaos around them.

All of them were there—Virginia, Memphis, Ithaca, and Winston, and below them in the coffin that was now slowly settling into the muddy earth lay the lifeless body of the fifth member of their guild—Christian.

Christian had been a big brother to the three youngest members and a kind of adopted son to Winston. The five of them had been as close as family—closer even, growing up together and learning from each other's mistakes as they trained and explored the world around them and the fabric of the universe that held it all together. They'd laughed and fought and cried with each other, and together they had somehow shouldered the great responsibilities that came with being an Elemental.

But now, all that was finished. Three nights ago, on a dark, tree-lined street, Christian's life was snuffed out in a flash of tires and screeching metal. He was dead, and for nothing more than a stupid car accident, the kind of tragedy that strikes friends and families a hundred times a day all across the world. Christian was dead, and if losing their dear friend wasn't traumatic enough, the very existence of their guild was now in jeopardy. Everything they'd worked so hard for was in question.

Virginia had absolutely no idea what they were going to do.

She reached into her pocket and squeezed the petra stone that she always carried with her; she could feel its power, and took comfort in it as she closed her eyes to block out the tears and falling rain.

What are we going to do? Virginia asked herself.

Christian would have to be replaced; otherwise, their guild would fall. But how could anyone ever replace him? They could never love anyone the way they had loved him.

When the priest finished the ceremony, the mourners began to shuffle slowly back to their waiting cars. Some of them stopped by with words of wisdom and comfort for the four of them—how sorry they were, how time heals all wounds, and how no one can know the sometimes terrible cost that all of us have to pay for being human. But none of the mourners had any idea what the five of them had been through together, or how Christian's death threatened to unravel all of their lives.

Virginia's father leaned down to whisper in her ear. He and her mother would wait in the car, and she should take all the time she needed to say good-bye. He smiled at her—a weak and helpless smile full of love and caring—before Virginia's mother gave her a hug, and the two of them walked off, melting into the crowd of other black clothes and umbrellas making their way through the forest of gray headstones.

"I know it seems impossible," Winston said after everyone else was out of earshot, and just the four of them were left standing by the grave that was cut like a scar into the side of the hill. "But we'll find another to take his place. The guild will live on, and so will Christian's spirit."

The three of them looked up at Winston as he gazed off distantly toward the horizon. A slash of lightning cut through the sky in the east followed by a peal of thunder that washed over the landscape like a thunderous, breaking wave.

Winston was right. There was no other choice, and they all knew it, but that didn't make the lacerating pain of loss any easier to bear.

Every guild must consist of five members, or the guild must disband.

They all knew the rules. They'd been living by them all of their lives.

The second sample chapter I have for you today is from the next installment in the on-going adventures of Kitty Hawk. Please check out this sample chapter from....

Kitty Hawk and the Tragedy of the R.M.S. Titanic

Book Four of the Kitty Hawk Flying Detective Agency Series

Chapter One

"Ladies and gentlemen!" the sharply-dressed man out at the centre of the podium said excitedly. "Welcome to Dublin and the grand opening of the Grafton Street location of Wasabi Willy's Family Sushi Restaurant!"

The crowd him below cheered and clapped enthusiastically. And this was understandable since they would soon be sampling some free sushi as a part of the opening ceremony activities. I myself, on the other hand, was a bit less enthusiastic as I watched the sharp-dressed man continue to address the crowd. The man's name was Kevin O'Donnell and he was the head manager of the Wasabi Willy's restaurant chain in Ireland.

"We have a lot of exciting things lined up today for you guys," Kevin continued. "Including some free sushi giveaways for anyone who wants to try a few of the delicious items from our menu. But first I would like to welcome a very special guest to today's grand opening. This young lady has come to visit us all the way from Canada and she's stopping here in Dublin to have some sushi before she continues on her amazing solo flight around the world. Ladies and gentlemen, will you please welcome the incredible and remarkable young female pilot, Ms. Kitty Hawk!"

The crowd burst into another round of energetic applause and cheers - fuelled, I suppose, by the promise of free sushi and less by the prospect of meeting me. With a big smile I stepped out into view and struggled to wave to the crowd as I waddled across the stage toward Kevin.

You might be wondering why I was struggling and waddling. The reason was quite simple. I was dressed in a gigantic inflatable sumo wrestler suit.

"Thank you very much," I said after I reached the centre of the podium and Kevin handed me his microphone. "Thank you for such a warm welcome to your beautiful country. I am thrilled to be here to support this grand opening of a restaurant that I know and love so much."

I was reciting some pre-written text that Kevin and I had agreed upon earlier but the fact was that I *did* know the Wasabi Willy's restaurant fairly well. I had eaten there twelve months earlier, before I was swept along on my adventures up the Chilkoot Trail and into the Yukon and was still doing my humpback whale research in Juneau, Alaska. The restaurant atmosphere was great and the food even better, but I did have my doubts about their colourful mascot, a giant blob of maniacally smiling wasabi in a sumo-wrestler loincloth.

Of course I didn't say anything to Kevin about my feelings toward their mascot. The company was, after all, financing my flight around the world in exchange for my promoting the company and participating in events such as the grand opening I was currently attending. Oh yes, and let's not forget that they painted the giant smiling wasabi logo on the side of my De Havilland Beaver seaplane.

My friend Charlie back in Alaska had made all the arrangements for me with the Wasabi Willy company and for that I was eternally grateful, but as I wobbled and teetered precariously out on that stage in my enormous sumo suit I did have to wonder how in the world I'd gotten myself into all of this.

I looked out across the small sea of smiling faces and did my best to smile back as I handed the microphone back to Kevin so he could continue with the grand opening festivities. As I scanned the crowd I noticed a handsome young man standing by himself off to one side. He was wearing a dark suit with a pale grey tie and his forehead was wrinkled into a slightly worried expression. I watched him for a few moments, wondering why he was looking so serious while everyone else in the crowd around him was smiling. After a few seconds he noticed me looking at him and immediately broke into a wide smile as he nodded in my direction.

Busted! I thought to myself and quickly tried to look elsewhere, pretending that I hadn't been staring at him so intently. In my embarrassment I blushed bright red and averted my eyes but I was smiling to myself as I did so. Whoever he was, he was very good looking and who can help but be happy when someone smiles at them like that.

"Thank you Kitty," Kevin's said as he continued with the opening ceremony. "We're happy to have you here with us in Ireland and I hope that you'll join us for some free sushi in just a few minutes."

"I certainly will," I replied, keeping my eyes straight forward and resisting the urge to look over to the side where out of the corner of my eye I could still see the young man in the dark suit standing there.

"But first," Kevin continued, his voice deep and booming loudly through the microphone like an announcer in a boxing match. "It's time to introduce your opponent for today's sumo wrestling challenge. Ladies and gentlemen, in the opposite corner, weighing in at a staggering three hundred and forty seven kilograms, please allow me to introduce the reigning heavyweight champion... Wasabiiiii Willyyyyyy!!!"

I resisted the urge to roll my eyes as dramatic music began to play and Kevin gestured flamboyantly across to the opposite side of the stage.

"Y'all ready for this?" Kevin bellowed to the crowd. "Let's get ready to rumblllllllle!!!"

As the pulsing electronic beat of a dance mix filled the air I turned to look over to the side of the stage where a gigantic Wasabi Willy was pounding out onto the podium. I couldn't help but laugh as I watched the enormous costume make its way out to centre stage. I knew that underneath the huge inflatable costume there was a tiny young woman named Ciara, whom I'd met before the show. I was amazed that despite her very small size she was able to move around in the Wasabi Willy costume like it didn't weigh a thing.

As Wasabi Willy broke into a comical dance the crowd below us clapped and danced along to the deafening beat of the music. Above our heads confetti cannons exploded a deluge of tissue paper wasabi blobs into the air and as they showered down on the crowd a cheerleading squad in short wasabi green skirts erupted from both sides of the stage and joined Willy in his ridiculous dance at centre stage.

I really couldn't stop myself from smiling ear-to-ear and laughing. There was a time in my life when I'd probably have nearly died of embarrassment from being involved in such a outlandish spectacle, but it was so completely insane and over-the-top that I simply couldn't help but laugh at the craziness of it all.

"Be aggressive! B - E - Aggressive!" the cheerleaders cheered as they kicked and flipped their way around the stage. "Whoop, there it is! Whoop, there it is!"

The cheerleaders continued their frenetic dance around the stage and then just as quickly as they'd appeared they circled around and disappeared backstage once again. At the front of the stage Wasabi Willy led the audience in one final cheer as the music began to fade then lumbered back to the side of the wrestling ring where he crouched over into a traditional sumo wrestler's stance.

"You're up," Kevin said, grinning as he slapped me on the back of my inflatable sumo suit. "Good luck."

Still laughing and smiling I waddled over to my side of the circle and tried to lean over into a proper wrestling stance. The whole thing was crazy but if this is what Wasabi Willy's restaurant wanted me to do in exchange for funding my flight around the world, then who was I to complain? I was going to enjoy every second of it even if they expected me to sumo wrestle a ridiculous big-head costume version of their mascot. And that, of course, was exactly what I was about to do.

A Message From The Author

First off, before I say anything else, thank you so very much for buying my book and sharing in the adventures of Kitty Hawk. While I was out for a walk this morning I was counting the number of books I expect to have in the complete series and the number I settled on was thirteen. So you and I have a ways to go yet. That is, if you're up for it.

And speaking of having a ways to go yet (not to mention the number 13)... I was thinking the other day about who should write the Kitty Hawk theme song IF (big "if") they ever make a Kitty Hawk movie. And the answer was obvious. Taylor Swift, right? So help me convince Taylor Swift to write a Kitty Hawk movie theme song by signing my online petition:

http://www.ipetitions.com/petition/taylor-swift-kitty-hawk-theme-song/

(Or if that's too much typing you can also go to www.kittyhawkworld.com and click on the link from there.)

And speaking of music... If you're interested in hearing some of the music I write and record in my spare time, please check it out (for FREE) at www.secretworldonline.com.

And finally, on a more serious note... You might have noticed that at the end of this book I have included sample chapters for TWO future books. One of these, of course, is for the next installment in the adventures of Kitty Hawk but the other one is for another books series that I am thinking of writing called The Guild Of The Wizards Of Waterfire. I sometimes have trouble deciding which one to concentrate on next so if you have any thoughts about this, let me know.

That's about it, I guess. Thank you again for buying this book. You have no idea how much that means to me.

Talk to you again soon... in the next adventure.